Robert Harris is the author of four other novels – *Fatherland*, *Enigma*, *Archangel* and *Pompeii* – all of which were number one bestsellers. His work has been translated into thirty-three languages. He was born in Nottingham in 1957 and is a graduate of Cambridge University. He worked as a reporter on the BBC's *Newsnight* and *Panorama* programmes, before becoming Political Editor of the *Observer* in 1987, and then a columnist on the *Sunday Times* and the *Daily Telegraph*. In 2003 he was named Columnist of the Year in the British Press Awards. He lives near Hungerford in Berkshire with his wife and their four children.

ROBERT HARRIS

IMPERIUM

HUTCHINSON
LONDON

First published by Hutchinson in 2006

5 7 9 10 8 6 4

Copyright © Robert Harris 2006

Robert Harris has asserted his right under the Copyright, Designs
and Patents Act, 1988 to be identified as the author of this work

Map of Republican Rome by Reginald Piggott

HUTCHINSON
The Random House Group Limited
20 Vauxhall Bridge Road, London SW1V 2SA

www.rbooks.co.uk

Addresses for companies within the Random House Group Limited can be found at:
www.randomhouse.co.uk/offices.htm

The Random House Group Limited Reg. No. 954009

A CIP catalogue record for this book
is available from the British Library

The Random House Group Limited supports The Forest Stewardship
Council (FSC), the leading international forest certification organisation. All our
titles that are printed on Greenpeace approved FSC certified paper carry the FSC logo. Our paper
procurement policy can be found at www.rbooks.co.uk/environment

Mixed Sources
Product group from well-managed
forests and other controlled sources
www.fsc.org Cert no. TT-COC-2139
© 1996 Forest Stewardship Council
FSC

Typeset in 12.5/16.5pt Dante MT by
Palimpsest Book Production Limited, Grangemouth, Stirlingshire
Printed and bound in the UK by CPI Mackays, Chatham ME5 8TD

ISBN 9780091931193

IN MEMORY OF
Audrey Harris
1920–2005
and for
Sam

TIRO, M. Tullius, the secretary of Cicero. He was not only the amanuensis of the orator, and his assistant in literary labour, but was himself an author of no mean reputation, and the inventor of the art of shorthand, which made it possible to take down fully and correctly the words of public speakers, however rapid their enunciation. After the death of Cicero, Tiro purchased a farm in the neighbourhood of Puteoli, to which he retired, and lived, according to Hieronymous, until he reached his hundredth year. Asconius Pedianus (in *Milon.* 38) refers to the fourth book of a life of Cicero by Tiro.

Dictionary of Greek and Roman Biography and Mythology, Vol. III, edited by William L. Smith, London, 1851

'*Innumerabilia tua sunt in me officia, domestica, forensia, urbana, provincialia, in re privata, in publica, in studiis, in litteris nostris . . .*'

'Your services to me are beyond count – in my home and out of it, in Rome and abroad, in private affairs and public, in my studies and literary work . . .'

Cicero, letter to Tiro, 7 November 50 BC

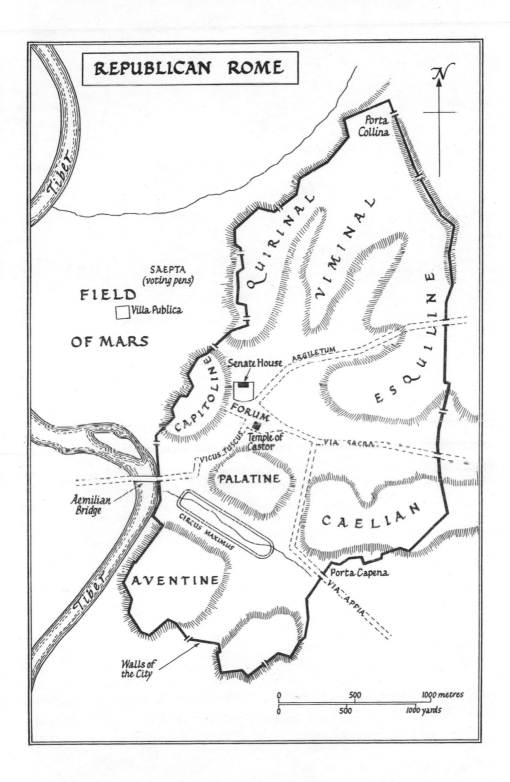

REPUBLICAN ROME

N

Tiber

Porta
Collina

QUIRINAL

VIMINAL

ESQUILINE

SAEPTA
(voting pens)

FIELD

Villa Publica

OF MARS

CAPITOLINE

Senate House

ARGILETUM

FORUM

Temple of
Castor

VIA SACRA

Vicus Tuscus

PALATINE

Aemilian
Bridge

CAELIAN

CIRCUS MAXIMUS

AVENTINE

Porta Capena

VIA APPIA

Tiber

Walls of
the City

| 0 | 500 | 1000 metres |
| 0 | 500 | 1000 yards |

PART ONE

SENATOR

79–70 BC

'Urbem, urbem, mi Rufe, cole et in ista luce vive!'

'Rome! Stick to Rome, my dear fellow, and live in the limelight!'

Cicero, letter to Caelius, 26 June 50 BC

I

My name is Tiro. For thirty-six years I was the confidential secretary of the Roman statesman Cicero. At first this was exciting, then astonishing, then arduous, and finally extremely dangerous. During those years I believe he spent more hours with me than with any other person, including his own family. I witnessed his private meetings and carried his secret messages. I took down his speeches, his letters and his literary works, even his poetry — such an outpouring of words that I had to invent what is commonly called shorthand to cope with the flow, a system still used to record the deliberations of the senate, and for which I was recently awarded a modest pension. This, along with a few legacies and the kindness of friends, is sufficient to keep me in my retirement. I do not require much. The elderly live on air, and I am very old – almost a hundred, or so they tell me.

In the decades after his death, I was often asked, usually in whispers, what Cicero was really like, but always I held my silence. How was I to know who was a government spy and who was not? At any moment I expected to be purged. But since my life is almost over, and since I have no fear of anything any more – not even torture, for I would not last an instant at the hands of the carnifex or his assistants – I have decided to offer this work as my answer. I shall base it on my memory, and on the documents

3

entrusted to my care. Because the time left to me inevitably must be short, I propose to write it quickly, using my shorthand system, on a few dozen small rolls of the finest paper – Hieratica, no less – which I have long hoarded for the purpose. I pray forgiveness in advance for all my errors and infelicities of style. I also pray to the gods that I may reach the end before my own end overtakes me. Cicero's final words to me were a request to tell the truth about him, and this I shall endeavour to do. If he does not always emerge as a paragon of virtue, well, so be it. Power brings a man many luxuries, but a clean pair of hands is seldom among them.

And it is of power and the man that I shall sing. By power I mean official, political power – what we know in Latin as *imperium* – the power of life and death, as vested by the state in an individual. Many hundreds of men have sought this power, but Cicero was unique in the history of the republic in that he pursued it with no resources to help him apart from his own talent. He was not, unlike Metellus or Hortensius, from one of the great aristocratic families, with generations of political favours to draw on at election time. He had no mighty army to back up his candidacy, as did Pompey or Caesar. He did not have Crassus's vast fortune to grease his path. All he had was his voice – and by sheer effort of will he turned it into the most famous voice in the world.

I was twenty-four years old when I entered his service. He was twenty-seven. I was a household slave, born on the family estate in the hills near Arpinum, who had never even seen Rome. He was a young advocate, suffering from nervous exhaustion, and struggling to overcome considerable natural disabilities. Few would have wagered much on either of our chances.

Cicero's voice at this time was not the fearsome instrument it later became, but harsh and occasionally prone to stutter. I believe the problem was that he had so many words teeming in his head that at moments of stress they jammed in his throat, as when a pair of sheep, pressed by the flock behind them, try at the same time to squeeze through a gate. In any case, these words were often too high-falutin for his audience to grasp. 'The Scholar', his restless listeners used to call him, or 'the Greek' – and the terms were not meant as compliments. Although no one doubted his talent for oratory, his frame was too weak to carry his ambition, and the strain on his vocal cords of several hours' advocacy, often in the open air and in all seasons, could leave him rasping and voiceless for days. Chronic insomnia and poor digestion added to his woes. To put it bluntly, if he was to rise in politics, as he desperately wished to do, he needed professional help. He therefore decided to spend some time away from Rome, travelling both to refresh his mind and to consult the leading teachers of rhetoric, most of whom lived in Greece and Asia Minor.

Because I was responsible for the upkeep of his father's small library, and possessed a decent knowledge of Greek, Cicero asked if he might borrow me, as one might remove a book on loan, and take me with him to the East. My job would be to supervise arrangements, hire transport, pay teachers and so forth, and after a year go back to my old master. In the end, like many a useful volume, I was never returned.

We met in the harbour of Brundisium on the day we were due to set sail. This was during the consulship of Servilius Vatia and Claudius Pulcher, the six hundred and seventy-fifth year after the foundation of Rome. Cicero then was nothing like the imposing figure he later became, whose features were so famous he could not walk down the quietest street unrecognised. (What

5

has happened, I wonder, to all those thousands of busts and portraits, which once adorned so many private houses and public buildings? Can they really *all* have been smashed and burned?) The young man who stood on the quayside that spring morning was thin and round-shouldered, with an unnaturally long neck, in which a large Adam's apple, as big as a baby's fist, plunged up and down whenever he swallowed. His eyes were protuberant, his skin sallow, his cheeks sunken; in short, he was the picture of ill health. *Well, Tiro,* I remember thinking, *you had better make the most of this trip, because it is not going to last long.*

We went first to Athens, where Cicero had promised himself the treat of studying philosophy at the Academy. I carried his bag to the lecture hall and was in the act of turning away when he called me back and demanded to know where I was going.

'To sit in the shade with the other slaves,' I replied, 'unless there is some further service you require.'

'Most certainly there is,' he said. 'I wish you to perform a very strenuous labour. I want you to come in here with me and learn a little philosophy, in order that I may have someone to talk to on our long travels.'

So I followed him in, and was privileged to hear Antiochus of Ascalon himself assert the three basic principles of stoicism – that virtue is sufficient for happiness, that nothing except virtue is good, and that the emotions are not to be trusted – three simple rules which, if only men could follow them, would solve all the problems of the world. Thereafter, Cicero and I would often debate such questions, and in this realm of the intellect the difference in our stations was always forgotten. We stayed six months with Antiochus and then moved on to the real purpose of our journey.

The dominant school of rhetoric at that time was the so-called

Asiatic method. Elaborate and flowery, full of pompous phrases and tinkling rhythms, its delivery was accompanied by a lot of swaying about and striding up and down. In Rome its leading exponent was Quintus Hortensius Hortalus, universally considered the foremost orator of the day, whose fancy footwork had earned him the nickname of 'the Dancing Master'. Cicero, with an eye to discovering his tricks, made a point of seeking out all Hortensius's mentors: Menippus of Stratonicea, Dionysius of Magnesia, Aeschylus of Cnidus, Xenocles of Adramyttium – the names alone give a flavour of their style. Cicero spent weeks with each, patiently studying their methods, until at last he felt he had their measure.

'Tiro,' he said to me one evening, picking at his customary plate of boiled vegetables, 'I have had quite enough of these perfumed prancers. You will arrange a boat from Loryma to Rhodes. We shall try a different tack, and enrol in the school of Apollonius Molon.'

And so it came about that, one spring morning just after dawn, when the straits of the Carpathian Sea were as smooth and milky as a pearl (you must forgive these occasional flourishes: I have read too much Greek poetry to maintain an austere Latin style), we were rowed across from the mainland to that ancient, rugged island, where the stocky figure of Molon himself awaited us on the quayside.

This Molon was a lawyer, originally from Alabanda, who had pleaded in the Rome courts brilliantly, and had even been invited to address the senate in Greek – an unheard-of honour – after which he had retired to Rhodes and opened his rhetorical school. His theory of oratory, the exact opposite of the Asiatics', was simple: don't move about too much, hold your head straight, stick to the point, make 'em laugh, make 'em cry, and when you've won their sympathy, sit down quickly – 'For nothing,' said Molon, 'dries more quickly than a tear.' This was far more to Cicero's taste, and he placed himself in Molon's hands entirely.

Molon's first action was to feed him that evening a bowl of hard-boiled eggs with anchovy sauce, and, when Cicero had finished that – not without some complaining, I can tell you – to follow it with a lump of red meat, seared over charcoal, accompanied by a cup of goat's milk. 'You need bulk, young man,' he told him, patting his own barrel chest. 'No mighty note was ever sounded by a feeble reed.' Cicero glared at him, but dutifully chewed until his plate was empty, and that night, for the first time in months, slept soundly. (I know this because I used to sleep on the floor outside his door.)

At dawn, the physical exercises began. 'Speaking in the forum,' said Molon, 'is comparable to running in a race. It requires stamina and strength.' He threw a fake punch at Cicero, who let out a loud 'Oof!' and staggered backwards, almost falling over. Molon had him stand with his legs apart, his knees rigid, then bend from the waist twenty times to touch the ground on either side of his feet. After that, he made him lie on his back with his hands clasped behind his head and repeatedly sit up without shifting his legs. He made him lie on his front and raise himself solely by the strength of his arms, again twenty times, again without bending his knees. That was the regime on the first day, and each day afterwards more exercises were added and their duration increased. Cicero again slept soundly, and now had no trouble eating, either.

For the actual declamatory training, Molon took his eager pupil out of the shaded courtyard and into the heat of midday, and had him recite his exercise pieces – usually a trial scene or a soliloquy from Menander – while walking up a steep hill without pausing. In this fashion, with the lizards scattering underfoot and only the scratching of the cicadas in the olive trees for an audience, Cicero strengthened his lungs and learned how to gain the maximum output of words from a single breath. 'Pitch your delivery in the middle range,' instructed Molon. 'That is where the power is. Nothing too high or low.' In the afternoons, for speech projection, Molon took him down to the shingle beach, paced out eighty yards (the maximum range of the human voice) and made him declaim against the boom and hiss of the sea – the nearest thing, he said, to the murmur of three thousand people in the open air, or the background mutter of several hundred men in conversation in the senate. These were distractions Cicero would have to get used to.

'But what about the content of what I say?' Cicero asked. 'Surely I will compel attention chiefly by the force of my arguments?'

Molon shrugged. 'Content does not concern me. Remember Demosthenes: "Only three things count in oratory. Delivery, delivery, and again: delivery."'

'And my stutter?'

'The st-st-stutter does not b-b-bother me either,' replied Molon with a grin and a wink. 'Seriously, it adds interest and a useful impression of honesty. Demosthenes himself had a slight lisp. The audience identifies with these flaws. It is only perfection which is dull. Now, move further down the beach and still try to make me hear.'

Thus was I privileged, from the very start, to see the tricks of oratory passed from one master to another. 'There should be no effeminate bending of the neck, no twiddling of the fingers. Do not move your shoulders. If you must use your fingers for a gesture, try bending the middle finger against the thumb and extending the other three – that is it, that is good. The eyes of course are *always* turned in the direction of the gesture, except when we have to reject: "O gods, avert such plague!" or "I do not think that I deserve such honour."'

Nothing was allowed to be written down, for no orator worthy of the name would dream of reading out a text or consulting a sheaf of notes. Molon favoured the standard method of memorising a speech: that of an imaginary journey around the speaker's house. 'Place the first point you want to make in the entrance hall, and picture it lying there, then the second in the atrium, and so on, walking round the house in the way you would naturally tour it, assigning a section of your speech not just to each room, but to every alcove and statue. Make sure each site is well lit, clearly defined, and distinctive. Otherwise you will go groping around like a drunk trying to find his bed after a party.'

Cicero was not the only pupil at Molon's academy that spring and summer. In time we were joined by Cicero's younger brother Quintus, and his cousin Lucius, and also by two friends of his: Servius, a fussy lawyer who wished to become a judge, and Atticus – the dapper, charming Atticus – who had no interest in oratory, for he lived in Athens, and certainly had no intention of making a career in politics, but who loved spending time with Cicero. All marvelled at the change which had been wrought in his health and appearance, and on their final evening together – for now it was autumn, and the time had come to return to Rome – they gathered to hear the effects which Molon had produced on his oratory.

I wish I could recall what it was that Cicero spoke about that night after dinner, but I fear I am the living proof of Demosthenes' cynical assertion that content counts for nothing beside delivery. I stood discreetly out of sight, among the shadows, and all I can picture now are the moths whirling like flakes of ash around the torches, the wash of stars above the courtyard, and the enraptured faces of the young men, flushed in the firelight, turned towards Cicero. But I do remember Molon's words afterwards, when his protégé, with a final bow of his head towards the imaginary jury, sat down. After a long silence he got to his feet and said, in a hoarse voice: 'Cicero, I congratulate you and I am amazed at you. It is Greece and her fate that I am sorry for. The only glory that was left to us was the supremecy of our eloquence, and now you have taken that as well. Go back,' he said, and gestured with those three outstretched fingers, across the lamp-lit terrace to the dark and distant sea, 'go back, my boy, *and conquer Rome.*'

Very well, then. Easy enough to say. But how do you do this? How do you 'conquer Rome' with no weapon other than your voice?

The first step is obvious: you must become a senator.

To gain entry to the senate at that time it was necessary to be at least thirty-one years old and a millionaire. To be exact, assets of one million sesterces had to be shown to the authorities simply to qualify to be a candidate at the annual elections in July, when twenty new senators were elected to replace those who had died in the previous year or had become too poor to keep their seats. But where was Cicero to get a million? His father certainly did not have that kind of money: the family estate was small and heavily mortgaged. He faced, therefore, the three traditional options. But making it would take too long, and stealing it would be too risky. Accordingly, soon after our return from Rhodes, he married it. Terentia was seventeen, boyishly flat-chested, with a head of short, tight black curls. Her half-sister was a vestal virgin, proof of her family's social status. More importantly, she was the owner of two slum apartment blocks in Rome, some woodland in the suburbs, and a farm; total value: one and a quarter million. (Ah, Terentia: plain, grand and rich – what a piece of work you were! I saw her only a few months ago, being carried on an open litter along the coastal road to Naples, screeching at her bearers to make better speed: white-haired and walnut-skinned but otherwise quite unchanged.)

So Cicero, in due course, became a senator – in fact, he topped the poll, being generally now regarded as the second-best advocate in Rome, after Hortensius – and then was sent off for the obligatory year of government service, in his case to the province of Sicily, before being allowed to take his seat. His official title was quaestor, the most junior of the magistracies. Wives were not permitted to accompany their husbands on these tours of duty, so Terentia – I am sure to his deep relief – stayed at home. But I went with him, for by this time I had become a kind of extension of himself, to be used unthinkingly, like an extra hand or foot. Part of the reason for my indispensability was that I had devised a method of taking down his words as fast as he could utter them. From small beginnings – I can modestly claim to be the man who invented the ampersand – my system eventually swelled to a handbook of some four thousand symbols. I found, for example, that Cicero was fond of repeating certain phrases, and these I learned to reduce to a line, or even a few dots – thus proving what most people already know, that politicians essentially say the same thing over and over again. He dictated to me from his bath and his couch, from inside swaying carriages and on country walks. He never ran short of words and I never ran short of symbols to catch and hold them for ever as they flew through the air. We were made for one another.

But to return to Sicily. Do not be alarmed: I shall not describe our work in any detail. Like so much of politics, it was dreary even while it was happening, without revisiting it sixty-odd years later. What was memorable, and significant, was the journey home. Cicero purposely delayed this by a month, from March to April, to ensure he passed through Puteoli during the senate recess, at exactly the moment when all the smart political set would be on the Bay of Naples, enjoying the mineral baths. I was ordered to hire the finest twelve-oared rowing boat I could find, so that he could enter the harbour in style, wearing for the first time the purple-edged toga of a senator of the Roman republic.

For Cicero had convinced himself that he had been such a great success in Sicily, he must be the centre of all attention back in Rome. In a hundred stifling market squares, in the shade of a thousand dusty, wasp-infested Sicilian plane trees, he had dispensed Rome's justice, impartially and with dignity. He had purchased a record amount of grain to feed the electors back in the capital, and had dispatched it at a record cheap price. His speeches at government ceremonies had been masterpieces of tact. He had even feigned interest in the conversation of the locals. He knew he had done well, and in a stream of official reports to the senate he boasted of his achievements. I must confess that occasionally I toned these down before I gave them to the official messenger, and tried to hint to him that perhaps Sicily was not entirely the centre of the world. He took no notice.

I can see him now, standing in the prow, straining his eyes at Puteoli's quayside, as we returned to Italy. What was he expecting? I wonder. A band to pipe him ashore? A consular deputation to present him with a laurel wreath? There was a crowd, all right, but it was not for him. Hortensius, who already had his eye on the consulship, was holding a banquet on several brightly coloured pleasure-craft moored nearby, and guests were waiting to be ferried out to the party. Cicero stepped ashore – ignored. He looked about him, puzzled, and at that moment a few of the revellers, noticing his freshly gleaming senatorial rig, came hurrying towards him. He squared his shoulders in pleasurable anticipation.

'Senator,' called one, 'what's the news from Rome?'

Cicero somehow managed to maintain his smile. 'I have not come from Rome, my good fellow. I am returning from my province.'

A red-haired man, no doubt already drunk, said, 'Ooooh! My *good fellow*! He's returning from his *province* . . .'

There was a snort of laughter, barely suppressed.

'What is so funny about that?' interrupted a third, eager to smooth things over. 'Don't you know? He has been in Africa.'

Cicero's smile was now heroic. 'Sicily, actually.'

There may have been more in this vein. I cannot remember. People began drifting away once they realised there was no city gossip to be had, and very soon Hortensius came along and ushered his remaining guests towards their boats. Cicero he nodded to, civilly enough, but pointedly did not invite to join him. We were left alone.

A trivial incident, you might think, and yet Cicero himself used to say that this was the instant at which his ambition hardened within him to rock. He had been humiliated – humiliated by his own vanity – and given brutal evidence of his smallness in the world. He stood there for a long time, watching Hortensius and his friends partying across the water, listening to the merry flutes, and when he turned away, he had changed. I do not exaggerate. I saw it in his eyes. *Very well*, his expression seemed to say, *you fools can frolic; I shall work.*

'This experience, gentlemen, I am inclined to think was more valuable to me than if I had been hailed with salvoes of applause. I ceased thenceforth from considering what the world was likely to hear about me: from that day I took care that I should be seen personally every day. I lived in the public eye. I frequented the forum. Neither my doorkeeper nor sleep prevented anyone from getting in to see me. Not even when I had nothing to do did I do nothing, and consequently absolute leisure was a thing I never knew.'

I came across that passage in one of his speeches not long ago and I can vouch for the truth of it. He walked away from the harbour like a man in a dream, up through Puteoli and out on to the main highway without once looking back. I struggled along behind him carrying as much luggage as I could manage. To begin with, his steps were slow and thoughtful, but gradually they picked up speed, until at last he was striding so rapidly in the direction of Rome I had difficulty keeping up.

And with this both ends my first roll of paper, and begins the real story of Marcus Tullius Cicero.

II

The day which was to prove the turning point began like any other, an hour before dawn, with Cicero, as always, the first in the household to rise. I lay for a little while in the darkness and listened to the thump of the floorboards above my head as he went through the exercises he had learned on Rhodes – a visit now six years in the past – then I rolled off my straw mattress and rinsed my face. It was the first day of November; cold.

Cicero had a modest two-storey dwelling on the ridge of the Esquiline Hill, hemmed in by a temple on one side and a block of flats on the other, although if you could be bothered to scramble up on to the roof you would be rewarded with a decent view across the smoky valley to the great temples on Capitol Hill about half a mile to the west. It was actually his father's place, but the old gentleman was in poor health nowadays and seldom left the country, so Cicero had it to himself, along with Terentia and their five-year-old daughter, Tullia, and a dozen slaves: me, the two secretaries working under me, Sositheus and Laurea, the steward, Eros, Terentia's business manager, Philotimus, two maids, a nurse, a cook, a valet and a doorkeeper. There was also an old blind philosopher somewhere, Diodotus the Stoic, who occasionally groped his way out of his room to join Cicero for dinner when his master needed an intellectual workout. So: fifteen of us in the household in all. Terentia complained endlessly about the cramped conditions, but Cicero would not move, for at this time he was still very much in his man-of-the-people phase, and the house sat well with the image.

The first thing I did that morning, as I did every morning, was to slip over my left wrist a loop of cord, to which was attached a small notebook of my own design. This consisted of not the usual one or two but four double-sided sheets of wax, each in a beechwood frame, very thin and so hinged that I could fold them all up and snap them shut. In this way I could take many more notes in a single session of dictation than the average secretary; but even so, such was Cicero's daily torrent of words, I always made sure to put spares in my pockets. Then I pulled back the curtain of my tiny room and walked across the courtyard into the tablinum, lighting the lamps and checking all was ready. The only piece of furniture was a sideboard, on which stood a bowl of chickpeas. (Cicero's name derived from *cicer*, meaning chickpea, and believing that an unusual name was an advantage in politics, he always took pains to draw attention to it.) Once I was satisfied, I passed through the atrium into the entrance hall, where the doorman was already waiting with his hand on the big metal lock. I checked the light through the narrow window, and when I judged it pale enough, gave a nod to the doorman, who slid back the bolts.

Outside in the chilly street, the usual crowd of the miserable and the desperate was already waiting, and I made a note of each man as he crossed the threshold. Most I recognised; those I did not, I asked for their names; the familiar no-hopers, I turned away. But the standing instruction was: 'If he has a vote, let him in', so the tablinum was soon well filled with anxious clients, each seeking a piece of the senator's time. I lingered by the entrance until I reckoned the queue had all filed in and was just stepping back when a figure with the dusty clothes, straggling hair and uncut beard of a man in mourning loomed in the doorway. He gave me a fright, I do not mind admitting.

'Tiro!' he said. 'Thank the gods!' And he sank against the door jamb, exhausted, peering out at me with pale, dead eyes. I guess he must have been about fifty. At first I could not place him, but it is one of the jobs of a political secretary to put names to faces, and gradually, despite his condition, a picture began to assemble in my mind: a large house overlooking the sea, an ornamental garden, a collection of bronze statues, a town somewhere in Sicily, in the north – Thermae, that was it.

'Sthenius of Thermae,' I said, and held out my hand. 'Welcome.'

It was not my place to comment on his appearance, nor to ask what he was doing hundreds of miles from home and in such obvious distress. I left him in the tablinum and went through to Cicero's study. The senator, who was due in court that morning to defend a youth charged with parricide, and who would also be expected to attend the afternoon session of the senate, was squeezing a small leather ball to strengthen his fingers, while being robed in his toga by his valet. He was listening to one letter being read out by young Sositheus, and at the same time dictating a message to Laurea, to whom I had taught the rudiments of my shorthand system. As I entered, he threw the ball at me – I caught it without thinking – and gestured for the list of callers. He read it greedily, as he always did. What had he caught overnight? Some prominent citizen from a useful tribe? A Sabatini, perhaps? A Pomptini? Or a businessman rich enough to vote among the first centuries in the consular elections? But today it was only the usual small fry and his face gradually fell until he reached the final name.

'Sthenius?' He interrupted his dictation. 'He's that Sicilian, is he not? The rich one with the bronzes? We had better find out what he wants.'

'Sicilians don't have a vote,' I pointed out.

'Pro bono,' he said, with a straight face. 'Besides, he does have bronzes. I shall see him first.'

So I fetched in Sthenius, who was given the usual treatment – the trademark smile, the manly double-grip handshake, the long and sincere stare into the eyes – then shown to a seat and asked what had brought him to Rome. I had started remembering more about Sthenius. We had stayed with him twice in Thermae, when Cicero heard cases in the town. Back then he had been one of the leading citizens of the province, but now all his vigour and confidence had gone. He needed help, he announced. He was facing ruin. His life was in terrible danger. He had been robbed.

'Really?' said Cicero. He was half glancing at a document on his desk, not paying too much attention, for a busy advocate hears many hard-luck stories. 'You have my sympathy. Robbed by whom?'

'By the governor of Sicily, Gaius Verres.'

The senator looked up sharply.

There was no stopping Sthenius after that. As his story poured out, Cicero caught my eye and performed a little mime of note-taking – he wanted a record of this – and when Sthenius eventually paused to draw breath, he gently interrupted and asked him to go back a little, to the day, almost three months earlier, when he had first received the letter from Verres. 'What was your reaction?'

'I worried a little. He already had a . . . *reputation*. People call him – his name meaning boar – people call him the Boar with Blood on his Snout. But I could hardly refuse.'

'You still have this letter?'

'Yes.'

'And in it did Verres specifically mention your art collection?'

'Oh yes. He said he had often heard about it and wanted to see it.'

'And how soon after that did he come to stay?'

'Very soon. A week at most.'

'Was he alone?'

'No, he had his lictors with him. I had to find room for them as well. Bodyguards are always rough types, but these were the worst set of thugs I ever saw. The chief of them, Sextius, is the official executioner for the whole of Sicily. He demands bribes from his victims by threatening to botch the job – you know, mangle them – if they do not pay up beforehand.' Sthenius swallowed and started breathing hard. We waited.

'Take your time,' said Cicero.

'I thought Verres might like to bathe after his journey, and then we could dine – but no, he said he wanted to see my collection straightaway.'

'You had some very fine pieces, I remember.'

'It was my life, Senator, I cannot put it plainer. Thirty years of travelling and haggling. Corinthian and Delian bronzes, pictures, silver – nothing I did not handle and choose myself. I had Myron's *The Discus Thrower* and *The Spear Bearer* by Polycleitus. Some silver cups by Mentor. Verres was complimentary. He said it deserved a wider audience. He said it was good enough for public display. I paid no attention till we were having dinner on the terrace and I heard a noise from the inner courtyard. My steward told me a wagon drawn by oxen had arrived and Verres's lictors were loading it with everything.'

Sthenius was silent again, and I could readily imagine the shame of it for such a proud man: his wife wailing, the household traumatised, the dusty outlines where the statues had once stood. The only sound in the study was the tap of my stylus on wax.

Cicero said: 'You did not complain?'

'Who to? The governor?' Sthenius laughed. 'No, Senator. I was alive, wasn't I? If he had just left it at that, I would have swallowed my losses, and you would never have heard a squeak from me. But collecting can be a sickness, and I tell you what: your Governor Verres has it badly. You remember those statues in the town square?'

'Indeed I do. Three very fine bronzes. But you are surely not telling me he stole those as well?'

'He tried. This was on his third day under my roof. He asked me whose they were. I told him they were the property of the town, and had been for centuries. You know they are four hundred years old? He said he would like permission to remove them to his residence in Syracuse, also as a loan, and asked me to approach the council. By then I knew what kind of a man he was, so I said I could not, in all honour, oblige him. He left that night. A few days after that, I received a summons for trial on the fifth day of October, on a charge of forgery.'

'Who brought the charge?'

'An enemy of mine named Agathinus. He is a client of Verres. My first thought was to face him down. I have nothing to fear as far as my honesty goes. I have never forged a document in my life. But then I heard the judge was to be Verres himself, and that he had already fixed on the punishment. I was to be whipped in front of the whole town for my insolence.'

'And so you fled?'

'That same night, I took a boat along the coast to Messana.'

Cicero rested his chin in his hand and contemplated Sthenius. I recognised that gesture. He was weighing the witness up. 'You say the hearing was on the fifth of last month. Have you heard what happened?'

'That is why I am here. I was convicted in my absence, sentenced to be flogged – and fined five thousand. But there is worse than that. At the hearing, Verres claimed fresh evidence had been produced against me, this time of spying for the rebels in Spain. There is to be a new trial in Syracuse on the first day of December.'

'But spying is a capital offence.'

'Senator – believe me – he plans to have me crucified. He boasts of it openly. I would not be the first, either. I need help. Please. Will you help me?'

I thought he might be about to sink to his knees and start kissing the senator's feet, and so, I suspect, did Cicero, for he quickly got up from his chair and started pacing about the room. 'It seems to me there are two aspects to this case, Sthenius. One, the theft of your property – and there, frankly, I cannot see what is to be done. Why do you think men such as Verres desire to be governors in the first place? Because they know they can take what they want, within reason. The second aspect, the manipulation of the legal process – that is more promising.

'I know several men with great legal expertise who live in Sicily – one, indeed, in Syracuse. I shall write to him today and urge him, as a particular favour to me, to accept your case. I shall even give him my opinion as to what he should do. He should apply to the court to have the forthcoming prosecution declared invalid, on the grounds that you are not present to answer. If that fails, and Verres goes ahead, your advocate should come to Rome and argue that the conviction is unsound.'

But the Sicilian was shaking his head. 'If it was just a lawyer in Syracuse I needed, Senator, I would not have come all the way to Rome.'

I could see Cicero did not like where this was leading. Such a case could tie up his practice for days, and Sicilians, as I had reminded him, did not have votes. Pro bono indeed!

'Listen,' he said reassuringly, 'your case is strong. Verres is obviously corrupt. He abuses hospitality. He steals. He brings false charges. He plots judicial murder. His position is indefensible. It can easily be handled by an advocate in Syracuse – really, I promise you. Now, if you will excuse me, I have many clients to see, and I am due in court in less than an hour.'

He nodded to me and I stepped forward, putting a hand on Sthenius's arm to guide him out. The Sicilian shook it off. 'But I need you,' he persisted.

'Why?'

'Because my only hope of justice lies here, not in Sicily, where Verres controls the courts. And everyone here tells me Marcus Cicero is the second-best lawyer in Rome.'

'Do they indeed?' Cicero's tone took on an edge of sarcasm: he hated that epithet. 'Well then, why settle for second best? Why not go straight to Hortensius?'

'I thought of that,' said his visitor artlessly, 'but he turned me down. He is representing Verres.'

I showed the Sicilian out and returned to find Cicero alone in his study, tilted back in his chair, staring at the wall, tossing the leather ball from one hand to the other. Legal textbooks cluttered his desk. *Precedents in Pleading* by Hostilius was one which he had open; Manilius's *Conditions of Sale* was another.

'Do you remember that red-haired drunk on the quayside at Puteoli, the day we came back from Sicily? "Ooooh! My *good fellow*! He's returning from his *province* . . ."'

I nodded.

'That was Verres.' The ball went back and forth, back and forth. 'The fellow gives corruption a bad name.'

'I am surprised at Hortensius for getting involved with him.'

'Are you? I'm not.' He stopped tossing the ball and contemplated it on his outstretched palm. 'The Dancing Master and the Boar . . .' He brooded for a while. 'A man in my position would have to be mad to tangle with Hortensius and Verres combined, and all for the sake of some Sicilian who is not even a Roman citizen.'

'True.'

'True,' he repeated, although there was an odd hesitancy in the way he said it which sometimes makes me wonder if he had not just then glimpsed the whole thing – the whole extraordinary set of possibilities and consequences, laid out like a mosaic in his mind. But if he had, I never knew, for at that moment his daughter Tullia ran in, still wearing her nightdress, with some childish drawing to show him, and suddenly his attention switched entirely on to her and he scooped her up and settled her on his knee. 'Did you do this? Did you *really* do this all by yourself . . . ?'

I left him to it and slipped away, back into the tablinum, to announce that we were running late and that the senator was about to leave for court. Sthenius was still moping around, and asked me when he could expect an answer, to which I could only reply that he would have to fall in with the rest. Soon after that

Cicero himself appeared, hand in hand with Tullia, nodding good morning to everyone, greeting each by name ('The first rule in politics, Tiro: never forget a face'). He was beautifully turned out, as always, his hair pomaded and slicked back, his skin scented, his toga freshly laundered; his red leather shoes spotless and shiny; his face bronzed by years of pleading in the open air; groomed, lean, fit: he *glowed*. They followed him into the vestibule, where he hoisted the beaming little girl into the air, showed her off to the assembled company, then turned her face to his and gave her a resounding kiss on the lips. There was a drawn-out 'Ahh!' and some isolated applause. It was not wholly put on for show – he would have done it even if no one had been present, for he loved his darling Tulliola more than he ever loved anyone in his entire life – but he knew the Roman electorate were a sentimental lot, and that if word of his paternal devotion got around, it would do him no harm.

And so we stepped out into the bright promise of that November morning, into the gathering noise of the city – Cicero striding ahead, with me beside him, notebook at the ready; Sositheus and Laurea tucked in behind, carrying the document cases with the evidence he needed for his appearance in court; and, on either side of us, trying to catch the senator's attention, yet proud merely to be in his aura, two dozen assorted petitioners and hangers-on, including Sthenius – down the hill from the leafy, respectable heights of the Esquiline and into the stink and smoke and racket of Subura. Here the height of the tenements shut out the sunlight and the packed crowds squeezed our phalanx of supporters into a broken thread that still somehow determinedly trailed along after us. Cicero was a well-known figure here, a hero to the shopkeepers and merchants whose interests he had represented, and who had watched him walking past for years. Without once breaking his rapid step, his sharp blue eyes registered every bowed head, every wave of greeting, and it was rare for me to need to whisper a name in his ear, for he knew his voters far better than I.

I do not know how it is these days, but at that time there were six or seven law courts in almost permanent session, each set up in a different part of the forum, so that at the hour when they all opened one could barely move for advocates and legal officers hurrying about. To make it worse, the praetor of each court would always arrive from his house preceded by half a dozen lictors to clear his path, and as luck would have it, our little entourage debouched into the forum at exactly the moment that Hortensius – at this time a praetor himself – went parading by towards the senate house. We were all held back by his guards to let the great man pass, and to this day I do not think it was his intention to cut Cicero dead, for he was a man of refined, almost effeminate manners: he simply did not see him. But the consequence was that the so-called second-best advocate in Rome, his cordial greeting dead on his lips, was left staring at the retreating back of the so-called best with such an intensity of loathing I was surprised Hortensius did not start rubbing at the skin between his shoulder blades.

Our business that morning was in the central criminal court, convened outside the Basilica Aemilia, where the fifteen-year-old Caius Popillius Laenas was on trial accused of stabbing his father to death through the eye with a metal stylus. I could already see a big crowd waiting around the tribunal. Cicero was due to make the closing speech for the defence. That was attraction enough. But if he failed to convince the jury, Popillius, as a convicted parricide, would be stripped naked, flayed till he bled, then sewn up in a sack together with a dog, a cock and a viper and thrown into the River Tiber. There was a whiff of bloodlust in the air, and as the onlookers parted to let us through, I caught a glimpse of Popillius himself, a notoriously violent youth, whose eyebrows merged to form a continuous thick black line. He was seated next to his uncle on the bench reserved for the defence, scowling defiantly, spitting at anyone who came too close. 'We really must secure an acquittal,' observed Cicero, 'if only to spare the dog, the cock and the viper the ordeal of being sewn up in a sack with Popillius.' He always maintained that it was no business of the advocate to worry whether his client was guilty or not: that was for the court. He undertook only to do his best, and in return the Popillii Laeni, who could boast four consuls in their family tree, would be obliged to support him whenever he ran for office.

Sositheus and Laurea set down the boxes of evidence, and I was just bending to unfasten the nearest when Cicero told me to leave it. 'Save yourself the trouble,' he said, tapping the side of his head. 'I have the speech up here well enough.' He bowed politely to his client – 'Good day, Popillius: we shall soon have this settled, I trust' – then continued to me, in a quieter voice: 'I have a more important task for you. Give me your notebook. I want you to go to the senate house, find the chief clerk, and see if there is a chance of having this put on the order paper this afternoon.' He was writing rapidly. 'Say nothing to our Sicilian friend just yet. There is great danger. We must take this carefully, one step at a time.'

It was not until I had left the tribunal and was halfway across the forum to the senate house that I risked taking a look at what he had written: *That in the opinion of this house the prosecution of persons in their absence on capital charges should be prohibited in the provinces.* I felt a tightening in my chest, for I saw at once what it meant. Cleverly, tentatively, obliquely, Cicero was preparing at last to challenge his great rival. I was carrying a declaration of war.

Gellius Publicola was the presiding consul for November. He was a blunt, delightfully stupid military commander of the old school. It was said, or at any rate it was said by Cicero, that when Gellius had passed through Athens with his army twenty years before, he had offered to mediate between the warring schools of philosophy: he would convene a conference at which they could thrash out the meaning of life once and for all, thus sparing themselves further pointless argument. I knew Gellius's secretary fairly well, and as the afternoon's agenda was unusually light, with nothing scheduled apart from a report on the military situation, he agreed to add Cicero's motion to the order paper. 'But you might warn your master,' he said, 'that the consul has heard his little joke about the philosophers, *and he does not much like it.*'

By the time I returned to the criminal court, Cicero was already well launched on his closing speech for the defence. It was not one of those which he afterwards chose to preserve, so unfortunately I do not have the text. All I can remember is that he won the case by the clever expedient of promising that young Popillius, if acquitted, would devote the rest of his life to military service – a pledge which took the prosecution, the jury, and indeed his client entirely by surprise. But it did the trick, and the moment the verdict was in, without pausing to waste another moment on the ghastly Popillius, or even to snatch a mouthful of food, he set off immediately westwards towards the senate house, still trailed by his original honour-guard of admirers, their number swelled by the spreading rumour that the great advocate had another speech planned.

Cicero used to say that it was not in the senate chamber that the real business of the republic was done, but outside, in the open-air lobby known as the senaculum, where the senators were obliged to wait until they constituted a quorum. This daily massing of white-robed figures, which might last for an hour or more, was one of the great sights of the city, and while Cicero plunged in among them, Sthenius and I joined the crowd of gawpers on the other side of the forum. (The Sicilian, poor fellow, still had no idea what was happening.)

It is in the nature of things that not all politicians can achieve greatness. Of the six hundred men who then constituted the senate, only eight could be elected praetor – to preside over the courts – in any one year, and only two of these could go on to achieve the supreme *imperium* of the consulship. In other words, more than half of those milling around the senaculum were doomed never to hold elected office at all. They were what the aristocrats sneeringly called the *pedarii*, the men who voted with their feet, shuffling dutifully to one side of the chamber or the other whenever a division was called. And yet, in their way, these citizens were the backbone of the republic: bankers, businessmen and landowners from all over Italy; wealthy, cautious and patriotic; suspicious of the arrogance and show of the aristocrats. Like Cicero, they were often 'new men', the first in their families to win election to the senate. These were his people, and observing him threading his way among them that afternoon was like watching a master-craftsman in his studio, a sculptor with his stone – here a hand resting lightly on an elbow, there a heavy arm clapped across a pair of meaty shoulders; with this man a coarse joke, with that a solemn word of condolence, his own hands crossed and pressed to his breast in sympathy; detained by a bore, he would seem to have all the hours of the day to listen to his dreary story, but then you would see his hand flicker out and catch some passer-by, and he would spin as gracefully as a dancer, with the tenderest backward glance of apology and regret, to work on someone else. Occasionally he would gesture in our direction, and a senator would stare at us, and perhaps shake his head in disbelief, or nod slowly to promise his support.

'What is he saying about me?' asked Sthenius. 'What is he going to do?'

I made no answer, for I did not know myself.

By now it was clear that Hortensius had realised something was going on, but was unsure exactly what. The order of business had been posted in its usual place beside the door of the senate house. I saw Hortensius stop to read it – *the prosecution of persons in their absence on capital charges should be prohibited in the provinces* – and turn away, mystified. Gellius Publicola was sitting in the doorway on his carved ivory chair, surrounded by his attendants, waiting until the entrails had been inspected and the auguries declared favourable before summoning the senators inside. Hortensius approached him, palms spread wide in enquiry. Gellius shrugged and pointed irritably at Cicero. Hortensius swung round to discover his ambitious rival surrounded by a conspiratorial circle of senators. He frowned, and went over to join his own aristocratic friends: the three Metellus brothers – Quintus, Lucius and Marcus – and the two elderly ex-consuls who really ran the empire, Quintus Catulus (whose sister was married to Hortensius), and the double-triumphator Publius Servilius Vatia Isauricus. Merely writing their names after all these years raises the hairs on my neck, for these were such men, stern and unyielding and steeped in the old republican values, as no longer exist. Hortensius must have told them about the motion, because slowly all five turned to look at Cicero.

Immediately thereafter a trumpet sounded to signal the start of the session and the senators began to file in.

The old senate house was a cool, gloomy, cavernous temple of government, split by a wide central aisle of black and white tile. Facing across it on either side were long rows of wooden benches, six deep, on which the senators sat, with a dais at the far end for the chairs of the consuls. The light on that November afternoon was pale and bluish, dropping in shafts from the unglazed windows just beneath the raftered roof. Pigeons cooed on the sills and flapped across the chamber, sending small feathers and even occasionally hot squirts of excrement down on to the senators below. Some held that it was lucky to be shat on while speaking, others that it was an ill omen, a few that it depended on the colour of the deposit. The superstitions were as numerous as their interpretations. Cicero took no notice of them, just as he took no notice of the arrangement of sheep's guts, or whether a peal of thunder was on the left or the right, or the particular flight path of a flock of birds – idiocy all of it, as far as he was concerned, even though he later campaigned enthusiastically for election to the College of Augurs.

By ancient tradition, then still observed, the doors of the senate house remained open so that the people could hear the debates. The crowd, Sthenius and I among them, surged across the forum to the threshold of the chamber, where we were held back by a simple rope. Gellius was already speaking, relating the dispatches of the army commanders in the field. On all three fronts, the news was good. In southern Italy, the vastly rich Marcus Crassus – he who once boasted that no man could call himself wealthy until he could keep a legion of five thousand solely out of his income – was putting down Spartacus's slave revolt with great severity. In Spain, Pompey the Great, after six years' fighting, was mopping up the last of the rebel armies. In Asia Minor, Lucius Lucullus was enjoying a glorious run of victories over King Mithradates. Once their reports had been read, supporters of each man rose in turn to praise his patron's achievements and subtly denigrate those of his rivals. I knew the politics of this from Cicero and passed them on to Sthenius in a superior whisper: 'Crassus hates Pompey and is determined to defeat Spartacus before Pompey can return with his legions from Spain to take all the credit. Pompey hates Crassus and wants the glory of finishing off Spartacus so that he can rob him of a triumph. Crassus and Pompey both hate Lucullus because he has the most glamorous command.'

'And whom does Lucullus hate?'

'Pompey and Crassus, of course, for intriguing against him.'

I felt as pleased as a child who has just successfully recited his lesson, for it was all just a game then, and I had no idea that we would ever get drawn in. The debate came to a desultory halt, without the need for a vote, and the senators began talking among themselves. Gellius, who must have been well into his sixties, held the order paper up close to his face and squinted at it, then peered around the chamber, trying to locate Cicero, who, as a junior senator, was confined to a distant back bench near the door. Eventually Cicero stood to show himself, Gellius sat, the buzz of voices died away, and I picked up my stylus. There was a silence, which Cicero allowed to grow, an old trick to increase tension. And then, when he had waited so long it seemed that something must be wrong, he began to speak – very quietly and hesitantly at first, forcing his listeners to strain their ears, the rhythm of his words hooking them without their even knowing it.

'Honourable members, compared to the stirring accounts of

our men in arms to which we have lately listened, I fear what I say will sound small indeed.' And now his voice rose. 'But if the moment has come when this noble house no longer has ears for the pleas of an innocent man, then all those courageous deeds are worthless, and our soldiers bleed in vain.' There was a murmur of agreement from the benches beside him. 'This morning there came into my home just such an innocent man, whose treatment by one of our number has been so shameful, so monstrous and so cruel that the gods themselves must weep to hear of it. I refer to the honourable Sthenius of Thermae, recently resident in the miserable, misgoverned, misappropriated province of Sicily.'

At the word 'Sicily', Hortensius, who had been sprawling on the front bench nearest the consul, twitched slightly. Without taking his eyes from Cicero he turned and began whispering to Quintus, the eldest of the Metellus brothers, who promptly leaned behind him and beckoned to Marcus, the junior of the fraternal trio. Marcus squatted on his haunches to receive his instructions, then, after a brief bow to the presiding consul, came hurrying down the aisle towards me. For a moment I thought I was about to be struck – they were tough, swaggering fellows, those Metelli – but he did not even look at me. He lifted the rope, ducked under it, pushed through the crowd and disappeared.

Cicero, meanwhile, was hitting his stride. After our return from Molon, with the precept 'Delivery, delivery, delivery' carved into his mind, he had spent many hours at the theatre, studying the methods of the actors, and had developed a considerable talent for mime and mimicry. Using only the smallest touch of voice or gesture, he could, as it were, populate his speeches with the characters to whom he referred. He treated the senate that afternoon to a command performance: the swaggering arrogance of Verres

33

was contrasted with the quiet dignity of Sthenius, the long-suffering Sicilians shrank before the vileness of the public executioner, Sextius. Sthenius himself could hardly believe what he was witnessing. He had been in the city but a day, and here he was, the subject of a debate in the Roman senate itself. Hortensius, meanwhile, kept glancing towards the door, and as Cicero began to work towards his peroration – 'Sthenius seeks our protection, not merely from a thief, but from the very man who is supposed to punish thieves!' – he finally sprang to his feet. Under the rules of the senate, a serving praetor always took precedence over a humble member of the *pedarii*, and Cicero had no choice but to give way.

'Senators,' boomed Hortensius, 'we have sat through this long enough! This is surely one of the most flagrant pieces of opportunism ever seen in this noble house! A vague motion is placed before us, which now turns out to relate to one man only. No notice is given to us about what is to be discussed. We have no means of verifying whether what we are hearing is true. Gaius Verres, a senior member of this order, is being defamed with no opportunity to defend himself. I move that this sitting be suspended immediately!'

Hortensius sat to a patter of applause from the aristocrats. Cicero stood. His face was perfectly straight.

'The senator seems not to have read the motion,' he said, in mock puzzlement. 'Where is there any mention here of Gaius Verres? Gentlemen, I am not asking this house to vote on Gaius Verres. It would not be fair to judge Gaius Verres in his absence. Gaius Verres is not here to defend himself. And now that we have established that principle, will Hortensius please extend it to my client, and agree that he should not be tried in his absence either? Or is there to be one law for the aristocrats and another for the rest of us?'

That raised the temperature well enough and set the *pedarii* around Cicero and the crowd at the door roaring with delight. I felt someone pushing roughly behind me and Marcus Metellus shouldered his way back into the chamber and walked quickly up the aisle towards Hortensius. Cicero watched his progress, at first with an expression of puzzlement, and then with one of realisation. He quickly held up his hand for silence. 'Very well. Since Hortensius objects to the vagueness of the original motion, let us reframe it so that there can be no doubt. I propose an amendment: *That whereas Sthenius has been prosecuted in his absence, it is agreed that no trial of him in his absence shall take place, and that if any such trial has already taken place, it shall be invalid.* And I say: let us vote on it now, and in the highest traditions of the Roman senate save an innocent man from the dreadful punishment of crucifixion!'

To mingled cheers and cat-calls, Cicero sat and Gellius rose. 'The motion has been put,' declared the consul. 'Does any other member wish to speak?'

Hortensius, the Metellus brothers and a few others of their party, such as Scribonius Curio, Sergius Catilina and Aemilius Alba, were in a huddle around the front bench, and it briefly seemed that the house would move straight to a division, which would have suited Cicero perfectly. But when the aristocrats finally settled back in their places, the bony figure of Catulus was revealed to be still on his feet. 'I believe I shall speak,' he said. 'Yes, I believe I shall have something to say.' Catulus was as hard and heartless as flint – the great-great-great-great-great-grandson (I believe that is the correct number of greats) of that Catulus who had triumphed over Hamilcar in the First Punic War – and a full two centuries of history were distilled into his vinegary old voice. 'I shall speak,' he repeated, 'and what I shall say first is that that young man' – pointing at Cicero – 'knows nothing whatsoever about "the highest traditions of the Roman senate", for if he did he would realise that no senator ever attacks another, except to his face. It shows a lack of breeding. I look at him there, all clever and eager in his place, and do you know what I think, gentlemen? I think of the wisdom of the old saying: "An ounce of heredity is worth a pound of merit"!'

Now it was the aristocrats who were rocking with laughter. Catilina, of whom I shall have much more to say later, pointed at Cicero, and then drew his finger across his throat. Cicero flushed pink but kept his self-control. He even managed a thin smile. Catulus turned with delight to the benches behind him, and I caught a glimpse of his grinning profile, sharp and beak-nosed, like a head on a coin. He swivelled back to face the chamber. 'When I first entered this house, in the consulship of Claudius Pulcher and Marcus Perperna . . .' His voice settled into a confident drone.

Cicero caught my eye. He mouthed something, glanced up at the windows, then gestured with his head towards the door. I understood at once what he meant, and as I pushed my way back through the spectators and into the forum, I realised that Marcus Metellus must have been dispatched on exactly the same errand. In those days, when time-keeping was cruder than it is now, the last hour of the day's business was deemed to begin when the sun dropped west of the Maenian Column. I guessed that must be about to happen, and sure enough, the clerk responsible for making the observation was already on his way to tell the consul. It was against the law for the senate to sit after sunset. Clearly, Hortensius and his friends were planning to talk out the remainder of the session, preventing Cicero's motion from being put to the vote. By the time I had quickly confirmed the sun's position for myself, run back across the forum and wriggled my way through the crowd to the threshold of the chamber, Gellius was making the announcement: 'The last hour!'

Cicero was instantly on his feet, wanting to make a point of order, but Gellius would not take it, and the floor was still with Catulus. On and on Catulus went, giving an interminable history of provincial government, virtually from the time since the she-wolf suckled Romulus. (Catulus's father, also a consul, had famously died by shutting himself up in a sealed room, kindling a charcoal fire, and suffocating himself with the fumes: Cicero used to say he must have done it to avoid listening to another speech by his son.) When he did eventually reach some sort of conclusion, he promptly yielded the floor to Quintus Metellus. Again Cicero rose, but again he was defeated by the seniority rule. Metellus had praetorian rank, and unless he chose to give way, which naturally he did not, Cicero had no right of speech. For a time Cicero stood his ground, against a swelling roar of protest, but the men on either side of him – one of whom was Servius, his lawyer friend, who had his interests at heart and could see he was in danger of making a fool of himself – pulled at his toga, and finally he surrendered and sat down.

It was forbidden to light a lamp or a brazier inside the chamber. As the gloom deepened, the cold sharpened and the white shapes of the senators, motionless in the November dusk, became like a parliament of ghosts. After Metellus had droned on for an eternity, and sat down in favour of Hortensius – a man who could talk on anything for hours – everyone knew the debate was over, and very soon afterwards Gellius dissolved the house. He limped down the aisle, an old man in search of his dinner, preceded by four lictors carrying his curule chair. Once he had passed through the doors, the senators streamed out after him and Sthenius and

I retreated a short distance into the forum to wait for Cicero. Gradually the crowd around us dwindled. The Sicilian kept asking me what was happening, but I felt it wiser to say nothing, and we stood in silence. I pictured Cicero sitting alone on the back benches, waiting for the chamber to empty so that he could leave without having to speak to anyone, for I feared he had badly lost face. But to my surprise he strolled out chatting with Hortensius and another, older senator, whom I did not recognise. They talked for a while on the steps of the senate house, shook hands and parted.

'Do you know who that was?' asked Cicero, coming over to us. Far from being cast down, he appeared highly amused. 'That was Verres's father. He has promised to write to his son, urging him to drop the prosecution, if we agree not to bring the matter back to the senate.'

Poor Sthenius was so relieved, I thought he might die from gratitude. He dropped to his knees and began kissing the senator's hands. Cicero made a sour face and gently raised him to his feet. 'Really, my dear Sthenius, save your thanks until I have actually achieved something. He has only promised to write, that is all. It is not a guarantee.'

Sthenius said, 'But you will accept the offer?'

Cicero shrugged. 'What choice do we have? Even if I re-table the motion, they will only talk it out again.'

I could not resist asking why, in that case, Hortensius was bothering to offer a deal at all.

Cicero nodded slowly. 'Now that is a good question.' There was a mist rising from the Tiber, and the lamps in the shops along the Argiletum shone yellow and gauzy. He sniffed the damp air. 'I suppose it can only be because he is embarrassed. Which in his case, of course, takes quite a lot. Yet it seems that even *he* would prefer not to be associated too publicly with such a flagrant criminal as Verres. So he is trying to settle the matter quietly. I wonder how much his retainer is from Verres: it must be an enormous sum.'

'Hortensius was not the only one who came to Verres's defence,' I reminded him.

'No.' Cicero glanced back at the senate house, and I could see that something had just occurred to him. 'They are all in it together, aren't they? The Metellus brothers are true aristocrats – they would never lift a finger to help anyone apart from them selves, unless it was for money. As for Catulus, the man is frantic for gold. He has undertaken so much building on the Capitol over the past ten years, it is almost more of a shrine to him than it is to Jupiter. I estimate we must have been looking at half a million in bribes this afternoon, Tiro. A few Delian bronzes – however fine, Sthenius, forgive me – would not be sufficient to buy that kind of protection. What *is* Verres up to down there in Sicily?' He suddenly began working his signet ring over his knuckle. 'Take this to the National Archive, Tiro, and show it to one of the clerks. Demand in my name to see all the official accounts submitted to the senate by Gaius Verres.'

My face must have registered my dismay. 'But the National Archive is run by Catulus's people. He is sure to hear word of what you are doing.'

'That cannot be helped.'

'But what am I looking for?'

'Anything interesting. You will know it when you see it. Go quickly, while there is still some light.' He put his arm round the shoulders of the Sicilian. 'As for you, Sthenius – you will come to dinner with me tonight, I hope? It is only family, but I am sure my wife will be delighted to meet you.'

I rather doubted that, but naturally it was not my place to say so.

The National Archive, which was then barely six years old, loomed over the forum even more massively than it does today, for back then it had less competition. I climbed that great flight of steps up to the first gallery, and by the time I found an attendant my heart was racing. I showed him the seal, and demanded, on behalf of Senator Cicero, to see Verres's accounts. At first he claimed never to have heard of Cicero, and besides, the building was closing. But then I pointed in the direction of the Carcer and told him firmly that if he did not desire to spend a month in chains in the state prison for impeding official business, he had better fetch those records now. (One lesson I had learned from Cicero was how to hide my nerves.) He scowled a bit and thought about it, then told me to follow him.

The Archive was Catulus's domain, a temple to him and his clan. Above the vaults was his inscription – *Q. Lutatius Catulus, son of Quintus, grandson of Quintus, consul, by a decree of the Senate, commissioned the erection of this National Archive, and approved it satisfactory* – and beside the entrance stood his life-size statue, looking somewhat more youthful and heroic than he had appeared in the senate that afternoon. Most of the attendants were either his slaves or his freedmen, and wore his emblem, a little dog, sewn on to their tunics. I shall tell you the kind of man Catulus was. He blamed the suicide of his father on the populist praetor Gratidianus – a distant relative of Cicero – and after the victory of the aristocrats in the civil war between Marius and Sulla he took the opportunity for revenge. His young protégé, Sergius Catilina, at his behest, seized Gratidianus, and whipped him through the streets to the Catulus family tomb. There, his arms and legs were broken, his ears and nose cut off, his tongue pulled out of his mouth and severed, and his eyes gouged out. In this ghastly condition his head was then lopped off, and Catilina bore it in triumph to Catulus, who was waiting in the forum. Do you wonder now why I was nervous as I waited for the vaults to be opened?

The senatorial records were kept in fireproof strongrooms, built to withstand a lightning strike, tunnelled into the rock of the Capitol, and when the slaves swung back the big bronze door I had a glimpse of thousands upon thousands of rolled papyri, receding into the shadows of the sacred hill. Five hundred years of history were encompassed in that one small space: half a millennium of magistracies and governorships, proconsular decrees and judicial rulings, from Lusitania to Macedonia, from Africa to Gaul, and most of them made in the names of the same few families: the Aemilii, the Claudii, the Cornelii, the Lutatii, the Metelli, the Servilii. This was what gave Catulus and his kind the confidence to look down upon such provincial equestrians as Cicero.

They kept me waiting in an antechamber while they searched for Verres's records, and eventually brought out to me a single document case containing perhaps a dozen rolls. From the labels on the ends I saw that these were all, with one exception, accounts from his time as urban praetor. The exception was a flimsy piece of papyrus, barely worth the trouble of unrolling, covering his work as a junior magistrate twelve years previously, at the time of the war between Sulla and Marius, and on which was written just three sentences: *I received 2,235,417 sesterces. I expended on wages, grain, payments to legates, the proquaestor, the praetorian cohort 1,635,417 sesterces. I left 600,000 at Ariminum.* Remembering the scores of rolls of meticulous accounts which Cicero's term as a junior magistrate on Sicily had generated, all of which I had written out for him, I could barely refrain from laughing.

'Is this all there is?'

The attendant assured me it was.

'But where are the accounts from his time in Sicily?'

'They have not yet been submitted to the treasury.'

'Not yet submitted? He has been governor for almost two years!'

The fellow looked at me blankly, and I could see that there was no point in wasting any more time with him. I copied out the three lines relating to Verres's junior magistracy and went out into the evening.

While I had been in the National Archive, darkness had fallen over Rome. In Cicero's house the family had already gone into dinner. But the master had left instructions with the steward, Eros, that I was to be shown straight into the dining room the moment I returned. I found Cicero lying on a couch beside Terentia. His brother, Quintus, was also there, with his wife, Pomponia. The third couch was occupied by Cicero's cousin Lucius and the hapless Sthenius, still clad in his dirty mourning clothes and squirming with unease. I could sense the strained atmosphere as soon as I entered, although Cicero was in good spirits. He always liked a dinner party. It was not the quality of the food and drink which mattered to him, but the company and the conversation. Quintus and Lucius, along with Atticus, were the three men he loved most.

'Well?' he said to me. I told him what had happened and showed him my copy of Verres's quaestorian accounts. He scanned it, grunted, and tossed the wax tablet across the table. 'Look at that, Quintus. The villain is too lazy even to lie adequately. Six hundred thousand – what a nice round sum, not a penny either side of it

– and where does he leave it? Why, in a town which is then conveniently occupied by the opposition's army, so the loss can be blamed on them! And no accounts submitted from Sicily for *two years*? I am obliged to you, Sthenius, for bringing this rogue to my attention.'

'Oh yes, *so* obliged,' said Terentia, with savage sweetness. '*So* obliged – for setting us at war with half the decent families in Rome. But presumably we can socialise with Sicilians from now on, so that will be all right. Where did you say you came from again?'

'Thermae, your ladyship.'

'Thermae. I have never heard of it, but I am sure it is delightful. You can make speeches to the town council, Cicero. Perhaps you will even get elected there, now that Rome is forever closed to you. You can be the consul of Thermae and I can be the first lady.'

'A role I am sure you will perform with your customary charm, my darling,' said Cicero, patting her arm.

They could needle away at one another like this for hours. Sometimes I believe they rather enjoyed it.

'I still fail to see what you can do about it,' said Quintus. He was fresh from military service: four years younger than his brother, and possessed of about half the brains. 'If you raise Verres's conduct in the senate, they will talk it out. If you try to take him to court, they will make sure he is acquitted. Just keep your nose out of it is my advice.'

'And what do you say, cousin?'

'I say no man of honour in the Roman senate can stand by and see this sort of corruption going on unchecked,' replied Lucius. 'Now that you know the facts, you have a duty to make them public.'

'Bravo!' said Terentia. 'Spoken like a true philosopher who has never stood for office in his life.'

Pomponia yawned noisily. 'Can we talk about something else? Politics is so dull.'

She was a tiresome woman whose only obvious attraction, apart from her prominent bust, was that she was Atticus's sister. I saw the eyes of the two Cicero brothers meet and my master give a barely perceptible shake of his head: ignore her, his expression said, it is not worth arguing over. 'All right,' he conceded, 'enough of politics. But I propose a toast.' He raised his cup and the others did the same. 'To our old friend Sthenius. If nothing else, may this day have seen the beginning of the restoration of his fortunes. Sthenius!'

The Sicilian's eyes were wet with tears of gratitude.

'Sthenius!'

'And Thermae, Cicero,' added Terentia, her small dark eyes, her shrew's eyes, bright with malice over the rim of her drink. 'Do not let us forget Thermae.'

I took my meal alone in the kitchen and went exhausted to bed with my lamp and a book of philosophy which I was too tired to read. (I was free to borrow whatever I liked from the household's small library.) Later, I heard the guests all leave and the bolts slam shut on the front door. I heard Cicero and Terentia mount the stairs in silence and go their separate ways, for she had long since taken to sleeping in another part of the house to avoid being woken by him before dawn. I heard Cicero's footsteps on the boards above my head, and then I blew out my lamp, and that was the last sound I heard as I surrendered myself to sleep – his footsteps pacing, up and down, up and down.

It was six weeks later that we heard the news from Sicily. Verres had ignored the entreaties of his father. On the first day of December, in Syracuse, exactly as he had threatened, he had judged Sthenius in his absence, found him guilty of espionage, sentenced him to be crucified, and dispatched his officials to Rome to arrest him and return him for execution.

III

The governor of Sicily's contemptuous defiance caught Cicero off his guard. He had been convinced he had struck a gentlemen's agreement which would safeguard his client's life. 'But then of course,' he complained bitterly, 'none of them is a gentleman.' He stormed around the house in an uncharacteristic rage. He had been tricked! They had played him for a fool! He would march down to the senate house right there and then and expose their villainous lies! I knew he would calm down before long, for he was only too aware that he lacked the rank simply to demand a hearing in the senate: he would risk humiliation.

But there was no escaping the fact that he was under a heavy obligation to protect his client, and on the morning after Sthenius had learned his fate, Cicero convened a meeting in his study to determine how best to respond. For the first time that I can remember, all his usual callers were turned away, and six of us crammed into that small space: Cicero, brother Quintus, cousin Lucius, Sthenius, myself (to take notes), and Servius Sulpicius, already widely regarded as the ablest jurist of his generation. Cicero began by inviting Servius to give his legal opinion.

'In theory,' said Servius, 'our friend has a right of appeal in

Syracuse, but only to the governor, that is to Verres himself; so that avenue is closed to us. To bring a prosecution against Verres is not an option: as a serving governor he has executive immunity; besides, Hortensius is the praetor of the extortion court until January; and besides both of these, the jury will be composed of senators who will never convict one of their own. You could table another motion in the senate, but you have already tried that, and presumably if you tried again you would merely meet with the same result. Continuing to live openly in Rome is not an option for Sthenius – anyone convicted of a capital crime is automatically subject to banishment from the city, so it is impossible for him to remain here. Indeed, Cicero, you are liable to prosecution yourself if you harbour him under your roof.'

'So what is your advice?'

'Suicide,' said Servius. Sthenius let out a terrible groan. 'No, really, I am afraid you should consider it. Before they catch hold of you. You do not want to suffer the scourge, the hot irons, or the torments of the cross.'

'Thank you, Servius,' said Cicero, cutting him off swiftly before he had an opportunity to describe those torments in further detail. 'Tiro, we need to find Sthenius a place where he can hide. He cannot stay here any longer. It is the first place they will look. As for the legal situation, Servius, your analysis strikes me as faultless. Verres is a brute, but a cunning brute, which is why he felt strong enough to press ahead with the conviction. In short, having thought about the matter overnight, it seems to me that there is only one slim possibility.'

'Which is?'

'To go to the tribunes.'

This suggestion produced an immediate stir of unease, for the tribunes were at that time an utterly discredited group.

Traditionally, they had checked and balanced the power of the senate by voicing the will of the common people. But ten years earlier, after Sulla had defeated the forces of Marius, the aristocrats had stripped them of their powers. They could no longer summon meetings of the people, or propose legislation, or impeach the likes of Verres for high crimes and misdemeanours. As a final humiliation, any senator who became a tribune was automatically disqualified from standing for senior office, that is the praetorship or the consulship. In other words, the tribuneship was designed to be a political dead end – a place to confine the ranting and the rancorous, the incompetent and the unpromotable: the effluent of the body politic. No senator of any nobility or ambition would go anywhere near it.

'I know your objections,' said Cicero, waving the room to be silent. 'But the tribunes still have one small power left to them, do they not, Servius?'

'That is true,' agreed Servius. 'They do have a residual *potestas auxilii ferendi*.' Our blank looks gave him obvious satisfaction. 'It means,' he explained with a smile, 'that they have the right to offer their protection to private persons against the unjust decisions of magistrates. But I must warn you, Cicero, that your friends, among whom I have long counted it an honour to number myself, will think much the less of you if you start dabbling in the politics of the mob. Suicide,' he repeated. 'Where is the objection? We are all mortal. For all of us it is only a matter of time. And this way you go with honour.'

'I agree with Servius about the danger we run if we approach the tribunes,' said Quintus. (It was usually 'we' when Quintus spoke about his elder brother.) 'Whether we like it or not, power in Rome nowadays lies with the senate and with the nobles. That's why our strategy has always been to build your reputation carefully, through your advocacy in the courts. We shall do ourselves irreparable damage with the men who really matter if the feeling gets around that you are merely another rabble-rouser. Also . . . I hesitate to raise this, Marcus, but have you considered Terentia's reaction if you were to follow this course?'

Servius guffawed at that. 'You will never conquer Rome, Cicero, if you cannot rule your wife.'

'Conquering Rome would be child's play, Servius, believe me, compared with ruling my wife.'

And so the debate went on. Lucius favoured an immediate approach to the tribunes, no matter what the consequences. Sthenius was too numb with misery and fear to have a coherent opinion on anything. At the very end, Cicero asked me what I thought. In other company this might have caused surprise, a slave's view not counting for much in most Romans' eyes, but these men were used to the way that Cicero sometimes turned to me for advice. I replied cautiously that it seemed to me that Hortensius would not be happy to learn of Verres's action, and that the prospect of the case becoming a public scandal might yet force him to put more pressure on his client to see sense: going to the tribunes was a risk, but on balance it was one worth taking. The answer pleased Cicero.

'Sometimes,' he said, summing up the discussion with an aphorism I have never forgotten, 'if you find yourself stuck in politics, the thing to do is start a fight – start a fight, even if you do not know how you are going to win it, because it is only when a fight is on, and everything is in motion, that you can hope to see your way through. Thank you, gentlemen.' And with that the meeting was adjourned.

★　★　★

There was no time to waste, for if the news from Syracuse had already reached Rome, it was a fair assumption that Verres's men were not far behind. Even while Cicero was talking, I had conceived an idea for a possible hiding place for Sthenius, and the moment the conference was over I went in search of Terentia's business manager, Philotimus. He was a plump and lascivious young man, generally to be found in the kitchen, pestering the maids to satisfy one or other, or preferably both, of his vices. I asked him if there was a spare apartment available in one of his mistress's tenement blocks, and when he replied that there was, I bullied him into giving me the key. I checked the street outside the house for suspicious loiterers, and when I was sure that it was safe I persuaded Sthenius to follow me.

He was in a state of complete dejection, his dreams of returning to his homeland dashed, in hourly terror of being arrested. And I fear that when he first saw the squalid building in Subura in which I said he would now have to live, he must have felt that even we had abandoned him. The stairs were rickety and gloomy. There was evidence of a recent fire on the walls. His room, on the fifth floor, was barely more than a cell, with a straw mattress in the corner and a tiny window which offered no view, except across the street to another, similar apartment, close enough for Sthenius to reach out and shake hands with his neighbour. For a latrine he had a bucket. But if it did not offer him comfort, it at least offered him security – dropped, unknown, into this warren of slums, it would be almost impossible for him to be found. He asked me, in a plaintive tone, to sit with him a while, but I had to get back and gather all the documents relating to his case, so that Cicero could present them to the tribunes. We were fighting time, I told him, and left at once.

The headquarters of the tribunes were next door to the senate house, in the old Basilica Porcia. Although the tribunate was only a shell, from which all the succulent flesh of power had been sucked, people still hung around its building. The angry, the dispossessed, the hungry, the militant – these were the denizens of the tribunes' basilica. As Cicero and I walked across the forum, we could see a sizeable crowd jostling on its steps to get a view of what was happening inside. I was carrying a document case, but still I cleared a way for the senator as best I could, receiving some kicks and curses for my pains, as these were not citizens with any great love for a purple-bordered toga.

There were ten tribunes, elected annually by the people, and they always sat on the same long wooden bench, beneath a mural depicting the defeat of the Carthaginians. It was not a large building, but packed, noisy and warm, despite the December cold outside. A young man, bizarrely barefoot, was haranguing the mob as we entered. He was an ugly, raw-faced youth with a brutal, grating voice. There were always plenty of cranks in the Basilica Porcia, and I took him at first to be just another, as his entire speech seemed to be devoted to arguing why one particular pillar should not, on any account, be demolished, or even moved one inch, to give the tribunes more room. And yet for some curious reason he compelled attention. Cicero began listening to him very carefully, and after a while he realised – from the constant references to 'my ancestor' – that this peculiar creature was none other than the great-grandson of the famous Marcus Porcius Cato who had originally built the basilica and given it his name.

I mention this here because young Cato – he was then twenty-three – was to become such an important figure, in both the life of Cicero and the death of the republic. Not that one would have guessed it at the time. He looked destined for nowhere more significant than the asylum. He finished his speech, and as he went by, wild-eyed and unseeing, he knocked into me. What remains in my mind is the animal stink of him, his hair matted with damp and the patches of sweat the size of dinner plates spreading under the armpits of his tunic. But he had won his point, and that pillar stayed absolutely in its place for as long as the building stood – which was not, alas, to be many years longer.

However, returning to my story, the tribunes were a poor lot on the whole, but there was one among them who stood out for his talent and his energy, and that was Lollius Palicanus. He was a proud man, but of low birth, from Picenum in the Italian north-east, the power base of Pompey the Great. It had been assumed that when Pompey returned from Spain he would use his influence to try to gain his fellow countryman a praetorship, and Cicero had been as surprised as everybody else earlier in the summer when Palicanus had suddenly announced his candidacy for the tribunate. But on this particular morning he looked happy enough with his lot. The fresh crop of tribunes always began their term of office on the tenth day of December, so he must have been very new in the job. 'Cicero!' he bellowed, the moment he saw us. 'I had been wondering when you would show up!'

He told us that he had already heard the news from Syracuse, and he wanted to talk about Verres. But he wanted to talk in private, for there was more at stake, he said mysteriously, than the fate of one man. He proposed meeting us at his house on the Aventine Hill in an hour, to which Cicero agreed, whereupon he immediately ordered one of his attendants to guide us, saying he would follow separately.

It turned out to be a rough and unpretentious place, in keeping with the man, close to the Lavernan Gate, just outside the city wall. The thing I remember most clearly is the larger-than-life-size bust of Pompey, posed in the headgear and armour of Alexander the Great, which dominated the atrium. 'Well,' said Cicero, after he had contemplated it for a while, 'I suppose it makes a change from the 'Three Graces.' This was exactly the sort of droll but inappropriate comment which used to get repeated around the town, and which invariably found its way back to its victim. Luckily, only I was present on this occasion, but I took the opportunity to pass on what the consul's clerk had said regarding his joke about Gellius mediating between the philosophers. Cicero pretended to be sheepish and promised to be more circumspect in future – he knew, he said, that people liked their statesmen to be dull – but naturally he soon forgot his resolution.

'That was a good speech you made the other week,' said Palicanus, the moment he arrived. 'You have the stuff in you, Cicero, you really have, if I may say so. But those blue-blooded bastards screwed you over, and now you are in the shit. So what exactly are you planning to do about it?' (This was more or less how he spoke – rough words in a rough accent – and the aristocrats used to have some sport with him over his elocution.)

I opened my case and handed the documents to Cicero, and he quickly laid out the situation regarding Sthenius. When he had finished he asked what chance there was of receiving any help from the tribunes.

'That depends,' said Palicanus, with a quick lick of his lips and a grin. 'Come and sit down and let us see what is to be done.'

He took us through into another room, small and completely overwhelmed by a huge wall painting of a laurelled Pompey, this time dressed as Jupiter, complete with lightning bolts shooting from his fingers.

'Do you like it?' asked Palicanus.

'It is remarkable,' said Cicero.

'Yes, it is,' he said, with some satisfaction. '*That* is art.'

I took a seat in the corner, beneath the Picenean deity, while Cicero, whose eye I dared not meet, settled himself at the opposite end of the couch to our host.

'What I am about to tell you, Cicero, is not to be repeated outside this house. Pompey the Great' – Palicanus nodded to the painting, in case we were in any doubt as to whom he meant – 'will soon be returning to Rome for the first time in six years. He will come with his army, so there can be no fancy double-dealing from our noble friends. He will seek the consulship. And he will get the consulship. And he will get it unopposed.'

He leaned forward eagerly, expecting shock or surprise, but Cicero received this sensational intelligence as coolly as if he were being told the weather.

'So in return for your helping me over Sthenius, I am to support you over Pompey?'

'You are a canny one, Cicero, you have the stuff in you. What do you think?'

Cicero rested his chin in his hand and gazed at Palicanus. 'Quintus Metellus will not be happy, for a start. You know the old poem – "In Rome Metelli are, 'tis fate,/Elected to the consulate." He has been scheduled since birth to have his turn next summer.'

'Has he indeed? Well he can kiss my backside. How many legions did Quintus Metellus have behind him, the last time you looked?'

'Crassus has legions,' Cicero pointed out. 'So has Lucullus.'

'Lucullus is too far away, and besides, he has his hands full. As for Crassus – well, it is true that Crassus hates Pompey's guts.

But the thing about Crassus is that he is not a proper soldier. He is a businessman, and that type always cuts a deal.'

'And then there is the little matter of its being completely unconstitutional. You have to be forty-two at the time of the consular election, and Pompey is how old?'

'Just thirty-four.'

'Indeed. Almost a year younger than me. And a consul is also required to have been elected to the senate and to have served as praetor, neither of which Pompey has achieved. He has never made a political speech in his life. To put the matter simply, Palicanus, seldom has a man been less qualified for the post.'

Palicanus made a dismissive gesture. 'All that may be true, but let us face facts – Pompey has run whole countries for years, and done it with proconsular authority to boot. He *is* a consul, in all but name. Be realistic, Cicero. You cannot expect a man such as Pompey to come back to Rome and start at the bottom, running for quaestor like some political hack. What would that do to his dignity?'

'I appreciate his feelings, but you asked my opinion, and I am giving it to you, and I tell you the aristocrats will not stand for it. All right, perhaps if he has ten thousand men outside the city they will have no choice but to let him become consul, but sooner or later his army will go home and then how will he— Ha!' Cicero suddenly threw back his head and started laughing. 'That is very clever.'

'You have seen it?' said Palicanus, with a grin.

'I have seen it.' Cicero nodded appreciatively. 'Very good.'

'Well, I am offering you the chance to be a part of it. And Pompey the Great does not forget his friends.'

At the time I had not the least idea of what they were talking about. Only when we were walking home afterwards did Cicero explain everything to me. Pompey was planning to seek the consulship on the platform of a full restoration of tribunician power. Hence Palicanus's surprising move in becoming a tribune. The strategy was not born of some altruistic desire on Pompey's part to give the Roman people greater liberty – although I suppose it is just possible he was occasionally pleased to lie in his bath in Spain and fancy himself a champion of citizens' rights – no: it was purely a matter of self-interest. Pompey, as a good general, saw that by advocating such a programme, he would trap the aristocrats in a pincer movement, between his soldiers encamped beyond the walls of Rome and the common people on the city's streets. Hortensius, Catulus, Metellus and the rest would have no choice but to concede both Pompey's consulship and the tribunes' restoration, or risk annihilation. And once they did, Pompey could send his army home, and if necessary rule by circumventing the senate and appealing directly to the people. He would be unassailable. It was, as Cicero described it to me, a brilliant stroke, and he had seen it in that flash of insight as he sat on Palicanus's couch.

'What exactly would be in it for me?' asked Cicero.

'A reprieve for your client.'

'And nothing else?'

'That would depend on how good you were. I cannot make specific promises. That will have to wait until Pompey himself gets back.'

'It is rather a weak offer, if I may say so, my dear Palicanus.'

'Well, you are in rather a weak position, if I may say so, my dear Cicero.'

Cicero stood. I could see he was put out. 'I can always walk away,' he said.

'And leave your client to die in agony on one of Verres's crosses?'

Palicanus also stood. 'I doubt it, Cicero. I doubt you are that hard.' He took us out then, past Pompey as Jupiter, past Pompey as Alexander. 'I shall see you and your client at the basilica tomorrow morning,' he said, shaking hands with Cicero on the doorstep. 'After that you will be in our debt, and we shall be watching.' The door closed with a confident slam.

Cicero turned on his heel and stepped into the street. 'If that is the kind of art he puts on public display,' he said, 'what do you suppose he keeps in the latrine? And do not warn me to guard my tongue, Tiro, because I do not care who hears it.'

He walked on ahead of me through the city gate, his hands clasped behind his back, his head hunched forward, brooding. Of course, Palicanus was right. Cicero had no choice. He could not abandon his client. But I am sure he must have been weighing the political risks of moving beyond a simple appeal to the tribunes to a full-blooded campaign for their restoration. It would cost him the support of the moderates, such as Servius.

'Well,' he said with a wry smile, when we reached his house, 'I wanted to get into a fight, and it seems I have succeeded.'

He asked Eros, the steward, where Terentia was, and looked relieved when he learned she was still in her room. At least that saved him from having to tell her the news for a few more hours. We went into his study, and he had just started dictating to me his speech to the tribunes – 'Gentlemen, it is an honour to stand before you for the first time' – when we heard shouts and a thump from the entrance. Cicero, who always liked to think on his feet and was prowling around, ran out to find out what was happening. I hurried after him. Six rough-looking fellows were crowded in the vestibule, all wielding sticks. Eros was rolling on the ground, clutching his stomach, with blood pouring from a split lip. Another stranger, armed not with a stick but with an official-looking document, stepped up to Cicero and announced that he had the authority to search the house.

'The authority of whom?' Cicero was calm – calmer than I would have been in his shoes.

'Gaius Verres, pro-praetor of Sicily, issued this warrant in Syracuse on the first day of December.' He held it up before Cicero's face for an insultingly short time. 'I am searching for the traitor Sthenius.'

'You will not find him here.'

'I shall be the judge of that.'

'And who are you?'

'Timarchides, freedman of Verres, and I shall not be kept talking while he escapes. You,' he said, turning to the nearest of his men, 'secure the front. You two take the back. The rest of you come with me. We shall start with your study, Senator, if you have no objection.'

Very soon the house was filled with the sounds of the search – boots on marble tile and wooden board, the screams of the female slaves, harsh male voices, the occasional crash as something was knocked and broken. Timarchides worked his way through the study upending document cases, watched by Cicero from the door.

'He is hardly likely to be in one of those,' said Cicero. 'He is not a dwarf.'

Finding nothing in the study, they moved on up the stairs to the senator's spartan bedroom and dressing room. 'Be assured, Timarchides,' said Cicero, still keeping his cool, but obviously with greater difficulty as he watched his bed being overturned, 'that you and your master will be repaid for this, one hundred-fold.'

'Your wife,' said Timarchides. 'Where does she sleep?'

'Ah,' said Cicero quietly. 'Now I really would not do that, if I were you.'

But Timarchides had his blood up. He had come a long way, was finding nothing, and Cicero's manner was chafing on his nerves. He ran along the passage, followed by three of his men, shouted, 'Sthenius! We know you're in there!' and threw open the door of Terentia's bedroom. The screech that followed and the sharp crack of her hand across the invader's face rang through the house. Then came such a volley of colourful abuse, delivered in such an imperious voice, and at such a volume, that Terentia's distant ancestor who had commanded the Roman line against Hannibal at Cannae a century and a half before must surely have sat bolt upright in his tomb. 'She fell on that wretched freedman,' Cicero used to say afterwards, 'like a tigress out of a tree. I almost felt sorry for the fellow.'

Timarchides must have realised his mission had failed and decided to cut his losses, for in short order he and his ruffians were retreating down the stairs, followed by Terentia, with little Tullia hiding behind her skirts and occasionally brandishing her tiny fists in imitation of her mother. We heard Timarchides calling to his men, heard a running of feet and the slam of the door, and after that the old house was silent except for the distant wailing of one of the maids.

'And this,' said Terentia, taking a deep breath and rounding on Cicero, her cheeks flushed, her narrow bosom rising and falling rapidly, '*this* is all because you spoke in the senate on behalf of that dreary Sicilian?'

'I am afraid it is, my darling,' he said sadly. 'They are determined to scare me off.'

'Well, you must not let them, Cicero.' She put her hands on either side of his head, gripped it tight – a gesture not at all of tenderness but of passion – and glared furiously into his eyes. 'You must *crush* them.'

The upshot was that the following morning, when we set out for the Basilica Porcia, Quintus was on one side of Cicero, Lucius was on the other, and behind him, magnificently turned out in the formal dress of a Roman matron and carried in a litter hired specially for the occasion, came Terentia. It was the first time she had ever troubled to see him speak, and I swear he was more nervous of appearing before her than he was of appearing before the tribunes. He had a big retinue of clients to back him up as he left the house, and we picked up more along the way, especially after we stopped off halfway down the Argiletum to retrieve Sthenius from his bolt-hole. A hundred or more of us must have surged across the forum and into the tribunes' hall. Timarchides followed at a distance with his gang, but there were far too many of us for him to risk an attack, and he knew that if he tried anything in the basilica itself he would be torn to bits.

The ten tribunes were on the bench. The hall was full. Palicanus rose and read the motion – *That in the opinion of this body the proclamation of banishment from Rome does not apply to Sthenius* – and Cicero stepped up to the tribunal, his face clenched white with nerves. Quite often he was sick before a major speech, as he had been on this occasion, pausing at the door to vomit into the gutter. The first part of his oration was more or less the same as the one he had given in the senate, except that now he could call his client to the front and gesture to him as need arose to stir the pity of the judges. And certainly a more perfect illustration of a dejected victim was never paraded before a Roman court than Sthenius on that day. But Cicero's peroration was entirely new, not at all like his normal forensic oratory, and marked a decisive shift in his political position. By the time he reached it, his nerves were gone and his delivery was on fire.

'There is an old saying, gentlemen, among the merchants in the Macellum, that a fish rots from the head down, and if there is something rotten in Rome today – and who can doubt that there is? – I tell you plainly that it has started in the head. It has started at the top. It has started in the senate.' Loud cheers and stamping of feet. 'And there is only one thing to do with a stinking, rotten fish-head, those merchants will tell you, and that is to cut it off – cut it off and throw it out!' Renewed cheers. 'But it will need quite a knife to sever this head, for it is an aristocratic head, and we all know what they are like!' Laughter. 'It is a head swollen with the poison of corruption and bloated with pride and arrogance. And it will need a strong hand to wield that knife, and it will need a steady nerve besides, because they have necks of brass, these aristocrats, I tell you: brass necks, all of them!' Laughter. 'But that man will come. He is not far away. Your powers will be restored, I promise you, however hard the struggle.' A few brighter sparks started shouting out Pompey's name. Cicero held up his hand, three fingers outstretched. 'To you now falls the great test of being worthy of this fight. Show courage, gentlemen. Make a start today. Strike a blow against tyranny. Free my client. And then free Rome!'

Later, Cicero was so embarrassed by the rabble-rousing nature of this speech that he asked me to destroy the only copy, so I must confess I am writing here from memory. But I recollect it very clearly – the force of his words, the passion of his delivery, the excitement of the crowd as he whipped them up, the wink he exchanged with Palicanus as he left the tribunal, and Terentia not moving a muscle, simply staring straight ahead as the common people around her erupted in applause. Timarchides, who had been standing at the back, slipped out before the ovation ended, no doubt to ride at full gallop to Sicily and report to his master what had happened – for the motion, I need hardly add, was passed by ten votes to nil, and Sthenius, as long as he stayed in Rome, was safe.

IV

Another of Cicero's maxims was that if you must do something unpopular, you might as well do it wholeheartedly, for in politics there is no credit to be won by timidity. Thus, although he had never previously expressed an opinion about Pompey or the tribunes, neither cause now had a more devoted adherent. And the Pompeians were naturally delighted to welcome such a brilliant recruit to their ranks.

That winter was long and cold in the city, and for no one, I suspect, more than Terentia. Her personal code of honour required her to support her husband against the enemies who had invaded her home. But having sat among the smelly poor, and listened to Cicero haranguing her own class, she now found her drawing room and dining room invaded at all hours by his new political cronies: men from the uncouth north who spoke with ugly accents and who liked to put their feet up on her furniture and plot late into the night. Palicanus was the chief of these, and on his second visit to the house in January he brought with him one of the new praetors, Lucius Afranius, a fellow senator from Pompey's homeland of Picenum. Cicero went out of his way to be charming, and in earlier years, Terentia, too, would have felt it an honour to have a praetor in her house. But Afranius had no decent family or breeding of any sort. He actually had the nerve to ask her if she liked dancing, and, when she drew back in horror, declared that personally he loved nothing more. He pulled up his toga, showed her his legs and demanded to know if she had ever seen a finer pair of calves.

These men were Pompey's representatives in Rome and they brought with them something of the whiff and manners of the army camp. They were blunt to the point of brutality; but then, perhaps, they had to be, given what they were planning. Palicanus's daughter, Lollia – a blowsy young piece, very much not to Terentia's taste – occasionally joined the menfolk, for she was married to Aulus Gabinius, another of Pompey's Picenean lieutenants, currently serving with the general in Spain. This Gabinius was a link with the legionary commanders, who in turn provided intelligence on the loyalty of the centuries – an important consideration, for, as Afranius put it, there was no point in bringing the army all the way to Rome to restore the powers of the tribunes, only to find that the legions would happily go over to the aristocrats if they were offered a big enough bribe.

At the end of January, Gabinius sent word that the final rebel strongholds of Uxama and Calagurris had been taken, and that Pompey was ready to march his legions home. Cicero had been active among the *pedarii* for weeks, drawing senators aside as they waited for debates, convincing them that the rebel slaves in the Italian north posed a gathering threat to their businesses and trade. He lobbied well. When the issue came up for discussion in the senate, despite the intense opposition of the aristocrats and the supporters of Crassus, the house voted narrowly to let Pompey keep his Spanish army intact and bring it back to the mother country to crush Spartacus's northern recruits. From that point on, the consulship was as good as his, and on the day the motion passed, Cicero came home smiling. True, he had been snubbed by the aristocrats, who now loathed him more than any other man in Rome, and the presiding consul, the super-snobbish Publius Cornelius Lentulus Sura, had even refused to recognise him when he tried to speak. But what did that matter? He was in the inner circle of Pompey the Great, and, as every fool knows, the quickest way to get ahead in politics is to get yourself close to the man at the top.

Throughout these busy months, I am ashamed to say, we neglected Sthenius of Thermae. He would often turn up in the mornings, and hang around the senator for the entire day in the hope of securing an interview. He was still living in Terentia's squalid tenement block. He had little money. He was unable to venture beyond the walls of the city, as his immunity ended at the boundaries of Rome. He had not shaved his beard nor cut his hair, nor, by the smell of him, changed his clothes since October. He reeked – not of madness exactly, but of obsession, forever producing small pieces of paper, which he would fumble and drop in the street.

Cicero kept making excuses not to see him. Doubtless he felt he had discharged his obligations already. But that was not the sole explanation. The truth is that politics is a country idiot, capable of concentrating only on one thing at a time, and poor Sthenius had become yesterday's topic. All anyone could talk about now was the coming confrontation between Crassus and Pompey; the plight of the Sicilian was a bore.

In the late spring, Crassus – having finally defeated the main force of Spartacus's rebels in the heel of Italy, killing Spartacus and taking six thousand prisoners – had started marching towards Rome. Very soon afterwards, Pompey crossed the Alps and wiped out the slave rebellion in the north. He sent a letter to the consuls which was read out in the senate, giving only the faintest credit to Crassus for his achievement and instead proclaiming that it was really he who had finished off the slave war 'utterly and entirely'. The signal to his supporters could not have been clearer: only one general would be triumphing that year, and it would not be Marcus Crassus. Finally, lest there be any remaining doubt, at the end of his dispatch Pompey announced that he too was moving on Rome. Little wonder that amid these stirring historical events, Sthenius was forgotten.

Sometime in May, it must have been, or possibly early June – I cannot find the exact date – a messenger arrived at Cicero's house bearing a letter. With some reluctance the man let me take it, but refused to leave the premises until he had received a reply: those, he said, were his orders. Although he was wearing civilian clothes, I could tell he was in the army. I carried the message into the study and watched Cicero's expression darken as he read it. He handed it to me, and when I saw the opening – *From Marcus Licinius Crassus, Imperator, to Marcus Tullius Cicero: Greetings* – I understood the reason for his frown. Not that there was anything threatening in the letter. It was simply an invitation to meet the victorious general the next morning on the road to Rome, close to the town of Lanuvium, at the eighteenth milestone.

'Can I refuse?' asked Cicero, but then he answered his own question. 'No, I can't. That would be interpreted as a mortal insult.'

'Presumably he is going to ask for your support.'

'Really?' said Cicero sarcastically. 'What makes you think that?'

'Could you not offer him some limited encouragement, as long as it does not clash with your undertakings to Pompey?'

'No. That is the trouble. Pompey has made that very clear. He expects absolute loyalty. So Crassus will pose the question: "Are you for me or against me?" and then I shall face the politician's worst nightmare: the requirement to give a straight answer.' He sighed. 'But we shall have to go, of course.'

We left soon after dawn the following morning, in a two-wheeled open carriage, with Cicero's valet doubling up as coachman for the occasion. It was the most perfect time of day at the most perfect time of year, already hot enough for people to be bathing in the public pool beside the Capena Gate, but cool enough for the air to be refreshing. There was none of the usual dust thrown up from the road. The leaves of the olive trees were a glossy fresh green. Even the tombs that line the Appian Way so thickly along that particular stretch just beyond the wall gleamed bright and cheerful in the first hour of the sun. Normally, Cicero liked to draw my attention to some particular monument and give me a lecture on it – the statue of Scipio Africanus, perhaps, or the tomb of Horatia, murdered by her brother for displaying excessive grief at the death of her lover. But on this morning his usual good spirits had deserted him. He was too preoccupied with Crassus.

'Half of Rome belongs to him – these tombs as well, I should not wonder. You could house an entire family in one of these! Why not? Crassus would! Have you ever seen him in operation? Let us say he hears there is a fire raging and spreading through a particular neighbourhood: he sends a team of slaves round all the apartments, offering to buy out the owners for next to nothing. When the poor fellows have agreed, he sends another team equipped with water-carts to put the fires out! That is just one of his tricks. Do you know what Sicinnius calls him – always bearing in mind, by the way, that Sicinnius is afraid of no one? He calls Crassus "the most dangerous bull in the herd".'

His chin sank on to his chest and that was all he said until we had passed the eighth milestone and were deep into open country, not far from Bovillae. That was when he drew my attention to something odd: military pickets guarding what looked like small timber yards. We had already passed four or five, spaced out at regular half-mile intervals, and the further down the road we went, the greater the activity seemed – hammering, sawing, digging. It was Cicero who eventually supplied the answer. The legionaries were making crosses. Soon afterwards, we encountered a column of Crassus's infantry tramping towards us, heading for Rome, and we had to pull over to the far side of the road to let them pass. Behind the legionaries came a long, stumbling procession of prisoners, hundreds of them, vanquished rebel slaves, their arms pinioned behind their backs – a terrible, emaciated, grey army of ghosts, heading for a fate which we had seen being prepared for them, but of which they were presumably ignorant. Our driver muttered a spell to ward off evil, flicked his whip over the flanks of the horses and we jolted forwards. A mile or so later, the killing started, in little huddles off on either side of the road, where the prisoners were being nailed to the crosses. I try not to remember it, but it comes back to me occasionally in my dreams, especially, for some reason, the crosses with their impaled and shrieking victims being pulled upright by soldiers heaving on ropes, each wooden upright dropping with a thud into the deep hole that had been dug for it. That I remember, and also the moment when we passed over the crest of a hill and saw a long avenue of crosses running straight ahead for mile after mile, shimmering in the mid-morning heat, the air seeming to tremble with the moans of the dying, the buzz of the flies and the screams of the circling crows.

'So this is why he dragged me out of Rome,' muttered Cicero furiously, 'to intimidate me by showing me these poor wretches.'

He had gone very white, for he was squeamish about pain and death, even when inflicted on animals, and for that reason tried to avoid attending the games. I suppose this also explains his aversion to all matters military. He had done the bare minimum of army service in his youth, and was quite incapable of wielding a sword or hurling a javelin; throughout his career he had to put up with the taunt that he was a draft-dodger.

At the eighteenth milestone, surrounded by a ditch and ramparts, we found the bulk of Crassus's legions encamped beside the road, giving off that dusty smell of sweat and leather which always lingers over an army in the field. Standards fluttered over the gate, beside which Crassus's own son, Publius, then a brisk young junior officer, was waiting to conduct Cicero to the general's tent. A couple of other senators were being shown out as we arrived, and suddenly there was Crassus himself at the entrance, instantly recognisable – 'Old Baldhead', as his soldiers called him – wearing the scarlet cloak of a commander, despite the heat. He was all affability, waving goodbye to his previous visitors, wishing them a safe journey, and greeting us equally heartily – even me, whose hand he shook as warmly as if I were a senator myself, rather than a slave who might in other circumstances have been howling from one of his crosses. And looking back on it, and trying to fix precisely what it was about him which made him so disconcerting, I think it was this: his indiscriminate and detached friendliness, which you knew would never waver or diminish even if he had just decided to have you killed. Cicero had told me he was worth at least two hundred million, but Crassus talked as easily to any man as a farmer leaning on a gate, and his army tent – like his house in Rome – was modest and unadorned.

He led us inside – me as well: he insisted – apologising for the gruesome spectacle along the Appian Way, but he felt it was necessary. He seemed particularly proud of the logistics which had enabled him to crucify six thousand men along three hundred and fifty miles of road, from the victorious battlefield to the gates of Rome, without, as he put it, 'any scenes of violence'. That was seventeen crucifixions to the mile, which meant one hundred and seventeen paces between each cross – he had a wonderful head for figures – and the trick was not to cause a panic among the prisoners, or else one would have had another battle on one's hands. So, after every mile – or sometimes two or three, varying it to avoid arousing suspicion – the requisite number of recaptured slaves would be halted by the roadside as the rest of the column marched on, and not until their comrades were out of sight did the executions begin. In this way the job had been done with the minimum amount of disruption for the maximum deterrent effect – the Appian Way being the busiest road in Italy.

'I doubt whether many slaves, once they hear of this, will rise against Rome in the future,' smiled Crassus. 'Would you, for example?' he said to me, and when I replied very fervently that I most certainly would not, he pinched my cheek and ruffled my hair. The touch of his hand made my flesh shrivel. 'Is he for sale?' he asked Cicero. 'I like him. I'd give you a good price for him. Let us see . . .' He named an amount that was at least ten times what I was worth, and for a terrible moment I thought the offer might be accepted and I would lose my place in Cicero's life – a banishment I could not have borne.

'He is not for sale, at any price,' said Cicero. The journey had upset him; there was a hoarsenes to his voice. 'And to avoid any misunderstanding, Imperator, I believe I should tell you right away that I have pledged my support to Pompey the Great.'

'Pompey the who?' mocked Crassus. 'Pompey the *Great*? As great as what?'

'I would rather not say,' replied Cicero. 'Comparisons can be odious.' At which remark even Crassus, for all his ironclad bonhomie, drew back his head a little.

There are certain politicians who cannot stand to be in the same room as one another, even if mutual self-interest dictates that they should try to get along, and it quickly became apparent to me that Cicero and Crassus were two such men. This is what the Stoics fail to grasp when they assert that reason rather than emotion should play the dominant part in human affairs. I am afraid the reverse is true, and always will be, even – perhaps especially – in the supposedly calculating world of politics. And if reason cannot rule in politics, what hope is there for it in any other sphere? Crassus had summoned Cicero in order to seek his friendship. Cicero had come determined to keep Crassus's goodwill. Yet neither man could quite conceal his distaste for the other, and the meeting was a disaster.

'Let us get to the point, shall we?' said Crassus, after he had invited Cicero to sit down. He took off his cloak and handed it to his son, then settled on the couch. 'There are two things I would like to ask of you, Cicero. One is your support for my candidacy for the consulship. I am forty-four, so I am more than old enough, and I believe this ought to be my year. The other is a triumph. For both I am willing to pay whatever is your current market rate. Normally, as you know, I insist on an exclusive contract, but, given your prior commitments, I suppose I shall have to settle for half of you. Half of Cicero,' he added with a slight bow of his head, 'being worth twice as much as the entirety of most men.'

'That is flattering, Imperator,' responded Cicero, bridling at the implication. 'Thank you. My slave cannot be bought, but I can, is that it? Perhaps you will allow me to think about it.'

'What is there to think about? Every citizen has two votes for the consulship. Give one to me and one to whomever else you please. Just make sure your friends all follow your example. Tell them Crassus never forgets those who oblige him. Or those who disoblige him, for that matter.'

'I would still have to think about it, I am afraid.'

Some shadow moved across Crassus's friendly face, like a pike in clear water. 'And my triumph?'

'Personally, I absolutely believe you have earned the honour. But, as you know, to qualify for a triumph it is necessary for the military action concerned to have extended the dominion of the state. The senate has consulted the precedents. Apparently, it is not enough merely to regain territory that has been lost previously. For example, when Fulvius won back Capua after its defection to Hannibal, he was not allowed a triumph.' Cicero explained all this with what seemed genuine regret.

'But this is a technicality, surely? If Pompey can be a consul without meeting any of the necessary requirements, why cannot I at least have a triumph? I know you are unfamiliar with the difficulties of military command, or even,' he added sinuously, 'with military service, but surely you would agree that I have met all the other requirements – killed five thousand in battle, fought under the auspices, been saluted imperator by the legions, brought peace to the province, withdrawn my troops? If someone of influence such as yourself were to put down a motion in the senate, he would find me very generous.'

There was a long pause, and I wondered how Cicero would escape from his dilemma.

'*There* is your triumph, Imperator!' he said suddenly, pointing in the direction of the Appian Way. 'That is the monument to the kind of man you are! For as long as Romans have tongues to speak, they will remember the name of Crassus as the man who crucified six thousand slaves over three hundred and fifty miles, with one hundred and seventeen paces between the crosses. None of our other great generals would ever have done such a thing. Scipio Africanus, Pompey, Lucullus . . .' He flicked them away with contempt. 'None of them would even have *thought* of it.'

Cicero sat back and smiled at Crassus; Crassus smiled in return. Time went on. I felt myself begin to sweat. It became a contest to see whose smile would crack first. Eventually, Crassus stood and held out his hand to Cicero. 'Thank you so much for coming, my young friend,' he said.

When the senate met a few days later to determine honours, Cicero voted with the majority to deny Crassus a triumph. The vanquisher of Spartacus had to settle for an ovation, an altogether second-class award. Rather than entering the city riding on a chariot drawn by four horses, he would have to walk in; the customary fanfare of trumpets would be replaced by the trilling of flutes; and instead of the usual wreath of laurel he would only be permitted to wear myrtle. 'If the man has any sense of honour,' said Cicero, 'he will turn it down.' I need hardly add that Crassus quickly sent word of his acceptance.

Once the discussion moved on to honours for Pompey, Afranius pulled a clever trick. He used his praetorian rank to rise early in the debate and declare that Pompey would accept with humble gratitude whatever the house chose to grant him: he would be arriving outside the city with ten thousand men the following day, and hoped to thank as many of the senators in person as possible. *Ten thousand men?* After that, even the aristocrats were unwilling publicly to snub the conqueror of Spain, and the consuls were instructed by a unanimous vote to attend on Pompey at his earliest convenience and offer him a full triumph.

The next morning Cicero dressed with even more care than usual and consulted with Quintus and Lucius as to what line he should take in his discussions with Pompey. He decided on a bold approach. The following year he would be thirty-six, just eligible to stand for an aedileship of Rome, four of which were elected annually. The functions of the office – the maintenance of public buildings and public order, the celebration of various festivals, the issuing of trading licences, distribution of grain and so on – were a useful means of consolidating political support. That was what he would ask for, it was agreed: Pompey's backing for an aedileship. 'I believe I have earned it,' said Cicero.

After that was settled, we joined the throngs of citizens heading west towards the Field of Mars, where it was rumoured that Pompey intended to halt his legions. (It was, at least in those days, illegal to possess military *imperium* within the sacred boundaries of Rome; thus both Crassus and Pompey were obliged, if they wanted to keep command of their armies, to do their scheming from beyond the city's walls.) There was intense interest in seeing what the great man looked like, for the Roman Alexander, as Pompey's followers called him, had been away fighting for nearly seven years. Some wondered how much he might have changed; others – of whom I was one – had never set eyes on him at all. Cicero had already heard from Palicanus that Pompey intended to set up his headquarters in the Villa Publica, the government guest house next to the voting enclosures, and that was where we made for – Cicero, Quintus, Lucius and I.

The place was encircled with a double cordon of soldiers, and by the time we had fought our way through the crowds to the perimeter wall, no one was being allowed into the grounds unless they had authorisation. Cicero was most offended that none of the guards had even heard of him, and we were lucky that Palicanus was at that moment passing close to the gate: he was able to fetch his son-in-law, the legionary commander Gabinius, to vouch for us. Once we were inside we found that half of official Rome was already there, strolling around the shaded colonnades, humming with curiosity at being this close to power.

'Pompey the Great arrived in the middle of the night,' Palicanus informed us, adding grandly: 'The consuls are with him now.' He promised to return with more information as soon as he had any, then disappeared, self-importantly, between the sentries into the house.

Several hours passed, during which there was no further sign of Palicanus. Instead we noted the messengers rushing in and out, hungrily witnessed food being delivered, saw the consuls leave, and then watched Catulus and Isauricus, the elder statesmen, arrive. Waiting senators, knowing Cicero to be a fervent partisan of Pompey and believing him to be in his inner counsels, kept coming up to him and asking what was really happening. 'All in good time,' he would reply, 'all in good time.' Eventually I guess he must have found this formula embarrassing, for he sent me off to find him a stool, and when I returned, he set it against a pillar, leaned back and closed his eyes. Towards the middle of the afternoon, Hortensius arrived, squeezing his way through the curious onlookers held back by the soldiers, and was admitted immediately into the villa. When he was followed soon afterwards by the three Metellus brothers, it was impossible even for Cicero to pretend this was anything other than a humiliation. Brother Quintus was dispatched to see if he could pick up any gossip outside the senate house, while Cicero paced up and down the colonnades and ordered me for the twentieth time to try to find Palicanus or Afranius or Gabinius – anyone who could get him in to that meeting.

I hung around the crowded entrance, rising on tiptoe, trying to see over all the jostling heads. A messenger came out and briefly left the door half open, and for a moment I glimpsed white-robed figures, laughing and talking, standing around a heavy marble table with documents spread across it. But then I was distracted by a commotion from the street. With shouts of 'Hail Imperator!' and much cheering and yelling, the gate was swung open and, flanked by bodyguards, in stepped Crassus. He took off his plumed helmet and handed it to one of his lictors, wiped his forehead and looked around him. His gaze fell upon Cicero. He gave him a slight nod of the head accompanied by another of his plain man's smiles, and that was one of the few occasions, I should say, when Cicero was entirely lost for words. Then Crassus swept his scarlet cloak around him – rather magnificently, it must be admitted – and marched into the Villa Publica, while Cicero plonked down heavily on his stool.

I have frequently observed this curious of aspect of power: that it is often when one is physically closest to its source that one is least well informed as to what is actually going on. For example, I have seen senators obliged to step out of the senate chamber and dispatch their slaves to the vegetable market to find out what was happening in the city they were supposedly running. Or I have known of generals, surrounded by legates and ambassadors, who have been reduced to intercepting passing shepherds to discover the latest events on the battlefield. So it was that afternoon with Cicero, who sat within twenty feet of the room in which Rome was being carved up like a cooked chicken, but who had to hear the news of what had been decided from Quintus, who had picked it up from a magistrate in the forum, who had heard it from a senate clerk.

'It's bad,' said Quintus, although one could already tell that from his face. 'Pompey for consul and the rights of the tribunes restored, and with no opposition to be offered by the aristocrats. But in return – listen to this – *in return*, Hortensius and Quintus Metellus are to be consuls in the following year, with the full support of Pompey, while Lucius Metellus is to replace Verres as governor of Sicily. Finally, Crassus – *Crassus!* – is to rule with Pompey as joint consul, with both their armies to be dissolved on the day they take office.'

'But I should have been in there,' said Cicero, staring with dismay at the villa. '*I should have been in there!*'

'Marcus,' said his brother sadly, putting his hand on his shoulder, 'none of them would have you.'

Cicero looked stunned at the scale of this reversal – himself excluded, his enemies rewarded, Crassus elevated to the consulship – but then he shook his shoulder free and made angrily towards the doors. And perhaps his career might have been ended there by the sword of one of Pompey's sentries, for I believe, in his desperation, Cicero had resolved to force his way through to the negotiating table and demand his share. But it was too late. The big men, their deal struck, were already coming out, their aides scampering ahead of them, their guards stamping to attention as they passed. Crassus emerged first, and then, from the shadows, Pompey, his identity obvious at once not only from the aura of power around him – the way the proximate air seemed almost to crackle as he moved – but from the cast of his features. He had a broad face, wide cheekbones, and thick wavy hair that rose in a quiff, like the prow of a ship. It was a face full of weight and command, and he possessed the body to go with it, wide shoulders and a strong chest – the torso of a wrestler. I could see why, when he was younger, and famed for his ruthlessness, he had been called the Butcher Boy.

And so off they went, Baldhead and the Butcher Boy, noticeably neither talking nor even looking at one another, heading towards the gate, which swung open as they approached. A stampede of senators, seeing what was happening, set off in pursuit, and we were swept along in the rush, borne out of the Villa Publica and into what felt like a solid wall of noise and heat. Twenty thousand people must have gathered on the Field of Mars that afternoon, all bellowing their approval. A narrow avenue had been cleared by the soldiers, straining arms chain-linked at the elbows, feet scrabbling in the dust to hold back the crowd. It was just wide enough for Pompey and Crassus to walk abreast, although what their expressions were and whether they had started talking I could not see, as we were far back in the procession. They made slow progress towards the tribunal, where the officials traditionally stand at election time. Pompey heaved himself up first, to a renewed surge of applause, which he basked in for a while, turning his wide and beaming face this way and that, like a cat in sunshine. Then he reached down and hauled Crassus up after him. At this demonstration of unity between the two notorious rivals, the crowd let out another roar, and it came again and even louder when Pompey seized hold of Crassus's hand and raised it above his head.

'What a sickening spectacle,' said Cicero. He had to shout into my ear to make himself heard. 'The consulship demanded and conceded at the point of the sword. We are witnessing the beginning of the end of the republic, Tiro, remember my words!' I could not help reflecting, however, that if *he* had been in that conference, and had helped engineer this joint ticket, he would now be hailing it as a masterpiece of statecraft.

Pompey waved at the crowd for quiet, then began speaking in his parade-ground voice. 'People of Rome! The leaders of the senate have graciously conveyed to me the offer of a triumph, and I am pleased to accept it. They have also told me that I will be allowed to stand as a candidate for the consulship, and I am pleased to accept that as well. The only thing that pleases me more is that my old friend Marcus Licinius Crassus will be my colleague.' He concluded by promising that the following year he would hold a great festival of games, dedicated to Hercules, in honour of his victories in Spain.

Well, these were fine words, no doubt, but he spoke them all too quickly, forgetting to leave the necessary pause after every sentence, which meant that those few who had managed to hear what he said had no opportunity to repeat it to those behind who had not. I doubt if more than a few hundred out of that vast assembly knew what he was saying, but they cheered in any case, and they cheered even more when Crassus immediately, and cunningly, upstaged him.

'I hereby dedicate,' he said, in the booming voice of a trained orator, 'at the same time as Pompey's games – on the same day as Pompey's games – one tenth of my fortune – one tenth of my *entire* fortune – to providing free food to the people of Rome – free food for every one of you, for *three months* – and a great banquet in the streets – a banquet for every citizen – a banquet in honour of Hercules!'

The crowd went into fresh ecstasies. 'The villain,' said Cicero admiringly. 'A tenth of his fortune is a bribe of twenty million! But cheap at the price. See how he turns a weak position into a strong one? I bet you were not expecting *that*,' he called out to Palicanus, who was struggling towards us from the tribunal. 'He has made himself look Pompey's equal. You should never have allowed him a platform.'

'Come and meet the imperator,' urged Palicanus. 'He wants to thank you in person.' I could see Cicero was in two minds, but Palicanus was insistent, tugging at his sleeve, and I suppose he thought he ought to try to salvage something from the day.

'Is he going to make a speech?' shouted Cicero, as we followed Palicanus towards the tribunal.

'He doesn't really make speeches,' replied Palicanus over his shoulder. 'Not yet, anyway.'

'That is a mistake. They will expect him to say something.'

'Well, they will just have to be disappointed, won't they?'

'What a waste,' Cicero muttered to me in disgust. 'What I would not give to have an audience such as this! How often do you see so many voters in one place?'

But Pompey had little experience of public oratory, and besides, he was accustomed to commanding men, not pandering to them. With a final wave to the crowd, he clambered down from the platform. Crassus followed suit and the applause slowly died away. There was a palpable sense of anticlimax, as people stood around wondering what they should do next. 'What a waste,' repeated Cicero. '*I* would have given them a show.'

Behind the tribunal was a small enclosed area, where it was the custom for the magistrates to wait before going up to offi-ciate on election-day. Palicanus conducted us into it, past the guards, and here, a moment or two later, Pompey himself appeared. A young black slave handed him a cloth and he began dabbing at his sweating face and wiping the back of his neck. A dozen senators waited to greet him and Palicanus thrust Cicero into the middle of the line, then drew back with Quintus, Lucius and myself to watch. Pompey was moving down the queue, shaking hands with each of the senators in turn, Afranius at his back to tell him who was who. 'Good to meet you,' said Pompey. 'Good to meet you. Good to meet you.' As he came closer I had a better opportunity to study him. He had a noble face, no question of it, but there was also a disagreeable vanity in those fleshy features, and his grand, distracted manner only emphasised his obvious boredom at meeting all these tedious civilians. He reached Cicero very quickly.

'This is Marcus Cicero, Imperator,' said Afranius.

'Good to meet you.'

He was about to move on, but Afranius took his elbow and whispered, 'Cicero is considered one of the city's foremost advocates, and was very useful to us in the senate.'

'Was he? Well, then – keep up the good work.'

'I shall,' said Cicero quickly, 'for I hope next year to be aedile.'

'Aedile?' Pompey scoffed at the very idea. 'No, no, I do not think so. I have other plans in that direction. But I'm sure we can always find a use for a clever lawyer.'

And with that he really did move on – 'Good to meet you . . . Good to meet you . . .' – leaving Cicero staring straight ahead and swallowing hard.

V

That night, for the first and last time in all my years in his service, Cicero drank too much. I could hear him arguing over dinner with Terentia – not one of their normal, witty, icily courteous disputes, but a row which echoed throughout the small house, as she berated him for his stupidity in ever trusting such an obviously dishonourable gang: Piceneans, all of them, not even proper Romans! 'But then of course, you are not a proper Roman either' – a dig at Cicero's lowly provincial origins which invariably got under his skin. Ominously, I did not hear what he said back to her – it was delivered in such a quiet, malevolent tone – but whatever it was, it must have been devastating, for Terentia, who was not a woman easily shaken, ran from the dining room in tears and disappeared upstairs.

I thought it best to leave him well alone. But an hour later I heard a crash, and when I went in Cicero was on his feet and swaying slightly, staring at a broken plate. The front of his tunic was stained with wine. 'I really do not feel well,' he said.

I got him up to his room by hooking his arm over my shoulder – not an easy procedure, as he was heavier than I – laid him on his bed, and unlaced his shoes. 'Divorce,' he muttered into his pillow, 'that is the answer, Tiro – divorce, and if I have to leave the senate because I can't afford it – well, so what? Nobody would miss me. Just another "new man" who came to nothing. Oh dear, Tiro!' I managed to get his chamber pot in front of him just before he was sick. Head down, he addressed his own vomit. 'We shall go to Athens, my dear fellow, and live with Atticus and study philosophy and no one here will miss us . . .' these last few words all running together into a long, self-pitying burble of slurred syllables and sibilant consonants which no shorthand symbol of mine could ever have reconstructed. I set the pot beside him, blew out the lamp and he was snoring even before I reached the door. I confess I went to bed that night with a troubled heart.

And yet, the next morning, I was woken at exactly the usual pre-dawn hour by the sound of him going through his exercises – a little more slowly than usual, perhaps, but then it was awfully early, for this was the height of summer, and he can hardly have had more than a few hours' sleep. Such was the nature of the man. Failure was the fuel of his ambition. Each time he suffered a humiliation be it as an advocate in his early days when his constitution failed him, or on his return from Sicily, or now, with Pompey's offhand treatment – the fire in him was temporarily banked, but only that it might flare up again even more fiercely. 'It is perseverance,' he used to say, 'and not genius that takes a man to the top. Rome is full of unrecognised geniuses. Only perseverance enables you to move forward in the world.' And so I heard him preparing for another day of struggle in the Roman forum and felt the old, familiar rhythm of the house reassert itself.

I dressed. I lit the lamps. I told the porter to open the front door. I checked the callers. Then I went into Cicero's study and gave him his list of clients. No mention was ever made, either then or in the future, of what had happened the previous night, and I suspect this helped draw us even closer. To be sure, he looked a little green, and he had to screw up his eyes to focus on the names, but otherwise he was entirely normal. 'Sthenius!' he groaned, when he saw who was waiting, as usual, in the tablinum. 'May the gods have mercy upon us!'

'He is not alone,' I warned him. 'He has brought two more Sicilians with him.'

'You mean to say he is multiplying?' He coughed to clear his throat. 'Right. Let us have him in first and get rid of him once and for all.'

As in some curious recurring dream from which one cannot wake, I found myself yet again conducting Sthenius of Thermae into Cicero's presence. His companions he introduced as Heraclius of Syracuse and Epicrates of Bidis. Both were old men, dressed like him in the dark garb of mourning, with uncut hair and beards.

'Now listen, Sthenius,' said Cicero sternly, after he had shaken hands with the grim-looking trio, 'this has got to stop.'

But Sthenius was in that strange and remote private kingdom into which outside sounds seldom penetrate: the land of the obsessive litigant. 'I am most grateful to you, Senator. Firstly, now that I have obtained the court records from Syracuse,' he said, pulling a piece of paper from his leather bag and thrusting it into Cicero's hands, 'you can see what the monster has done. This is what was written before the verdict of the tribunes. And this,' he said, giving him another, 'is what was written after-wards.'

With a sigh, Cicero held the two documents side by side and squinted at them. 'So what is this? This is the official record of your trial for treason, in which I see it is written that you were present during the hearing. Well, we know that is nonsense. And here . . .' his words began to slow as he realised the implications, 'here it says that you were *not* present.' He looked up, his bleary eyes starting to clear. 'So Verres is falsifying the proceedings of his own court, and then he is falsifying his own falsification?'

'Exactly!' cried Sthenius. 'When he realised you had produced me before the tribunes, and that all of Rome knew I could hardly have been in Syracuse on the first day of December, he had to obliterate the record of his lie. But the first document was already on its way to me.'

'Well, well,' said Cicero, continuing to scrutinise the paper, 'perhaps he is more worried than we thought. And I see it also says here that you had a defence attorney representing you that day: "Gaius Claudius, son of Gaius Claudius, of the Palatine tribe." You are a fortunate man, to have your very own Roman lawyer. Who is he?'

'He is Verres's business manager.'

Cicero studied Sthenius for a moment or two. 'What else do you have in that bag of yours?' he said.

Out it all came then, tipped over the study floor on that hot summer's morning: letters, names, scraps of official records, scribbled notes of gossip and rumours – seven months' angry labour by three desperate men, for it transpired that Heraclius and Epicrates had also been swindled out of their estates by Verres, one worth sixty thousand, the other thirty. In both cases, Verres had abused his office to bring false accusations and secure illegal verdicts. Both had been robbed at around the same time as Sthenius. Both had been, until then, the leading men in their communities. Both had been obliged to flee the island penniless and seek refuge in Rome. Hearing of Sthenius's appearance before the tribunes, they had sought him out and proposed cooperation.

'As single victims, they were weak,' said Cicero, years later, reminiscing about the case, 'but when they joined in common cause, they found they had a network of contacts which spread across the entire island: Thermae in the north, Bidis in the south, Syracuse in the east. These were men sagacious by nature, shrewd by experience, accomplished by education, and their fellow countrymen had opened up the secrets of their suffering to them, as they would never have done to a Roman senator.'

Outwardly, Cicero still seemed the calm advocate. But as the sun grew stronger and I blew out the lamps, and as he picked up one document after another, I could sense his gathering excitement. Here was the sworn affidavit of Dio of Halaesa, from whom Verres had first demanded a bribe of ten thousand to bring in a not guilty verdict, and then stolen all his horses, tapestries and gold and silver plate. Here were the written testimonies of priests whose temples had been robbed – a bronze Apollo, signed in silver by the sculptor Myron, and presented by Scipio a century and a half earlier, stolen from the shrine of Aesculapius at Agrigentum; a statue of Ceres carried away from Catina, and of Victory from Henna; the sacking of the ancient shrine of Juno in Melita. Here was the evidence of farmers in Herbita and Agyrium, threatened with being flogged to death unless they paid protection money to Verres's agents. Here was the story of the wretched Sopater of Tyndaris, seized in midwinter by Verres's lictors and bound naked to an equestrian statue in full view of the entire community, until he and his fellow citizens agreed to hand over a valuable municipal bronze of Mercury that stood in the local gymnasium. 'It is not a province Verres is running down there,' murmured Cicero, in wonder, 'it is a fully fledged criminal state.' There were a dozen more of these grim stories.

With the agreement of the three Sicilians, I bundled the papers together and locked them in the senator's strongbox. 'It is vital, gentlemen, that not a word of this leaks out,' Cicero told them. 'By all means continue to collect statements and witnesses, but please do it discreetly. Verres has used violence and intimidation many times before, and you can be sure he will use them again to protect himself. We need to take the rascal unawares.'

'Does that mean,' asked Sthenius, hardly daring to hope, 'that you will help us?'

Cicero looked at him but did not answer.

Later that day, when he returned from the law courts, the senator made up his quarrel with his wife. He dispatched young Sositheus down to the old flower market in the Forum Boarium, in front of the Temple of Portunus, to buy a bouquet of fragrant summer blooms. These he then gave to little Tullia, telling her solemnly that he had a vital task for her. She was to take them in to her mother and announce they had come for her from a rough provincial admirer. ('Have you got that, Tulliola? A rough provincial admirer.') She disappeared very self-importantly into Terentia's chamber, and I guess they must have done the trick, for that evening, when – at Cicero's insistence – the couches were carried up to the roof and the family dined beneath the summer stars, the flowers had a place of honour at the centre of the table.

I know this because, as the meal was ending, I was unexpectedly sent for by Cicero. It was a still night, without a flicker of wind to disturb the candles, and the night-time sounds of Rome down in the valley mingled with the scent of the flowers in the warm June air – snatches of music, voices, the call of the watchmen along the Argiletum, the distant barking of the guard dogs set loose in the precincts of the Capitoline Triad. Lucius and Quintus were still laughing at some joke of Cicero's, and even Terentia could not quite hide her amusement as she flicked her napkin at her husband and scolded him that that was quite enough. (Pomponia, thankfully, was away visiting her brother in Athens.)

'Ah,' said Cicero, looking round, 'now here is Tiro, the master politician of us all, which means I can proceed to make my little declaration. I thought it appropriate that he should be present to hear this as well. I have decided to stand for election as aedile.'

'Oh, very good!' said Quintus, who thought it was all still part of Cicero's joke. Then he stopped laughing and said in a puzzled way, 'But that is not funny.'

'It will be if I win.'

'But you can't win. You heard what Pompey said. He doesn't want you to be a candidate.'

'It is not for Pompey to decide who is to be a candidate. We are free citizens, free to make our own choices. I choose to run for aedile.'

'There is no sense in running and losing, Marcus. That is the sort of pointlessly heroic gesture Lucius here believes in.'

'Let us drink to pointless heroism,' said Lucius, raising his glass.

'But we cannot win against Pompey's opposition,' persisted Quintus. 'And what is the point of incurring Pompey's enmity?'

To which Terentia retorted: 'After yesterday, one might better ask, "What is the point of incurring Pompey's friendship?"'

'Terentia is right,' said Cicero. 'Yesterday has taught me a lesson. Let us say I wait a year or two, hanging on Pompey's every word in the hope of favour, running errands for him. We have all seen men like that in the senate – growing older, waiting for half-promises to be fulfilled. They are hollowed out by it. And before they even know it, their moment has passed and they have nothing left with which to bargain. I would sooner clear out of politics right now than let that happen to me. If you want power, there is a time when you have to seize it. This is my time.'

'But how is this be accomplished?'

'By prosecuting Gaius Verres for extortion.'

So there it was. I had known he would do it since early morning, and so, I am sure, had he, but he had wanted to take his time about it – to try on the decision, as it were, and see how it fitted him. And it fitted him very well. I had never seen him more determined. He looked like a man who believed he had the force of history running through him. Nobody spoke.

'Come on!' he said with a smile. 'Why the long faces? I have not lost yet! And I do not believe I shall lose, either. I had a visit from the Sicilians this morning. They have gathered the most damning testimony against Verres, have they not, Tiro? We have it under lock and key downstairs. And when we do win – think of it! I defeat Hortensius in open court, and all this "second best advocate" nonsense is finished for ever. I assume the rank of the man I convict, according to the traditional rights of the victorious prosecutor, which means I become a praetorian overnight – so no more jumping up and down on the back benches in the senate, hoping to be called. And I place myself so firmly before the gaze of the Roman people that my election as aedile is assured. But the best thing of all is that I do it – I, Cicero – and I do it without owing favours to anyone, least of all Pompey the Great.'

'But what if we lose?' said Quintus, finding his voice at last. 'We are defence attorneys. We never prosecute. You have said it yourself a hundred times: defenders win friends; prosecutors just make enemies. If you don't bring Verres down, there is a good chance he will eventually be elected consul. Then he will never rest until you are destroyed.'

'That is true,' conceded Cicero. 'If you are going to kill a dangerous animal, you had better make sure you do it with the first thrust. But then – don't you see? This way I can win everything. Rank, fame, office, dignity, authority, independence, a base of clients in Rome and Sicily. It opens my way clear through to becoming consul.'

This was the first time I had heard him mention his great ambition, and it was a measure of his renewed confidence that he felt able to utter the word at last. *Consul*. For every man in public life, this was the apotheosis. The very years themselves were distinguished from one another on all official documents and foundation stones by the names of the presiding consuls. It was the nearest thing below heaven to immortality. How many nights and days must he have thought of it, dreamed of it, nursed it, since his gawky adolescence? Sometimes it is foolish to articulate an ambition too early – exposing it prematurely to the laughter and scepticism of the world can destroy it before it is even properly born. But sometimes the opposite occurs, and the very act of mentioning a thing makes it suddenly seem possible, even plausible. That was how it was that night. When Cicero pronounced the word 'consul' he planted it in the ground like a standard for us all to admire. And for a moment we glimpsed the brilliant, starry future through his eyes, and saw that he was right: that if he took down Verres, he had a chance; that he might just – with luck – go all the way to the summit.

There was much to be done over the following months, and as usual a great deal of the work fell upon me. First, I drew up a large chart of the electorate for the aedileship. At that time, this consisted of the entire Roman citizenry, divided into their thirty-five tribes. Cicero himself belonged to the Cornelia, Servius to the Lemonia, Pompey to the Clustumina, Verres to the Romilia, and so forth. A citizen cast his ballot on the Field of Mars as a member of his tribe, and the results of each tribe's vote were then read out by the magistrates. The four candidates who secured the votes of the greatest number of tribes were duly declared the winners.

There were several advantages for Cicero in this particular electoral college. For one thing – unlike the system for choosing praetors and consuls – each man's vote, whatever his wealth, counted equally, and as Cicero's strongest support was among the men of business and the teeming poor, the aristocrats would find it harder to block him. For another, it was a relatively easy electorate to canvass. Each tribe had its own headquarters some-where in Rome, a building large enough to lay on a show or a dinner. I went back through our files and compiled a list of every man Cicero had ever defended or helped over the past six years, arranged according to his tribe. These men were then contacted and asked to make sure that the senator was invited to speak at any forthcoming tribal event. It is surely amazing how many favours there are to be called in after six years of relentless advo-cacy and advice. Cicero's campaign schedule was soon filled with engagements, and his working day became even longer. After the courts or the senate had adjourned, he would hurry home, quickly bathe and change, and then rush out again to give one of his rousing addresses. His slogan was 'Justice and Reform'.

Quintus, as usual, acted as Cicero's campaign manager, while cousin Lucius was entrusted with organising the case against Verres. The governor was due to return from Sicily at the end of the year, whereupon – at the very instant he entered the city – he would lose his *imperium*, and with it his immunity from prosecution. Cicero was determined to strike at the first opportunity, and, if possible, give Verres no time to dispose of evidence or intimidate witnesses. For this reason, to avoid arousing suspicion, the Sicilians stopped coming to the house, and Lucius became the conduit between Cicero and his clients, meeting them in secret at various locations across the city. I thus came to know Lucius much better, and the more I saw of him the more I liked him. He was in many respects very similar to Cicero. He was almost the same age, clever and amusing, a gifted philosopher. The two had grown up together in Arpinum, been schooled together in Rome, and travelled together in the East. But there was one huge difference: Lucius entirely lacked worldly ambition. He lived alone, in a small house full of books, and did nothing all day except read and think – a most dangerous occupation for a man which in my experience leads invariably to dyspepsia and melancholy. But oddly enough, despite his solitary disposition, he soon came to relish leaving his study every day and was so enraged by Verres's wickedness that his zeal to bring him to justice eventually exceeded even Cicero's. 'We shall make a lawyer of you yet, cousin,' Cicero remarked admiringly, after Lucius had produced yet another set of damning affidavits.

Towards the end of December an incident occurred which finally brought together, and in dramatic fashion, all these separate strands of Cicero's life. I opened the door one dark morning to find, standing at the head of the usual queue, the man we had recently seen in the tribunes' basilica, acting as defence attorney for his great-grandfather's pillar – Marcus Porcius Cato. He was alone, without a slave to attend him, and looked as though he had slept out in the street all night. (I suppose he might have done, come to think of it, although Cato's appearance was usually dishevelled – like that of a holy man or mystic – so that it was hard to tell.) Naturally, Cicero was intrigued to discover why a man of such eminent birth should have turned up on his doorstep, for Cato, bizarre as he was, dwelt at the very heart of the old republican aristocracy, connected by blood and marriage to a webwork of Servilii, Lepidi and Aemilii. Indeed, such was Cicero's pleasure at having so high-born a visitor, he went out to the tablinum himself to welcome him, and conducted him into the study personally. This was the sort of client he had long dreamed of finding in his net one morning.

I settled myself in the corner to take notes, and young Cato, never a man for small talk, came straight to the point. He was in need of a good advocate, he said, and he had liked the way Cicero had handled himself before the tribunes, for it was a monstrous thing when any man such as Verres considered himself above the ancient laws. To put it briefly: he was engaged to be married to his cousin, Aemilia Lepida, a charming girl of eighteen, whose young life had already been blighted by tragedy. At the age of thirteen, she had been humiliatingly jilted by her fiancé, the haughty young aristocrat Scipio Nasica. At fourteen, her mother had died. At fifteen, her father had died. At sixteen, her brother had died, leaving her completely alone.

'The poor girl,' said Cicero. 'So I take it, if she is your cousin, that she must be the daughter of the consul of six years ago, Aemilius Lepidus Livianus? He was, I believe, the brother of your late mother, Livia?' (Like many supposed radicals, Cicero had a surprisingly thorough knowledge of the aristocracy.)

'That is correct.'

'Why, then, I congratulate you, Cato, on a most brilliant match. With the blood of those three families in her veins, and with her nearest relatives all dead, she must be the richest heiress in Rome.'

'She is,' said Cato bitterly. 'And that is the trouble. Scipio Nasica, her former suitor, who has just come back from Spain after fighting in the army of Pompey the so-called Great, has found out how rich she has become, now that her father and brother are gone, and he has reclaimed her as his own.'

'But surely it is for the young lady herself to decide?'

'She has,' said Cato. 'She has decided on him.'

'Ah,' replied Cicero, sitting back in his chair, 'in that case, you may be in some difficulties. Presumably, if she was orphaned at fifteen, she must have had a guardian appointed. You could always talk to him. He is probably in a position to forbid the marriage. Who is he?'

'That would be me.'

'You? You are the guardian of the woman you want to marry?'

'I am. I am her closest male relative.'

Cicero rested his chin in his hand and scrutinised his prospective new client – the ragged hair, the filthy bare feet, the tunic unchanged for weeks. 'So what do you wish me to do?'

'I want you to bring legal proceedings against Scipio, and against Lepida if necessary, and put a stop to this whole thing.'

'These proceedings – would they be brought by you in your role as rejected suitor, or as the girl's guardian?'

'Either.' Cato shrugged. 'Both.'

Cicero scratched his ear. 'My experience of young women,' he said carefully, 'is as limited as my faith in the rule of law is boundless. But even I, Cato, *even I* have to say that I doubt whether the best way to a girl's heart is through litigation.'

'A girl's heart?' repeated Cato. 'What has a girl's heart got to do with anything? This is a matter of principle.'

And money, one would have added, if he had been any other man. But Cato had that most luxurious prerogative of the very rich: little interest in money. He had inherited plenty, and gave it away without even noticing. No: it was principle that always motivated Cato – the relentless desire never to compromise on principle.

'We would have to go to the embezzlement court,' said Cicero, 'and lay charges of breach of promise. We would have to prove the existence of a prior contract between you and the Lady Lepida, and that she was therefore a cheat and a liar. We would have to prove that Scipio was a double-dealing, money-grubbing knave. I would have to put them both on the witness stand and tear them to pieces.'

'Do it,' said Cato, with a gleam in his eye.

'And at the end of all that, we would probably still lose, for juries love nothing more than star-crossed lovers, save perhaps for orphans – and she is both – and you would have been made the laughing stock of Rome.'

'What do I care what people think of me?' said Cato scornfully.

'And even if we win – well, imagine it. You might end up having to drag Lepida kicking and screaming from the court through the streets of Rome, back to her new marital home. It would be the scandal of the year.'

'So this is what we have descended to, is it?' demanded Cato bitterly. 'The honest man is to step aside so that the rascal triumphs? And this is Roman justice?' He leapt to his feet. 'I need a lawyer with steel in his bones, and if I cannot find anyone to help me, then I swear I shall lay the prosecution myself.'

'Sit down, Cato,' said Cicero gently, and when Cato did not move, he repeated it: 'Sit, Cato, and I shall tell you something about the law.' Cato hesitated, frowned, and sat, but only on the edge of his chair, so that he could leap up again at the first hint that he should moderate his convictions. 'A word of advice, if I may, from a man ten years your senior. You must not take everything head-on. Very often the best and most important cases never even come to court. This looks to me like one of them. Let me see what I can do.'

'And if you fail?'

'Then you can proceed however you like.'

After he had gone, Cicero said to me: "That young man seeks opportunities to test his principles as readily as a drunk picks fights in a bar.' Nevertheless, Cato had agreed to let Cicero approach Scipio on his behalf, and I could tell that Cicero relished the opportunity this would give him to scrutinise the aristocracy at first hand. There was literally no man in Rome with grander lineage than Quintus Caecilius Metellus Pius Cornelius Scipio Nasica – Nasica meaning 'pointed nose', which he carried very firmly in the air – for he was not only the natural son of a Scipio, but the adopted son of Metellus Pius, pontifex maximus and the titular head of the Metelli clan. Father and adopted son had only recently returned from Spain, and were presently on Pius's immense country estate at Tibur. They were expected to enter the city on the twenty-ninth day of December, riding behind Pompey in his triumph. Cicero decided to arrange a meeting for the thirtieth.

The twenty-ninth duly arrived, and what a day that was – Rome had not seen such a spectacle since the days of Sulla. As I waited by the Triumphal Gate it seemed that everyone in the city had turned out to line the route. First to pass through the gate from the Field of Mars was the entire body of the senate, including Cicero, on foot, led by the consuls and the other magistrates. Then the trumpeters, sounding the fanfares. Then the carriages and litters laden with the spoils of the Spanish war – gold and silver, coin and bullion, weapons, statues, pictures, vases, furniture, precious stones and tapestries – and wooden models of the cities Pompey had conquered and sacked, and placards with their names, and the names of all the famous men he had killed in battle. Then the massive, plodding white bulls, destined for sacrifice, with gilded horns hung with ribbons and floral garlands, driven by the slaughtering-priests. Then trudging elephants – the heraldic symbol of the Metellii – and lumbering ox-carts bearing cages containing the wild beasts of the Spanish mountains, roaring and tearing at their bars in rage. Then the arms and insignia of the beaten rebels, and then the prisoners themselves, the defeated followers of Sertorius and Perperna, shuffling in chains. Then the crowns and tributes of the allies, borne by the ambassadors of a score of nations. Then the twelve lictors of the imperator, their rods and axes wreathed in laurel. And now at last, to a tumult of applause from the vast crowd, the four white horses of the imperator's chariot came trotting through the gate, and there was Pompey himself, in the barrel-shaped, gem-encrusted chariot of the triumphator. He wore a gold-embroidered robe with a flowered tunic. In his right hand he held a laurel bough and in his left a sceptre. There was a wreath of Delphic laurel on his head, and his handsome face and muscled body had been painted with red lead, for on this day he truly was the embodiment of Jupiter. Standing beside him was his eight-year-old son, the golden-curled Gnaeus, and behind him a public slave to whisper in his ear that he was only human and all this would pass. Behind the chariot, riding on a black war-horse, came old Metellus Pius, his leg tightly bandaged, evidence of a wound incurred in battle. Next to him was Scipio, his adopted son – a handsome young fellow of twenty-four: no wonder, I thought, that Lepida preferred him to Cato – and then the legionary commanders, including Aulus Gabinius, followed by all the knights and cavalry, armour glinting in the pale December sun. And finally the legions of Pompey's infantry, in full marching order, thousand upon thousand of sunburnt veterans, the crash of their tramping boots seeming to shake the very earth, roaring at the top of their voices, '*Io Triumphe!*' and chanting hymns to the gods and singing filthy songs about their commander-in-chief, as they were traditionally permitted to do in this, the hour of his glory.

It took half the morning for them all to pass, the procession winding through the streets towards the forum, where, according to tradition, as Pompey ascended the steps of the Capitol to sacrifice before the Temple of the Jupiter, his most eminent prisoners were lowered into the depths of the Carcer and garrotted – for what could be more fitting than that the day which ended the military authority of the conqueror should also end the lives of the conquered? I could hear the distant cheering inside the city but spared myself that sight, and hung around the Triumphal Gate with the dwindling crowd to see the entry of Crassus for his ovation. He made the best of it, marching with his sons beside him, but despite the efforts of his agents to whip up some enthusiasm, it was a poor show after the magnificence of Pompey's dazzling pageant. I am sure he must have resented it mightily, picking his way between the horse shit and elephant dung left behind by his consular colleague. He did not even have many prisoners to parade, the poor fellow, having slaughtered almost all of them along the Appian Way.

The following day, Cicero set out for the house of Scipio, with myself in attendance, carrying a document case – a favourite trick of his to try to intimidate the opposition. We had no evidence; I had simply filled it with old receipts. Scipio's residence was on the Via Sacra, fronted by shops, although naturally these were not your average shops, but exclusive jewellers, who kept their wares behind metal grilles. Our arrival was expected, Cicero having sent notice of his intention to visit, and we were shown immediately by a liveried footman into Scipio's atrium. This has been described as 'one of the wonders of Rome', and indeed it was, even at that time. Scipio could trace his line back for at least eleven generations, nine of which had produced consuls. The walls around us were lined with the wax masks of the Scipiones, some of them centuries old, yellowed with smoke and grime (later, Scipio's adoption by Pius was to bring a further six consular masks crowding into the atrium), and they exuded that thin, dry compound of dust and incense which is to me the smell of antiquity. Cicero went round studying the labels. The oldest mask was three hundred and twenty-five years old. But naturally, it was that of Scipio Africanus, conqueror of Hannibal, which fascinated him the most, and he spent a long time bent down studying it. It was a noble, sensitive face – smooth, unlined, ethereal, more like the representation of a soul than of flesh and blood. 'Prosecuted, of course, by the great-grandfather of our present client,' sighed Cicero, as he straightened. 'Contrariness runs thick in the blood of the Catos.'

The footman returned and we followed him through into the tablinum. There, young Scipio lounged on a couch surrounded by a jumble of precious objects – statues, busts, antiques, rolls of carpet and the like. It looked like the burial chamber of some Eastern potentate. He did not stand when Cicero entered (an insult to a senator), nor did he invite him to sit, but merely asked him in a drawling voice to state his business. This Cicero proceeded to do, firmly but courteously, informing him that Cato's case was legally watertight, given that Cato was both formally betrothed to the young lady, and also her guardian. He gestured to the document case, which I held before me like a serving boy with a tray, and ran through the precedents, concluding by saying that Cato was resolved to bring an action in the embezzlement court, and would also seek a motion *obsignandi gratia*, preventing the young lady from having further contact with any person or persons material to the case. There was only one sure way of avoiding this humiliation, and that was for Scipio to give up his suit immediately.

'He really is a crackpot, isn't he?' said Scipio languidly, and lay back on his couch with his hands behind his head, smiling at the painted ceiling.

'Is that your only answer?' said Cicero.

'No,' said Scipio, 'this is my only answer. Lepida!' And at that, a demure young woman appeared from behind a screen, where she had obviously been listening, and moved gracefully across the floor to stand beside the couch. She slipped her hand into Scipio's. 'This is my wife. We were married yesterday evening. What you see around you are the wedding gifts of our friends. Pompey the Great came directly from sacrificing on the Capitol to be a witness.'

'Jupiter himself could have been a witness,' retorted Cicero, 'but that would not suffice to make the ceremony legal.' Still, I could see by the way his shoulders slumped slightly that the fight had gone out of him. Possession, as the jurists say, is nine tenths of the law, and Scipio had not merely the possession, but obviously the eager acquiescence, of his new bride. 'Well,' Cicero said, looking around at the wedding presents, 'on my behalf, I suppose, if not that of my client, I offer you both congratulations. Perhaps my wedding gift to you should be to persuade Cato to recognise reality.'

'That,' said Scipio, 'would be the rarest gift ever bestowed.'

'My cousin is a good man at heart,' said Lepida. 'Will you convey my best wishes, and my hopes that one day we shall be reconciled?'

'Of course,' said Cicero, with a gentlemanly bow, and he was just turning to go when he stopped abruptly. 'Now that is a pretty piece. That is a very pretty piece.'

It was a bronze statue of a naked Apollo, perhaps half the size of a man, playing on a lyre – a sublime depiction of graceful masculinity, arrested in mid-dance, with every hair of his head and string of his instrument perfectly delineated. Worked into his thigh in tiny silver letters was the name of the sculptor: Myron.

'Oh, that,' said Scipio, very offhand, 'that was apparently given to some temple by my illustrious ancestor, Scipio Africanus. Why? Do you know it?'

'If I am not mistaken, it is from the shrine of Aesculapius at Agrigentum.'

'That is the place,' said Scipio. 'In Sicily. Verres got it off the priests there and gave it to me last night.'

In this way Cicero learned that Gaius Verres had returned to Rome and was already spreading the tentacles of his corruption across the city. 'Villain!' exclaimed Cicero as he walked away down the hill. He clenched and unclenched his fists in impotent fury. 'Villain, villain, *villain!*' He had good cause to be alarmed, for it was fair to assume that if Verres had given a Myron to young Scipio, then Hortensius, the Metellus brothers and all his other prominent allies in the senate would have received even heftier bribes – and it was precisely from among such men that the jury at any future trial would be drawn. A secondary blow was the discovery that Pompey had been present at the same wedding feast as Verres and the leading aristocrats. Pompey had always had strong links with Sicily – as a young general he had restored order on the island, and had even stayed overnight in the house of Sthenius. Cicero had looked to him if not exactly for support – he had learned his lesson there – then at least for benign neutrality. The awful possibility now occurred to him that if he went ahead with the prosecution he might have every powerful faction in Rome united against him

But there was no time to ponder the implications of that now. Cato had insisted on hearing the results of Cicero's interview immediately, and was waiting for him at the house of his half-sister, Servilia, which was also on the Via Sacra, only a few doors down from Scipio's residence. As we entered, three young girls – none I would guess more than five years old – came running out into the atrium, followed by their mother. This was the first occasion, I believe, on which Cicero met Servilia, who was later to become the most formidable woman among the many formid-able women who lived in Rome. She was nearly thirty, hand-some but not at all pretty, about five years older than Cato. By her late first husband, Marcus Brutus, she had given birth to a son when she was still only fifteen; by her second, the feeble Junius Silanus, she had produced these three daughters in quick succession. Cicero greeted them as if he had not a care in the world, squatting on his haunches to talk to them while Servilia looked on. She insisted that they meet every caller, and so become familiar with adult ways, for they were her great hope for the future, and she wished them to be sophisticated.

Eventually a nurse came and took the girls away and Servilia showed us through to the tablinum. Here, Cato was waiting with Antipater the Tyrian, a Stoic philosopher who seldom left his side. Cato took the news of Lepida's marriage quite as badly as one would have predicted, striding around and swearing, which reminds me of another of Cicero's witticisms – that Cato was always the perfect Stoic, as long as nothing went wrong.

'Do calm yourself, Cato,' said Servilia after a while. 'It is perfectly obvious the matter is finished, and you might as well get used to it. You did not love her – you do not know what love is. You do not even need her money – you have plenty of your own. She is a drippy little thing. You can find a hundred better.'

'She asked me to bring you her best wishes,' said Cicero, which provoked another outpouring of abuse from Cato.

'I shall not put up with it!' he shouted.

'Yes you will,' said Servilia. She pointed at Antipater, who quailed. 'You tell him, philosopher. My brother thinks his fine principles are all the product of his intellect, whereas they are simply girlish emotions tricked out by false philosophers as manly points of honour.' And then, to Cicero again: 'If he had had more experience of the female sex, Senator, he would see how foolish he is being. But you have never even lain with a woman, have you, Cato?'

Cicero looked embarrassed, for he always had the equestrian class's slight prudishness about sexual matters, and was unused to the free ways of the aristocrats.

'I believe it weakens the male essence, and dulls the power of thought,' said Cato sulkily, producing such a shriek of laughter from his sister that his face turned as red as Pompey's had been painted the previous day, and he stamped out of the room, trailing his Stoic after him.

'I apologise,' said Servilia, turning to Cicero. 'Sometimes I almost think he is slow-witted. But then, when he does get hold of a thing, he will never let go of it, which is a quality of sorts, I suppose. He praised your speech to the tribunes about Verres. He made you sound a very dangerous fellow. I rather like dangerous fellows. We should meet again.' She held out her hand to bid Cicero goodbye. He took it, and it seemed to me that she held it rather longer than politeness dictated. 'Would you be willing to take advice from a woman?'

'From you,' said Cicero, eventually retrieving his hand, 'of course.'

'My other brother, Caepio – my full brother, that is – is betrothed to the daughter of Hortensius. He told me that Hortensius was speaking of you the other day – that he suspects you plan to prosecute Verres, and has some scheme in mind to frustrate you. I know no more than that.'

'And in the unlikely event that I was planning such a prosecution,' said Cicero, with a smile, 'what would be your advice?'

'That is simple,' replied Servilia, with the utmost seriousness. 'Drop it.'

VI

Far from deterring him, this conversation with Servilia and his visit to Scipio convinced Cicero that he would have to move even more quickly than he had planned. On the first day of January, in the six hundred and eighty-fourth year since the foundation of Rome, Pompey and Crassus took office as consuls. I escorted Cicero to the inaugural ceremonies on Capitol Hill, and then stood with the crowd at the back of the portico. The rebuilt Temple of Jupiter was at that time nearing completion under the guiding hand of Catulus, and the new marble pillars shipped from Mount Olympus and the roof of gilded bronze gleamed in the cold sunshine. According to tradition, saffron was burnt on the sacrificial fires, and those crackling yellow flames, the smell of spice, the shiny clarity of the winter air, the golden altars, the shuffling creamy bullocks awaiting sacrifice, the white and purple robes of the watching senators – all of it made an unforgettable impression on me. I did not recognise him, but Verres was also there, Cicero told me afterwards, standing with Hortensius: he was aware of the two of them looking at him, and laughing at some shared joke.

For several days thereafter nothing could be done. The senate met and heard a stumbling speech from Pompey, who had never before set foot in the chamber, and who was only able to follow what was happening by constant reference to a bluffer's guide to procedure which had been written out for him by the famous scholar Varro, who had served under him in Spain. Catulus, as usual, was given the first voice, and he made a notably states-manlike speech, conceding that, although he opposed it person-ally, the demand for the restoration of the tribunes' rights could not be resisted, and that the aristocrats had only themselves to blame for their unpopularity. ('You should have seen the looks on the faces of Hortensius and Verres when he said *that*,' Cicero told me later.) Afterwards, following the ancient custom, the new consuls went out to the Alban Mount to preside over the cele-brations of the Latin Festival, which lasted four days. These were followed by another two days of religious observance, during which the courts were closed. So it was not until the second week of the new year that Cicero was finally able to begin his assault.

On the morning that Cicero planned to make his announce-ment, the three Sicilians – Sthenius, Heraclius and Epicrates – came openly to the house for the first time in half a year, and together with Quintus and Lucius they escorted Cicero down the hill into the forum. He also had a few tribal officials in his train, mainly from the Cornelia and the Esquilina, where his support was particularly strong. Some onlookers called out to Cicero as he passed, asking where he was going with his three strange-looking friends, and Cicero responded cheerfully that they should come along and see – they would not be disappointed. He always liked a crowd, and in this way he ensured he had one as he approached the tribunal of the extortion court.

In those days, this court always met before the Temple of Castor and Pollux, at the very opposite end of the forum to the senate house. Its new praetor was Acilius Glabrio, of whom little was known, except that he was surprisingly close to Pompey. I say surprisingly because as a young man he had been required by the dictator Sulla to divorce his wife, even though she was then pregnant with his child, and yield her in marriage to Pompey. Subsequently, this unfortunate woman, whose name was Aemilia, died in childbirth in Pompey's house, whereupon Pompey returned the infant – a son – to his natural father; the boy was now twelve, and the joy of Glabrio's life. This bizarre episode was said to have made the two men not enemies but friends, and Cicero gave much thought as to whether this was likely to be helpful to his cause or not. In the end he could not decide.

Glabrio's chair had just been set up for him, the signal that the court was ready to open for business, and it must have been cold, for I have a very clear memory of Glabrio wearing mittens and sitting beside a charcoal brazier. He was stationed on that platform which runs along the front of the temple, halfway up the stairs. His lictors, their bundled rods slung over their shoulders, were standing in line, stamping their feet, on the steps beneath him. It was a busy spot, for as well as housing the extortion court, the temple was also the venue of the Bureau of Standards, where tradesmen went to check their weights and measures. Glabrio looked surprised to see Cicero with his train of supporters advancing towards him, and many other curious passers-by turned to watch. The praetor waved to his lictors to let the senator approach the bench. As I opened the document case and handed Cicero the *postulatus*, I saw anxiety in his eyes, but also relief that the waiting was finally over. He mounted the steps and turned to address the spectators.

'Citizens,' he said, 'today I come to offer my life in service to the Roman people. I wish to announce my intention to seek the office of aedile of Rome. I do this not out of any desire for personal glory, but because the state of our republic demands that honest men stand up for justice. You all know me. You know what I believe in. You know that I have long been keeping an eye on certain aristocratic gentlemen in the senate!' There was a murmur of approval. 'Well, I have in my hand an application to prosecute – a *postulatus*, as we lawyers call it. And I am here to serve notice of my intention to bring to justice Gaius Verres for the high crimes and misdemeanours committed during his term as governor of Sicily.' He waved it above his head, finally extracting a few muted cheers. 'If he is convicted he will not only have to pay back what he has stolen; he will lose all civil rights as a citizen. Exile or death will be his only choices. He will fight like a cornered animal. It will be a long, hard battle, make no mistake, and on its outcome I hereby wager everything – the office I seek, my hopes for the future, the reputation which I have risen early and toiled in the heat to gain – but I do so in the firm conviction that right will prevail!'

And with that he swung round and marched up the remaining few steps to Glabrio, who was looking mightily bemused, and gave him his application to prosecute. The praetor glanced at it quickly, then passed it to one of his clerks. He shook Cicero's hand – and that was it. The crowd began to disperse and there was nothing left to do except walk back up to the house. I am afraid the whole business had fallen embarrassingly flat, the trouble being that Rome was constantly witnessing individuals declaring their intention to run for some office or another – at least fifty were elected annually – and nobody saw Cicero's announcement in quite the same historic terms as he did. As for the prosecution, it was more than a year since he had stirred up the original excitement about Verres, and people, as he frequently remarked, have short memories; they had forgotten all about the wicked governor of Sicily. I could see that Cicero was suffering a dreadful sense of anticlimax, which even Lucius, who was usually good at making him laugh, could not shake him out of.

We reached the house, and Quintus and Lucius tried to amuse him by picturing the responses of Verres and Hortensius when they learned that a charge had been laid: the slave running back from the forum with the news, Verres turning white, a crisis meeting summoned. But Cicero would have none of it. I guessed he was thinking of the warning Servilia had given him, and the way Hortensius and Verres had laughed at him on inauguration day. 'They knew this was coming,' he said. "They have a plan. The question is: what? Do they know our evidence is too weak? Is Glabrio in their pocket? What?'

The answer was in his hands before the morning was out. It came in the form of a writ from the extortion court, served upon him by one of Glabrio's lictors. He took it with a frown, broke open the seal, read it quickly, and then said a soft 'Ah . . .'

'What is it?' asked Lucius.

'The court has received a second application to prosecute Verres.'

'That is impossible,' said Quintus. 'Who else would want to do that?'

'A senator,' replied Cicero, studying the writ. 'Caecilius Niger.'

'I know him,' piped up Sthenius. 'He was Verres's quaestor, in the year before I had to flee the island. It was rumoured that he and the governor quarrelled over money.'

'Hortensius has informed the court that Verres has no objection to being prosecuted by Caecilius, on the grounds that he seeks "personal redress", whereas I, apparently, merely seek "public notoriety".'

We all looked at one another in dismay. Months of work seemed to be turning to dust.

'It is clever,' said Cicero ruefully. 'You have to say that for Hortensius. What a clever devil he is! I assumed he would try to have the whole case dismissed without a hearing. I never imagined that instead he would seek to control the prosecution as well as the defence.'

'But he cannot do that!' spluttered Quintus. 'Roman justice is the fairest system in the world!'

'My dear Quintus,' replied Cicero, with such patronising sarcasm it made me wince, 'where *do* you find these slogans? In nursery books? Do you suppose that Hortensius has dominated the Roman bar for the best part of twenty years by playing *fair*? This is a writ. I am summoned before the extortion court tomorrow morning to argue why I should be allowed to bring the prosecution rather than Caecilius. I have to plead my worth before Glabrio and a full jury. A jury, let me remind you, that will be composed of thirty-two senators, many of whom, you may be sure, will recently have received a new year's gift of bronze or marble.'

'But we Sicilians are the victims!' exclaimed Sthenius. 'Surely it must be for us to decide whom we wish to have as our advocate?'

'Not at all. The prosecutor is the official appointee of the court, and as such a representative of the Roman people. Your opinions are of interest, but they are not decisive.'

'So we are finished?' asked Quintus plaintively.

'No,' said Cicero, 'we are not finished,' and already I could see that some of the old fight was coming back into him, for nothing roused him to greater energy than the thought of being outwitted by Hortensius. 'And if we are finished, well then, at least let us go down with a fight. I shall start preparing my speech, and you, Quintus, will see if you can prepare me a crowd. Call in every favour. Why not give them your line about Roman justice being the fairest in the world, and see if you can persuade a couple of respectable senators to escort me to the forum? Some might even believe it. When I step up to that tribunal tomorrow, I want Glabrio to feel that the whole of Rome is watching him.'

No one can really claim to know politics properly until he has stayed up all night, writing a speech for delivery the following day. While the world sleeps, the orator paces around by lamp-light, wondering what madness ever brought him to this occupation in the first place. Arguments are prepared and discarded. Versions of openings and middle sections and perorations lie in drifts across the floor. The exhausted mind ceases to have any coherent grip upon the purpose of the enterprise, so that often – usually an hour or two after midnight – there comes a point where failing to turn up, feigning illness and hiding at home seem the only realistic options. And then, somehow, under pressure of panic, just as humiliation beckons, the parts cohere, and there it is: a speech. A second-rate orator now retires gratefully to bed. A Cicero stays up and commits it to memory.

Taking only a little fruit and cheese and some diluted wine to sustain him, this was the process Cicero went through that evening. Once he had the sections in order, he released me to get some sleep, but I do not believe that he saw his own bed for even an hour. At dawn he washed in freezing-cold water to revive himself and dressed with care. When I went in to see him, just before we left for court, he was as restless as any prizefighter limbering up in the ring, flexing his shoulders and rocking from side to side on the balls of his feet.

Quintus had done his job well, and immediately the door was opened we were greeted by a noisy crowd of well-wishers, jammed right the way up the street. In addition to the ordinary people of Rome, three or four senators with a particular interest in Sicily had turned out to demonstrate their support. I remember the taciturn Gnaeus Marcellinus, the righteous Calpurnius Piso Frugi – who had been praetor in the same year as Verres, and despised him as a scoundrel – and at least one member of the Marcelli clan, the traditional patrons of the island. Cicero waved from the doorstep, hoisted up Tullia and gave her one of his resounding kisses, and showed her to his supporters. Then he returned her to her mother, with whom he exchanged a rare public embrace, before Quintus, Lucius and I cleared a passage for him and he thrust his way into the centre of the throng.

I tried to wish him luck, but by then, as so often before a big speech, he was unreachable. He looked at people but he did not see them. He was primed for action, playing out some inner drama, rehearsed since childhood, of the lone patriot, armed only with his voice, confronting everything that was corrupt and despicable in the state. As if sensing their part in this fantastic pageant the crowd gradually swelled in number, so that by the time we reached the Temple of Castor there must have been two or three hundred to clap him vigorously into court. Glabrio was already in his place between the great pillars of the temple, as were the panel of jurors, among whom sat the menacing spectre of Catulus himself. I could see Hortensius on the bench reserved for distinguished spectators, examining his beautifully manicured hands and looking as calm as a summer morning. Next to him, also very easy with himself, was a man in his mid-forties with reddish, bristling hair and a freckled face, whom I realised must be Gaius Verres. It was curious for me actually to set eyes on this monster, who had occupied our thoughts for so long, and to find him so ordinary-looking – more fox, in fact, than boar.

Two chairs had been put out for the contesting prosecutors. Caecilius was already seated, with a bundle of notes in his lap, and did not look up when Cicero arrived, but nervously pre-occupied himself with study. The court was called to order and Glabrio told Cicero that he, as the original applicant, must go first – a significant disadvantage. Cicero shrugged and rose, waited for absolute quiet, and started slowly as usual, saying that he assumed people might be surprised to see him in this role, as he had never before sought to enter any arena as a prosecutor. He had not wanted to do it now, he said. Indeed, privately he had urged the Sicilians to give the job to Caecilius. (I almost gasped at that.) But in truth, he said, he was not doing it simply for the Sicilians. 'What I am doing I do for the sake of my country.' And very deliberately he walked across the court to where Verres was sitting and slowly raised his arm to point at him. 'Here is a human monster of unparalleled greed, impu-dence and wickedness. If I bring this man to judgement, who can find fault with me for doing this? Tell me, in the name of all that is just and holy, what better service I can do my country at the present time!' Verres was not in the least put out, but grinned defiantly at Cicero, and shook his head. Cicero stared at him with contempt for a while longer, then turned to face the jury. 'The charge against Gaius Verres is that during a period of three years he has laid waste the province of Sicily – that he has plundered Sicilian communities, stripped bare Sicilian homes, and pillaged Sicilian temples. Could all Sicily speak with a single voice, this is what she would say: "All the gold, all the silver, all the beautiful things that once were in my cities, houses and temples: all these things you, Verres, have plundered and stolen from me; and on this account I sue you in accordance with the law for the sum of one million sesterces!" These are the words all Sicily would utter, if she could speak with a single voice, and as she cannot, she has chosen me to conduct her case for her. So what incredible impudence it is that *you'* – and now he finally turned to Caecilius – 'should dare to try to undertake their case when they have already said they will not have you!'

He strolled across to Caecilius, and stood behind him. He gave an exaggerated sigh of sadness. 'I am now going to speak to you as one friend to another,' he said, and patted Caecilius's shoulder, so that his rival had to twist round in his seat to see him – a fidgety movement which drew a good deal of laughter. 'I earnestly advise you to examine your own mind. Recollect yourself. Think of what you are, and what you are fit for. This prosecution is a very formidable and a very painful undertaking. Have you the powers of voice and memory? Have you the intelligence and the ability to sustain such a burden? Even if you had the advantage of great natural gifts, even if you had received a thorough education, could you hope to stand the strain? We shall find out this morning. If you can reply to what I am now saying, if you can use one single expression that is not contained in some book of extracts compiled from other people's speeches and given to you by your schoolteacher, then perhaps you will not be a failure at the actual trial.'

He moved towards the centre of the court, and now he addressed the crowd in the forum as well as the jury. '"Well," you may say, "what if that is so? Do *you* then possess all these qualities yourself?" Would that I did, indeed! Still, I have done my best, and worked hard from boyhood, in order to acquire them if I could. Everyone knows that my life has centred around the forum and the law courts; that few men, if any, of my age have defended more cases; that all the time I can spare from the business of my friends I spend in the study and hard work which this profession demands, to make myself fitter and readier for forensic practice. Yet even I, when I think of the great day when the accused man is summoned to appear and I have to make my speech, am not only anxious, but tremble physically from head to foot. *You*, Caecilius, have no such fears, no such thoughts, no such anxieties. You imagine that, if you can learn by heart a phrase or two out of some old speech, like "I beseech almighty and most merciful God" or "I could wish, gentlemen, had it only been possible", you will be excellently prepared for your entrance into court.

'Caecilius, you are nothing, and you count for nothing. Hortensius will *destroy* you! But he will never crush me with his cleverness. He will never lead me astray by any display of ingenuity. He will never employ his great powers to weaken and dislodge me from my position.' He looked towards Hortensius, and bowed to him in mock humility, to which Hortensius responded by standing and bowing back, eliciting more laughter. 'I am well acquainted with all this gentleman's methods of attack,' continued Cicero, 'and all his oratorical devices. However capable he may be, he will feel, when he comes to speak against me, that the trial is among other things a trial of his own capacities. And I give the gentleman fair warning well beforehand, that if you decide that I am to conduct this case, he will have to make a radical change in his methods of defence. If *I* conduct the case, he will have no reason to think that the court can be bribed without serious danger to a large number of people.'

The mention of bribery produced a brief uproar, and brought

the normally equable Hortensius to his feet, but Cicero waved him back into his place. On and on he went, his rhetoric hammering down upon his opponents like the ringing blows of a blacksmith in a forge. I shall not quote it all: the speech, which lasted at least an hour, is readily available for those who wish to read it. He smashed away at Verres for his corruption, and at Caecilius for his previous links with Verres, and at Hortensius for desiring a second-rate opponent. And he concluded by challenging the senators themselves, walking over to the jury and looking each of them in the eye. 'It rests with you, then, gentlemen, to choose the man whom you think best qualified by good faith, industry, sagacity and weight of character to maintain this great case before this great court. If you give Quintus Caecilius the preference over me, I shall not think I have been beaten by the better man. But Rome may think that an honourable, strict and energetic prosecutor like myself was not what you desired, and not what senators would ever desire.' He paused, his gaze coming to rest at last on Catulus, who stared straight back at him, and then he said very quietly: 'Gentlemen, see that this does not happen.'

There was loud applause, and now it was Caecilius's turn. He had risen from very humble origins, much more humble than Cicero's, and he was not entirely without merit. One could even say he had some prior claim to prosecute, especially when he began by pointing out that his father had been a freed Sicilian slave, that he had been born in the province, and that the island was the place he loved most in the world. But his speech was full of statistics about falling agricultural production and Verres's system of accounting. He sounded peevish rather than impassioned. Worse, he read it all out from notes, and in a monotone, so that when, after an hour, he approached his peroration,

Cicero slumped to one side and pretended to fall asleep. Caecilius, who was facing the jury and therefore could not see what everyone was laughing at, was seriously knocked off his stride. He struggled through to the end and then sat down, crimson with embarrassment and rage.

In terms of rhetoric, Cicero had scored a victory of annihilating proportions. But as the voting tablets were passed among the jury, and the clerk of the court stood ready with his urn to collect them, Cicero knew, he told me afterwards, that he had lost. Of the thirty-two senators, he recognised at least a dozen firm enemies, and only half as many friends. The decision, as usual, would rest with the floaters in the middle, and he could see that many of these were craning their necks for a signal from Catulus, intent on following his lead. Catulus marked his tablet, showed it to the men on either side of him, then dropped it in the urn. When everyone had voted, the clerk took the urn over to the bench, and in full view of the court tipped it out and began counting the tablets. Hortensius, abandoning his pretence of coolness, was on his feet, and so was Verres, trying to see how the tally was going. Cicero sat as still as a statue. Caecilius was hunched in his chair. All around me people who made a habit of attending the courts and knew the procedure as well as the judges were whispering that it was close, that they were re-counting. Eventually the clerk passed the tally up to Glabrio, who stood and called for silence. The voting, he said, was fourteen for Cicero – my heart stopped: he had lost! – thirteen for Caecilius, with five abstentions, and that Marcus Tullius Cicero was therefore appointed special prosecutor (*nominis delator*) in the case of Gaius Verres. As the spectators applauded and Hortensius and Verres sat down stunned, Glabrio told Cicero to stand and raise his right hand, and then had him swear the traditional oath to conduct the prosecution in good faith.

The moment that was finished, Cicero made an application for an adjournment. Hortensius swiftly rose to object: why was this necessary? Cicero said he wished to travel to Sicily to subpoena evidence and witnesses. Hortensius interrupted to say it was outrageous for Cicero to demand the right to prosecute, only to reveal in his next breath that he lacked an adequate case to bring to court! This was a valid point, and for the first time I realised how unconfident Cicero must be of the strength of his position. Glabrio seemed inclined to agree with Hortensius, but Cicero pleaded that it was only now, since Verres had left his province, that his victims felt it safe to speak out. Glabrio pondered the issue, checked the calendar, then announced, reluctantly, that the case would stand adjourned for one hundred and ten days. 'But be sure you are ready to open immediately after the spring recess,' he warned Cicero. And with that, the court was dismissed.

To his surprise, Cicero later discovered that he owed his victory to Catulus. This hard and snobbish old senator was, nevertheless, a patriot to his marrow, which was why his opinions commanded such respect. He took the view that the people had the right, under the ancient laws, to see Verres subjected to the most rigorous prosecution available, even though Verres was a friend of his. Family obligations to his brother-in-law, Hortensius, naturally prevented him from voting for Cicero outright, so instead he abstained, taking four waverers with him.

Grateful to be still in 'the Boar Hunt', as he called it, and delighted to have outwitted Hortensius, Cicero now flung himself into the business of preparing his expedition to Sicily. Verres's official papers were sealed by the court under an order *obsignandi gratia*. Cicero laid a motion before the senate demanding that the former governor submit his official accounts for the past three years (he never did). Letters were dispatched to every large town on the island, inviting them to submit evidence. I reviewed our files and extracted the names of all the leading citizens who had offered Cicero hospitality when he was a junior magistrate, for we would need accommodation throughout the province. Cicero also wrote a courtesy letter to the governor, Lucius Metellus, informing him of his visit and requesting official co-operation – not that he expected anything other than official harassment, but he reasoned it might be useful to have the notification in writing, to show that he had at least tried. He decided to take his cousin with him – Lucius having worked on the case for six months already – and to leave his brother behind to manage his election campaign. I was to go, too, along with both of my juniors, Sositheus and Laurea, for there would be much copying and note-taking. The former praetor, Calpurnius Piso Frugi, offered Cicero the services of his eighteen-year-old son, Gaius – a young man of great intelligence and charm, to whom everyone soon took a liking. At Quintus's insistence, we also acquired four strong and reliable slaves, ostensibly to act as porters and drivers, but also to serve as bodyguards. It was lawless country down in the south at that time – many of Spartacus's followers still survived in the hills; there were pirates; and no one could be sure what measures Verres might adopt.

All of this required money, and although Cicero's legal practice was now bringing in some income – not in the form of direct payments, of course, which were forbidden, but in gifts and legacies from grateful clients – he had nothing like the amount of ready cash necessary to mount a proper prosecution. Most ambitious young men in his position would have gone to see Crassus, who always gave loans to rising politicians on generous terms. But just as Crassus liked to show that he rewarded support, so he also took care to let people see how he punished opposition. Ever since Cicero had declined to join his camp, he had gone out of his way to demonstrate his enmity. He cut him dead in public. He poor-mouthed him behind his back. Perhaps if Cicero had grovelled sufficiently, he would have condescended to change his mind: his principles were infinitely malleable. But, as I have already said, the two men found it difficult even to stand within ten feet of one another.

So Cicero had no choice but to approach Terentia, and a painful scene ensued. I only became involved because Cicero, in a rather cowardly way, at first dispatched *me* to see her business manager, Philotimus, to enquire how difficult it would be to raise one hundred thousand from her estate. With characteristic malevolence, Philotimus immediately reported my approach to his mistress, who stormed down to find me in Cicero's study, and demanded to know how I dared poke my nose into her affairs. Cicero came in while this was happening and was consequently obliged to explain why he needed the money.

'And how is this sum to be repaid?' demanded Terentia.

'From the fine levied on Verres once he is found guilty,' replied her husband.

'And you are sure he *will* be found guilty?'

'Of course.'

'Why? What is your case? Let me hear it.' And with that she sat down in his chair and folded her arms. Cicero hesitated, but knowing his wife and seeing she was not to be shifted, told me to open the strongbox and fetch out the Sicilians' evidence. He took her through it, piece by piece, and at the end of it she regarded him with unfeigned dismay. 'But that is not enough, Cicero! You have wagered everything on *that*? Do you really think a jury of senators will convict one of their own because he has rescued some important statues from provincial obscurity and brought them back to Rome – where they properly belong?'

'You may be right, my dear,' conceded Cicero. 'That is why I need to go to Sicily.'

Terentia regarded her husband – arguably the greatest orator and the cleverest senator in Rome at that time – with the sort of look a matron might reserve for a child who has made a puddle on the drawing room floor. She would have said something, I am sure, but she noticed I was still there, and thought the better of it. Silently, she rose and left the study.

The following day, Philotimus sought me out and handed me a small money chest containing ten thousand in cash, with authorisation to draw a further forty thousand as necessary.

'Exactly half of what I asked for,' said Cicero, when I took it in to him 'That is a shrewd businesswoman's assessment of my chances, Tiro – and who is to say she is wrong?'

VII

We left Rome on the Ides of January, on the last day of the Festival of the Nymphs, with Cicero riding in a covered wagon so that he could continue to work – although I found it a torment even attempting to read, let alone write, in that rattling, creaking, lurching *carruca*. It was a miserable journey, freezing cold, with flurries of snow across the higher ground. By this time, most of the crosses bearing the crucified rebel slaves had been removed from the Appian Way. But some still stood as a warning, stark against the whitened landscape, with a few rotted fragments of bodies attached. Gazing at them, I felt as if Crassus's long arm had reached out after me from Rome and was once again pinching my cheek.

Because we had departed in such a hurry, it had proved impossible to arrange places to stay all along our route, and on three or four nights when no inns were available we were reduced to sleeping by the roadside. I lay with the other slaves, huddled around the campfire, while Cicero, Lucius and young Frugi slept in the wagon. In the mountains I would wake at dawn to find my clothes starched with ice. When at last we reached the coast at Velia, Cicero decided it would be quicker to board a ship and hug the coast – this despite the risk of winter storms and pirates, and his own marked aversion to travelling by boat, for he had been warned by a sibyl that his death would somehow be connected with the sea.

Velia was a health resort, with a well-known temple to Apollo Oulius, then a fashionable god of healing. But it was all shuttered up and out of season, and as we made our way down to the harbour front, where the grey sea battered against the wharf, Cicero remarked that he had seldom seen a less enticing holiday spot. Aside from the usual collection of fishing boats, the port contained one huge vessel, a cargo ship the size of a trireme, and while we were negotiating our journey with the local sailors, Cicero happened to ask to whom it belonged. It was, we were told, a gift from the citizens of the Sicilian port of Messana to their former governor, Gaius Verres, and had been moored here for a month.

There was something infinitely sinister about that great ship, sitting low in the water, fully crewed and ready to move at a moment's warning. Our appearance in the deserted harbour had clearly already been registered and was causing something of a panic. Even as Cicero led us cautiously towards the vessel, we heard three short blasts sounded on a trumpet, and saw it sprout oars, like some immense water beetle, and edge away from the quayside. It moved a short distance out to sea, and dropped anchor. As the ship turned into the wind, the lanterns at its prow and stern danced bright yellow in the gloomy afternoon, and figures deployed along its heaving decks. Cicero debated with Lucius and young Frugi what to do. In theory, his warrant from the extortion court gave him authority to board and search any vessel he suspected of connection with the case. In truth, we lacked the resources, and by the time reinforcements could be summoned, the ship would be long gone. What it showed beyond doubt was that Verres's crimes were on a scale vastly bigger than anything even Cicero had imagined. He decided we should press on south at redoubled speed.

I guess it must be a hundred and twenty miles from Velia down to Vibo, running straight along the shin bone to the toe of Italy. But with a favourable wind and strong rowing we did it in just two days. We kept always within sight of the shore, and put in for one night to sleep on the sandy beach, where we cut down a thicket of myrtle to make a campfire and used our oars and sail for a tent. From Vibo we took the coast road to Regium, and here we chartered a second boat to sail across the narrow straits to Sicily. It was a misty early morning when we set off, with a saturating drizzle falling. The distant island appeared on the horizon as a dreary black hump. Unfortunately, there was only one place to make for, especially in midwinter, and that was Verres's stronghold of Messana. He had bought the loyalty of its inhabitants by exempting them from taxes throughout all his three years as governor, and alone of the towns on the island it had refused to offer Cicero any cooperation. We steered towards its lighthouse, and as we drew closer realised that what we had perceived as a large mast at the entrance to the harbour was not part of a ship at all, but a cross, facing directly across the straits to the mainland.

'That is new,' said Cicero, frowning as he wiped the rain from his eyes. 'This was never a place of execution in our day.'

We had no option but to sail straight past it, and the sight fell across our waterlogged spirits like a shadow.

Despite the general hostility of the people of Messana towards the special prosecutor, two citizens of the town – Basiliscus and Percennius – had bravely agreed to offer him hospitality, and were waiting on the quayside to greet us. The moment he stepped ashore, Cicero queried them about the cross, but they begged to be excused from answering until they had transported us away from the wharf. Only when we were in the compound of Basiliscus's house did they feel it safe to tell the story. Verres had spent his last days as governor living full-time in Messana, supervising the loading of his loot aboard the treasure ship which the grateful town had built for him. There had been a festival in his honour about a month ago, and almost it seemed as part of the entertainment, a Roman citizen had been dragged from the prison, stripped naked in the forum, publicly flogged, tortured, and finally crucified.

'A Roman citizen?' repeated Cicero incredulously. He gestured at me to begin making notes. 'But it is illegal to execute a Roman citizen without a full trial. Are you sure that is what he was?'

'He cried out that his name was Publius Gavius, that he was a merchant from Spain, and that he had done military service in the legions. Throughout his whipping he screamed, "I am a Roman citizen!" every time he received a blow.'

'"I am a Roman citizen",' repeated Cicero, savouring the phrase. '"I am a Roman citizen . . ." But what was alleged to be his crime?'

'Spying,' replied our host. 'He was on the point of boarding a ship for Italy. But he made the mistake of telling everyone he met that he had escaped from the Stone Quarries in Syracuse and was going straight to Rome to expose all Verres's crimes. The elders of Messana had him arrested and held until Verres arrived. Then Verres ordered him to be scourged, tortured with hot irons and executed on a cross looking out across the straits to Regium, so that he could see the mainland throughout his final agonies. Imagine that – being only five miles from safety! The cross has been left standing by the followers of Verres as a warning to anyone else who feels tempted to talk too freely.'

'There were witnesses to this crucifixion?'

'Of course. Hundreds.'

'Including Roman citizens?'

'Yes.'

'Could you identify any of them?'

He hesitated. 'Gaius Numitorius, a Roman knight from Puteoli. The Cottius brothers from Tauromenium. Lucceius – he is from Regium. There must have been others.'

I took down their names. Afterwards, while Cicero was having a bath, we gathered beside his tub to discuss this development. Lucius said, 'Perhaps this man Gavius really was a spy.'

'I would be more inclined to believe that,' replied Cicero, 'if Verres had not brought exactly the same charge against Sthenius, who is no more a spy than you or I. No, this is the monster's favoured method of operation: he arranges a trumped-up charge, then uses his position as supreme justice in the province to reach a verdict and pronounce sentence. The question is: why did he pick on Gavius?'

Nobody had an answer; nor did we have the spare time to linger in Messana and try to find one. Early the following morning we had to leave for our first official engagement, in the northern coastal town of Tyndaris. This visit set the pattern for a score which followed. The council came out to greet Cicero with full honours. He was conducted into the municipal square. He was shown the standard-issue statue of Verres, which the citizens had been obliged to pay for, and which they had now pulled down and smashed. Cicero made a short speech about Roman justice. His chair was set up. He listened to the complaints of the locals. He then selected those which were most eye-catching or most easily proved – in Tyndaris it was the story of Sopater, bound naked to a statue until the town yielded up its bronze of Mercury – and finally either I or one of my two assistants moved in to take statements, which would be witnessed and signed.

From Tyndaris we travelled on to Sthenius's home city of Thermae, where we saw his wife in his empty house, who sobbed as Cicero delivered letters from her exiled husband, and then ended the week in the fortress port of Lilybaeum, on the extreme western tip of the island. Cicero knew this place well, having been based here when he was a junior magistrate. We stayed, as so often in the past, at the home of his old friend Pamphilius. Over dinner on the first night, Cicero noticed that the usual decorations of the table – a beautiful jug and goblets, all family heirlooms – were missing, and when he asked what had become of them, was told that Verres had seized them. It quickly transpired that all the other guests in the dining room had similar tales to tell. Young Gaius Cacurius had been obliged to give up all his furniture, and Lutatius a citrus-wood table at which Cicero had regularly eaten. Lyso had been robbed of his precious statue of Apollo, and Diodorus of a set of chased silver cups by Mentor. The list was endless, and I should know, for I was the one summoned to compile it. After taking statements from each of them, and subsequently from all their friends, I began to think that Cicero had gone a little mad – did he plan to catalogue every stolen spoon and cream jug on the island? – but of course he was being cleverer than I, as events were to show.

We moved on a few days later, rattling down the unmade tracks from Lilybaeum to the temple city of Agrigentum, then up into the mountainous heart of the island. The winter was unusually harsh; the land and sky were iron. Cicero caught a bad cold and sat wrapped in his cloak in the back of our cart.

At Henna, a town built precipitously into the cliffs and surrounded by lakes and woods, the ululating priests all came out to greet us, wearing their elaborate robes and carrying their sacred boughs, and took us to the shrine of Ceres, from which Verres had removed the goddess's statue. And here for the first time our escort became involved in scuffles with the lictors of the new governor, Lucius Metellus. These brutes with their rods and axes stood to one side of the market square and shouted threats of dire penalties for any witness who dared to testify against Verres. Nevertheless, Cicero persuaded three prominent citizens of Henna – Theodorus, Numenius and Nicasio – to undertake to come to Rome and give their evidence.

Finally, we turned south-east towards the sea again, into the fertile plains below Mount Aetna. This was state-owned land, administered on behalf of the Roman treasury by a revenue-collection company, which in turn awarded leases to local farmers. When Cicero had first been on the island, the plains of Leontini had been the granary of Rome. But now we drove past deserted farmhouses and grey, untended fields, punctuated by drifting columns of brown smoke, where the homeless former tenants now lived in the open. Verres and his friends in the tax company had fanned out across the region like a ravaging army, commandeering crops and livestock for a fraction of their true value, and raising rents far beyond what most could pay. One farmer who had dared to complain, Nymphodorus of Centuripae, had been seized by Verres's tithe collector, Apronius, and hanged from an olive tree in the market place of Aetna. Such stories enraged Cicero, and drove him to fresh exertions. I still cherish the memory of this most urban of gentlemen, his toga hoisted around his knees, his fine red shoes in one hand, his warrant in the other, picking his way daintily across a muddy field in the pouring rain to take evidence from a farmer at his plough. By the time we came at last to Syracuse, after more than thirty days of arduous travels around the province, we had the statements of nearly two hundred witnesses.

Syracuse is by far the largest and fairest of Sicily's cities. It is four towns, really, which have merged into one. Three of these – Achradina, Tycha and Neapolis – have spread themselves around the harbour, and in the centre of this great natural bay sits the fourth settlement, known simply as the Island, the ancient royal seat, which is linked to the others by a bridge. This walled city-within-a-city, forbidden at night to Sicilians, is where the Roman governor has his palace, close by the great temples of Diana and Minerva. We had feared a hostile reception, given that Syracuse was said to be second only to Messana in its loyalty to Verres, and its senate had recently voted him a eulogy. In fact, the opposite was the case. News of Cicero's honesty and diligence had preceded him, and we were escorted through the Agrigentine gate by a crowd of cheering citizens. (One reason for Cicero's popularity was that, as a young magistrate, he had located in the overgrown municipal cemetery the one-hundred-and-thirty-year-old lost tomb of the mathematician Archimedes, the greatest man in the history of Syracuse. Typically, he had read somewhere that it was marked by a cylinder and a sphere, and once he had found the monument, he paid to have the weeds and brambles cleared away. He had then spent many hours beside it, pondering the transience of human glory. His generosity and respect had not been forgotten by the local population.)

But to resume. We were lodged in the home of a Roman

knight, Lucius Flavius, an old friend of Cicero's, who had plenty of stories of Verres's corruption and cruelty to add to our already bulging stock. There was the tale of the pirate captain, Heracleo, who had been able to sail right into Syracuse at the head of a squadron of four small galleys, pillage the warehouses, and leave without encountering any resistance. Captured some weeks later, further up the coast at Megara, neither he nor his men had been paraded as prisoners, and there were rumours that Verres had exchanged him for a large ransom. Then there was the horrible business of the Roman banker from Spain, Lucius Herennius, who had been dragged into the forum of Syracuse one morning, summarily denounced as a spy and, on Verres's orders, beheaded – this despite the pleadings of his friends and business associates, who had come running to the scene when they heard what was happening. The similarity of Herennius's case to that of Gavius in Messana was striking: both Romans, both from Spain, both involved in commerce, both accused of spying, and both executed without a hearing or a proper trial.

That night, after dinner, Cicero received a messenger from Rome. Immediately he had read the letter, he excused himself, and took Lucius, young Frugi and myself aside. The dispatch was from his brother Quintus, and it contained grave news. It seemed that Hortensius was up to his old tricks again. The extortion court had unexpectedly given permission for a prosecution to be brought against the former governor of Achaia. The prosecutor, Dasianus, a known associate of Verres, had undertaken to travel to Greece and back and present his evidence two days before the deadline set for Cicero's return from Sicily. Quintus urged his brother to return to Rome as quickly as possible to retrieve the situation.

'It's a trap,' declared Lucius immediately, 'to make you panic, and cut short your expedition here.'

'Probably so,' agreed Cicero. 'But I can't afford to take the risk. If this other prosecution slips into the court's schedule ahead of ours, and if Hortensius spins it out as he likes to do, our case could be pushed back until after the elections. By then Hortensius and Quintus Metellus will be consuls-elect. That youngest Metellus brother will no doubt be a praetor-elect, and this third will still be governor here. How will that be for having the odds stacked against us?'

'So what are we going to do?'

'We have wasted too much time pursuing the small fry in this investigation,' said Cicero. 'We need to take the war into the enemy's camp, and loosen some tongues among those who really know what has been going on – the Romans themselves.'

'I agree,' said Lucius. 'The question is: how?'

Cicero glanced around and lowered his voice before replying. 'We shall carry out a raid,' he announced. 'A raid on the offices of the revenue collectors.'

Even Lucius looked slightly green at that, for short of marching up to the governor's palace and attempting to arrest Metellus, this was about the most provocative gesture Cicero could make. The revenue collectors were a syndicate of well-connected men, of equestrian rank, operating under statutory protection, whose investors would certainly include some of the wealthiest senators in Rome. Cicero himself, as a specialist in commercial law, had built up a network of supporters among exactly this class of businessman. He knew it was a risky strategy, but he was not to be dissuaded, for it was here, he was sure, that the dark heart of Verres's murderous corruption was to be found. He sent the messenger back to Rome that same night with a letter for Quintus, announcing that he had only one more thing left to do, and that he would depart from the island within a few days.

Cicero now had to make his preparations with great speed and secrecy. He deliberately timed his raid to take place two days hence, at the least-expected hour – just before dawn on a major public holiday, Terminalia. The fact that this is the day sacred to Terminus, the ancient god of boundaries and good neighbours, only made it more symbolically attractive as far as he was concerned. Flavius, our host, agreed to come with us to point out the location of the offices. In the interim, I went down to the harbour in Syracuse and found the same trusty skipper I had used years before, when Cicero made his ill-judged return to Italy. From him I hired a ship and crew and told him to be ready to sail before the end of the week. The evidence we had already collected was packed in trunks and stowed aboard. The ship was placed under guard.

None of us got much sleep on the night of the raid. In the darkness before dawn we positioned our hired ox-carts at either end of the street to block it, and when Cicero gave the signal we all jumped out carrying our torches. The senator hammered on the door, stood aside without waiting for a reply, and a couple of our burliest attendants took their axes to it. The instant it yielded, we poured through into the passage, knocking aside the elderly nightwatchman, and secured the company's records. We quickly formed a human chain – Cicero, too – and passed the boxes of wax tablets and papyrus rolls from hand to hand, out into the street and on to the back of our carts.

I learned one valuable lesson that day, which is that if you seek popularity, there is no surer way of achieving it than raiding a syndicate of tax collectors. As the sun rose and news of our activity spread through the neighbourhood, an enthusiastic honour guard of Syracusans formed themselves around us, more than large enough to deter the director of the company, Carpinatius, when he arrived to reoccupy the building with a detachment of legionaries lent to him for the purpose by Lucius Metellus. He and Cicero fell into a furious argument in the middle of the road, Carpinatius insisting that provincial tax records were protected by law from seizure, Cicero retorting that his warrant from the extortion court overrode such technicalities. In fact, as Cicero conceded afterwards, Carpinatius was right. 'But,' he added, 'he who controls the street controls the law' – and on this occasion, at least, it was Cicero who controlled the street.

In all, we must have transported more than four cartloads of records back to the house of Flavius. We locked the gates, posted sentries, and then began the wearying business of sorting through them. Even now, remembering the size of the task that confronted us, I find myself starting to break into a sweat of apprehension. These records, which went back years, not only covered all the state land on Sicily, but itemised every farmer's number and quality of grazing animals, and every crop he had ever sown, its size and yield. Here were details of loans issued and taxes paid and correspondence entered into. And it quickly became clear that other hands had already been through this mass of material, and removed every trace of the name of Verres. A furious message arrived from the governor's palace, demanding that Cicero appear before Metellus when the courts reopened the following day, to answer a writ from Carpinatius that he return the documents. Meanwhile, yet another large crowd had started gathering outside and was chanting Cicero's name. I thought of Terentia's prediction, that her husband and she would be

ostracised by Rome and end their days as consul and first lady
of Thermae, and never did a prophecy seem more prescient than
at that moment. Only Cicero retained his cool. He had represented enough shady revenue collectors in his time to know most
of their tricks. Once it became apparent that the files specifically
relating to Verres had been excised, he dug out an old list of all
the company's managers, and hunted through it until he came
to the name of the firm's financial director during the period of
Verres's governorship.

'I'll tell you one thing, Tiro,' he said to me. 'I have never come
across a financial director yet who didn't keep an extra set of
records for himself when he handed over to his successor, just
to be on the safe side.'

And with that we set off on our second raid of the morning.

Our quarry was a man named Vibius, who was at that moment
celebrating Terminalia with his neighbours. They had set up an
altar in the garden and there was some grain upon it, also some
honeycombs and wine, and Vibius had just sacrificed a sucking
pig. ('Always very pious, these crooked accountants,' observed
Cicero.) When he saw the senator bearing down upon him, he
looked a little like a sucking pig himself, but once he had read
the warrant, which had Glabrio's praetorian seal attached to it,
he reluctantly decided there was nothing he could do except
cooperate. Excusing himself from his bemused guests, he led us
inside to his tablinum and opened up his strongbox. Among the
title deeds, account books and jewellery, there was a little packet
of letters marked 'Verres', and as Cicero broke it open, Vibius's
face bore an expression of utter terror. I guess he must have been
told to destroy it, and had either forgotten or had thought to
make some profit out of it.

At first sight, it was nothing much – merely some correspond-

ence from a tax inspector, Lucius Canuleius, who was responsible for collecting export duty on all goods passing through
Syracuse harbour. The letters concerned one particular shipment
of goods which had left Syracuse two years before, and upon
which Verres had failed to pay any tax. The details were attached:
four hundred casks of honey, fifty dining room couches, two
hundred chandeliers and ninety bales of Maltese cloth. Another
prosecutor might not have spotted the significance, but Cicero
saw it at once.

'Take a look at that,' he said, handing it to me. 'These are not
goods seized from a number of unfortunate individuals. *Four
hundred* casks of honey? *Ninety* bales of foreign cloth?' He turned
his furious gaze on the hapless Vibius. 'This is a *cargo*, isn't it?
Your Governor Verres must have stolen *a ship*.'

Poor Vibius never stood a chance. Glancing nervously over his
shoulder at his bewildered guests, who were staring open-
mouthed in our direction, he confirmed that this was indeed a
ship's cargo, and that Canuleius had been instructed never again
to attempt to levy tax on any of the governor's exports.

'How many more such shipments did Verres make?' demanded
Cicero.

'I am not sure.'

'Guess then.'

'Ten,' said Vibius fearfully. 'Perhaps twenty.'

'And no duty was ever paid? No records kept?'

'No.'

'And where did Verres acquire all these cargoes?' demanded
Cicero.

Vibius was almost swooning with terror. 'Senator, please . . .'

'I shall have you arrested,' said Cicero. 'I shall have you transported to Rome in chains. I shall break you on the witness stand

before a thousand spectators in the Forum Romanum and feed what's left of you to the dogs of the Capitoline Triad.'

'From ships, Senator,' said Vibius, in a little mouse voice. 'They came from ships.'

'What ships? Ships from where?'

'From everywhere, Senator. Asia. Syria. Tyre. Alexandria.'

'So what happened to these ships? Did Verres have them impounded?'

'Yes, Senator.'

'On what grounds?'

'Spying.'

'Ah, spying! Of course! Did ever a man,' said Cicero to me, 'root out so many spies as our vigilant Governor Verres? So tell us,' he said, turning back to Vibius, 'what became of the crews of these spy ships?'

'They were taken to the Stone Quarries, Senator.'

'And what happened to them then?'

He made no reply.

The Stone Quarries was the most fearsome prison in Sicily, probably the most fearsome in the world – at any rate, I never heard of a worse one. It was six hundred feet long and two hundred wide, gouged deep into the solid rock of that fortified plateau known as Epipolae, which overlooks Syracuse from the north. Here, in this hellish pit, from which no scream could carry, exposed without protection to the burning heat of summer and the cold downpours of winter, tormented by the cruelty of their guards and the debased appetites of their fellow prisoners alike, the victims of Verres suffered and died.

Cicero, with his notorious aversion to military life, was often charged with cowardice by his enemies, and certainly he was prone to nerves and squeamishness. But I can vouch that he was brave enough that day. He went back to our headquarters and collected Lucius, leaving young Frugi behind to continue his search of the tax records. Then, armed only with our walking sticks and the warrant issued by Glabrio, and followed by the now-usual crowd of Syracusans, we climbed the steep path to Epipolae. As always, the news of Cicero's approach and the nature of his mission had preceded him, and the captain of the guard, after receiving a withering harangue from the senator, threatening all manner of dire repercussions if his demands were not met, allowed us to pass through the perimeter wall and on to the plateau. Once inside, refusing to heed warnings that it was too dangerous, Cicero insisted on being allowed to inspect the Quarries himself.

This vast dungeon, the work of Dionysius the Tyrant, was already more than three centuries old. An ancient metal door was unlocked and we proceeded into the mouth of a tunnel, guided by prison guards who carried burning torches. The glistening walls, cankerous with lime and fungi, the scuttling of the rats in the shadows, the stench of death and waste, the cries and groans of the abandoned souls – truly this was a descent into Hades. Eventually we came to another massive door, and when this was unlocked and unbolted we stepped on to the floor of the prison. What a spectacle greeted our eyes! It was as if some giant had filled a sack with hundreds of manacled men and had then tipped them out into a hole. The light was weak, almost subaquatic, and everywhere, as far as one could see, there were prisoners. Some shuffled about, a few huddled in groups, but most lay apart from their fellows, mere yellowing sacks of bones. The day's corpses had not yet been cleared, and it was hard to distinguish the living skeletons from the dead.

We picked our way among the bodies – those who had already died, and those whose end had yet to come: there was no discernible difference – and occasionally Cicero stopped and asked a man his name, bending to catch the whispered reply. We found no Romans, only Sicilians. 'Is any man here a Roman citizen?' he demanded loudly. 'Have any of you been taken from ships?' There was silence. He turned and called for the captain of the watch and demanded to see the prison records. Like Vibius, the wretch struggled between fear of Verres and fear of the special prosecutor, but eventually he succumbed to Cicero's pressure.

Built into the rock walls of the quarry were separate special cells and galleries, where torture and execution were done, and where the guards ate and slept. (The favoured method of execution, we discovered afterwards, was the garrotte.) Here, too, was housed the administration of the prison, such as it was. Boxes of damp and musty rolls were fetched out for us, containing long lists of prisoners' names, with the dates of their arrival and departure. Some men were recorded as having been released, but against most was scratched the Sicilian word *edikaiothesan* – meaning 'the death penalty was inflicted upon them'.

'I want a copy of every entry for the three years when Verres was governor,' Cicero said to me, 'and you,' he said to the prison captain, 'when it is done, will sign a statement to say that we have made a true likeness.'

While I and the other two secretaries set to work, Cicero and Lucius searched through the records for Roman names. Although the majority of those held in the Quarries during

Verres's time were obviously Sicilian, there was also a considerable proportion of races from all across the Mediterranean – Spaniards, Egyptians, Syrians, Cilicians, Cretans, Dalmatians. When Cicero asked why they had been imprisoned, he was told they were pirates – pirates and spies. All were recorded as having been put to death, among them the infamous pirate captain Heracleo. The Romans, on the other hand, were officially described as 'released' – including the two men from Spain, Publius Gavius and Lucius Herennius, whose executions had been described to us.

'These records are a nonsense,' said Cicero quietly to Lucius, 'the very opposite of the truth. No one saw Heracleo die, although the spectacle of a pirate on the cross invariably draws an enthusiastic crowd. But plenty saw the Romans executed. It looks to me as though Verres simply switched the two about – killed the innocent ships' crews and freed the pirates, no doubt on payment of a fat ransom. If Gavius and Herennius had discovered his treachery, that would explain why Verres had been so anxious to kill them quickly.'

I thought poor Lucius was going to be sick. He had surely come a long way from his philosophy books in sunlit Rome to find himself studying death lists by the guttering light of candles, eighty feet beneath the dripping earth. We finished as quickly as we could, and never have I been more glad to escape from anywhere than I was to climb the tunnel out of the Stone Quarries and rejoin humanity on the surface. A slight breeze had sprung up, blowing in across the sea, and I remember as if it were this afternoon rather than an afternoon more than half a century ago the way we all instinctively turned our faces to it and gratefully drank in the taste of that cold clear air.

'Promise me,' said Lucius after a while, 'that if ever you achieve this *imperium* you desire so much, you will never preside over cruelty and injustice such as this.'

'I swear it,' replied Cicero. 'And if ever, my dear Lucius, you should question why good men forsake philosophy to seek power in the real world, promise me in return that you will always remember what you witnessed in the Stone Quarries of Syracuse.'

By this time it was late afternoon, and Syracuse, thanks to Cicero's activities, was in a tumult. The crowd which had followed us up the steep slope to the prison was still waiting for us outside the walls of Epipolae. Indeed, it had grown larger, and had been joined by some of the most distinguished citizens of the city, among them the chief priest of Jupiter, all dressed up in his sacred robes. This pontificate, traditionally reserved for the highest-ranking Syracusan, was presently held by none other than Cicero's client, Heraclius, who had returned privately from Rome to help us – at considerable personal risk. He came with a request that Cicero should immediately accompany him to the city's senate chamber, where the elders were waiting to give him a formal civic welcome. Cicero was in two minds. He had much work to do, and not long left to do it, and it was undoubtedly a breach of protocol for a Roman senator to address a local assembly without the permission of the governor. However, it also promised to be a wonderful opportunity to further his enquiries. After a short hesitation, he agreed to go, and we duly set off on foot back down the hill with a huge escort of respectful Sicilians.

The senate chamber was packed. Beneath a gilded statue of Verres himself, the house's most senior senator, the venerable Diodorus, welcomed Cicero in Greek, and apologised for the fact that they had so far offered him no assistance: not until the events of today had they truly believed he was in earnest. Cicero, also speaking in Greek, and fired up by the scenes he had just witnessed, then proceeded to make a most brilliant off-the-cuff speech, in which he promised to dedicate his life to righting the injustices done to the people of Sicily. At the end of it, the Syracusan senators voted almost unanimously to rescind their eulogy to Verres (which they swore they had only agreed to after being pressured into it by Metellus). Amid loud cheers, several younger members threw ropes around the neck of Verres's statue and pulled it down, while others – more importantly – fetched out of the senate's own secret archives a wealth of new evidence which they had been collecting about Verres's crimes. These outrages included the theft of twenty-seven priceless portraits from the Temple of Minerva – even the highly decorated doors of the sanctuary had been carried away! – as well as details of all the bribes Verres had demanded to bring in 'not guilty' verdicts when he was a judge.

News of this assembly and the toppling of the statue had by now reached the governor's palace, and when we tried to leave the senate house we found the building ringed with Roman soldiers. The meeting was dissolved on Metellus's orders, Heraclius arrested, and Cicero ordered to report to the governor at once. There could easily have been a bloody riot, but Cicero leapt up on to the back of a cart and told the Sicilians to calm themselves, that Metellus would not dare to harm a Roman senator acting on the authority of a praetor's court – although he did add, and only half in jest, that if he had not emerged by nightfall, they might perhaps make enquiries as to his whereabouts. He then clambered down and we allowed ourselves to be conducted over the bridge and on to the Island.

The Metellus family were at this time approaching the zenith of their power. In particular, the branch of the clan that had produced the three brothers, Quintus, Lucius and Marcus – all then in their forties – looked set to dominate Rome for years to come. It was, as Cicero said, a three-headed monster, and this middle head – the second brother, Lucius – was in many ways the most formidable of all. He received us in the royal chamber of the governor's palace with the full panoply of his *imperium* – an imposing, handsome figure, seated in his curule chair beneath the unyielding marble gaze of a dozen of his predecessors, flanked by his lictors, with his junior magistrate and his clerks behind him, and an armed sentry on the door.

'It is a treasonable offence,' he began, without rising and without preliminaries, 'to foment rebellion in a Roman province.'

'It is also a treasonable offence,' retorted Cicero, 'to insult the people and senate of Rome by impeding their appointed representative in his duties.'

'Really? And what kind of Roman representative addresses a Greek senate in its native tongue? Everywhere you have gone in this province, you have stirred up trouble. I shall not have it! We have too small a garrison to keep order among so many natives. You are making this place ungovernable, with your damned agitation.'

'I assure you, Governor, the resentment is against Verres, not against Rome.'

'Verres!' Metellus banged the arm of his chair. 'Since when did you care about Verres? I shall tell you when. Since you saw a chance to use him as a way of advancing yourself, you shitty little seditious lawyer!'

'Take this down, Tiro,' Cicero said, without removing his steady gaze from Metellus. 'I want a verbatim record. Such intimidation is entirely admissible in court.'

But I was too frightened even to move, for there was a lot of shouting now from the other men in the room, and Metellus had jumped to his feet. 'I order you,' he said, 'to return the documents you stole this morning!'

'And I remind the governor,' replied Cicero calmly, 'with the greatest respect, that he is not on the parade ground, that he is addressing a free Roman citizen, and I shall discharge the duty I have been assigned!'

Metellus had his hands on his hips and was leaning forward, his broad chin thrust out. 'You will undertake to return those documents now, in private – or you will be ordered to return them tomorrow in court, before the whole of Syracuse!'

'I choose to take my chance in court, as always,' said Cicero, with a tiny inflection of his head. 'Especially knowing what an impartial and honourable judge I shall have in you, Lucius Metellus – the worthy heir of Verres!'

I know I have this conversation exactly right, because the moment we were outside the chamber which was very soon after this last exchange Cicero and I reconstructed it while it was still fresh in our memories, in case he did indeed have occasion to use it in court. ('The fair copy remains to this day among his papers.)

'That went well,' he joked, but his hand and voice were trembling, for it was now plain that his whole mission, perhaps even his mortal safety, was in the gravest peril. 'But if you seek power,' he said, almost to himself, 'and if you are a new man, this is what you have to do. Nobody is ever going simply to hand it to you.'

We returned at once to the house of Flavius and worked all night, by the weak light of smoky Sicilian candles and stuttering oil lamps, to prepare for court the following morning. Frankly,

I did not see what Cicero could possibly hope to achieve, except humiliation. Metellus was never going to award judgement in his favour, and besides – as Cicero had privately conceded – the right of law lay with the tax company. But fortune, as the noble Terence has it, favours the brave, and she certainly favoured Cicero that night. It was young Frugi who made the breakthrough. I have not mentioned Frugi as often in this narrative as I should have done, chiefly because he had that kind of quiet decency which does not attract much comment, and which is only noticed when its possessor has gone. He had spent the day on the tax company records, and in the evening, despite having caught Cicero's cold, he refused to go to bed, and switched his attention instead to the evidence collected by the Syracusan senate. It must have been long after midnight when I suddenly heard him utter a cry, and then he beckoned us all over to the table. Laid out across it was a series of wax tablets, detailing the company's banking activities. Taken on their own, the lists of names, dates and sums loaned meant little. But once Frugi compared it with the list compiled by the Syracusans of those who had been forced to pay a bribe to Verres, we could see they tallied exactly: his victims had raised the funds they needed to buy him off by borrowing. Better still was the effect produced when he laid out a third set of accounts: the company's receipts. On the same dates exactly the same sums had been redeposited with the tax company by a character named 'Gaius Verrucius'. The depositor's identity was so crudely forged, we all burst out laughing, for obviously the name originally entered had been 'Verres', but in every case the last two letters had been scraped off and 'ucius' added as a replacement.

'So Verres demanded a bribe,' said Cicero, with growing

excitement, 'and insisted his victim borrow the necessary cash from Carpinatius – no doubt at an extortionate rate of interest. Then he reinvested the bribe with his friends in the tax company, so that he not only protected his capital but earned an extra share of the profits as well! Brilliant villain! Brilliant, greedy, stupid villain!' And after executing a brief dance of delight, he flung his arms around the embarrassed Frugi and kissed him warmly on both cheeks.

Of all Cicero's courtroom triumphs, I should say that the one he enjoyed the following day was among the sweetest – especially considering that technically it was not a victory at all but a defeat. He selected the evidence he needed to take back to Rome, and Lucius, Frugi, Sositheus, Laurea and I each carried a box of documents down to the Syracusan forum, where Metellus had set up his tribunal. An immense throng of local people had already gathered. Carpinatius was sitting waiting for us. He fancied himself as quite a lawyer, and presented his own case, quoting all the relevant statutes and precedents establishing that tax records could not be removed from a province, and generally giving the impression that he was merely the humble victim of an over-mighty senator. Cicero hung his head and put on such a mime of dejection I found it hard to keep a straight face. When at last he got to his feet he apologised for his actions, conceded he was wrong in law, begged forgiveness from the governor, promised gladly to return the documents to Carpinatius, but – he paused – *but* there was one small point he did not understand, which he would be very grateful to have cleared up first. He picked up one of the wax tablets and studied it in bafflement. 'Who exactly is Gaius Verrucius?'

Carpinatius, who had been smiling happily, looked like a man struck in the chest by an arrow fired from very short range, while

Cicero, in a puzzled manner, as if it were all a mystery far beyond his comprehension, pointed out the coincidence of names, dates and sums in the tax company's records and the claims of bribery compiled by the Syracusan senate.

'And there is another thing,' said Cicero pleasantly. 'This gentleman, who did so much business with you, does not appear in your accounts before his near-namesake, Gaius Verres, came to Sicily, and he has not done any business with you since Gaius Verres left. But in those three years when Verres was here, he was your biggest client.' He showed the accounts to the crowd. 'And it is unfortunate – do you see? – that whenever the slave who wrote up your records came to put down his name, he always made the same slip of his stylus. But there we are. I am sure there is nothing suspicious about it. So perhaps you could simply tell the court who this Verrucius is, and where he can be found.'

Carpinatius looked helplessly towards Metellus, as someone in the crowd shouted, 'He does not exist!' 'There never was anyone in Sicily called Verrucius!' yelled another. 'It is Verres!' And the crowd started chanting: 'It is Verres! It is Verres!'

Cicero held up his hand for silence. 'Carpinatius insists I cannot remove these records from the province, and I concede in law he is correct. But nowhere in law does it say I cannot make a copy, as long as it is fair, and properly witnessed. All I need is help. Who here will help me copy these records, so that I can take them back to Rome and bring this swine Verres to justice for his crimes against the people of Sicily?'

A plantation of hands sprang up. Metellus tried to call for silence, but his words were lost in the din of people shouting their support. Cicero, with Flavius to help him, picked out all the most eminent men in the city – Sicilian and Roman alike –

and invited them to come forward and take a share of the evidence, whereupon I handed each volunteer a tablet and stylus. I could see Carpinatius out of the corner of my eye frantically trying to struggle across to Metellus, and I could see Metellus with his arms folded scowling furiously down from his raised bench at the chaos of his court. Eventually, he simply turned on his heel and strode angrily up the steps and into the temple behind him.

Thus ended Cicero's visit to Sicily. Metellus, I am sure, would dearly have liked to have arrested him, or at least prevented him from removing evidence. But Cicero had won over too many adherents in both the Roman and the Sicilian communities. To have seized him would have caused an insurrection, and as Metellus had conceded, he did not have the troops to control the entire population. By the end of that afternoon, the copies of the tax company's records had been witnessed, sealed and transferred to our guarded ship in the harbour, where they joined the other trunks of evidence. Cicero himself remained only one more night on the island, drawing up the list of witnesses he wished to bring to Rome. Lucius and Frugi agreed to remain behind in Syracuse to arrange their transportation.

The following morning they came down to the dock to see Cicero off. The harbour was packed with well-wishers, and he made a gracious speech of thanks. 'I know that I carry in this fragile vessel the hopes of this entire province. In so far as it lies within my power, I shall not let you down.' Then I helped him on to the deck, where he stood with fresh tears shining on his cheeks. Consummate actor that he was, I knew that he could summon any emotion at will, but I am sure that on that day his feelings were unfeigned. I wonder, indeed, looking back on it, if he somehow knew that he would never return to the island again. The oars dipped and stroked us out into the channel. The faces on the quayside blurred, the figures dwindled and disappeared, and slowly we headed out through the mouth of the harbour and into open water.

VIII

The journey back from Regium to Rome was easier than our progress south had been, for by now it was early spring, and the mainland was soft and welcoming. Not that we had much opportunity to admire the birds and flowers. Cicero worked every mile of the way, propped up, swaying and pitching in the back of his covered wagon, assembling the outline of his case against Verres. I would fetch documents from the baggage cart as he needed them, and trot along at the rear of his carriage taking down his dictation, which was no easy feat. His plan, as I understood it, was to separate the mass of evidence into four sets of charges – corruption as a judge, extortion in collecting taxes and official revenues, the plundering of private and municipal property, and, finally, illegal and tyrannical punishments. Witness statements and records were grouped accordingly, and even as he bounced along, he began drafting whole passages of his opening speech. (Just as he had trained his body to carry the weight of his ambition, so he had, by effort of will, cured himself of travel sickness, and over the years he was to do a vast amount of work while journeying up and down Italy.) In this manner, almost without his noticing where he was, we completed the trip in less than a fortnight and came at last to Rome on the Ides of March, exactly two months after we had left the city.

Hortensius, meanwhile, had not been idle, and an elaborate decoy prosecution was now underway. Of course, as Cicero had suspected, it had been designed partly as a trap to lure him into leaving Sicily early. Dasianus had not bothered to travel to Greece to collect any evidence. He had never even left Rome. But that had not stopped him from bringing charges against the former governor of Achaia in the extortion court, and the praetor, Glabrio, with nothing to do until Cicero returned, had found himself with little option but to let him proceed. And so there he was, day after day, this long-forgotten nonentity, droning away before a bored-looking jury of senators, with Hortensius at his side. And when Dasianus's loquacity flagged, the Dancing Master would rise in his graceful way, and pirouette about the court, making his own elaborate points.

Quintus, ever the well-trained staff officer, had prepared a daily campaign schedule while we had been away, and had set it up in Cicero's study. Cicero went to inspect it the moment he entered the house, and one glance revealed the shape of Hortensius's plan. Blobs of red dye marked the festivals when the court would not be sitting. Once those were removed, there were only twenty full working days until the senate went into recess. The recess itself lasted a further twenty days, and was followed immediately by the five-day Festival of Flora. Then there was the Day of Apollo, the Tarentine Games, the Festival of Mars, and so on. Roughly one day in four was a holiday. 'To put it simply,' said Quintus, 'judging by the way it is going, I think Hortensius will have no trouble occupying the court until almost the consular elections at the end of July. Then you yourself have to face the elections for aedile at the beginning of August. The earliest we are likely to be able to get into court, therefore, is the fifth. But then in the middle of August, Pompey's games begin – and they are scheduled to last for a full fifteen days. And then of course there are the Roman Games, and the Plebeian Games—'

'For pity's sake,' exclaimed Cicero, peering at the chart, 'does nobody in this wretched town do anything except watch men and animals kill one other?' His high spirits, which had sustained him all the way from Syracuse, seemed visibly to leak from him at that moment, like air from a bladder. He had come home ready for a fight, but Hortensius was far too shrewd to meet him head-on in open court. Blocking and attrition: these were to be his tactics, and they were nicely judged. Everyone knew that Cicero's resources were modest. The longer it took him to get his case to court, the more money it would cost him. Within a day or two, our first few witnesses would start arriving in Rome from Sicily. They would expect to have their travel and accommodation costs defrayed, and to be compensated for their loss of earnings. On top of this, Cicero was having to fund his election campaign for aedile. And assuming he won, he would then have to find the money to maintain himself in the office for a year, repairing public buildings and staging two more sets of official games. He could not afford to skimp these duties: the voters never forgave a cheapskate.

So there was nothing for it but to endure another painful session with Terentia. They dined alone together on the night of his return from Syracuse, and later I was summoned by Cicero and told to bring him the draft passages of his opening speech. Terentia was lying stiffly on her couch when I went in, stabbing irritably at her food; Cicero's plate, I noticed, was untouched. I was glad to hand him the document case and escape immediately. Already the speech was vast and would have taken at least two days to deliver. Later, I heard him pacing up and down, declaiming parts of it, and I realised she was making him rehearse his case, before deciding whether to advance him any more money. She must have liked what she heard, for the following morning Philotimus arranged for us to draw a line of credit for another fifty thousand. But it was humiliating for Cicero, and it is from around this time that I date his increasing preoccupation with money, a subject which had never previously interested him in the least.

I sense that I am dawdling in this narrative, having already reached my eighth roll of Hieratica, and need to speed it up a little, else either I shall die on the job, or you will be worn out reading. So let me dispense with the next four months very quickly. Cicero was obliged to work even harder than before. First of all in the mornings he had to deal with his clients (and of course there was a great backlog of casework to get through, which had built up while we were in Sicily). Then he had to appear in court or the senate, whichever was in session. He kept his head down in the latter, anxious in particular to avoid falling into conversation with Pompey the Great, fearful either that Pompey might ask him to drop his prosecution of Verres and give up his candidacy for aedile, or – worse – offer to help, which would leave him beholden to the mightiest man in Rome, an obligation he was determined to avoid. Only when the courts and senate adjourned for public holidays and recesses was he was able to transfer all his energies to the Verres prosecution, sorting out and mastering the evidence, and coaching the witnesses. We were bringing around one hundred Sicilians to Rome, and as for virtually all of them it was their first visit, they needed to have their hands held, and this task fell to me. I became a kind of one-man tour agent, running around the city, trying to stop them falling prey to Verres's spies, or turning into drunks, or getting into fights – and a homesick Sicilian, let me tell you, is no easy charge. It was a relief when young Frugi returned from Syracuse to lend me a hand (cousin Lucius having remained in Sicily to keep the supply of witnesses and evidence flowing). Finally, in the early evenings, accompanied by Quintus, Cicero resumed his visits to the tribal headquarters to canvass for the aedileship.

Hortensius was also active. He kept the extortion court tied up with his tedious prosecution, using his mouthpiece Dasianus. Really, there was no end to his tricks. For example, he went out of his way to be friendly to Cicero, greeting him whenever they were standing around in the senaculum, waiting for a senate quorum, and ostentatiously steering him away for a private word about the general political situation. At first, Cicero was flattered, but then he discovered that Hortensius and his supporters were putting it about that he had agreed to take an enormous bribe deliberately to bungle the prosecution, hence the public embraces. Our witnesses, cooped up in their apartment blocks around the city, heard the rumours and started fluttering in panic, like chickens in a henhouse when a fox is about, and Cicero had to visit each in turn and reassure him. The next time Hortensius approached him with his hand outstretched, he showed him his back. Hortensius smiled, shrugged and turned away – what did he care? Everything was going his way.

I should perhaps say a little more about this remarkable man – 'the King of the Law Courts', as his claque of supporters called him – whose rivalry with Cicero lit up the Roman bar for a generation. The foundation of his success was his memory. In more than twenty years of advocacy, Hortensius had never been known to use a note. It was no trouble to him to memorise a four-hour speech, and deliver it perfectly, either in the senate or in the forum. And this phenomenal memory was not a dull thing, born of night-time study; it shone quick in the daylight. He had an alarming capacity to remember everything his opponents had said, whether in statement or cross-examination, and could hurl it back in their faces whenever he chose. He was like some doubly armoured gladiator in the arena of the law, lunging with sword and trident, protected by net and shield. He was forty-four years old that summer, and lived with his wife and teenaged son and daughter in an exquisitely decorated house on the Palatine Hill, next door to his brother-in-law, Catulus. *Exquisite* – that is the *mot juste* for Hortensius: exquisite in manners, exquisite in dress, in hairstyle, in scent, exquisite in his taste for all fine things. He never said a rude word to anyone. But his besetting sin was greed, which was already swelling to outrageous proportions – a palace on the Bay of Naples, a private zoo, a cellar containing ten thousand casks of the finest Chianti, a picture by Cydias bought for one hundred and fifty thousand, eels dressed in jewellery, trees watered with wine, the first man to serve peacock at dinner: the whole world knows the stories. It was this extravagance which had led him to form his alliance with Verres, who showered him with stolen gifts – the most notorious of which was a priceless sphinx, carved out of a single piece of ivory – and who paid for his campaign for the consulship.

Those consular elections were fixed to be held on the twenty-seventh day of July. On the twenty-third, the jury in the extortion court voted to acquit the former governor of Achaia of all the charges against him. Cicero, who had hurried down from working on his opening speech at home to await the result, listened impassively as Glabrio announced that he would begin hearing the case against Verres on the fifth day of August – 'when I trust your addresses to the court will be slightly shorter,' he said to Hortensius, who replied with a smirk. All that remained was to select a jury. This was accomplished the following day.

Thirty-two senators, drawn by lot, was the number laid down by the law. Each side was entitled to make six objections, but despite using up all his challenges, Cicero still faced a dauntingly hostile jury, including – yet again – Catulus and his protégé Catilina, as well as that other grand old man of the senate, Servilius Vatia Isauricus; even Marcus Metellus slipped on to the panel. Apart from these aristocratic hard-liners, we had also to write off cynics such as Aemilius Alba, Marcus Lucretius and Antonius Hybrida, for they would invariably sell themselves to the highest bidder, and Verres was lavish with his funds. I do not think I ever knew the true meaning of that old expression about someone looking like the cat that got the cream until I saw Hortensius's face on the day that jury was sworn in. He had it all. The consulship was in the bag, and with it, he was now confident, the acquittal of Verres.

The days which followed were the most nerve-racking Cicero had endured in public life. On the morning of the consular election he was so dispirited he could hardly bring himself to go out to the Field of Mars to vote, but of course he had to be seen to be an active citizen. The result was never in doubt, from the moment the trumpets sounded and the red flag was hoisted over the Janiculum Hill. Hortensius and Quintus Metellus were backed by Verres and his gold, by the aristocrats, and by the supporters of Pompey and Crassus. Nevertheless, there was always a race-day atmosphere on these occasions, with the candidates and their supporters streaming out of the city in the early-morning sunshine towards the voting pens, and the enterprising shop-keepers piling their stalls with wine and sausages, dice and para-sols, and all else necessary to enjoy a good election. Pompey, as senior consul, in accordance with the ancient custom, was already standing at the entrance to the returning officer's tent, with an augur beside him. The moment all the candidates for consul and praetor, perhaps twenty senators, had lined up in their whitened togas, he mounted the platform and read out the traditional prayer. Soon afterwards the voting started and there was nothing for the thousands of electors to do except mill around and gossip until it was their turn to enter the enclosures.

This was the old republic in action, the men all voting in their allotted centuries, just as they had in ancient times, when as soldiers they elected their commander. Now that the ritual has become meaningless, it is hard to convey how moving a spectacle it was, even for a slave such as I, who did not have the franchise. It embodied something marvellous – some impulse of the human spirit that had sparked into life half a millennium before among that indomitable race who dwelled amid the hard rocks and soft marshland of the Seven Hills: some impulse towards the light of dignity and freedom, and away from the darkness of brute subservience. This is what we have lost. Not that it was a pure, Aristotelian democracy, by any means. Precedence among the centuries – of which there were one hundred and ninety-three – was determined by wealth, and the richest classes always voted earliest and declared first: a significant advantage. These centuries also benefited by having fewer members, whereas the centuries of the poor, like the slums of Subura, were vast and teeming; as a consequence, a rich man's vote counted for more. Still, it was freedom, as it had been practised for hundreds of years, and no man on the Field of Mars that day would have dreamed that he might live to see it taken away.

Cicero's century, one of the twelve consisting entirely of members of the equestrian order, was called around mid-morning, just as it was starting to get hot. He strolled with his fellows into the roped-off enclosure and proceeded to work the throng in his usual way – a word here, a touch of the elbow there. Then they formed themselves into a line and filed by the table at which sat the clerks, who checked their names and handed them their voting counters. If there was to be any intimidation, this was generally the place where it occurred, for the partisans of each candidate could get up close to the voters and whisper their threats or promises. But on this day all was quiet, and I watched Cicero step across the narrow wooden bridge and disappear behind the boards to cast his ballot. Emerging on the other side, he passed along the line of candidates and their friends, who were standing beneath an awning, paused briefly to talk to Palicanus – the roughly spoken former tribune was standing for a praetorship – and then exited without giving Hortensius or Metellus a second glance.

Like all those before it, Cicero's century backed the official slate – Hortensius and Quintus Metellus for consul; Marcus Metellus and Palicanus for praetor – and now it was merely a question of going on until an absolute majority was reached. The poorer men must have known they could not affect the outcome, but such was the dignity conveyed by the franchise, they stood all afternoon in the heat, awaiting their turn to collect their ballots and shuffle over the bridge. Cicero and I went up and down the lines as he canvassed support for the aedileship, and it was marvellous how many he knew personally – not just the voters' names, but their wives' names and the number of their children, and the nature of their employment: all done without any prompting from me. At the eleventh hour, when the sun was just starting to dip towards the Janiculum, a halt was called at last and Pompey proclaimed the winners. Hortensius had topped the poll for consul, with Quintus Metellus second; Marcus Metellus had won most votes for praetor. Their jubilant supporters crowded round them, and now for the first time we saw the red-headed figure of Gaius Verres slip into the front rank – 'The puppet-master comes to take his bow,' observed Cicero – and one would have thought that *he* had won the consulship by the way the aristocrats shook his hand and pounded him on the back. One of them, a former consul, Scribonius Curio, embraced Verres and said, loudly enough for all to hear, 'I hereby inform you that today's election means your acquittal!'

There are few forces in politics harder to resist than a feeling that something is inevitable, for humans move as a flock, and will always rush like sheep towards the safety of a winner. On every side now, one heard the same opinion: Cicero was done for, Cicero was finished, the aristocrats were back in charge, no jury would ever convict Gaius Verres. Aemilius Alba, who fancied himself a wit, told everyone he met that he was in despair: the bottom had dropped out of the market for Verres's jurors, and he could not sell himself for more than three thousand. Attention now switched to the forthcoming elections for aedile, and it was not long before Cicero detected Verres's hand at work behind the scenes here, as well. A professional election agent, Ranunculus, who was well disposed towards Cicero and was afterwards employed by him, came to warn the senator that Verres had called a night-time meeting at his own house of all the leading bribery merchants, and had offered five thousand to every man who could persuade his tribe not to vote for Cicero. I could see that both Cicero and his brother were worried. Worse was to follow. A few days later, on the eve of the actual election, the senate met with Crassus in the chair, to witness the praetors-elect draw lots to determine which courts they would preside over when they took office in January. I was not present, but

Cicero was in the chamber, and he returned home afterwards looking white and limp. The unbelievable had happened: Marcus Metellus, already a juror in the Verres case, had drawn the extortion court!

Even in his darkest imaginings, Cicero had never contemplated such an outcome. He was so shocked he had almost lost his voice. 'You should have heard the uproar in the house,' he whispered to Quintus. 'Crassus must have rigged the draw. Everyone believes he did it, but nobody knows *how* he did it. That man will not rest until I am broken, bankrupt and in exile.' He shuffled into his study and collapsed into his chair. It was a stiflingly hot day, the third of August, and there was hardly room to move among all the accumulated material from the Verres case: the piles of tax records and affidavits and witness statements, roasting and dusty in the heat. (And these were only a fraction of the total: most were locked in boxes in the cellar.) His draft speech – his immense opening speech, which kept on growing and growing, like some proliferating madness – was stacked in tottering piles across his desk. I had long since given up trying to keep track of it. Only he knew how it might come together. It was all in his head, the sides of which he now began massaging with the tips of his fingers. He asked in a croaking voice for a cup of water. I turned away to fetch it, heard a sigh and then a thump, and when I looked round he had slumped forwards, knocking his skull against the edge of his desk. Quintus and I rushed to either side of him and pulled him up. His cheeks were dead grey, with a livid streak of bright red blood trickling from his nose; his mouth hung slackly open.

Quintus was in a panic. 'Fetch Terentia!' he shouted at me. 'Quickly!'

I ran upstairs to her room and told her the master was ill. She came down at once and was magnificent in the way she took command. Cicero by now was feebly conscious, his head between his knees. She knelt beside him, called for water, pulled a fan from her sleeve, and starting waving it vigorously to cool his cheeks. Quintus in the meantime, still wringing his hands, had dispatched the two junior secretaries to fetch whatever doctors were in the neighbourhood, and each soon returned with a Greek medic in tow. The wretched quacks immediately began arguing between themselves about whether it was best to purge or bleed. Terentia sent both packing. She also refused to allow Cicero to be carried up to bed, warning Quintus that word of this would quickly get around, and the widespread belief that her husband was finished would then become an accomplished fact. She made him rise unsteadily to his feet and, holding his arm, took him out into the atrium, where the air was fresher. Quintus and I followed. 'You are not finished!' I could hear her saying sternly to him. 'You have your case – now make it!' Cicero mumbled something in reply.

Quintus burst out: 'That is all very well, Terentia, but you do not understand what has just happened.' And he told her about Metellus's appointment as the new president of the extortion court, and its implications. There was no chance of a guilty verdict being returned once *he* was in the judge's chair, which meant their only hope was to have the hearing concluded by December. But that was impossible, given Hortensius's ability to spin it out. There was simply too much evidence for the time available: only ten days in court before Pompey's games, and Cicero's opening statement alone would take up most of it. No sooner would he have finished outlining his case than the court would be in recess for the best part of a month, and by the time they came back the jury would have forgotten his brilliant points. 'Not that it matters,' Quintus concluded gloomily, 'as most of them are in the pay of Verres already.'

'It's true, Terentia,' said Cicero. He looked around him distractedly, as if he had only just woken up and realised where he was. 'I must pull out of the election for aedile,' he muttered. 'It would be humiliating enough to lose, but even more humiliating to win and not be able to discharge the duties of the office.'

'Pathetic,' replied Terentia, and she angrily pulled her arm free of his. 'You don't deserve to be elected, if this is how you surrender at the first setback, without putting up a fight!'

'My dear,' said Cicero beseechingly, pressing his hand to his forehead, 'if you will tell me how I am supposed to defeat time itself, then I will fight it bravely. But what am I to do if I only have ten days to set out my prosecution before the court goes into recess for weeks on end?'

Terentia leaned in close to him, so that her face was only inches from his. 'Make your speech shorter!' she hissed.

After his wife had retired to her corner of the house, Cicero, still not fully recovered from his fit of nerves, retreated to his study and sat there for a long time, staring at the wall. We left him alone. Sthenius came by just before sunset to report that Quintus Metellus had summoned all the Sicilian witnesses to his house, and that a few of the more timid souls had foolishly obeyed. From one of these, Sthenius had obtained a full report of how Metellus had tried to intimidate them into retracting their evidence. 'I am consul-elect,' he had thundered at them. 'One of my brothers is governing Sicily, the other is going to preside over the extortion court. Many steps have been taken to ensure that no harm can befall Verres. We shall not forget those who go

against us.' I took down the exact quotation and tentatively went
in to see Cicero. He had not moved in several hours. I read out
Metellus's words, but he gave no sign of having heard.

By this stage I was becoming seriously concerned, and would
have fetched his brother or wife again, if his mind had not
suddenly re-emerged from wherever it had been wandering.
Staring straight ahead, he said in a grim tone: 'Go and make an
appointment for me to see Pompey this evening.' When I hesitated, wondering if this was another symptom of his malady, he
glared at me. 'Go!'

It was only a short distance to Pompey's house, which was in
the same district of the Esquiline Hill as Cicero's. The sun had
just gone down but it was still light, and swelteringly hot, with
a torpid breeze wafting gently from the east – the worst possible
combination at the height of summer, because it carried into the
neighbourhood the stench of the putrefying corpses in the great
common graves beyond the city wall. I believe the problem is
not so acute these days, but sixty years ago the Esquiline Gate
was the place where everything dead and not worth a proper
funeral was taken to be dumped – the bodies of dogs and cats,
horses, donkeys, slaves, paupers and still-born babies, all mixed
up and rotting together, along with the household refuse. The
stink always drew great flocks of crying gulls, and I remember
that on this particular evening it was especially acute: a rancid
and pervasive smell, which one tasted on the tongue as much as
one absorbed it through the nostrils.

Pompey's house was much grander than Cicero's, with a couple
of lictors posted outside and a crowd of sightseers gathered opposite. There were also half a dozen canopied litters set down in
the lee of the wall, their bearers squatting nearby playing bones
– evidence that a big dinner party was in progress. I gave my

message to the gatekeeper, who vanished inside, and returned a little later with the praetor-elect, Palicanus, who was dabbing at his greasy chin with a napkin. He recognised me, asked what it was all about, and I repeated my message. 'Right you are,' said Palicanus, in his blunt way. 'You can tell him from me that the consul will see him immediately.'

Cicero must have known Pompey would agree to meet, for when I returned he had already changed into a fresh set of clothes and was ready to go out. He was still very pale. He exchanged a last look with Quintus, and then we set off. There was no conversation between us as we walked, because Cicero, who hated any reminder of death, kept his sleeve pressed to his mouth and nose to ward off the smell from the Esquiline Field. 'Wait here,' he said, when we reached Pompey's house, and that was the last I saw of him for several hours. The daylight faded, the massy purple twilight ripened into darkness and the stars began to appear in clusters above the city. Occasionally, when the door was opened, the muffled sounds of voices and laughter reached the street, and I could smell meat and fish cooking, although on that foul night they all reeked of death to me, and I wondered how Cicero could possibly find the stomach for it, for by now it was clear that Pompey had asked him to join his dinner party.

I paced up and down, leaned against the wall, attempted to think up some new symbols for my great shorthand system, and generally tried to occupy myself as the night went on. Eventually, Pompey's guests started reeling out, half of them too drunk to stand properly, and it was the usual crew of Piceneans – Afranius, the former praetor and lover of the dance; Palicanus, of course; and Gabinius, Palicanus's son-in-law, who also had a reputation for loving women and song – a real old soldiers' reunion, it must have been, and I found it hard to imagine that Cicero could have enjoyed himself much. Only the austere and scholarly Varro – 'the man who showed Pompey where the senate house was', in Cicero's cutting phrase – would have been remotely congenial company, especially as he at least emerged sober. Cicero was the last to leave. He set off up the street and I hurried after him. There was a good yellow moon and I had no difficulty in making out his figure. He still kept his hand up to his nose, for neither the heat nor the smell had much diminished, and when he was a decent distance from Pompey's house, he leaned against the corner of an alley and was violently sick.

I came up behind him and asked him if he needed assistance, at which he shook his head and responded, 'It is done.' That was all he said to me, and all he said to Quintus, too, who was waiting up anxiously for him at the house when he got in: 'It is done.'

At dawn the following day we made the two-mile walk back to the Field of Mars for the second round of elections. Although these did not carry the same prestige as those for the consulship and the praetorship, they nevertheless had the advantage of always being much more exciting. Thirty-four men had to be elected (twenty senators, ten tribunes and four aediles), which meant there were simply too many candidates for the poll to be easily controlled: when an aristocrat's vote carried no more weight than a pauper's, anything could happen. Crassus, as junior consul, was the presiding officer at this supplementary election – 'But presumably even he,' said Cicero darkly, as he pulled on his red leather shoes, 'cannot rig this ballot.'

He had woken in an edgy, preoccupied mood. Whatever had been agreed with Pompey the previous night had obviously disturbed his rest, and he snapped irritably at his valet that his shoes were not as clean as they ought to be. He donned the same brilliant white toga he had worn on this day six years earlier, when he had first been elected to the senate, and braced himself before the front door was opened, as if he were about to shoulder a great weight. Once again, Quintus had done a fine job, and a marvellous crowd was waiting to escort him out to the voting pens. When we reached the Field of Mars, we found it was packed right down to the river's edge, for there was a census in progress, and tens of thousands had come to the city to register. You can imagine the noisy roar of it. There must have been a hundred candidates for those thirty-four offices, and all across the vast open field one could see these gleaming figures passing to and fro, accompanied by their friends and supporters, trying to gather every last vote before polling opened. Verres's red head was also conspicuous, darting all over the place, with his father beside him, and his son, and his freedman, Timarchides – the creature who had invaded our house – making extravagant promises to any who would vote against Cicero. The sight seemed to banish Cicero's ill humour instantly, and he plunged in to canvass. I thought on several occasions that our groups might collide, but the crowd was so huge it never happened.

When the augur pronounced himself satisfied, Crassus came out of the sacred tent and the candidates gathered at the base of his tribunal. Among them, I should record, making his first attempt to enter the senate, was Julius Caesar, who stood beside Cicero and engaged him in friendly conversation. They had known one another a long time, and indeed it was on Cicero's recommendation that the younger man had gone to Rhodes to study rhetoric under Apollonius Molon. Much hagiography now clusters around Caesar's early years, to the extent that you would think he had been marked out by his contemporaries as a genius ever since the cradle. Not so, and anyone who saw him in his whitened toga that morning, nervously fiddling with his thinning hair, would have been hard put to distinguish him from any of the other well-bred young candidates. There was one great difference, though: few can have been as poor. To stand for election, he must have borrowed heavily, for he lived in very modest accommodation in the Subura, in a house full of women – his mother, his wife, and his little daughter – and I picture him at this stage not as the gleaming hero waiting to conquer Rome, but as a thirty-year-old man lying sleepless at night, kept awake by the racket of his impoverished neighbourhood, brooding bitterly on the fact that he, a scion of the oldest family in Rome, had been reduced to such circumstances. His antipathy towards the aristocrats was consequently far more dangerous to them than Cicero's ever was. As a self-made man, Cicero merely resented and envied them. But Caesar, who believed he was a direct descendant of Venus, viewed them with contempt, as interlopers.

But now I am running ahead of myself, and committing the same sin as the hagiographers, by shining the distorting light of the future on to the shadows of the past. Let me simply record that these two outstanding men, with six years' difference in their ages but much in common in terms of brains and outlook, stood chatting amiably in the sun, as Crassus mounted the platform and read out the familiar prayer: 'May this matter end well and happily for me, for my best endeavours, for my office, and for the People of Rome!' And with that the voting started.

The first tribe into the pens, in accordance with tradition, were the Suburana. But despite all Cicero's efforts over the years, they did not vote for him. This must have been a blow, and certainly suggested Verres's bribery agents had earned their cash. Cicero, however, merely shrugged: he knew that many influential men who had yet to vote would be watching for his reaction, and it was important to wear a mask of confidence. Then, one after another, came the three other tribes of the city: the Esquilina, the Collina and the Palatina. Cicero won the support of the first two, but not the third, which was scarcely surprising, as it was easily the most aristocratically inclined of Rome's neighbourhoods. So the score was two–two: a tenser start than he would have liked. And now the thirty-one rustic tribes started lining up: the Aemilia, Camilia, Fabia, Galeria . . . I knew all their names from our office files, could tell you who were the key men in each, who needed a favour and who owed one. Three of these four went for Cicero. Quintus came up and whispered in his ear, and for the first time he could perhaps afford to relax, as Verres's money had obviously proved most tempting to those tribes composed of a majority of city-dwellers. The Horatia, Lemonia, Papiria, Menenia . . . On and on, through the heat and the dust, Cicero sitting on a stool between counts but always rising whenever the voters passed in front of him after casting their ballots, his memory working to retrieve their names, thanking them, and passing on his respects to their families. The Sergia, Voltina, Pupina, Romilia . . . Cicero failed in the last tribe, not surprisingly, as it was Verres's own, but by the middle of the afternoon he had won the support of sixteen tribes and needed only two more for victory. Yet still Verres had not given up, and could be seen in huddled groups with his son and Timarchides. For a terrible hour, the balance seemed to tilt his way. The Sabatini did not go for Cicero, and nor did the Publilia. But then he just scraped in with the Scaptia, and finally it was the Falerna from northern Campania who put him over the top: eighteen tribes out of the thirty which had so far voted, with five left to come

– but what did they matter? He was safely home, and at some
point when I was not looking Verres quietly removed himself
from the election field to calculate his losses. Caesar, whose own
elevation to the senate had just been confirmed, was the first to
turn and shake Cicero's hand. I could see Quintus triumphantly
brandishing his fists in the air, Crassus staring angrily into the
distance. There were cheers from the spectators who had been
keeping their own tallies – those curious zealots who follow elections as fervently as other men do chariot racing – and who
appreciated what had just happened. The victor himself looked
stunned by his achievement, but no one could deny it, not even
Crassus, who would shortly have to read it out, even though the
words must have choked him. Against all odds, Marcus Cicero
was an aedile of Rome.

A big crowd – they are always bigger after a victory – escorted
Cicero from the Field of Mars all the way back to his house,
where the domestic slaves were assembled to applaud him over
the threshold. Even Diodotus the blind Stoic put in a rare appearance. All of us were proud to belong to such an eminent figure;
his glory reflected on every member of his household; our worth
and self-esteem increased with his. From the atrium, Tullia
darted forward with a cry of 'Papa!' and wrapped her arms
around his legs, and even Terentia stepped up and embraced
him, smiling. I still hold that image of the three of them frozen
in my mind – the triumphant young orator with his left hand
on the head of his daughter and his right clasped about the
shoulders of his happy wife. Nature bestows this gift, at least,
on those who rarely smile: when they do, their faces are transformed, and I saw at that moment how Terentia, for all her

complaints about her husband, nonetheless relished his brilliance and success.

It was Cicero who reluctantly broke the embrace. 'I thank you all,' he declared, looking around at his admiring audience. 'But this is not the time for celebrations. That will only come when Verres is defeated. Tomorrow, at long last, I shall open the prosecution in the forum, and let us pray to the gods that before too many days have passed, fresh and far greater honour will descend upon this household. So what are you waiting for?' He smiled and clapped his hands. 'Back to work!'

Cicero retired with Quintus to his study, and beckoned to me to follow. He threw himself into his chair with a gasp of relief and kicked off his shoes. For the first time in more than a week the tension in his face seemed to have eased. I assumed he would now want to begin on the urgent task of pulling together his speech, but apparently he had other plans for me. I was to go back out into the city with Sositheus and Laurea, and between us we were to visit all the Sicilian witnesses, give them the news of his election, check that they were holding firm, and instruct them all to present themselves in court the following morning.

'All?' I repeated in astonishment. 'All one hundred?'

'That is right,' he replied. The old decisiveness was back in his voice. 'And tell Eros to hire a dozen porters – reliable men – to carry every box of evidence down to court at the same time as I go down tomorrow.'

'All the witnesses . . . A dozen porters . . . Every box of evidence . . .' I was making a list of his orders. 'But this is going to take me until midnight,' I said, unable to conceal my bewilderment.

'Poor Tiro. But do not worry – there will be time enough to sleep when we are dead.'

'I am not worried about my sleep, Senator,' I said stiffly. 'I was wondering when I was going to have time to help you with your speech.'

'I shall not require your help,' he said with a slight smile, and raised a finger to his lips, to warn me that I must say nothing. But as I had no idea of the significance of his remark, there was hardly any danger of my revealing his plans, and not for the first time I left his presence in a state of some confusion.

IX

And so it came about that on the fifth day of August, in the consulship of Gnaeus Pompey Magnus and Marcus Licinius Crassus, one year and nine months after Sthenius had first come to see Cicero, the trial of Gaius Verres began.

Bear in mind the summer heat. Calculate the number of victims with an interest in seeing Verres brought to justice. Remember that Rome was, in any case, swarming with citizens in town for the census, the elections and the impending games of Pompey. Consider that the hearing pitched the two greatest orators of the day in head-to-head combat ('a duel of real magnitude', as Cicero later called it). Put all this together, and you may begin to guess something of the atmosphere in the extortion court that morning. Hundreds of spectators, determined to have a decent vantage point, had slept out in the forum overnight. By dawn, there was nowhere left to stand that offered any shade. By the second hour, there was nowhere left at all. In the porticoes and on the steps of the Temple of Castor, in the forum itself and in the colonnades surrounding it, on the rooftops and balconies of the houses, on the sides of the hills – anywhere that human beings could squeeze themselves into, or hang off, or perch on – there you would find the people of Rome.

Frugi and I scurried around like a pair of sheepdogs, herding our witnesses into court, and what an exotic and colourful assembly they made, in their sacred robes and native dress, victims from every stage of Verres's career, drawn by the promise of vengeance – priests of Juno and Ceres, the mystagogues of the Syracusan Minerva and the sacred virgins of Diana; Greek nobles whose descent was traced to Cecrops or Eurysthenes or to the great Ionian and Minyan houses, and Phoenicians whose ancestors had been priests of Tyrian Melcarth, or claimed kindred with the Zidonian Iah; eager crowds of impoverished heirs and their guardians, bankrupt farmers and grain merchants and ship owners, fathers bewailing their children carried off to slavery, children mourning for their parents dead in the governor's dungeons; deputations from the foot of Mount Taurus, from the shores of the Black Sea, from many cities of the Grecian mainland, from the islands of the Aegean and of course from every city and market town of Sicily.

I was so busy helping to ensure that all the witnesses were admitted, and that every box of evidence was in its place and securely guarded, that only gradually did I come to realise what a spectacle Cicero had stage-managed. Those evidence boxes, for example, now included public testimony collected by the elders of virtually every town in Sicily. It was only when the jurors started shouldering their way through the masses and taking their places on the benches that I realised – showman that he was – why Cicero had been so insistent on having *everything* in place at once. The impression on the court was overwhelming. Even the hard-faces, like old Catulus and Isauricus, registered astonishment. As for Glabrio, when he came out of the temple preceded by his lictors, he paused for a moment on the top step, and swayed half a pace backwards when confronted by that wall of faces.

Cicero, who had been standing apart until the last possible moment, squeezed through the crowd and climbed the steps to his place on the prosecutor's bench. There was a sudden quietness; a silent quiver of anticipation in the still air. Ignoring the shouts of encouragement from his supporters, he turned and shielded his eyes against the sun and scanned the vast audience, squinting to right and left, as I imagine a general might check the lie of the land and position of the clouds before a battle. Then he sat down, while I stationed myself at his back so that I could pass him any document he needed. The clerks of the court set up Glabrio's curule chair – the signal that the tribunal was in session – and everything was ready, save for the presence of Verres and Hortensius. Cicero, who was as cool as I had ever seen him, leaned back and whispered to me, 'After all that, perhaps he is not coming.' Needless to say, he *was* coming – Glabrio sent one of his lictors to fetch him – but Hortensius was giving us a foretaste of his tactics, which would be to waste as much time as possible. Eventually, perhaps an hour late, to ironic applause, the immaculate figure of the consul-elect eased through the press of spectators, followed by his junior counsel – none other than young Scipio Nasica, the love rival of Cato – then Quintus Metellus, and finally came Verres himself, looking redder than usual in the heat. For a man with any shred of conscience, it would surely have been a vision out of hell, to see those ranks of his victims and accusers, all ranged against him. But this monster merely bowed at them, as if he were delighted to greet old acquaintances.

Glabrio called the court to order, but before Cicero could rise to begin his speech, Hortensius jumped up to make a point of order: under the Cornelian Law, he declared, a prosecutor was entitled to call no more than forty-eight witnesses, but this prosecutor had brought to court at least double that number, purely for the purpose of intimidation! He then embarked on a long, learned and elegant speech about the origins of the extortion court, which lasted for what felt like another hour. At length, Glabrio cut him off, saying there was nothing in the law about restricting the number of witnesses present in court, only the number giving verbal evidence. Once again, he invited Cicero to open his case, and once again, Hortensius intervened with another point of order. The crowd began to jeer, but he pressed on, as he did repeatedly whenever Cicero rose to speak, and thus the first few hours of the day were lost in vexatious legal point-scoring.

It was not until the middle of the afternoon, when Cicero was wearily getting to his feet for the ninth or tenth time, that Hortensius at last remained seated. Cicero looked at him, waited, then slowly spread his arms wide in mock-amazement. A wave of laughter went round the forum. Hortensius responded by gesturing with a foppish twirl of his hand to the well of the court, as if to say, 'Be my guest.' Cicero bowed courteously and came forward. He cleared his throat.

There could scarcely have been a worse moment at which to begin such an immense undertaking. The heat was unbearable. The crowd was now bored and restless. Hortensius was smirking. There were only perhaps two hours left before the court adjourned for the evening. And yet this was to be one of the most decisive moments in the history of our Roman law – indeed, in the history of all law, everywhere, I should not wonder.

'Gentlemen of the court,' said Cicero, and I bent my head over my tablet and noted the words in shorthand. I waited for him to continue. For almost the first time before a major speech, I had no idea what he was going to say. I waited a little longer, my heart thumping, and then nervously glanced up to find him walking across the court away from me. I thought he was going to stop and confront Verres, but instead he walked straight past him and halted in front of the senators in the jury.

'Gentlemen of the court,' he repeated, addressing them directly, 'at this great political crisis, there has been offered to you, not through man's wisdom but almost as the direct gift of heaven, the very thing you most need – a thing that will help more than anything else to mitigate the unpopularity of your order and the suspicion surrounding these courts. A belief has become established – as harmful to the republic as it is to yourselves – that these courts, with you senators as the jury, will never convict any man, however guilty, if he has sufficient *money*.'

He put a wonderful, contemptuous stress on the last word. 'You are not wrong there!' shouted a voice in the crowd.

'But the character of the man I am prosecuting,' continued Cicero, 'is such that you may use him to restore your own good name. Gaius Verres has robbed the treasury and behaved like a pirate and a destroying pestilence in his province of Sicily. You have only to find this man guilty, and respect in you will be rightly restored. But if you do not – if his immense wealth is sufficient to shatter your honesty – well then, I shall achieve one thing at least. The nation will not believe Verres to be right and me wrong – but they will certainly know all they need to know about a jury of Roman senators!'

It was a nice stroke to start off with. There was a rustle of approval from the great crowd that was like a wind moving through a forest, and in some curious sense the focus of the trial seemed to shift all at once twenty paces to the left. It was as if the senators, sweating in the hot sun and squirming uncomfortably on their wooden benches, had become the accused, while the vast press of witnesses, drawn from every corner of the Mediterranean, was the jury. Cicero had never addressed such an immense throng before, but Molon's training on the seashore stood him in good stead, and when he turned to the forum his voice rang clear and true.

'Let me tell you of the impudent and insane plan that is now in Verres's mind. It is plain to him that I am approaching this case so well prepared that I shall be able to pin him down as a robber and a criminal, not merely in the hearing of this court but in the eyes of the whole world. But in spite of this, he holds so low an opinion of the aristocracy, he believes the senatorial courts to be so utterly abandoned and corrupt, that he goes about boasting openly that he has bought the safest date for his trial, he has bought the jury, and just to be on the safe side he has also bought the consular election for his two titled friends who have tried to intimidate my witnesses!'

This was what the crowd had come to hear. The rustle of approval became a roar. Metellus jumped up in anger, and so did Hortensius – yes, even Hortensius, who normally greeted any taunt in the arena with nothing more strenuous than a raised eyebrow. They began gesticulating angrily at Cicero.

'What?' he responded, turning on them. 'Did you count on my saying nothing of so serious a matter? On my caring for anything, except my duty and my honour, when the country and my own reputation are in such danger? Metellus, I am amazed at you. To attempt to intimidate witnesses, especially these timorous and calamity-stricken Sicilians, by appealing to their awe of you as consul-elect, and to the power of your two brothers – if this is not judicial corruption, I should be glad to know what is! What would you not do for an innocent kinsman if you abandon duty and honour for an utter rascal who is no kin of yours at all? Because I tell you this: Verres has been going round saying that you were only made consul because of his exertions, and that by January he will have the two consuls and the president of the court to suit him!'

I had to stop writing at this point, because the noise was too great for me to hear. Metellus and Hortensius both had their hands cupped to their mouths and were bellowing at Cicero. Verres was gesturing angrily at Glabrio to put a stop to this. The jury of senators sat immobile – most of them, I am sure, wishing they were anywhere but where they were – while individual spectators were having to be restrained by the lictors from storming the court. Eventually, Glabrio managed to restore order, and Cicero resumed, in a much calmer voice.

'So these are their tactics. Today the court did not start its business until the middle of the afternoon – they are already reckoning that today does not count at all. It is only ten days to the games of Pompey the Great. These will occupy fifteen days and will be followed immediately by the Roman Games. So it will not be until after an interval of nearly forty days that they expect to begin their reply. They count on being able then, with the help of long speeches and technical evasions, to prolong the trial until the Games of Victory begin. These games are followed without a break by the Plebeian Games, after which there will be very few days, or none at all, on which the court can sit. In this way they reckon that all the impetus of the prosecution will be spent and exhausted, and that the whole case will come up afresh before Marcus Metellus, who is sitting there on this jury.

'So what am I to do? If I spend upon my speech the full time allotted me by law, there is the gravest danger that the man I am prosecuting will slip through my fingers. "Make your speech shorter" is the obvious answer I was given a few days ago, and that is good advice. But, having thought the matter over, I shall go one better. Gentlemen, *I shall make no speech at all.*'

I glanced up in astonishment. Cicero was looking at Hortensius, and his rival was staring back at him with the most wonderful frozen expression on his face. He looked like a man who has been walking through a wood cheerfully enough, thinking himself safely alone, and has suddenly heard a twig snap behind him and has stopped dead in alarm.

'That is right, Hortensius,' said Cicero. 'I am not going to play your game and spend the next ten days in the usual long address. I am not going to let the case drag on till January, when you and Metellus as consuls can use your lictors to drag my witnesses before you and frighten them into silence. I am not going to allow you gentlemen of the jury the luxury of forty days to forget my charges, so that you can then lose yourselves and your consciences in the tangled thickets of Hortensius's rhetoric. I am not going to delay the settlement of this case until all these multitudes who have come to Rome for the census and the games have dispersed to their homes in Italy. I am going to call my witnesses at once, beginning now, and this will be my procedure: I shall read out the individual charge. I shall comment and elaborate upon it. I shall bring forth the witness who supports it, and question him, and then you, Hortensius, will have the same opportunity as me for comment and cross-examination. I shall do all this and I shall rest my case within the space of ten days.'

All my long life I have treasured – and for what little remains of it I shall continue to treasure – the reactions of Hortensius, Verres, Metellus and Scipio Nasica at that moment. Of course, Hortensius was on his feet as soon as he had recovered his breath and was denouncing this break with precedent as entirely illegal. But Glabrio was ready for him, and told him brusquely that it was up to Cicero to present his case in whatever manner he wished, and that he, for one, was sick of interminable speeches, as he had made clear in this very court before the consular elections. His remarks had obviously been prepared beforehand, and Hortensius rose again to accuse him of collusion with the prosecution. Glabrio, who was an irritable man at the best of times, told him bluntly he had better guard his tongue, or he would have his lictors remove him from the court – consul-elect or no. Hortensius sat down furiously, folded his arms and scowled at his feet, as Cicero concluded his opening address, once again by turning on the jury.

'Today the eyes of the world are upon us, waiting to see how far the conduct of each man among us will be marked by obedience to his conscience and observance of the law. Even as you will pass your verdict upon the prisoner, so the people of Rome will pass its verdict upon yourselves. The case of Verres will determine whether, in a court composed of senators, the condemnation of a very guilty and very rich man can possibly occur. Because all the world knows that Verres is distinguished by nothing except his monstrous offences and his immense wealth. Therefore if he is acquitted it will be impossible to imagine any explanation except the most shameful. So I advise you, gentlemen, for your own sakes, to see that this does not occur.' And with that he turned his back on them. 'I call my first witness – Sthenius of Thermae.'

I doubt very strongly whether any of the aristocrats on that jury – Catulus, Isauricus, Metellus, Catilina, Lucretius, Aemilius and the rest – had ever been addressed with such insolence before, especially by a new man without a single ancestral mask to show on his atrium wall. How they must have loathed being made to sit there and take it, especially given the deliriums of ecstasy with which Cicero was received by the vast crowd in the forum when he sat down. As for Hortensius, it was possible almost to feel sorry for him. His entire career had been founded on his ability to memorise immense orations and deliver them with the aplomb of an actor. Now he was effectively struck mute; worse, he was faced with the prospect of having to deliver four dozen mini-speeches in reply to each of Cicero's witnesses over the next ten days. He had not done sufficient research even remotely to attempt this, as became cruelly evident when Sthenius took the witness stand. Cicero had called him first as a mark of respect for the originator of this whole fantastic undertaking, and the Sicilian did not let him down. He had waited a long time for his day in court, and he made the most of it, giving a heart-wringing account of the way Verres had abused his hospitality, stolen his property, trumped up charges against him, fined him and tried to have him flogged, sentenced him to death in his absence and then forged the records of the Syracusan court – records which Cicero produced in evidence, and passed around the jury.

But when Glabrio called upon Hortensius to cross-examine the witness, the Dancing Master, not unnaturally, showed some reluctance to take the floor. The one golden rule of cross-examination is never, under any circumstances, to ask a question to which you do not know the answer, and Hortensius simply had no idea what Sthenius might say next. He shuffled a few documents, held a whispered consultation with Verres, then approached the witness stand. What could he do? After a few petulant questions, the implication of which was that the Sicilian was fundamentally hostile to Roman rule, he asked him why, of all the lawyers available, he had chosen to go straight to Cicero – a man known to be an agitator of the lower classes. Surely his whole motivation from the start was merely to stir up trouble?

'But I did not go straight to Cicero,' replied Sthenius in his ingenuous way. 'The first advocate I went to was you.'

Even some of the jury laughed at that.

Hortensius swallowed, and attempted to join in the merriment. 'Did you really? I can't say that I remember you.'

'Well you wouldn't, would you? You are a busy man. But I remember you, Senator. You said you were representing Verres. You said you didn't care how much of my property he had stolen – no court would ever believe the word of a Sicilian over a Roman.'

Hortensius had to wait for the storm of cat-calls to die down. 'I have no further questions for this witness,' he said in a grim voice, and with that the court was adjourned until the following day.

It had been my intention to describe in detail the trial of Gaius Verres, but now I come to set it down, I see there is no point. After Cicero's tactical masterstroke on that first day, Verres and his advocates resembled nothing so much as the victims of a siege: holed up in their little fortress, surrounded on every side by their enemies, battered day after day by a rain of missiles, and with tunnels undermining their crumbling walls. They had no means of fighting back. Their only hope was somehow to withstand the onslaught for the full nine days remaining, and then try to regroup during the lull enforced by Pompey's games. Cicero's objective was equally clear: to obliterate Verres's defences so completely that by the time he had finished laying out his case not even the most corrupt senatorial jury in Rome would dare to acquit him.

He set about this mission with his usual discipline. The prosecution team would gather before dawn. While Cicero performed his exercises, was shaved and dressed, I would read out the testimony of the witnesses he would be calling that day, and run through our schedule of evidence. He would then dictate to me the rough outline of what he intended to say. For an hour or two he would familiarise himself with the day's brief and thoroughly memorise his remarks, while Quintus, Frugi and I ensured that all his witnesses and evidence boxes were ready. We would then parade down the hill to the forum – and parades they were, for the general view around Rome was that Cicero's performance in the extortion court was the greatest show in town. The crowds were as large on the second and third days as they had been on the first, and the witnesses' performances were often heartbreaking, as they collapsed in tears recounting their ill treatment. I remember in particular Dio of Halaesa, swindled out of ten thousand sesterces, and two brothers from Agyrium forced to hand over their entire inheritance of four thousand. There would have been more, but Lucius Metellus had actually refused to let a dozen witnesses leave the island to testify, among them Heraclius of Syracuse, the chief priest of Jupiter – an outrage against justice which Cicero neatly turned to his advantage. 'Our allies' rights,' he boomed, 'do not even include permission to complain of their sufferings!' Throughout all this, Hortensius, amazing to relate, never said a word. Cicero would finish his examination of a witness, Glabrio would offer the King of the Law Courts his chance to cross-examine, and His Majesty would regally shake his head, or declare grandly, 'No questions for this witness.' On the fourth day, Verres pleaded illness and tried to be excused attendance, but Glabrio was having none of it, and told him he would be carried down to the forum on his bed if necessary.

It was on the following afternoon that Cicero's cousin Lucius

at last returned to Rome, his mission in Sicily accomplished.
Cicero was overjoyed to find him waiting at the house when we
got back from court, and embraced him tearfully. Without
Lucius's support in dispatching witnesses and boxes of evidence
back to the mainland, Cicero's case would not have been half as
strong. But the seven-month effort had clearly exhausted Lucius,
who had not been a strong man to begin with. He was now
alarmingly thin, and had developed a painful, racking cough. Even
so, his commitment to bringing Verres to justice was unwavering
– so much so that he had missed the opening of the trial in order
to take a detour on his journey back to Rome. He had stayed in
Puteoli and tracked down two more witnesses: the Roman knight
Gaius Numitorius, who had witnessed the crucifixion of Gavius
in Messana, and a friend of his, a merchant named Marcus Annius,
who had been in Syracuse when the Roman banker Herennius
had been judicially murdered.

'And where are these gentlemen?' asked Cicero eagerly.

'Here,' replied Lucius. 'In the tablinum. But I must warn you,
they do not want to testify.'

Cicero hurried through to find two formidable men of middle
age – 'The perfect witnesses from my point of view,' as he afterwards described them, 'prosperous, respectable, sober, and   above
all – not Sicilian.' As Lucius had predicted, they were reluctant to
get involved. They were businessmen, with no desire to make
powerful enemies, and did not relish the prospect of taking starring
roles in Cicero's great anti-aristocratic production in the Roman
forum. But he wore them down, for they were not fools, either, and
could see that in the ledger of profit and loss, they stood to gain
most by aligning themselves with the side that was winning. 'Do
you know what Pompey said to Sulla, when the old man tried to
deny him a triumph on his twenty-sixth birthday?' asked Cicero.

'He told me over dinner the other night: "More people worship a rising than a setting sun."' This potent combination of name-dropping and appeals to patriotism and self-interest at last won them round, and by the time they went into dinner with Cicero and his family, they had pledged their support.

'I knew if I had them in your company for a few moments,' whispered Lucius, 'they would do whatever you wanted.'

I had expected Cicero to put them on the witness stand the very next day, but he was too smart for that. 'A show must always end with a climax,' he said. By now he was ratcheting up the level of outrage with each new piece of evidence, having moved on through judicial corruption, extortion and straight-forward robbery, to cruel and unusual punishment. On the eighth day of the trial, he dealt with the testimony of two Sicilian naval captains, Phalacrus of Centuripa and Onasus of Segesta, who described how they and their men had only escaped floggings and executions by bribing Verres's freedman, Timarchides (present in court, I am glad to say, to experience his humiliation personally). Worse: the families of those who had not been able to raise sufficient funds to secure the release of their relatives had been told they would still have to pay a bribe to the official executioner, Sextius, or he would deliber-ately make a mess of the beheadings. 'Think of that unbear-able burden of pain,' declaimed Cicero, 'of the anguish that racked those unhappy parents, thus compelled to purchase for their children by bribery not life but a speedy death!' I could see the senators on the jury shaking their heads at this, and muttering to one another, and each time Glabrio invited Hortensius to cross-examine the witnesses, and Hortensius simply responded yet again, 'No questions,' they groaned. Their position was becoming intolerable, and that night the first rumours reached us that Verres had already packed up the contents of his house and was preparing to flee into exile.

Such was the state of affairs on the ninth day, when we brought Annius and Numitorius into court. If anything, the crowd in the forum was bigger than ever, for there were now only two days left until Pompey's great games. Verres came late, and obviously drunk. He stumbled as he climbed the steps of the temple up to the tribunal, and Hortensius had to steady him as the crowd roared with laughter. As he passed Cicero's place, he flashed him a shattered, red-eyed look of fear and rage the hunted, cornered look of an animal at bay. Cicero got straight down to business and called as his first witness Annius, who described how he had been inspecting a cargo down at the harbour in Syracuse one morning, when a friend had come running to tell him that their business associate, Herennius, was in chains in the forum and pleading for his life.

'So what did you do?'

'Naturally, I went at once.'

'And what was the scene?'

'There were perhaps a hundred people crying out that Herennius was a Roman citizen, and could not be executed without a proper trial.'

'How did you all know that Herennius was a Roman? Was he not a banker from Spain?'

'Many of us knew him personally. Although he had business in Spain, he had been born to a Roman family in Syracuse and had grown up in the city.'

'And what was Verres's response to your pleas?'

'He ordered Herennius to be beheaded immediately.'

There was a groan of horror around the court.

'And who dealt the fatal blow?'

'The public executioner, Sextius.'

'And did he make a clean job of it?'

'I am afraid he did not, no.'

'Clearly,' said Cicero, turning to the jury, 'Herennius had not paid Verres and his gang of thieves a large enough bribe.'

For most of the trial, Verres had sat slumped in his chair, but on this morning, fired by drink, he jumped up and began shouting that he had never taken any such bribe. Hortensius had to pull him down. Cicero ignored him and went on calmly questioning his witness.

'This is an extraordinary situation, is it not? A hundred of you vouch for the identity of this Roman citizen, yet Verres does not even wait an hour to establish the truth of who he is. How do you account for it?'

'I can account for it easily, Senator. Herennius was a passenger on a ship from Spain which was impounded with all its cargo by Verres's agents. He was sent to the Stone Quarries, along with everyone else on board, then dragged out to be publicly executed as a pirate. What Verres did not realise was that Herennius was not from Spain at all. He was known to the Roman community in Syracuse and would be recognised. But by the time Verres discovered his mistake, Herennius could not be allowed to go free, because he knew too much about what the governor was up to.'

'Forgive me, I do not understand,' said Cicero, playing the innocent. 'Why would Verres want to execute an innocent passenger on a cargo ship as a pirate?'

'He needed to show a sufficient number of executions.'

'Why?'

'Because he was being paid bribes to let the real pirates go free.'

Verres was up on his feet again shouting that it was a lie, and this time Cicero did not ignore him, but took a few paces towards him. 'A lie, you monster? A lie? Then why in your own prison records does it state that Herennius was released? And why do they further state that the notorious pirate captain, Heracleo, was executed, when no one on the island ever saw him die? I shall tell you why – because you, the Roman governor, responsible for the safety of the seas, were all the while taking bribes from the very pirates themselves!'

'Cicero, the great lawyer, who thinks himself so clever!' said Verres bitterly, his words slurred by drink. 'Who thinks he knows everything! Well, here is something you don't know. I have Heracleo in my private custody, here in my house in Rome, and he can tell you all himself that it's a lie!'

Amazing now, to reflect that a man could blurt out something so foolish, but the facts are there – they are in the record – and amid the pandemonium in court, Cicero could be heard demanding of Glabrio that the famous pirate be fetched from Verres's house by the lictors and placed in official custody, 'for the public safety'. Then, while that was being done, he called as his second witness of the day Gaius Numitorius. Privately, I thought that Cicero was rushing it too much: that he could have milked the admission about Heracleo for more. But the great advocate had sensed that the moment for the kill had arrived, and for months, ever since we had first landed in Sicily, he had known exactly the blade he wished to use. Numitorius swore an oath to tell the truth and took the stand, and Cicero quickly led him through his testimony to establish the essential facts about Publius Gavius: that he was a merchant travelling on a ship from Spain; that his ship had been impounded and the passengers all taken to the Stone Quarries, from which

Gavius had somehow managed to escape; that he had made his way to Messana to take a ship to the mainland, had been apprehended as he went aboard, and handed over to Verres when he visited the town. The silence of the listening multitudes was intense.

'Describe to the court what happened next.'

'Verres convened a tribunal in the forum of Messana,' said Numitorius, 'and then he had Gavius dragged before him. He announced to everyone that this man was a spy, for which there was only one just penalty. Then he ordered a cross set up overlooking the straits to Regium, so that the prisoner could gaze upon Italy as he died, and had Gavius stripped naked and publicly flogged before us all. Then he was tortured with hot irons. And then he was crucified.'

'Did Gavius speak at all?'

'Only at the beginning, to swear that the accusation was not true. He was not a foreign spy. He was a Roman citizen, a councillor from the town of Consa, and a former soldier in the Roman cavalry, under the command of Lucius Raecius.'

'What did Verres say to that.'

'He said that these were lies, and commanded that the execution begin.'

'Can you describe how Gavius met his dreadful death?'

'He met it very bravely, Senator.'

'Like a Roman?'

'Like a Roman.'

'Did he cry out at all?' (I knew what Cicero was after.)

'Only while he was being whipped, and he could see the irons being heated.'

'And what did he say?'

'Every time a blow landed, he said, "I am a Roman citizen."'

'Would you repeat what he said, more loudly please, so that all can hear.'

'He said, "I am a Roman citizen."'

'So just that?' said Cicero. 'Let me be sure I understand you. A blow lands' – he put his wrists together, raised them above his head and jerked forwards, as if his back had just been lashed – 'and he says, through gritted teeth, "I am a Roman citizen." A blow lands' – and again he jerked forwards – '"I am a Roman citizen." A blow lands. "*I am a Roman citizen –* "'

These flat words of mine cannot begin to convey the effect of Cicero's performance upon those who saw it. The hush around the court amplified his words. It was as if all of us now were witnesses to this monstrous miscarriage of justice. Some men and women – friends of Gavius, I believe – began to scream, and there was a growing swell of outrage from the masses in the forum. Yet again, Verres shook off Hortensius's restraining hand and stood up. 'He was a filthy spy!' he bellowed. 'A spy! He only said it to delay his proper punishment!'

'*But he said it!*' said Cicero, triumphantly, wheeling on him, his finger jabbing in outrage. 'You admit he said it! Out of your own mouth I accuse you – the man claimed to be a Roman citizen and you did nothing! This mention of his citizenship did not lead you to hesitate or delay, even for a little, the infliction of this cruel and disgusting death! If you, Verres, had been made a prisoner in Persia or the remotest part of India, and were being dragged off to execution, what cry would you be uttering, except that you were a Roman citizen? What then of this man whom you were hurrying to his death? Could not that statement, that claim of citizenship, have saved him for an hour, for a day, while its truth was checked? No, it could not – not with you in the judgement seat! And yet the poorest man, of humblest birth, in whatever savage land, has always until now had the confidence to know that the cry "I am a Roman citizen" is his final defence and sanctuary. It was not Gavius, not one obscure man, whom you nailed upon that cross of agony: it was the universal principle that Romans are free men!'

The roar which greeted the end of Cicero's tirade was terrifying. Rather than diminishing after a few moments, it gathered itself afresh and rose in volume and pitch, and I became aware, at the periphery of my vision, of a movement towards us. The awnings under which some of the spectators had been standing as protection against the sun began to collapse with a terrible tearing sound. A man dropped off a balcony on to the crowd beneath. There were screams. What was unmistakably a lynch mob began storming the steps to the platform. Hortensius and Verres stood up so quickly in their panic that they knocked over the bench behind them. Glabrio could be heard yelling that the court was adjourned, then he and his lictors hastened up the remaining steps towards the temple, with the accused and his eminent counsel in undignified pursuit. Some of the jury also fled into the sanctuary of the holy building (but not Catulus: I distinctly remember him standing like a sharp rock, staring unflinchingly ahead, as the current of bodies broke and swirled around him). The heavy bronze doors slammed shut. It was left to Cicero to try to restore order by climbing on to his own bench and gesturing for calm, but four or five men, rough-looking fellows, ran up and seized his legs and lifted him away. I was terrified, for both his safety and my own, but he stretched out his arms as if he was embracing the whole world. When they had settled him on their shoulders they spun him around to face the forum. The blast of applause was like the opening of a furnace door and the chant of 'Cic-er-o! Cic-er-o! Cic-er-o!' split the skies of Rome.

And that, at last, was the end of Gaius Verres. We never learned exactly what went on inside the temple after Glabrio suspended the sitting, but Cicero's belief was that Hortensius and Metellus made it clear to their client that further defence was useless. Their own dignity and authority were in tatters: they simply had to cut him adrift before any more harm was done to the reputation of the senate. It no longer mattered how lavishly he had bribed the jury – no member of it would dare to vote to acquit him after the scenes they had just witnessed. At any rate, Verres slipped out of the temple when the mob had dispersed, and fled the city at nightfall – disguised, some say, as a woman – riding full pelt for southern Gaul. His destination was the port of Massilia, where exiles could traditionally swap their hard-luck stories over grilled mullet and pretend they were on the Bay of Naples.

All that remained to do now was to fix the level of his fine, and when Cicero returned home he convened a meeting to discuss the appropriate figure. Nobody will ever know the full value of what Verres stole during his years in Sicily – I have heard an estimate of forty million – but Lucius, as usual, was eager for the most radical course: the seizure of every asset Verres possessed. Quintus thought ten million would be about right. Cicero was curiously silent for a man who had just recorded such a stupendous victory, and sat in his study moodily toying with a metal stylus. Early in the afternoon, we received a letter from Hortensius, relaying an offer from Verres to pay one million into court as compensation. Lucius was particularly appalled –

'an insult', he called it – and Cicero had no hesitation in sending the messenger away with a flea in his ear. An hour later he was back, with what Hortensius called his 'final figure': a settlement of one and a half million. This time, Cicero dictated a longer reply:

> From: Marcus Tullius Cicero
> To: Quintus Hortensius Hortalus
> Greetings!
> In view of the ludicrously low sum your client is proposing as compensation for his unparalleled wickedness, I intend asking Glabrio to allow me to continue the prosecution tomorrow, when I shall exercise my right to address the court on this and other matters.

'Let us see how much he and his aristocratic friends relish the prospect of having their noses rubbed further into their own filth,' he exclaimed to me. I finished sealing the letter, and when I returned from giving it to the messenger, Cicero set about dictating the speech he proposed to deliver the next day – a slashing attack on the aristocrats for prostituting their great names, and the names of their ancestors, in defence of such a scoundrel as Verres. Urged on by Lucius in particular, he poured out his loathing. 'We are aware with what jealousy, with what dislike, the merit and energy of "new men" are regarded by certain of the "nobles"; that we have only to shut our eyes for a moment to find ourselves caught in some trap; that if we leave them the smallest opening for any suspicion or charge of misconduct, we have to suffer for it at once; that we must never relax our vigilance, and never take a holiday. We have enemies – let us face them; tasks to perform – let us shoulder them; not forgetting that an open and declared enemy is less formidable than one who hides himself and says nothing!'

'There go another thousand votes,' muttered Quintus.

The afternoon wore on in this way, without any answer from Hortensius, until, at length, not long before dusk, there was a commotion from the street, and soon afterwards Eros came running into the study with the breathless news that Pompey the Great himself was in the vestibule. This was indeed an extra-ordinary turn-up, but Cicero and his brother had time to do no more than blink at one another before that familiar military voice could be heard barking, 'Where is he? Where is the greatest orator of the age?'

Cicero muttered an oath beneath his breath, and went out into the tablinum, followed by Quintus, then Lucius, and finally myself, just in time to see the senior consul come striding out of the atrium. The confines of that modest house made him bulk even larger than he did normally. 'And there he is!' he exclaimed, 'There is the man whom everyone comes to see!' He made straight for Cicero, threw his powerful arms around him, and embraced him in a bear hug. From where I was standing, just behind Cicero, I could see Pompey's crafty grey eyes taking in each of us in turn, and when he released his embarrassed host, he insisted on being introduced, even to me, so that I – a humble domestic slave from Arpinum – could now boast, at the age of thirty-four, that I had shaken hands with both the ruling consuls of Rome.

He had left his bodyguards out in the street and had come into the house entirely alone, a significant mark of trust and favour. Cicero, whose manners as always were impeccable, ordered Eros to tell Terentia that Pompey the Great was downstairs, and I was instructed to pour some wine.

'Only a little,' said Pompey, putting his large hand over the cup. 'We are on our way to dinner, and shall only stay a moment. But we could not pass our neighbour without calling in to pay our respects. We have been watching your progress, Cicero, over these past few days. We have been receiving reports from our friend Glabrio. Magnificent. We drink your health.' He raised his cup, but not a drop, I noticed, touched his lips. 'And now that this great enterprise is successfully behind you, we hope that we may see a little more of you, especially as I shall soon be merely a private citizen again.'

Cicero gave a slight bow. 'That would be my pleasure.'

'The day after tomorrow, for example – how are you placed?'

'That is the day of the opening of your games. Surely you will be occupied? Perhaps some other time . . .'

'Nonsense. Come and watch the opening from our box. It will do you no harm to be seen in our company. Let the world observe our friendship,' he added grandly. 'You enjoy the games, do you not?'

Cicero hesitated, and I could see his brain working through the consequences, of both refusal and acceptance. But really he had no choice. 'I adore the games,' he said. 'I can think of nothing I would rather do.'

'Excellent,' beamed Pompey. At that moment Eros returned, with a message that Terentia was lying down, unwell, and sent her apologies. 'That is a pity,' said Pompey, looking slightly put out. 'But let us hope there will be some future opportunity.' He handed me his untouched wine. 'We must be on our way. No doubt you have much to do. Incidentally,' he said, turning on the threshold of the atrium, 'have you settled on the level of the fine yet?'

'Not yet,' replied Cicero.

'What have they offered?'

'One and a half million.'

'Take it,' said Pompey. 'You have covered them in shit. No need to make them eat it, too. It would be embarrassing to me person-ally and injurious to the stability of the state to proceed with this case further. You understand me?' He nodded in a friendly way and walked out. We heard the front door open and the commander of his bodyguard call his men to attention. The door closed. For a little while, nobody spoke.

'What a ghastly man,' said Cicero. 'Bring me another drink.' As I fetched the jug, I saw Lucius frowning.

'What gives him the right to talk to you like that?' he asked. 'He said it was a social visit.'

'A social visit! Oh, Lucius!' Cicero laughed. 'That was a visit from the rent collector.'

'The rent collector? What rent do you owe him?' Lucius might have been a philosopher, but he was not a complete idiot, and he realised then what had happened. 'Oh, I understand!' A look of disgust came across his face, and he turned away.

'Spare me your superiority,' said Cicero, catching his arm. 'I had no choice. Marcus Metellus had just drawn the extortion court. The jury was bribed. The hearing was fixed to fail. I was this far' – Cicero measured an inch with his thumb and fore-finger – 'from abandoning the whole prosecution. And then Terentia said to me, "Make your speech shorter," and I realised that was the answer – to produce every document and every witness, and do it all in ten days, and *shame* them – that was it, Lucius: you understand me? – *shame* them before the whole of Rome, so they had no alternative except to find him guilty.'

In such a way did he speak, working all his persuasive powers upon his cousin, as if Lucius were a one-man jury which he needed to convince – reading his face, trying to find within it clues to the right words and arguments which would unlock his support.

'But *Pompey*,' said Lucius, bitterly. 'After what he did to you before!'

'All I needed, Lucius, was one thing – one tiny, tiny favour – and that was the assurance that I could proceed as I wished, and call my witnesses straight away. No bribery was involved; no corruption. I just knew I had to be sure to secure Glabrio's consent beforehand. But I could hardly, as the prosecutor, approach the praetor of the court myself. So I racked my brains: who could?'

Quintus said, 'There was only one man in Rome, Lucius.'

'Exactly!' cried Cicero. 'Only one man to whom Glabrio was honour-bound to listen. The man who had given him his son back, when his divorced wife died – Pompey.'

'But it was not a tiny favour,' said Lucius. 'It was a massive interference. And now there is a massive price to be paid for it – and not by you, but by the people of Sicily.'

'The people of Sicily?' repeated Cicero, beginning to lose his temper. 'The people of Sicily have never had a truer friend than me. There would never have been a prosecution without me. There would never have been an offer of one and a half million without me. By heaven, Gaius Verres would have been *consul* in two years' time but for me! You cannot reproach me for abandoning the people of Sicily!'

'Then refuse to pay his rent,' said Lucius, seizing hold of his hand. 'Tomorrow, in court, press for the maximum damages, and to hell with Pompey. You have the whole of Rome on your side. That jury will not dare to go against you. Who cares about Pompey? In five months' time, as he says himself, he will not even be consul. Promise me.'

Cicero clasped Lucius's hand fervently in both of his and gazed deep into his eyes – the old double-grip sincere routine, which I had seen so often in this very room. 'I promise you,' he said. 'I promise you I shall think about it.'

Perhaps he did think about it. Who am I to judge? But I doubt it can have occupied his mind for more than an instant. Cicero was no revolutionary. He never desired to set himself at the head of a mob, tearing down the state: and that would have been his only hope of survival, if he had turned Pompey against him as well as the aristocracy. 'The trouble with Lucius,' he said putting his feet up on the desk after his cousin had gone, 'is that he thinks politics is a fight for justice. Politics is a profession.'

'Do you think Verres bribed Pompey to intervene, to lower the damages?' asked Quintus, voicing exactly the possibility which had occurred to me.

'It could be. More likely he simply wants to avoid being caught in the middle of a civil war between the people and the senate. Speaking for myself, I would be happy to seize everything Verres possesses, and leave the wretch to live on Gaulish grass. But that is not going to happen,' he sighed, 'so we had better see how far we can make this one and a half million stretch.'

The three of us spent the rest of the evening compiling a list of the most worthy claimants, and after Cicero had deducted his own costs, of close to one hundred thousand, we reckoned he could just about manage to fulfil his obligations, at least to the likes of Sthenius, and to those witnesses who had travelled all the way to Rome. But what could one say to the priests? How could one put a price on looted temple statues made of gems and precious metals, long since broken up and melted down by

Verres's goldsmiths? And what payment could ever recompense the families and friends of Gavius and Herennius and the other innocents he had murdered? The work gave Cicero his first real taste of what it is like to have power – which is usually, when it comes down to it, a matter of choosing between equally unpalatable options – and fairly bitter he found it.

We went into court in the usual manner the following morning, and there was the usual big crowd in their usual places – everything the same, in fact, except for the absence of Verres, and the presence of twenty or thirty men of the magistrates' patrol, stationed around the perimeter of the tribunal. Glabrio made a short speech, opening the session and warning that he would not tolerate any disturbances similar to those which had occurred the previous day. Then he called on Hortensius to make a statement.

'Due to ill health,' Hortensius began, and there was the most wonderful shout of laughter from all sides. It was some time before he was able to proceed. 'Due to ill health,' he repeated, 'brought on by the strain of these proceedings, and wishing to spare the state any further disruption, my client Gaius Verres no longer proposes to offer a defence to the charges brought by the special prosecutor.'

He sat down. There was applause from the Sicilians at this concession, but little response from the spectators. They were waiting to take their lead from Cicero. He stood, thanked Hortensius for his statement – 'somewhat shorter than the speeches he is in the habit of making in these surroundings' – and demanded the maximum penalty under the Cornelian Law: a full loss of civil rights, in perpetuity, 'so that never again can the shadow of Gaius Verres menace his victims or threaten the just administration of the Roman republic'. This elicited the first real cheer of the morning.

'I wish,' continued Cicero, 'that I could undo his crimes, and restore to both men and gods all that he has robbed from them. I wish I could give back to Juno the offerings and adornments of her shrines at Melita and Samos. I wish Minerva could see again the decorations of her temple at Syracuse. I wish Diana's statue could be restored to the town of Segesta, and Mercury's to the people of Tyndaris. I wish I could undo the double injury to Ceres, whose images were carried away from both Henna and Catina. But the villain has fled, leaving behind only the stripped walls and bare floors of his houses here in Rome and in the country. These are the only assets which can be seized and sold. His counsel assesses the value of these at one and a half million sesterces, and this is what I must ask for and accept as recompense for his crimes.'

There was a groan, and someone shouted, 'Not enough!'

'It is not enough. I agree. And perhaps some of those in this court, who defended Verres when his star was rising, and others who promised him their support if they found themselves among his jurors, might inspect their consciences – might inspect, indeed, the contents of their villas!'

This brought Hortensius to his feet to complain that the prosecutor was talking in riddles.

'Well,' responded Cicero in a flash, 'as Verres provided him with an ivory sphinx, the consul-elect should find no difficulty solving riddles.'

It cannot have been a premeditated joke, as Cicero had no idea what Hortensius was going to say. Or perhaps, on second thoughts, having written that, I am being naïve, and it was actually part of that store of spontaneous witticisms which Cicero regularly laid up by candlelight to use should the opportunity arise. Whatever the truth, it was proof of how important humour can be on a public occasion, for nobody now remembers a thing about that last day in court except Cicero's crack about the ivory sphinx. I am not even sure, in retrospect, that it is particularly funny. But it brought the house down, and transformed what could have been an embarrassing speech into yet another triumph. 'Sit down quickly' – that was always Molon's advice when things were going well, and Cicero took it. I handed him a towel and he mopped his face and dried his hands as the applause continued. And with that, his exertions in the prosecution of Gaius Verres were at an end.

That afternoon, the senate met for its final debate before it went into a fifteen-day recess for Pompey's games. By the time Cicero had finished smoothing matters over with the Sicilians, he was late for the start of the session, and we had to run together from the Temple of Castor, right across the forum to the senate house. Crassus, as the presiding consul for the month, had already called the house to order and was reading the latest dispatch from Lucullus on the progress of the campaign in the East. Rather than interrupt him by making a conspicuous entry, Cicero stood at the bar of the chamber, and we listened to Lucullus's report. The aristocratic general had, by his own account, scored a series of crushing victories, entering the kingdom of Tigranes, defeating the king himself in battle, slaughtering tens of thousands of the enemy, advancing deeper into hostile territory to capture the city of Nisibisis, and taking the king's brother as hostage.

'Crassus must feel like throwing up,' Cicero whispered to me gleefully. 'His only consolation will be to know that Pompey is even more furiously jealous.' And, indeed, Pompey, sitting beside Crassus, his arms folded, did look sunk in a gloomy reverie.

When Crassus had finished speaking, Cicero took advantage of the lull to enter the chamber. The day was hot and the shafts of light from the high windows lit jewelled swirls of midges. He walked purposefully, head erect, watched by everyone, down the central aisle, past his old place in obscurity by the door, towards the consular dais. The praetorian bench seemed full, but Cicero stood patiently beside it, waiting to claim his rightful place, for he knew – and the house knew – that the ancient reward for a successful prosecutor was the assumption of the defeated man's rank. I do not know how long the silence went on, but it seemed an awfully long time to me, during which the only sound came from the pigeons in the roof. It was Afranius who finally beckoned to him to sit beside him, and who cleared sufficient space by roughly shoving his neighbours along the wooden seat. Cicero picked his way across half a dozen pairs of outstretched legs and wedged himself defiantly into his place. He glanced around at his rivals, and met and held the gaze of each. No one challenged him. Eventually, someone rose to speak, and in a grudging voice congratulated Lucullus and his victorious legions – it might have been Pompey, now I come to think of it. Gradually the low drone of background conversation resumed.

I close my eyes and I see their faces still in the golden light of that late-summer afternoon – Cicero, Crassus, Pompey, Hortensius, Catulus, Catilina, the Metellus brothers – and it is hard for me to believe that they, and their ambitions, and even the very building they sat in, are now all so much dust.

PART TWO

PRAETORIAN
68–64 BC

'Nam eloquentiam quae admirationem non habet nullam iudico.'

'Eloquence which does not startle I don't consider eloquence.'

Cicero, letter to Brutus, 48 BC

X

I propose to resume my account at a point more than two years after the last roll ended – an elision which I fear says much about human nature, for if you were to ask me: 'Tiro, why do you choose to skip such a long period in Cicero's life?' I should be obliged to reply: 'Because, my friend, those were happy years, and few subjects make more tedious reading than happiness.'

The senator's aedileship turned out to be a great success. His chief responsibility was to keep the city supplied with cheap grain, and here his prosecution of Verres reaped him a great reward. To show their gratitude for his advocacy, the farmers and grain merchants of Sicily not only helped him by keeping their prices low: on one occasion they even gave him an entire shipment for nothing. Cicero was shrewd enough to ensure that others shared the credit. From the aediles' headquarters in the Temple of Ceres, he passed this bounty on for distribution to the hundred or so precinct bosses who really ran Rome, and many, out of grati-tude, became his clients. With their help, over the following months, he built an electoral machine second to none (Quintus used to boast that he could have a crowd of two hundred on the streets within an hour whenever he chose), and henceforth little occurred in the city which the Ciceros did not know about. If some builders or a shopkeeper, for example, needed a particular licence, or wished to have their premises put on to the water supply, or were worried about the state of a local temple, sooner or later their problems were likely to come to the notice of the two brothers. It was this laborious attention to humdrum detail, as much as his soaring rhetoric, which made Cicero such a formidable politician. He even staged good games – or, rather, Quintus did, on his behalf – and at the climax of the Festival of Ceres, when, in accordance with tradition, foxes were released into the Circus Maximus with flaming torches tied to their backs, the entire crowd of two hundred thousand rose to acclaim him in the official box.

'That so many people can derive so much pleasure from such a revolting spectacle,' he said to me when he returned home that night, 'almost makes one doubt the very premise on which democracy is based.' But he was pleased nevertheless that the masses now thought of him as a good sport, as well as 'the Scholar' and 'the Greek'.

Matters went equally well with his legal practice. Hortensius, after a typically smooth and untroubled year as consul, spent increasingly lengthy periods on the Bay of Naples, communing with his bejewelled fish and wine-soaked trees, leaving Cicero in complete domination of the Roman bar. Gifts and legacies from grateful clients soon began flowing in such profusion that he was even able to advance his brother the million he needed to enter the senate – for Quintus had belatedly set his heart on a political career, even though he was a poor speaker and Cicero privately believed that soldiering was better suited to his temperament. But despite his increasing wealth and prestige, Cicero refused to move out of his father's house, fearing it would tarnish his image as the People's Champion to be seen swanking around on the Palatine Hill. Instead, without consulting Terentia, he borrowed heavily against his future earnings to buy a grand country villa, thirteen miles from the prying eyes of the city voters, in the Alban Hills near Tusculum. She pretended to be annoyed when he took her out to see it, and maintained that the elevated climate was bad for her rheumatics. But I could tell that she was secretly delighted to have such a fashionable retreat, only half a day's journey from Rome. Catulus owned the adjoining property, and Hortensius also had a house not far away, but such was the hostility between Cicero and the aristocrats that, despite the long summer days he spent reading and writing in his villa's cool and poplared glades, they never once invited him to dine. This did not disturb Cicero; rather, it amused him, for the house had once belonged to the nobles' greatest hero, Sulla, and he knew how much it must irritate them to see it in the hands of a new man from Arpinum. The villa had not been redecorated for more than a decade, and when he took possession an entire wall was devoted to a mural showing the dictator receiving a military decoration from his troops. Cicero made sure all his neighbours knew that his first act as owner was to have it whitewashed over.

Happy, then, was Cicero in the autumn of his thirty-ninth year: prosperous, popular, well rested after a summer in the country, and looking forward to the elections the following July, when he would be old enough to stand for a praetorship – the final stepping-stone before the glittering prize of the consulship itself.

And at this critical juncture in his fortunes, just as his luck was about to desert him and his life become interesting again, my narrative resumes.

At the end of September it was Pompey's birthday, and for the third year in succession Cicero received a summons to attend a dinner in his honour. He groaned when he opened the message, for he had discovered that there are few blessings in life more onerous than the friendship of a great man. At first, he had found it flattering to be invited into Pompey's inner circle. But after a while he grew weary of listening to the same old military anecdotes – usually illustrated by the manoeuvring of plates and decanters around the dinner table – of how the young general had outwitted three Marian armies at Auximum, or killed seventeen thousand Numidians in a single afternoon at the age of twenty-four, or finally defeated the Spanish rebels near Valencia. Pompey had been giving orders since he was seventeen and perhaps for this reason had developed none of Cicero's subtlety of intellect. Conversation as the senator enjoyed it – spontaneous wit, shared gossip, sharp observations which might be spun off mutually into some profound or fantastic dissertation on the nature of human affairs – all this was alien to Pompey. The general liked to hold forth against a background of respectful silence, assert some platitude, and then sit back and bask in the flattery of his guests. Cicero used to say he would sooner have all his teeth drawn by a drunken barber in the Forum Boarium than listen to another of these mealtime monologues.

The root of the problem was that Pompey was bored. At the end of his consulship, as promised, he had retired into private life with his wife, young son and baby daughter. But then what? Lacking any talent for oratory, there was nothing to occupy him in the law courts. Literary composition held no interest for him. He could only watch in a stew of jealousy as Lucullus continued his conquest of Mithradates. Not yet forty, his future, as the saying went, seemed all behind him. He would make occasional forays down from his mansion and into the senate, not to speak but to listen to the debates – processions for which he insisted on an immense escort of friends and clients. Cicero, who felt obliged to walk at least part of the way with him, observed that it was like watching an elephant trying to make itself at home in an anthill.

But still, he was the greatest man in the world, with a huge following among the voters, and not to be crossed, especially with an election less than a year away. Only that summer he had secured a tribuneship for his crony Gabinius: he still kept a hand in politics. So on the thirtieth day of September, Cicero went off as usual to the birthday party, returning later in the evening to regale Quintus, Lucius and myself with an account of events. Like a child, Pompey delighted in receiving presents, and Cicero had taken him a manuscript letter in the hand of Zeno, the founder of stoicism, two centuries old and extremely valuable, which had been acquired for him in Athens by Atticus. He would dearly have loved to have kept it for his own library in Tusculum, but he hoped that by giving it to Pompey he could begin to tempt the general into an interest in philosophy. Instead, Pompey had barely glanced at it before setting it aside in favour of a gift from Gabinius, of a silver rhino horn containing some Egyptian aphrodisiac made of baboon excrement. 'How I wish I could have retrieved that letter!' groaned Cicero, flopping down on to a couch, the back of his hand resting on his forehead. 'Even now it's probably being used by some kitchen maid to light the fire.'

'Who else was there?' asked Quintus eagerly. He had only been back in Rome for a few days, following his term as quaestor in Umbria, and was avid for the latest news.

'Oh, the usual cohort. Our fine new tribune-elect Gabinius, obviously, and his father-in-law, the art connoisseur Palicanus; Rome's greatest dancer, Afranius; that Spanish creature of

Pompey's, Balbus; Varro, the household polymath. Oh, and Marcus Fonteius,' he added lightly, but not so lightly that Lucius did not immediately detect the significance.

'And what did you talk about with Fonteius?' enquired Lucius, in the same clumsy attempt at an offhand manner.

'This and that.'

'His prosecution?'

'Naturally.'

'And who is defending the rascal?'

Cicero paused, and then said quietly, 'I am.'

I should explain, for those not familiar with the case, that this Fonteius had been governor of Further Gaul about five years earlier, and that one winter, when Pompey was particularly hard pressed fighting the rebels in Spain, he had sent the beleaguered general sufficient supplies and fresh recruits to enable him to survive until the spring. That had been the start of their friendship. Fonteius had gone on to make himself extremely rich, in the Verres manner, by extorting various illegal taxes out of the native population. The Gauls had at first put up with it, telling themselves that robbery and exploitation have ever been the handmaids of civilisation. But after Cicero's triumphant prosecution of the governor of Sicily, the chief of the Gauls, Induciomarus, had come to Rome to ask the senator to represent them in the extortion court. Lucius had been all for it; in fact it was he who had brought Induciomarus to the house: a wild-looking creature, dressed in his barbarian outfit of jacket and trousers – he gave me quite a shock when I opened the door to him one morning. Cicero, however, had politely declined. A year had passed, but now the Gauls had finally found a credible legal team in Plaetorius, who was a praetor-elect, and Marcus Fabius as his junior. The case would soon be in court.

'That is outrageous,' said Lucius, hotly. 'You cannot defend him. He is as guilty as Verres was.'

'Nonsense. He has neither killed anyone nor falsely imprisoned anyone either. The worse that can be said is that he once imposed excessive duties on the wine traders of Narbonne, and made some locals pay more than others to repair the roads. Besides,' added Cicero quickly, before Lucius could challenge this somewhat generous interpretation of Fonteius's activities, 'who are you or I to determine his guilt? It is a matter for the court to decide, not us. Or would you be a tyrant and deny him an advocate?'

'I would deny him *your* advocacy,' Lucius responded. 'You have heard from Induciomarus's own lips the evidence against him. Is all that to be cancelled out, simply because Fonteius is a friend of Pompey?'

'It has nothing to do with Pompey.'

'Then why do it?'

'Politics,' said Cicero, suddenly sitting up and swinging himself round so that his feet were planted on the floor. He fixed his gaze on Lucius and said very seriously: 'The most fatal error for any statesman is to allow his fellow countrymen, even for an instant, to suspect that he puts the interests of foreigners above those of his own people. That is the lie which my enemies spread about me after I represented the Sicilians in the Verres case, and that is the calumny which I can lay to rest if I defend Fonteius now.'

'And the Gauls?'

'The Gauls will be represented perfectly adequately by Plaetorius.'

'Not as well as they would be by you.'

'But you say yourself that Fonteius has a weak case. Let the weakest case be defended by the strongest advocate. What could be fairer than that?'

Cicero flashed him his most charming smile, but for once Lucius refused to be parted from his anger. Knowing, I suspect, that the only sure way to defeat Cicero in argument was to withdraw from the conversation altogether, he stood and limped across to the atrium. I had not realised until that moment how ill he looked, how thin and stooped; he had never really recovered from the strain of his efforts in Sicily. 'Words, words, words,' he said bitterly. 'Is there no end to the tricks you can make them perform? But, as with all men, your great strength is also your weakness, Marcus, and I am sorry for you, absolutely I am, because soon you will not be able to tell your tricks from the truth. And then you will be lost.'

'The truth,' laughed Cicero. 'Now there is a loose term for a philosopher to use!' But he was addressing his witticism to the air, for Lucius had gone.

'He will be back,' said Quintus.

But he did not come back, and over the following days Cicero went about his preparations for the trial with the determined expression of a man who has resigned himself to some distasteful but necessary surgical procedure. As for his client: Fonteius had been anticipating his prosecution for three years, and had used the time well, to acquire a mass of evidence to support his defence. He had witnesses from Spain and Gaul, including officers from Pompey's camp, and various sly and greedy tax farmers and merchants – members of the Roman community in Gaul, who would have sworn that night was day and land sea if it would have turned them a reasonable profit. The only trouble, as Cicero realised once he had mastered his brief, was that Fonteius was plainly guilty. He sat for a long time staring at the wall in his study, while I tiptoed around him, and it is important that I convey what he was doing, for it is necessary in order to understand his character. He was not merely trying, as a cynical and second-rate advocate might have done, to devise some clever tactic in order to outwit the prosecution. *He was trying to find something to believe in.* That was the core of his genius, both as an advocate and as a statesman. 'What convinces is conviction,' he used to say. 'You simply must believe the argument you are advancing, otherwise you are lost. No chain of reasoning, no matter how logical or elegant or brilliant, will win the case, if your audience senses that belief is missing.' Just one thing to believe in, that was all he needed, and then he could latch on to it, build out from it, embellish it, and transform it just for the space of an hour or two into the most important issue in the world, and deliver it with a passion that would obliterate the flimsy rationality of his opponents. Afterwards he would usually forget it entirely. And what did he believe in when it came to Marcus Fonteius? He gazed at the wall for many hours and concluded only this: that his client was a Roman, being assailed within his own city by Rome's traditional enemy, the Gauls, and that whatever the rights and wrongs of the case, that was a kind of treachery.

Such was the line which Cicero took when he found himself once again in the familiar surroundings of the extortion court before the Temple of Castor. The trial lasted from the end of October until the middle of November, and was most keenly fought, witness by witness, right up until the final day, when Cicero delivered the closing speech for the defence. From my place behind the senator, I had, from the opening day, kept an eye out for Lucius among the crowd of spectators, but it was only on that last morning that I fancied I saw him, a pale shadow, propped against a pillar at the very back of the audience. And if it was he – and I do not know it was – I have often wondered what he thought of his cousin's oratory, as he tore into the evidence of the Gauls, jabbing his finger at Induciomarus – 'Does he actually know what is meant by giving evidence? Is the greatest chief of the Gauls worthy to be set on the same level as even the meanest citizen of Rome?' – and demanding to know how a Roman jury could possibly believe the word of a man whose gods demanded human victims: 'For who does not know that to this very day they retain the monstrous and barbarous custom of sacrificing men?' What would he have said to Cicero's description of the Gaulish witnesses, 'swaggering from end to end of the forum, with proud and unflinching expressions on their faces and barbarian menaces upon their lips'? And what would he have made of Cicero's brilliant *coup de théâtre* at the very end, of producing in court, in the closing moments of his speech, Fonteius's sister, a vestal virgin, clad from head to toe in her official garb of a flowing white gown, with a white linen shawl around her narrow shoulders, and who raised her white veil to show the jury her tears – a sight which made her brother also break down weeping? Cicero laid his hand gently on his client's shoulder.

'From this peril, gentlemen, defend a gallant and blameless citizen. Let the world see that you place more confidence in the evidence of our fellow countrymen than in that of foreigners, that you have greater regard for the welfare of our citizens than for the caprice of our foes, that you set more store by the entreaties of she who presides over your sacrifices than by the effrontery of those who have waged war against the sacrifices and shrines of all the world. Finally, gentlemen, see to it – and here the dignity of the Roman people is most vitally engaged –

see to it that you show that the prayers of a vestal maid have more weight with you than the threats of Gauls.'

Well, that speech certainly did the trick, both for Fonteius, who was acquitted, and for Cicero, who was never again regarded as anything less than the most fervent patriot in Rome. I looked up after I had finished making my shorthand record, but it was impossible to discern individuals in the crowd any more — it had become a single, seething creature, aroused by Cicero's technique to a chanting ecstasy of national self-glorification. Anyway, I sincerely hope that Lucius was not present, and there must surely be a chance that he was not, for it was only a few hours later that he was discovered at his home quite dead.

Cicero was dining privately with Terentia when the message came. The bearer was one of Lucius's slaves. Scarcely more than a boy, he was weeping uncontrollably, so it fell to me to take the news in to the senator. He looked up blankly from his meal when I told him, and stared straight at me, and said irritably, 'No,' as if I had offered him the wrong set of documents in court. And for a long time that was all he said: 'No, no.' He did not move; he did not even blink. The working of his brain seemed locked. It was Terentia who eventually spoke, and suggested gently that he should go and find out what had happened, whereupon he started searching dumbly for his shoes. 'Keep an eye on him, Tiro,' she said quietly to me.

Grief kills time. All that I retain of that night, and of the days which followed, are fragments of scenes, like some luridly brilliant hallucinations left behind after a fever. I recall how thin and wasted Lucius's body was when we found it, lying on its right side in his cot, the knees drawn up, the left hand laid flat across his eyes, and how Cicero, in the traditional manner, bent over him with a candle, to call him back to life. 'What was he seeing?' – that was what he kept asking: 'What was he seeing?' Cicero was not, as I have indicated, a superstitious man, but he could not rid himself of the conviction that Lucius had been presented with a vision of unparalleled horror at the end, and that this had somehow frightened him to death. As to how he died – well here I must confess to carrying a secret all these years, of which I shall be glad now to unburden myself. There was a pestle and mortar in the corner of that little room, with what Cicero – and I, too, at first – took to be a bunch of fennel lying beside it. It was a reasonable supposition, for among Lucius's many chronic ailments was poor digestion, which he attempted to relieve by a solution of fennel oil. Only later, when I was clearing the room, did I rub those lacy leaves with my thumb, and detect the frightful, musty, dead-mouse odour of hemlock. I knew then that Lucius had tired of this life, and for whatever reason – despair at its injustices, weariness with his ailments – had chosen to die like his hero, Socrates. This information I always meant to share with Cicero and Quintus. But for some reason, in the sadness of those days, I kept it to myself, and then the proper time for disclosure had passed, and it seemed better to let them continue to believe he had died involuntarily.

I also recall how Cicero spent such a great sum on flowers and incense that, after Lucius had been cleaned and anointed and laid on his funeral couch in his finest toga, his skinny feet pointing towards the door, he seemed, even in that drab November, to be in an Elysian grove of petals and fragrant scent. I remember the surprising number, for such a solitary man, of friends and neighbours who came to pay their respects, and the funeral procession at dusk out to the Esquiline Field, with young Frugi weeping so hard he could not catch his breath. I recall the dirges and the music, and the respectful glances of the citizens along the route – for this was a Cicero they were bearing to meet his ancestors, and the name now counted for something in Rome. Out on the frozen field, the body lay on its pyre under the stars, and the great orator struggled to deliver a brief eulogy. But his words would not perform their tricks for him on that occasion, and he had to give up. He could not even collect himself sufficiently to apply the torch to ignite the wood, and passed the task instead to Quintus. As the flames shot high the mourners threw their gifts of scent and spices on to the bonfire, and the perfumed smoke, flecked with orange sparks, curled up to the Milky Way. That night I sat with the senator in his study as he dictated a letter to Atticus, and it is surely a tribute to the affection which Lucius also inspired in that noble heart that this was the first of Cicero's hundreds of letters which Atticus chose to preserve:

'Knowing me as well as you do, you can appreciate better than most how deeply my cousin Lucius's death has grieved me, and what a loss it means to me both in public and in private life. All the pleasure that one human being's kindness and charm can give another I had from him.'

Despite having lived in Rome for many years, Lucius had always said that he wished to have his ashes interred in the family vault in Arpinum. Accordingly, on the morning after the cremation, the Cicero brothers set off with his remains on the three-day journey east, accompanied by their wives, having sent word ahead to their father of what had happened. Naturally, I went too, for although Cicero was in the mourning period, his legal and political correspondence could not be neglected.

Nevertheless, for the first – and, I think, the only – time in all our years together, he transacted no official business on the road, but simply sat with his chin in his hand, staring at the passing countryside. He and Terentia were in one carriage, Quintus and Pomponia in another, endlessly bickering – so much so that I saw Cicero draw his brother aside and plead with him, for the sake of Atticus, if for no one else, to make the marriage work. 'Well,' retorted Quintus, with some justice, 'if the good opinion of Atticus is that important to you, why do *you* not marry her?' We stayed the first night at the villa in Tusculum, and had reached as far as Ferentium on the Via Latina when a message reached the brothers from Arpinum that their father had collapsed and died the previous day.

Given that he was in his sixties and had been ailing for many years, this was obviously less of a shock than the death of Lucius (the news of which had apparently proved the final blow to the old man's fragile health). But to leave one house festooned with the pine and cypress boughs of mourning and to arrive at another similarly adorned was the height of melancholy, made worse by the mischance that we reached Arpinum on the twenty-fifth day of November, that date kept sacred to Proserpina, Queen of Hades, who carries into effect the curses of men upon the souls of the dead. The Ciceros' villa lay three miles out of the town, down a winding stony road, in a valley ringed by high mountains. It was cold at this altitude, the peaks already draped with the vestal veils of snow which they would wear till May. I had not been back for ten years, and to see it all as I remembered aroused strange feelings in me. Unlike Cicero, I had always preferred the country to the town. I had been born here; my mother and father had both lived and died here; for the first quarter-century of my life, these springy meadows and crystal streams, with their tall poplars and verdant banks, had been the limit of my world. Seeing how much I was affected, and knowing how devoted I had been to the old master, Cicero invited me to accompany him and Quintus to the funeral couch, to say goodbye. In a way, I owed their father almost as much as they did, for he had taken a shine to me when I was a lad, and educated me so that I could help with his books, and then had given me the chance to travel with his son. As I bent to kiss his cold hand, I had a strong sense of returning home, and then the idea came to me that perhaps I could remain here, and act as steward, marry some girl of equal station, and have a child of my own. My parents, despite their status as domestic slaves rather than farm labourers, had both died in their early forties; I had to reckon on having, at best, only ten years left myself. (Little do we know how the fates will play us!) I ached to imagine that I might depart the earth without issue and I resolved to raise the matter with Cicero at the earliest opportunity.

Thus it was that I came to have rather a profound conversation with him. On the day after our arrival, the old master was buried in the family vault, then Lucius's ashes in their alabaster vase were interred beside him, and finally a pig was sacrificed to keep the spot holy. The next morning Cicero took a tour around his newly inherited estate, and I went with him in case he needed to dictate any notes, for the place (which was so heavily mortgaged as to be virtually worthless) was in a dilapidated state, and much work needed to be done. Cicero observed that it was originally his mother who had managed the property; his father had always been too much of a dreamer to cope with land agents and agricultural suppliers; after her death, he had slowly let it all go to ruin. This was, I think, the first time in more than a decade in his service that I had heard Cicero mention his mother. Helvia was her name. She had died twenty years earlier, when he was in his teens, by which time he had left for Rome to be educated. I could barely remember anything of her myself, except that she had a reputation for terrible strictness and meanness – the sort of mistress who marked the jars to check if the slaves had stolen anything, and took great pleasure in whipping them if she suspected that they had.

'Never a word of praise from her, Tiro,' he said, 'either for myself or my brother. Yet I tried so hard to please her.' He stopped and stared across the fields to the fast-moving, ice-cold river – the Fibrenus it was called – in the centre of which was a little island, with a wooded grove and a small pavilion, half tumbled down. 'That was where I used to go and sit as a boy,' he said wistfully. 'The hours I spent there! In my mind I was going to be another Achilles, albeit of the law courts rather than the battlefield. You know your Homer: "Far to excel, out-topping all the rest!"'

He was silent for a while, and I recognised this as my opportunity. And so I put my plan to him – I gabbled it out, fairly ineptly I suppose: that I might remain here and bring the farm back up to scratch for him – and all the while he kept looking at that childhood island of his. 'I know exactly what you mean,' he said with a sigh when I had finished. 'I feel it, too. This is the true fatherland of myself and my brother, for we are descended from a very ancient family of this place. Here are our ancestral cults, here is our race, here are many memorials of our forefathers. What more need I say?' He turned to look at me, and I noticed how very clear and blue his eyes were, despite all his recent weeping. 'But consider what we have seen this week – the empty, senseless shells of those we loved – and think what a terrible audit Death lays upon a man. Ah!' He shook his head vigorously, as if emptying it of a bad dream, then returned his attention to the landscape. After a while he said, in a very different voice: 'Well, I tell you, for my part, I do not propose to die leaving one ounce of talent unspent, or one mile of energy left in my legs. And it is your destiny, my dear fellow, to walk the road with me.' We were standing side by side; he prodded me gently in the ribs with his elbow. 'Come on, Tiro! A secretary who can take down my words almost as quickly as I can utter them? Such a marvel cannot be spared to count sheep in Arpinum! So let us have no more talk of such foolishness.'

And that was the end of my pastoral idyll. We walked back up to the house, and later that afternoon – or perhaps it was the following day: the memory plays such tricks – we heard the sound of a horse galloping very fast along the road from the town. It had started to rain, that much I do remember, and everyone was cooped up irritably indoors. Cicero was reading, Terentia sewing, Quintus practising drawing his sword, Pomponia lying down with a headache (She still maintained that politics was 'boring', which drove Cicero into a quiet frenzy. 'Such a stupid thing to say!' he once complained to me. 'Politics? Boring? Politics is history on the wing! What other sphere of human activity calls forth all that is most noble in men's souls, and all that is most base? Or has such excitement? Or more vividly exposes our strengths and weaknesses? Boring? You might as well say that life itself is boring!') Anyway, at the noise of hooves clattering to a halt, I went out to greet the rider, and took from him a letter bearing the seal of Pompey the Great. Cicero opened it himself and let out a shout of surprise. 'Rome has been attacked!' he announced, causing even Pomponia to rouse herself briefly from her couch. He read on rapidly. The consular war fleet had been set on fire in its winter anchorage at Ostia.

Two praetors, Sextilius and Bellinus, together with their lictors and staff, had been kidnapped. It was all the work of pirates and designed to spread terror, pure and simple. There was panic in the capital. The people were demanding action. 'Pompey wants me with him straightaway,' said Cicero. 'He is calling a council of war at his country estate the day after tomorrow.'

XI

Leaving the others behind and travelling hard in a two-wheeled carriage (Cicero never went on horseback if he could avoid it), we retraced our route, reaching the villa at Tusculum by nightfall the following day. Pompey's estate lay on the other side of the Alban Hills, only five miles to the south. The lazy household slaves were stunned to find their master back so quickly and had to scramble to put the place in order. Cicero bathed and went directly to bed, although I do not believe he slept well, for I fancied I heard him in the middle of the night, moving around his library, and in the morning I found a copy of Aristotle's *Nicomachean Ethics* half unrolled on his desk. But politicians are resilient creatures. When I went into his chamber he was already dressed and keen to discover what Pompey had in mind. As soon as it was light we set off. Our road took us around the great expanse of the Alban Lake, and when the sun broke pink over the snowy mountain ridge we could see the silhouettes of the fishermen pulling in their nets from the glittering waters. 'Is there any country in the world more beautiful than Italy?' Cicero murmured, inhaling deeply, and although he did not express it, I knew what he was thinking, because I was thinking it too: that it was a relief to have escaped the enfolding gloom of Arpinum, and that there is nothing quite like death to make one feel alive.

At length we turned off the road and passed through a pair of imposing gates on to a long driveway of white gravel lined with cypresses. The formal gardens to either side were filled with marble statues, no doubt acquired by the general during his various campaigns. Gardeners were raking the winter leaves and trimming the box hedges. The impression was one of vast, quiet, confident wealth. As Cicero strode through the entrance into the great house he whispered to me to stay close by, and I slipped in unobtrusively behind him, carrying a document case. (My advice to anyone, incidentally, who wishes to be inconspicuous, is always to carry documents: they cast a cloak of invisibility around their bearer that is the equal of anything in the Greek legends.) Pompey was greeting his guests in the atrium, playing the grand country seigneur, with his third wife, Mucia, beside him, and his son, Gnaeus – who must have been eleven by this time – and his infant daughter, Pompeia, who had just learned to walk. Mucia was an attractive, statuesque matron of the Metellus clan, in her late twenties and obviously pregnant again. One of Pompey's peculiarities, I later discovered, was that he always tended to love his wife, whoever she happened to be at the time. She was laughing at some remark which had just been made to her, and when the originator of this witticism turned I saw that it was Julius Caesar. This surprised me, and certainly startled Cicero, because up to this point we had seen only the familiar trio of Piceneans: Palicanus, Afranius and Gabinius. Besides, Caesar had been in Spain for more than a year, serving as quaestor. But here he was, lithe and well built, with his lean, intelligent face, his amused brown eyes, and those thin strands of dark hair which he combed so carefully across his sunburnt pate. (But why am I bothering to describe him? The whole world knows what he looked like!)

In all, eight senators gathered that morning: Pompey, Cicero and Caesar; the three Piceneans mentioned above; Varro, Pompey's house intellectual, then aged fifty; and Caius Cornelius, who had served under Pompey as his quaestor in Spain, and who was now, along with Gabinius, a tribune-elect. I was not as conspicuous as I had feared, as many of the principals had also brought along a secretary or bag-carrier of some sort; we all stood respectfully to one side. After refreshments had been served, and the children had been taken away by their nurses, and the Lady Mucia had graciously said goodbye to each of her husband's guests in turn – lingering somewhat over Caesar, I noticed – slaves fetched in chairs so that everyone could sit. I was on the point of leaving with the other attendants when Cicero suggested to Pompey that, as I was famous throughout Rome as the inventor of a marvellous new shorthand system – these were his words – I might stay and keep a minute of what was said. I blushed with embarrassment. Pompey looked at me suspiciously, and I thought he was going to forbid it, but then he shrugged and said, 'Very well. That might be useful. But there will only be one copy made, and I shall keep it. Is that acceptable to everyone?' There was a noise of assent, whereupon a stool was fetched for me and I found myself sitting in the corner with my notebook open and my stylus gripped in a sweaty hand.

The chairs were arranged in a semicircle, and when all his guests were seated, Pompey stood. He was, as I have said, no orator on a public platform. But on his own ground, among those whom he thought of as his lieutenants, he radiated power and authority. Although my verbatim transcript was taken from me, I can still remember much of what he said, because I had to write it up from my notes, and that always causes a thing to stick in my mind. He began by giving the latest details of the pirate attack on Ostia: nineteen consular war triremes destroyed, a couple of hundred men killed, grain warehouses torched, two praetors – one of whom had been inspecting the granaries and the other the fleet – seized in their official robes, along with their retinues and their symbolic rods and axes. A ransom demand for their release had arrived in Rome yesterday. 'But for my part,' said Pompey, 'I do not believe we should negotiate with such people, as it will only encourage them in their criminal acts.' (Everyone nodded in agreement.) The raid on Ostia, he continued, was a turning point in the history of Rome. This was not an isolated incident, but merely the most daring in a long line of such outrages, which included the kidnapping of the noble Lady Antonia from her villa in Misenum (she whose own father had led an expedition against the pirates!), the robbery of temple treasures from Croton, and the surprise attacks on Brundisium and Caieta. Where would be struck next? What Rome was facing was a threat very different from that posed by a conventional enemy. These pirates were a new type of ruthless foe, with no government to represent them and no treaties to bind them. Their bases were not confined to a single state. They had no unified system of command. They were a worldwide pestilence, a parasite which needed to be stamped out, otherwise Rome – despite her overwhelming military superiority – would never again know security or peace. The existing national security system, of giving men of consular rank a single command of limited duration in an individual theatre, was clearly inadequate to the challenge.

'Long before Ostia, I had been devoting much careful study to this problem,' declared Pompey, 'and I believe this unique

enemy demands a unique response. Now is our opportunity.'
He clapped his hands and a pair of slaves carried in a large
map of the Mediterranean, which they set up on a stand beside
him. His audience leaned forwards to get a better look, for
they could see mysterious lines had been drawn vertically across
both sea and land. 'The basis of our strategy from now on
must be to combine the military and the political spheres,' said
Pompey. 'We hit them with everything.' He took up a pointer
and rapped it on the painted board. 'I propose we divide the
Mediterranean into fifteen zones, from the Pillars of Hercules
here in the west to the waters of Egypt and Syria here in the
east, each zone to have its own legate, whose task will be to
scour his area clean of pirates and then to make treaties with
the local rulers to ensure the brigands' vessels never return to
their waters. All captured pirates are to be handed over to
Roman jurisdiction. Any ruler who refuses to cooperate will
be regarded as Rome's enemy. Those who are not with us are
against us. These fifteen legates will all report to one supreme
commander, who will have absolute authority over all the
mainland for a distance of fifty miles from the sea. I shall be
that commander.'

There was a long silence. It was Cicero who spoke first. 'Your
plan is certainly a bold one, Pompey, although some might
consider it a disproportionate response to the loss of nineteen
triremes. You do realise that such a concentration of power in a
single pair of hands has never been proposed in the entire history
of the republic?'

'As a matter of fact, I *do* realise that,' replied Pompey. He tried
to keep a straight face, but in the end he could not stop it breaking
into a broad grin, and quickly everyone was laughing, apart from
Cicero, who looked as if his world had just fallen apart – which

in a sense it had, because this was, as he put it afterwards, a plan for the domination of the world by one man, nothing less, and he had few doubts where it would lead. 'Perhaps I should have walked out there and then,' he mused to me later on the journey home. 'That is what poor, honest Lucius would have urged me to do. Yet Pompey would still have gone ahead, either with me or without me, and all I would have done is earned his enmity, and that would have put paid to my chances of a praetorship. Everything I do now must be viewed through the prism of that election.'

And so, of course, he stayed, as the discussion meandered on over the next few hours, from grand military strategy to grubby political tactics. The plan was for Gabinius to place a bill before the Roman people soon after he took office, which would be in about a week, setting up the special command and ordering it be given to Pompey; then he and Cornelius would dare any of the other tribunes to veto it. (One must remember that in the days of the republic only an assembly of the people had the power to make laws; the senate's voice was influential, but not decisive; their task was to implement the people's will.)

'What do you say, Cicero?' asked Pompey. 'You have been very quiet.'

'I say that Rome is indeed fortunate,' replied Cicero carefully, 'to have a man with such experience and global vision as yourself to call on in her hour of peril. But we must be realistic. There will be huge resistance to this proposal in the senate. The aristocrats, in particular, will say that it is nothing more than a naked grab for power dressed up as patriotic necessity.'

'I resent that,' said Pompey.

'Well, you may resent it all you like, but you will still need to demonstrate that it is not the case,' retorted Cicero, who knew that the surest way to a great man's confidence, curiously enough, is often to speak harshly back to him, thus conveying an appearance of disinterested candour. 'They will also say that this commission to deal with the pirates is simply a stepping-stone to your true objective, which is to replace Lucullus as commander of the Eastern legions.' To that, the great man made no response other than a grunt – he could not, because that really was his true objective. 'And finally, they will set about finding a tribune or two of their own, to veto Gabinius's bill.'

'It sounds to me as though you should not be here, Cicero,' sneered Gabinius. He was something of a dandy, with thick and wavy hair slicked back in a quiff, in imitation of his chief. 'To achieve our objective will require bold hearts, and possibly stout fists, not the quibbles of clever lawyers.'

'You will need hearts and fists *and* lawyers before you are done, Gabinius, believe me,' responded Cicero. 'The moment you lose the legal immunity conferred by your tribuneship, the aristocrats will have you in court and fighting for your life. You will need a clever lawyer, well enough, and so will you, Cornelius.'

'Let us move on,' said Pompey. 'Those are the problems. Do you have any solutions to offer?'

'Well,' replied Cicero, 'for a start, I strongly urge that your name should not appear anywhere in the bill setting up the supreme command.'

'But it was my idea!' protested Pompey, sounding exactly like a child whose game was being taken over by his playmates.

'True, but I still say it would be prudent not to specify the actual name of the commander at the very outset. You will be the focus of the most terrible envy and rage in the senate. Even the sensible men, whose support we can normally rely on, will baulk at this. You must make the central issue the defeat of the pirates, not the future of Pompey the Great. Everyone will know the post is designed for you; there is no need to spell it out.'

'But what am I to say when I lay the bill before the people?' asked Gabinius. 'That any fool off the street can hold the office?'

'Obviously not,' said Cicero, with a great effort at patience. 'I would strike out the name "Pompey" and insert the phrase "senator of consular rank". That limits it to the fifteen or twenty living ex-consuls.'

'So who might be the rival candidates?' asked Afranius.

'Crassus,' said Pompey at once: his old enemy was never far from his thoughts. 'Perhaps Catulus. Then there is Metellus Pius – doddery, but still a force. Hortensius has a following. Isauricus. Gellius. Cotta. Curio. Even the Lucullus brothers.'

'Well, I suppose if you are really worried,' said Cicero, 'we could always specify that the supreme commander should be any ex-consul whose name begins with a P.' For a moment, no one reacted, and I was certain he had gone too far. But then Caesar threw back his head and laughed, and the rest – seeing that Pompey was smiling weakly – joined in. 'Believe me, Pompey,' continued Cicero in a reassuring tone, 'most of these are far too old and idle to be a threat. Crassus will be your most dangerous rival, simply because he is so rich and jealous of you. But if it comes to a vote you will defeat him overwhelmingly, I promise you.'

'I agree with Cicero,' said Caesar. 'Let us clear our hurdles one at a time. First, the principle of the supreme command; then, the name of the commander.' I was struck by the authority with which he spoke, despite being the most junior man present.

'Very well,' said Pompey, nodding judiciously. 'It is settled. The central issue must be the defeat of the pirates, not the future of Pompey the Great.' And on that note, the conference adjourned for lunch.

There now followed a squalid incident which it embarrasses me to recall, but which I feel I must, in the interests of history, set down. For several hours, while the senators lunched, and afterwards strolled in the garden, I worked as rapidly as I could to translate my shorthand notes into a fair manuscript record of proceedings, which I could then present to Pompey. When I had finished, it occurred to me that perhaps I should check what I had written with Cicero, in case there might be something in it to which he objected. The chamber where the conference had been held was empty, and so was the atrium, but I could hear the senator's distinctive voice, and set off, clutching my roll of paper, in the direction from which I judged it was coming. I crossed a colonnaded courtyard, where a fountain played, then followed the portico round to another, inner garden. But now his voice had faded altogether. I stopped to listen. There was only birdsong, and the trickling of water. Then, suddenly, from somewhere very close, and loud enough to make me jump, I heard a woman groan, as if in agony. Like a fool, I turned, and took a few more steps, and through an open door was confronted by the sight of Caesar with Pompey's wife. The Lady Mucia did not see me. She had her head down between her forearms, her dress was bunched up around her waist, and she was bent over a table, gripping the edge so tightly her knuckles were white. But Caesar saw me well enough, for he was facing the door, thrusting into her from behind, his right hand cupped around her swollen belly, his left resting casually on his hip, like a dandy standing on a street corner. For exactly how long our eyes met I cannot say, but he stares back at me even now – those fathomless dark eyes of his gazing through the smoke and chaos of all the years that were to follow – amused, unabashed, challenging. I fled.

By this time, most of the senators had wandered back into the conference chamber. Cicero was discussing philosophy with Varro, the most distinguished scholar in Rome, of whose works on philology and antiquities I was deeply in awe. On any other occasion I would have been honoured to be introduced, but my head was still reeling from the scene I had just witnessed and I cannot remember a thing of what he said. I handed the minutes to Cicero, who skimmed them quickly, took my pen from me, and made a small amendment, all the while still talking to Varro. Pompey must have noticed what he was doing, for he came across with a big smile on his wide face, and pretended to be angry, taking the minutes away from Cicero and accusing him of inserting promises he had never made – 'though I think you can count on my vote for the praetorship,' he said, and slapped him on the back. Until a short while earlier, I had considered Pompey a kind of god among men – a booming, confident war hero – but now, knowing what I did, I thought him also sad. 'This is quite remarkable,' he said to me, as he ran his huge thumb down the columns of words. 'You have captured my voice exactly. How much do you want for him, Cicero?'

'I have already turned down an enormous sum from Crassus,' replied Cicero.

'Well, if ever there is a bidding war, be sure that I am included,' said Caesar, in his rasping voice, coming up behind us. 'I would dearly love to get my hands on Tiro.' But he said it in such a friendly way, accompanying it with a wink, that none of the others heard the menace in his words, while I felt almost faint with terror.

'The day that I am parted from Tiro,' said Cicero, prophetically as it turned out, 'is the day that I quit public life.'

'Now I am doubly determined to buy him,' said Caesar, and Cicero joined in the general laughter.

After agreeing to keep secret everything that had been discussed, and to meet in Rome in a few days' time, the group broke up. The moment we turned out of the gates and on to the road to Tusculum, Cicero let out a long-pent-up cry of frustration and struck the side of the carriage with the palm of his hand. 'A criminal conspiracy!' he said, shaking his head in despair. 'Worse – a *stupid* criminal conspiracy. This is the trouble, Tiro, when soldiers decide to play at politics. They imagine that all they need to do is issue an order, and everyone will obey. They never see that the very thing which makes them attractive in the first place – that they are supposedly these great patriots, above the squalor of politics – must ultimately defeat them, because either they *do* stay above politics, in which case they go nowhere, or they get down in the muck along with the rest of us, and show themselves to be just as venal as everyone else.' He stared out at the lake, darkening now in the winter light. 'What do you make of Caesar?' he said suddenly, to which I returned a noncommittal answer about his seeming very ambitious. 'He certainly is that. So much so, there were times today when it occurred to me that this whole fantastic scheme is actually not Pompey's at all, but Caesar's. That, at least, would explain his presence.'

I pointed out that Pompey had described it as his own idea.

'And no doubt Pompey thinks it is. But that is the nature of the man. You make a remark to him, and then you find it being repeated back to you, as if it were his own. "The central issue must be the defeat of the pirates, not the future of Pompey the Great." That is a typical example. Sometimes, just to amuse myself, I have argued against my own original assertion, and waited to see how long it was before I heard my rebuttal coming back at me too.' He frowned and nodded. 'I am sure I am right. Caesar is quite clever enough to have planted the seed and left it to flower on its own. I wonder how much time he has spent with Pompey. He seems very well bedded in.'

It was on the tip of my tongue then to tell him what I had witnessed, but a combination of fear of Caesar, my own shyness, and a feeling that Cicero would not think the better of me for spying – that I would in some sense be contaminated myself by describing the whole sordid business – caused me to swallow my words. It was not until many years later – after Caesar's death, in fact, when he could no longer harm me and I was altogether more confident – that I revealed my story. Cicero, then an old man, was silent for a long time. 'I understand your discretion,' he said at last, 'and in many ways I applaud it. But I have to say, my dear friend, that I wish you *had* informed me. Perhaps then things might have turned out differently. At least I would have realised earlier the kind of breathtakingly reckless man we were dealing with. But by the time I did understand, it was too late.'

The Rome to which we returned a few days later was jittery and full of rumours. The burning of Ostia had been clearly visible to the whole city as a red glow in the western night sky. Such an attack on the capital was unprecedented, and when Gabinius and Cornelius took office as tribunes on the tenth day of December, they moved quickly to fan the sparks of public anxiety into the flames of panic. They caused extra sentries to be posted at the city's gates. Wagons and pedestrians entering Rome were stopped and searched at random for weapons. The wharves and warehouses along the river were patrolled both day and night, and severe penalties were promulgated for citizens convicted of hoarding grain, with the inevitable result that the three great food markets of Rome in those days – the Emporium, the Macellum, and the Forum Boarium – immediately ran out of supplies. The vigorous new tribunes also dragged the outgoing consul, the hapless Marcius Rex, before a meeting of the people, and subjected him to a merciless cross-examination about the security lapses which had led to the fiasco at Ostia. Other witnesses were found to testify about the menace of the pirates, and that menace grew with every retelling. They had a thousand ships! They were not lone raiders at all, but an organised conspiracy! They had squadrons and admirals and fearsome weapons of poison tipped arrows and Greek fire! Nobody in the senate dared object to any of this, for fear of seeming complacent – not even when a chain of beacons was built all along the road to the sea, to be lit if pirate vessels were seen heading for the mouth of the Tiber. 'This is absurd,' Cicero said to me, on the morning we went out to inspect these most visible symbols of the national peril. 'As if any sane pirate would dream of sailing twenty miles up an open river to attack a defended city!' He shook his head in dismay at the ease with which a timorous population can be moulded by unscrupulous politicians. But what could he do? His closeness to Pompey had trapped him into silence.

On the seventeenth day of December, the Festival of Saturn began and lasted for a week. It was not the most enjoyable of holidays, for obvious reasons, and although the Cicero family went through the normal rituals of exchanging gifts, even allowing us slaves to have the day off and sharing a meal with us, nobody's heart was in it. Lucius used to be the life and soul of these events, and he was gone. Terentia, I believe, had hoped she was pregnant, but had discovered she was not, and was becoming seriously worried that she would never bear a son. Pomponia nagged away at Quintus about his inadequacies as a husband. Even little Tullia could not cheer the mood.

As for Cicero, he spent much of Saturnalia in his study, brooding on Pompey's insatiable ambition, and the implications it had for the country and for his own political prospects. The elections for the praetorship were barely eight months away, and he and Quintus had already compiled a list of likely candidates. From whichever of these men was eventually elected, he could probably expect to find his rivals for the consulship. The two brothers spent many hours discussing the permutations, and it seemed to me, although I kept it to myself, that they missed the wisdom of their cousin. For although Cicero used to joke that if he wanted to know what was politically shrewd, he would ask Lucius his opinion and then do precisely the opposite, nevertheless he had offered a fixed star to steer by. Without him, the Ciceros had only one another, and despite their mutual devotion, it was not always the wisest of relationships.

It was in this atmosphere, around the eighth or ninth day of January, when the Latin Festival was over and serious politics resumed, that Gabinius finally mounted the rostra to demand a new supreme commander. I am talking here, I should explain, about the old republican rostra, which was very different to the wretched ornamental footstool we have today. This ancient structure, now destroyed, was the heart of Rome's democracy: a long, curved platform, twelve feet high, covered with the statues of the heroes of antiquity, from which the tribunes and the consuls addressed the people. Its back was to the senate house, and it faced out boldly across the widest expanse of the forum, with six ships' battering rams, or 'beaks' – those *rostra* which gave the platform its name – thrusting from its heavy masonry (the beaks had been captured from the Carthaginians in a sea battle nearly three centuries earlier). The whole of its rear was a flight of steps, if you can imagine what I am saying, so that a magistrate might leave the senate house or the tribunes' headquarters, walk fifty paces, ascend the steps, and find himself on top of the rostra, facing a crowd of thousands, with the tiered façades of the two great basilicas on either side of him and the Temple of Castor straight ahead. This was where Gabinius stood on that January morning and declared, in his smooth and confident way, that what Rome needed was a strong man to take control of the war against the pirates.

Cicero, despite his misgivings, had done his best, with the help of Quintus, to turn out a good-sized crowd, and the Piceneans could always be relied upon to drum up a couple of hundred veterans. Add to these the regulars who hung about the Basilica Porcia, and those citizens going about their normal business in the forum, and I should say that close on a thousand were present to hear Gabinius spell out what was needed if the pirates were to be beaten – a supreme commander of consular rank with *imperium* lasting for three years over all territory up to fifty miles from the sea, fifteen legates of praetorian rank to assist him, free access to the treasury of Rome, five hundred warships and the right to levy up to one hundred and twenty thousand infantry and five thousand cavalry. These were staggering numbers and the demand caused a sensation. By the time Gabinius had finished the first reading of his bill, and had handed it to a clerk to be pinned up outside the tribunes' basilica, both Catulus and Hortensius had come hurrying into the forum to find out what was going on. Pompey, needless to say, was nowhere to be seen, and the other members of the group of seven (as the senators around Pompey had taken to calling themselves) took care to stand apart from one another, to avoid any suggestion of collusion. But the aristocrats were not fooled. 'If this is your doing,' Catulus snarled at Cicero, 'you can tell your master he will have a fight on his hands.'

The violence of their reaction was to prove even worse than Cicero had predicted. Once a bill had been given its first reading, three weekly market days had to pass before it could be voted on by the people (this was to enable country-dwellers to come into the city and study what was proposed). So the aristocrats had until the begining of February to organise against it, and they did not waste a moment. Two days later, the senate was summoned to debate the *lex Gabinia*, as it would be called, and despite Cicero's advice that he should stay away, Pompey felt that he was honour-bound to attend, and stake his claim to the job. He wanted a good-sized escort down to the senate house, and because there no longer seemed much point in secrecy, the seven senators formed an honour-guard around him. Quintus also joined them, in his brand-new senatorial toga: this was only his third or fourth visit to the chamber. As usual, I stayed close to Cicero. 'We should have known we were in trouble,' he lamented afterwards, 'when no other senator turned up.'

The walk down the Esquiline Hill and into the forum went well enough. The precinct bosses had played their part, delivering plenty of enthusiasm on the streets, with people calling out to Pompey to save them from the menace of the pirates. He waved to them like a landlord to his tenants. But the moment the group entered the senate house they were met by jeers from all sides, and a piece of rotten fruit flew across the chamber and splattered on to Pompey's shoulder, leaving a rich brown stain. Such a thing had never happened to the great general before, and he halted and looked around him in stupefaction. Afranius, Palicanus and Gabinius quickly closed ranks to protect him, just as if they were back on the battlefield, and I saw Cicero stretch out his arms to hustle all four to their places, no doubt reasoning that the sooner they sat down, the sooner the demonstration would be over. I was standing at the entrance to the chamber, held back with the other spectators by the familiar cordon of rope slung between the two doorposts. Of course, we were all supporters of Pompey, so the more the senators inside jeered him, the more we outside roared our approval, and it was a while before the presiding consul could bring the house to order.

The new consuls in that year were Pompey's old friend Glabrio, and the aristocratic Calpurnius Piso (not to be confused with the other senator of that name, who will feature later in this story, if the gods give me the strength to finish it). A sign of how desperate the situation was for Pompey in the senate was that Glabrio had chosen to absent himself, rather than be seen in open disagreement with the man who had given him back his son. That left Piso in the chair. I could see Hortensius, Catulus, Isauricus, Marcus Lucullus – the brother of the commander of the Eastern legions – and all the rest of the patrician faction poised to attack. The only ones no longer present to offer opposition were the three Metellus brothers: Quintus was abroad, serving as the governor of Crete, while the younger two, as if to prove the indifference of fate to the petty ambitions of men, had both died of the fever not long after the Verres trial. But what was most disturbing was that the *pedarii* – the unassuming, patient, plodding mass of the senate, whom Cicero had taken so much trouble to cultivate – even they were hostile, or at best sullenly unresponsive to Pompey's megalomania. As for Crassus, he was sprawled on the consular front bench opposite, with his arms folded and his legs casually outstretched, regarding Pompey with an expression of ominous calm. The reason for his sangfroid was obvious. Sitting directly behind him, placed there like a pair of prize animals just bought at auction, were two of that year's tribunes, Roscius and Trebellius. This was Crassus's way of telling the world that he had used his wealth to purchase not just one, but two vetoes, and that the *lex Gabinia*, whatever Pompey and Cicero chose to do, would never be allowed to pass.

Piso exercised his privilege of speaking first. 'An orator of the stationary or quiet type' was how Cicero condescendingly described him many years later, but there was nothing stationary or quiet about him that day. 'We know what you are doing!' he shouted at Pompey, as he came to the end of his harangue. 'You are defying your colleagues in the senate and setting yourself up as a second Romulus – slaying your brother so that you may rule alone! But you would do well to remember the fate of Romulus, who was murdered in his turn by his own senators, who cut up his body and carried the mangled pieces back to their homes!' That brought the aristocrats to their feet, and I could just make out Pompey's massive profile, stock still and staring straight ahead, obviously unable to believe what was happening.

Catulus spoke next, and then Isauricus. The worst, though, was Hortensius. For almost a year, since the end of his consulship, he had hardly been seen in the forum. His son-in-law, Caepio, the beloved elder brother of Cato, had recently died on army service in the East, leaving Hortensius's daughter a widow, and the word was that the Dancing Master no longer had the strength in his legs for the struggle. But now it seemed that Pompey's over-reaching ambition had brought him back into the arena revitalised, and listening to him reminded one of just how formidable he could be on a big set-piece occasion such as this. He never ranted or stooped to vulgarity, but eloquently restated the old republican case: that power must always be divided, hedged around with limitations, and renewed by annual votes, and that while he had nothing personally against Pompey – indeed, felt that Pompey was more worthy of supreme command than any other man in the state – it was a dangerous, un-Roman precedent that would be set by the *lex Gabinia*, and that ancient liberties were not to be flung aside merely because of some passing scare about pirates. Cicero was shifting in his place and I could not help but reflect that this was exactly the speech which he would have made if he had been free to speak his mind.

Hortensius had just about reached his peroration when the figure of Caesar rose from that obscure region at the back of the chamber, close to the door, which had once been occupied by Cicero, and asked Hortensius to give way. The respectful silence in which the great advocate had been heard fractured immediately, and one has to admit that it was brave of Caesar to take him on in such an atmosphere. Caesar stood his ground until at last he could be heard, and then he started to speak, in his clear, compelling, remorseless way. There was nothing un-Roman, he said, about seeking to defeat pirates, who were the scum of the sea; what was un-Roman was to will the end of a thing but not the means. If the republic functioned as perfectly as Hortensius said it did, why had this menace been allowed to grow? And now that it was grown monstrous, how was it to be defeated? He had himself been captured by pirates a few years back when he was on his way to Rhodes, and held to ransom, and when at last he had been released, he had gone back and hunted down every last man of his kidnappers, and carried out the promise he had made to them when he was their prisoner – had seen to it that the scoundrels were crucified! 'That, Hortensius, is the Roman way to deal with piracy – and that is what the *lex Gabinia* will enable us to do!'

He finished to a round of boos and cat-calls, and as he resumed his seat, with the most magnificent display of disdain, some kind of fight broke out at the other end of the chamber. I believe a senator threw a punch at Gabinius, who turned round and punched him back, and very quickly he was in difficulties, with bodies piling in on top of him. There was a scream and a crash as one of the benches toppled over. I lost sight of Cicero. A voice in the crowd behind me cried that Gabinius was being murdered and there was such a surge of pressure forwards that the rope was pulled from its fixings and we tumbled into the chamber. I was lucky to scramble to one side as several hundred of Pompey's plebeian supporters (who were a rough-looking lot, I must admit) poured down the aisle towards the consular dais and dragged Piso from his curule chair. One brute had him by the neck, and for a few moments it looked as though murder would be done. But then Gabinius managed to struggle free and pull himself up on to a bench to show that, although he had been somewhat knocked about, he was still alive. He appealed to the demonstrators to let go of Piso, and after a short argument the consul was reluctantly released. Rubbing his throat, Piso declared hoarsely that the session was adjourned without a vote – and so, by the very narrowest of margins, for the moment at least, the commonwealth was saved from anarchy.

Such violent scenes had not been witnessed in the heart of Rome's governing district for more than fourteen years, and they had a profound effect on Cicero, even though he had managed to escape the mêlée with barely a ruffle in his immaculate dress. Gabinius was streaming blood from his nose and lip and Cicero had to help him from the chamber. They came out some distance after Pompey, who walked on, looking neither right nor left, with the measured tread of a man at a funeral. What I remember most is the silence as the mingled crowd of senators and plebeians parted to let him through. It was as if both sides, at the very last moment, had realised that they were fighting on a cliff-edge, had come to their senses and drawn back. We went out into the forum, with Pompey still not saying anything, and when he turned into the Argiletum, in the direction of his house, his supporters all followed him, partly for want of anything else to do. Afranius, who was next to Pompey, passed the word back that the general wanted a meeting. I asked Cicero if there was anything he required and he replied, with a bitter smile, 'Yes, that quiet life in Arpinum!'

Quintus came up and said urgently, 'Pompey must withdraw, or be humiliated!'

'He already has been humiliated,' retorted Cicero, 'and we with him. Soldiers!' he said to me in disgust. 'What did I tell you? I would not dream of giving them orders on the battle-field. Why should they believe they know better than I about politics?'

We climbed the hill to Pompey's house and filed inside, leaving the muted crowd in the street. Ever since that first conference I had been accepted as the minute-taker for the group, and when I settled into my usual place in the corner, no one gave me a second glance. The senators arranged them-selves around a big table, Pompey at the head. The pride had entirely gone out of his massive frame. Slumped in his throne-like chair he reminded me of some great beast that had been captured, shackled, baffled and taunted in the arena by crea-tures littler than himself. He was utterly defeatist and kept repeating that it was all over – the senate would clearly never stand for his appointment, he had only the support of the dregs on the streets, Crassus's tame tribunes would veto the bill in any case: there was nothing left for it but death or exile. Caesar took the opposite view – Pompey was still the most popular man in the republic, he should go out into Italy and begin recruiting the legions he needed, his old veterans would provide the backbone of his new army, the senate would capitulate once he had sufficient force. 'There is only one thing to do if you lose a throw of the dice: double your stake and throw again. Ignore the aristocrats, and if necessary rule through the people and the army.'

I could see that Cicero was preparing himself to speak, and was sure he did not favour either of these extremes. But there is as much skill in knowing how to handle a meeting of ten as there is in manipulating a gathering of hundreds. He waited until everyone had had their say, and the discussion was exhausted, before coming fresh to the fray. 'As you know,

Pompey,' he began, 'I have had some misgivings about this undertaking from the outset. But after witnessing today's débâcle in the senate, I have to tell you, they have vanished entirely. Now we simply have to win this fight – for your sake, for Rome's, and for the dignity and authority of all those of us who have supported you. There can be no question of surrender. You are famously a lion on the battlefield; you cannot become a mouse in Rome.'

'You watch your language, lawyer,' said Afranius, wagging his finger at him, but Cicero took no notice.

'Can you conceive of what will happen if you give up now? The bill has been published. The people are clamouring for action against the pirates. If you do not assume the post, someone else will, and I can tell you who it will be: Crassus. You say yourself he has two tame tribunes. He will make sure this law goes through, only with his name written into it instead of yours. And how will you, Gabinius, be able to stop him? By vetoing your own legislation? Impossible! Do you see? We cannot abandon the battle now!'

This was an inspired argument, for if there was one thing guaranteed to rouse Pompey to a fight, it was the prospect of Crassus stealing his glory. He drew himself up, thrust out his jaw and glared around the table. I noticed both Afranius and Palicanus give him slight nods of encouragement. 'We have scouts in the legions, Cicero,' said Pompey, 'marvellous fellows who can find a way through the most difficult terrain – marshes, mountain ranges, forests which no man has penetrated since time began. But politics beats any obstacle I have ever faced. If you can show me a route out of this mess, you will have no truer friend than me.'

'Will you place yourself in my hands entirely?'

'You are the scout.'

'Very well,' said Cicero. 'Gabinius, tomorrow you must summon Pompey to the rostra, to ask him to serve as supreme commander.'

'Good,' said Pompey belligerently, clenching his massive fist. 'And I shall accept.'

'No, no,' said Cicero, 'you will refuse absolutely. You will say you have done enough for Rome, that you have no ambitions left in public life, and are retiring to your estate in the country.' Pompey's mouth fell open. 'Don't worry. I shall write the speech for you. You will leave the city tomorrow afternoon, and you will not come back. The more reluctant you seem, the more frantic the people will be for your recall. You will be our Cincinnatus, fetched from his plough to save the country from disaster. It is one of the most potent myths in politics, believe me.'

Some of those present were opposed to such a dramatic tactic, considering it too risky. But the idea of appearing modest appealed to Pompey's vanity. For is this not the dream of every proud and ambitious man? That rather than having to get down in the dust and fight for power, the people should come crawling to him, begging him to accept it as a gift? The more Pompey thought about it, the more he liked it. His dignity and authority would remain intact, he would have a comfortable few weeks, and if it all went wrong, it would be someone else's fault.

'This sounds very clever,' said Gabinius, who was dabbing at his split lip. 'But you seem to forget that it is not the people who are the problem; it is the senate.'

'The senate will come round once they wake up to the implications of Pompey's retirement. They will be faced with a choice of either doing nothing about the pirates, or awarding the supreme command to Crassus. To the great majority, neither will be acceptable. Apply a little grease and they will slide our way.'

'That is clever,' said Pompey admiringly. 'Is he not clever, gentlemen? Did I not tell you he was clever?'

'These fifteen legateships,' said Cicero. 'I propose you should use at least half of them to win over support inside the senate.' Palicanus and Afranius, seeing their lucrative commissions in jeopardy, immediately objected loudly, but Pompey waved them to be quiet. 'You are a national hero,' continued Cicero, 'a patriot above petty political squabbles and intrigue. Rather than using your patronage to reward your friends, you should use it to divide your enemies. Nothing will split the aristocratic faction more disastrously than if some can be persuaded to serve under you. They will tear each other's eyes out.'

'I agree,' said Caesar, with a decisive nod. 'Cicero's plan is better than mine. Be patient, Afranius. This is only the first stage. We can wait for our rewards.'

'Besides,' said Pompey sanctimoniously, 'the defeat of Rome's enemies should be reward enough for all of us.' I could see that in his mind's eye, he was already at his plough.

Afterwards, as we were walking home, Quintus said, 'I hope you know what you are doing.'

'I hope I know what I am doing,' replied Cicero.

'The nub of the problem, surely, is Crassus and those two tribunes of his, and his ability to veto the bill. How are you going to get round that?'

'I have no idea. Let us hope that a solution presents itself. One usually does.'

I realised then just how much Cicero was relying on his old dictum that sometimes you have to start a fight to discover how to win it. He said good night to Quintus and walked on, head down in thought. From being a reluctant participant in Pompey's grand ambition, he had now emerged as its chief organiser, and he knew that this would put him in a hard place, not least with his own wife. In my experience, women are far less willing than men to forget past slights and it was inexplicable to Terentia that her husband should still be dancing attendance on the 'Prince of Picenum', as she derisively called Pompey, especially after that day's scenes in the senate, about which the whole city was talking. She was waiting for Cicero in the tablinum when we arrived home, all drawn up in full battle order and ready to attack. She flew at him immediately. 'I cannot believe things have reached such a pass! There is the senate on one side and the rabble on the other – and where is my husband to be found? As usual, with the rabble! Surely even you will sever your connection with him now?'

'He is announcing his retirement tomorrow,' Cicero soothed her.

'What?'

'It is true. I am going to write his statement myself this evening. Which means I shall have to dine at my desk, I am afraid, if you will excuse me.' He eased past her, and once we were in his study he said, 'Do you think she believed me?'

'No,' I replied.

'Nor do I,' he said, with a chuckle. 'She has lived with me too long!'

He was rich enough by now to have divorced her if he wanted, and he could have made himself a better match, certainly a more beautiful one. He was disappointed she had not been able to give him a son. And yet, despite their endless arguments, he stayed with her. Love was not the word for it – not in the sense that the poets use it. Some stranger, stronger compound bound them.

She kept him sharp, that was part of it: the whetstone to his blade. At any rate, she did not bother us for the rest of that night, as Cicero dictated the words he thought that Pompey should say. He had never written a speech for anyone else before, and it was a peculiar experience. Nowadays, of course, most senators employ a slave or two to turn out their speeches; I have even heard of some who have no idea of what they are going to say until the text is placed in front of them: how these fellows can call themselves statesmen defeats me. But Cicero found that he rather enjoyed composing parts for others. It amused him to think of lines that great men ought to utter, if only they had the brains, and later he would use the technique to considerable effect in his books. He even thought of a phrase for Gabinius to deliver, which afterwards became quite famous: 'Pompey the Great was not born for himself alone, but for Rome!'

The statement was deliberately kept short and we finished it long before midnight, and early the following morning, after Cicero had performed his exercises and greeted only his most important callers, we went across to Pompey's house and gave him the speech. Overnight, Pompey had contracted a bad dose of cold feet, and now he fretted aloud whether retirement was such a good idea after all. But Cicero saw that it was nervousness about going up on to the rostra as much as anything else, and once Pompey had his prepared text in his hands, he began to calm down. Cicero then gave some notes to Gabinius, who was also present, but the tribune resented being handed his lines like an actor, and questioned whether he should really say that Pompey was 'born for Rome'. 'Why?' teased Cicero. 'Do you not believe it?' Whereupon Pompey gruffly ordered Gabinius to stop complaining and say the words as written. Gabinius fell silent, but he glowered at Cicero and from that moment I believe became

his secret enemy – a perfect example of the senator's reckless-
ness in causing offence by his repartee.

An enormous throng of spectators had gathered in the forum,
eager to see the sequel to the previous day's performance. We
could hear the noise as we came down the hill from Pompey's
house – that awesome, oblivious swelling sound of a great excited
multitude, which always reminds me of a huge sea rolling against
a distant shore. I felt my blood begin to pulse faster in anticipation. Most of the senate was there, and the aristocrats had brought
along several hundred supporters of their own, partly for their
protection, and also to howl down Pompey when, as they
expected, he declared his desire for the supreme command. The
great man briefly entered the forum escorted, as before, by Cicero
and his senatorial allies, but kept to the edge of it, and immediately went to the back of the rostra, where he paced around,
yawned, blew on his freezing hands, and generally gave every
indication of nerves, as the roar of the crowd increased in volume.
Cicero wished him luck, then went round to the front of the
rostra to stand with the rest of the senate, for he was keen to
observe their reactions. The ten tribunes filed up on to the platform and sat on their bench, then Gabinius stepped forward and
shouted dramatically, 'I summon before the people Pompey the
Great!'

How important appearance is in politics, and how superbly
Pompey was fashioned by nature to carry the look of greatness!
As that broad and familiar figure came plodding up the steps and
into view, his followers gave him the most tremendous ovation.
He stood there as solid as a full-grown bull, his massive head
tilted back slightly on his muscular shoulders, looking down on
the upturned faces, his nostrils flared as if inhaling the applause.
Normally, the people resented having speeches read to them

rather than delivered with apparent spontaneity, but on this occasion there was something in the way that Pompey unrolled his short text and held it up that reinforced the sense that these were words as weighty as the man delivering them – a man above the smooth oratorical tricks of the law and politics.

'People of Rome,' he bellowed into the silence, 'when I was seventeen I fought in the army of my father, Gnaeus Pompeius Strabo, to bring unity to the state. When I was twenty-three I raised a force of fifteen thousand, defeated the combined rebel armies of Brutus, Caelius and Carrinas, and was saluted imperator in the field. When I was twenty-four I conquered Sicily. When I was twenty-five I conquered Africa. On my twenty-sixth birthday, I triumphed. When I was thirty, and not even a senator, I took command of our forces in Spain with proconsular authority, fought the rebels for six years, and conquered. When I was thirty-six I returned to Italy, hunted down the last remaining army of the fugitive slave Spartacus, and conquered. When I was thirty-seven I was voted consul and triumphed for a second time. As consul, I restored to you the ancient rights of your tribunes, and staged games. Whenever danger has threatened this commonwealth, I have served it. My entire life has been nothing but one long special command. Now a new and unprecedented menace has arisen to threaten the republic. And to meet that danger, an office with new and unprecedented authority is rightly proposed. Whoever you choose to shoulder this burden must have the support of all ranks and all classes, for a great trust is involved in bestowing so much power on a single man. It is clear to me, after the meeting of the senate yesterday, that I do not have their trust, and therefore I want to tell you that however much I am petitioned, I shall not consent to be nominated; and if nominated, I shall not serve. Pompey the Great has had his fill of special commands. On this day I renounce all ambition for public office and retire from the city to till the soil like my forefathers before me.'

After a moment of shock, a terrible groan of disappointment broke from the crowd, and Gabinius darted to the front of the rostra, where Pompey was standing impassively.

'This cannot be permitted! Pompey the Great was not born for himself alone, but for Rome!'

Of course, the line provoked the most tremendous demonstration of approval, and the chant of 'Pompey! Pompey! Rome! Rome!' bounced off the walls of the basilicas and temples until one's ears ached with the noise. It was some time before Pompey could make himself heard.

'Your kindness touches me, my fellow citizens, but my continued presence in the city can only impede your deliberations. Choose wisely, O people of Rome, from the many able former consuls in the senate! And remember that although I now quit Rome altogether, my heart will remain among your hearths and temples for ever. Farewell!'

He raised his roll of papyrus as if it were a marshal's baton, saluted the wailing crowd, turned, and trudged implacably towards the back of the platform, ignoring all entreaties to remain. Down the steps he went, watched by the astonished tribunes, first the legs sinking from view, and then the torso, and finally the noble head with its crowning quiff. Some people standing close to me began weeping and tearing at their hair and clothes, and even though I knew the whole thing was a ruse, it was all I could do not to break into sobs myself. The assembled senators looked as if some weighty missile had dropped among them – a few were defiant, many were shaken, the majority simply blank with wonder. For almost as long as anyone could remember,

Pompey had been the foremost man in the state, and now he had – gone! Crassus's face in particular was a picture of conflicting emotions, which no artist ever born could have hoped to capture. Part of him knew that he must now, at last, after a lifetime in Pompey's shadow, be the favourite to seize the special command; the shrewder part knew that this had to be a trick, and that his whole position was threatened by some unforeseen jeopardy.

Cicero stayed just long enough to gauge the reactions to his handiwork, then hurried round to the back of the rostra to report. The Piceneans were there, and the usual crush of hangers on. Pompey's attendants had brought a closed litter of blue and gold brocade to ferry him to the Capena Gate, and the general was preparing to clamber into it. He was like many men I have seen immediately after they have delivered a big speech, in the same breath both arrogant with exhilaration and anxious for re-assurance. 'That went extremely well,' he said. 'Did you think it was all right?'

'Superb,' said Cicero. 'Crassus's expression is beyond description.'

'Did you like the line about my heart remaining among the hearths and temples of Rome for ever?'

'It was the consummate touch.'

Pompey grunted, highly pleased, and settled himself among the cushions of his litter. He let the curtain drop, then quickly pulled it aside again. 'You are sure this is going to work?'

'Our opponents are in disarray. That is a start.'

The curtain fell, then parted once more.

'How long before the bill is voted on?'

'Fifteen days.'

'Keep me informed. Daily at the least.'

Cicero stepped aside as the canopied chair was hoisted on to the shoulders of its bearers. They must have been strong young fellows, for Pompey was a great weight, yet they set off at the double, past the senate house and out of the forum – the heavenly body of Pompey the Great trailing his comet's tail of clients and admirers. 'Did I like the line about hearths and temples?' repeated Cicero under his breath as he watched him go. 'Well, naturally I did, you great booby – I wrote it!' I guess it must have been hard for him to devote so much energy to a chief he did not admire and a cause he believed to be fundamentally specious. But the journey to the top in politics often confines a man with some uncongenial fellow passengers and shows him strange scenery, and he knew there was no turning back now.

XII

For the next two weeks there was only one topic in Rome, and that was the pirates. Gabinius and Cornelius, in the phrase of the time, 'lived on the rostra' – that is, every day they kept the issue of the pirate menace before the people by issuing fresh proclamations and summoning more witnesses. Horror stories were their speciality. For example, it was put about that if one of the pirates' prisoners announced that he was a Roman citizen, his captors would pretend to be frightened, and beg forgiveness. They would even fetch a toga for him to wear, and shoes for his feet, and bow whenever he passed, and this game would go on for a long time, until at last, when they were far out at sea, they would let down a ladder and tell him he was free to go. If their victim refused to walk, he would be flung overboard. Such tales enraged the audience in the forum, who were accustomed to the magical incantation 'I am a Roman citizen' guaranteeing deference throughout the world.

Cicero himself did not speak from the rostra. Oddly enough, he had never yet done so, having decided early on to hold back until a moment in his career when he could make the maximum impact. He was naturally tempted to make this the issue on which he broke his silence, for it was a popular stick with which to beat the aristocrats. But in the end he decided against it, reasoning that the measure already had such overwhelming backing in the streets, he would be better employed behind the scenes, plotting strategy and trying to tempt over waverers in the senate. For this reason, his crucial importance has been frequently neglected. Instead of the fiery public orator he played the moderate for a change, working his way up and down the senaculum, listening to the complaints of the *pedarii*, promising to relay messages of commiseration and entreaty to Pompey, and dangling – very occasionally – half-offers of preferment to men of influence. Each day a messenger came to the house from Pompey's estate in the Alban Hills bearing a dispatch containing some fresh moan or enquiry or instruction ('Our new Cincinnatus does not seem to be spending much time ploughing,' observed Cicero with a wry smile), and each day the senator would dictate to me a soothing reply, often giving the names of men it might be useful for Pompey to summon out for interview. This was a delicate task, since it was important to maintain the pretence that Pompey was taking no further part in politics. But a combination of greed, flattery, ambition, realisation that some kind of special command was inevitable, and fear that it might go to Crassus eventually brought half a dozen key senators into Pompey's camp, the most significant of whom was Lucius Manlius Torquatus, who had only just finished serving as praetor and was certain to run for the consulship the following year.

Crassus remained, as always, the greatest threat to Cicero's schemes, and naturally he was not idle during this time either. He, too, went around making promises of lucrative commissions, and winning over adherents. For connoisseurs of politics it was fascinating to observe the perennial rivals, Crassus and Pompey, so evenly poised. Each had two tame tribunes; each could therefore veto the bill; and each had a list of secret supporters in the senate. Crassus's advantage over Pompey was the support of most of the aristocrats, who feared Pompey more than any other man in the republic; Pompey's advantage over Crassus was the popularity he enjoyed among the masses on the streets. 'They are like two scorpions, circling each other,' said Cicero, leaning back in his chair one morning, after he had dictated his latest dispatch to Pompey. 'Neither can win outright, yet each can kill the other.'

'Then how will victory ever be achieved?'

He looked at me, then suddenly lunged forward and slammed his palm down on his desk with a speed that made me jump. 'By the one which strikes the other by surprise.'

At the time he made that remark, there were only four days left before the *lex Gabinia* was due to be voted on by the people. He still had not thought of a means of circumventing Crassus's veto. He was wearied and discouraged, and once again began to talk of our retiring to Athens and studying philosophy. That day passed, and the next, and the next, and still no solution presented itself. On the final day before the vote, I rose as usual at dawn and opened the door to Cicero's clients. Now that he was known to be so close to Pompey, these morning levees had doubled in size compared to the old days, and the house was crowded with petitioners and well-wishers at all hours, much to Terentia's annoyance. Some of them had famous names: for example, on this particular morning, Antonius Hybrida, who was the second son of the great orator and consul Marcus Antonius, and who had just finished a term as tribune; he was a fool and a drunk, but protocol dictated he would have to be seen first. Outside it was grey and raining and the callers had brought in with them a wet-dog smell of moist stale clothes and damp hair. The black and white mosaic floor was streaked with tracks of mud and I was just contemplating summoning one of the household slaves to mop up when the door opened again and who should step in but Marcus Licinius Crassus himself. I was so startled, I briefly forgot to be alarmed, and gave him as natural a greeting as if he had been a nobody, come to request a letter of introduction.

'And a very good morning to you, Tiro,' he returned. He had only met me once, yet he still remembered my name, which frightened me. 'Might it be possible to have a word with your master?' Crassus was not alone but had brought with him Quintus Arrius, a senator who followed him around like a shadow, and whose ridiculously affected speech – always adding an aspirate to a vowel: 'Harrius' was how he pronounced his name – was to be so memorably parodied by that cruellest of poets, Catullus. I hurried through into Cicero's study, where he was doing his usual trick of dictating a letter to Sositheus while signing documents as quickly as Laurea could produce them.

'You will never guess who is here!' I cried.

'Crassus,' he replied, without looking up.

I was immediately deflated. 'You are not surprised?'

'No,' said Cicero, signing another letter. 'He has come to make a magnanimous offer, which is not really magnanimous at all, but which will show him in a better light when our refusal to agree to it becomes public. He has every reason to compromise, while we have none. Still, you had better show him in before he bribes all my clients away from me. And stay in the room and take a note, in case he tries to put words into my mouth.'

So I went out to fetch Crassus – who was indeed glad-handing his way around Cicero's tablinum, to the awed amazement of all concerned – and showed him into the study. The junior secretaries left, and there were just the four of us – Crassus, Arrius and Cicero all seated, and myself standing in the corner and taking notes.

'You have a very nice house,' said Crassus, in his friendly way. 'Small but charming. You must tell me if you think of selling.'

'If it ever catches fire,' responded Cicero, 'you will be the first to know.'

'Very droll,' said Crassus, clapping his hands and laughing with great good humour. 'But I am perfectly serious. An important man such as yourself should have a larger property, in a better neighbourhood. The Palatine, of course. I can arrange it. No, please,' he added, as Cicero shook his head, 'do not dismiss my offer. We have had our differences, and I should like to make a gesture of reconciliation.'

'Well, that is handsome of you,' said Cicero, 'but alas, I fear the interests of a certain gentleman still stand between us.'

'They need not. I have watched your career with admiration, Cicero. You deserve the place you have won in Rome. It is my view that you should achieve the praetorship in the summer, and the consulship itself two years after that. There – I have said it. You may have my support. Now what do you say in reply?'

This was indeed a stunning offer, and at that moment I grasped an important point about clever men of business – that it is not consistent meanness which makes them rich (as many vulgarly assume), but rather the capacity, when necessary, to be unexpectedly, even extravagantly generous. Cicero was entirely caught off balance. He was effectively being offered the consulship, his life's dream, on a platter – an ambition he had never even dared voice in the presence of Pompey, for fear of arousing the great man's jealousy.

'You overwhelm me, Crassus,' he said, and his voice was so

thick with emotion he had to cough to clear it before he could continue. 'But fate has once again cast us on different sides.'

'Not necessarily. On the day before the people vote, surely the time has arrived for a compromise? I accept that this supreme command is Pompey's conception. Let us share it.'

'A shared supreme command is an oxymoron.'

'We shared the consulship.'

'Yes, but the consulship is a joint office, based on the principle that political power should always be shared. Running a war is entirely different, as you know far better than I. In warfare, any hint of division at the top is fatal.'

'This command is so huge, there is easily room enough for two,' said Crassus airily. 'Let Pompey take the east, and I the west. Or Pompey the sea and I the land. Or vice versa. I do not mind. The point is that between us we can rule the world, with you as the bridge that links us.'

I am sure that Cicero had expected Crassus to come in threatening and aggressive, tactics which a career in the law courts had long since taught him how to handle. But this unexpectedly generous approach had him reeling, not least because what Crassus was suggesting was both sensible and patriotic. It would also be the ideal solution for Cicero, enabling him to win the friendship of all sides. 'I shall certainly put your offer to him,' promised Cicero. 'He shall have it in his hands before the day is out.'

'That is no use to me!' scoffed Crassus. 'If it were a matter of merely putting a proposal, I could have sent Arrius here out to the Alban Hills with a letter, could I not, Arrius?'

'Hindeed you could.'

'No, Cicero, I need you actually to bring this about.' He leaned in close and moistened his lips; there was something almost lecherous about the way Crassus talked of power. 'I shall be frank with you. I have set my heart upon resuming a military career. I have all the wealth a man could want, but that can only be a means and not an end in itself. Can you tell me what nation ever erected a statue to a man because he was rich? Which of the earth's many peoples mingles the name of some long-dead millionaire in its prayers because of the number of houses he once possessed? The only lasting glory is on the page – and I am no poet! – or on the battlefield. So you see, you really must deliver the agreement of Pompey for our bargain to stick.'

'He is not a mule to be driven to market,' objected Cicero, whom I could see was starting to recoil again from the crudeness of his old enemy. 'You know what he is like.'

'I do. Too well! But you are the most persuasive man in the world. You got him to leave Rome – do not deny it! Now surely you can convince him to come back?'

'His position is that he will come back as the sole supreme commander, or he will not come back at all.'

'Then Rome will never see him again,' snapped Crassus, whose friendliness was beginning to peel away like a thin layer of cheap paint on one of his less salubrious properties. 'You know perfectly well what is going to happen tomorrow. It will unfold as predictably as a farce at the theatre. Gabinius will propose your law and Trebellius, on my behalf, will veto it. Then Roscius, also on my instructions, will propose an amendment, setting up a joint command, and dare any tribune to veto *that*. If Pompey refuses to serve, he will look like a greedy child, willing to spoil the cake rather than share it.'

'I disagree. The people love him.'

'The people loved Tiberius Gracchus, but it did him no good in the end. That was a horrible fate for a patriotic Roman, which you might do well to remember.' Crassus stood. 'Look to your own interests, Cicero. Surely you can see that Pompey is leading you to political oblivion? No man ever became consul with the aristocracy united against him.' Cicero also rose and warily took Crassus's proferred hand. The older man grasped it hard and pulled him close. 'On two occasions,' he said in a very soft voice, 'I have offered the hand of friendship to you, Marcus Tullius Cicero. There will not be a third.'

With that, he strode out of the house, and at such a pace I could not get in front of him to show him out, or even open the door. I returned to the study to find Cicero standing exactly where I had left him, frowning at his hand. 'It is like touching the skin of a snake,' he said. 'Tell me – did I mishear him, or is he suggesting that Pompey and I might suffer the same fate as Tiberius Gracchus?'

'Yes: "a horrible fate for a patriotic Roman",' I read from my notes. 'What was the fate of Tiberius Gracchus?'

'Cornered like a rat in a temple and murdered by the nobles, while he was still tribune, and therefore supposedly inviolable. That must have been sixty years ago, at least. Tiberius Gracchus!' He clenched his hand into a fist. 'You know, for a moment, Tiro, he almost had me believing him. But I swear to you, I would sooner never be consul than feel that I had only achieved it because of Crassus.'

'I believe you, Senator. Pompey is worth ten of him.'

'A hundred, more like – for all his absurdities.'

I busied myself with a few things, straightening the desk and collecting the morning's list of callers from the tablinum, while Cicero remained motionless in the study. When I returned again, a curious expression had come over his face. I gave him the list and reminded him that he still had a houseful of clients to receive, including a senator. Absent-mindedly he selected a couple of names, among them Hybrida's, but then he suddenly said, 'Leave things here to Sositheus. I have a different task for you to perform. Go to the National Archive and consult the Annals for the consular year of Mucius Scaevola and Calpurnius Piso Frugi. Copy down everything relating to the tribuneship of Tiberius Gracchus and his agrarian bill. Tell nobody what you are doing. If anyone asks you, make something up. Well?' He smiled for the first time in a week and made a shooing gesture, flicking his fingers at me. 'Go on, man. Go!'

After so many years in his service I had become used to these bewildering and peremptory commands, and once I had wrapped myself up against the cold and wet I set off down the hill. Never had I known the city so grim and hard pressed – in the depths of winter, under a dark sky, freezing, short of food, with beggars on every corner, and even the occasional corpse in the gutter of some poor wretch who had died in the night. I moved quickly through the dreary streets, across the forum and up the steps to the Archive. This was the same building in which I had discovered the meagre official records of Gaius Verres and I had been back on many errands since, especially when Cicero was aedile, so my face was familiar to the clerks. They gave me the volume I needed without asking any questions. I took it over to a reading desk beside the window and unrolled it with my mittened fingers. The morning light was weak, it was very draughty, and I was not at all sure what I was looking for. The Annals, at least in those days before Caesar got his hands on them, gave a very straight and full account of what had happened in each year: the names of the magistrates, the laws passed, the wars fought, the famines endured, the eclipses and other natural phenomena observed. They were drawn from the official register that was written up each year by the pontifex maximus, and posted on the white board outside the headquarters of the college of priests.

History has always fascinated me. As Cicero himself once wrote: 'To be ignorant of what occurred before you were born is to remain always a child. For what is the worth of human life, unless it is woven into the life of our ancestors by the records of history?' I quickly forgot the cold and could have spent all day happily unwinding that roll, poring over the events of more than sixty years before. I discovered that in this particular year, Rome's six hundred and twenty-first, King Attalus III of Pergamon had died, bequeathing his country to Rome; that Scipio Africanus Minor had destroyed the Spanish city of Numantia, slaughtering all of its five thousand inhabitants, apart from fifty whom he saved to walk in chains in his triumph; and that Tiberius Gracchus, the famous radical tribune, had introduced a law to share out the public land among the common people, who were then, as always, suffering great hardship. Nothing changes, I thought. Gracchus's bill had infuriated the aristocrats in the senate, who saw it as threatening their estates, and they had persuaded or suborned a tribune named Marcus Octavius to veto the law. But because the people were unanimous in their support for the bill, Gracchus had argued from the rostra that Octavius was failing in his sacred duty to uphold their interests. He had therefore called upon the people to begin voting Octavius out of office, tribe by tribe, which they at once proceeded to do. When the first seventeen of the thirty-five tribes had voted overwhelmingly for Octavius's removal, Gracchus had suspended the polling and appealed to him to withdraw his veto. Octavius had refused, whereupon Gracchus had 'called upon the gods to witness that he did not willingly wish to remove his colleague', had balloted the eighteenth tribe, achieved a majority, and Octavius had been stripped of his tribuneship ('reduced to the rank of a private citizen he departed unobserved'). The agrarian law had then been passed. But the nobles, as Crassus had reminded Cicero, had exacted their revenge a few months later, when Gracchus had been surrounded in the Temple of Fides, beaten to death with sticks and clubs, and his body flung in the Tiber.

I unfastened the hinged notebook from my wrist and took out my stylus. I remember how I glanced around to make sure I was alone before I opened it and started copying the relevant passages from the Annals, for now I understood why Cicero had been so emphatic about the need for secrecy. My fingers were freezing and the wax was hard; the script I produced was atrocious. At one point, when Catulus himself, the patron of the Archive, appeared in the doorway and stared straight at me, I felt as if my heart would shatter the bones of my breast. But the old man was short-sighted, and I doubt he would have known who I was in any case; he was not that sort of politician. After talking for a while with one of his freedmen, he left. I finished my transcription and almost ran out of that place, down the icy steps and back across the forum towards Cicero's house, carrying my wax tablet pressed close to me, sensing I had never done a more significant morning's work in my life.

When I reached the house, Cicero was still ensconced with Antonius Hybrida, although as soon as he saw me waiting near the door, he drew their conversation to a close. Hybrida was one of those well-bred, fine-boned types, who had ruined himself and his looks with wine. I could smell his breath even from where I stood: it was like fruit rotting in a gutter. He had been thrown out of the senate a few years previously for bankruptcy and loose morals – specifically, corruption, drunkenness, and buying a beautiful young slave girl at an auction and living openly with her as his mistress. But the people, in that peculiar way of theirs, rather loved him for his rakish ways, and now that he had served a year as their tribune, he had worked his way back into the senate. I waited until he had gone before I gave Cicero my notes. 'What did he want?' I asked.

'My support in the elections for praetor.'

'He has a nerve!'

'I suppose he has. I promised to back him, though,' said Cicero carelessly, and seeing my surprise he explained: 'At least with him as praetor I shall have one fewer rival for the consulship.'

He laid my notebook on his desk and read it carefully. Then he put his elbows on either side of it, rested his chin in the palms of his hands, hunched forward and read it again. I pictured his quick thoughts running ahead in the way that water runs along the cracks in a tiled floor – first onwards, and then spreading to either side, blocked in one spot, advancing in another, widening and branching out, all the little possibilities and implications and likelihoods in shimmering fluid motion. Eventually, he said, half to himself and half to me, 'Such a tactic had never been tried before Gracchus used it, and has never been attempted since. One can see why. What a weapon to put into any man's hands! Win or lose, we should have to live with the consequences for years.' He looked up at me. 'I am not sure, Tiro. Perhaps it would be better if you erased it.' But when I made a move towards the desk, he said quickly, 'And then again perhaps not.' Instead, he told me to fetch Laurea and a couple of the other slaves and have them run around to all the senators in Pompey's inner group, asking them to assemble after the close of official business that afternoon. 'Not here,' he added quickly, 'but in Pompey's house.' Thereupon he sat down and began writing out, in his own hand, a dispatch to the general, which was sent off with a rider who had orders to wait and return with a reply. 'If Crassus wants to summon up the ghost of Gracchus,' he said grimly, when the letter had gone, 'he shall have him!'

Needless to say, the others were agog to hear why Cicero had summoned them, and once the courts and offices were shut for the day, everyone turned up at Pompey's mansion, filling all the seats around the table, except for the absent owner's great throne, which was left empty as a mark of respect. It may seem strange that such clever and learned men as Caesar and Varro were ignorant of the precise tactics which Gracchus had used as tribune, but remember that he had been dead by then for sixty-three years, that huge events had intervened, and that there was not yet the mania for contemporary history which was to develop over the coming decades. Even Cicero had forgotten it until Crassus's threat dislodged some distant memory from the time when he was studying for the bar. There was a profound hush as he read out the extract from the Annals, and when he had finished, an excited hubbub. Only the white-haired Varro, who was the oldest present, and who remembered hearing from his father about the chaos of the Gracchus tribunate, expressed reservations. 'You would create a precedent,' he said, 'by which any demagogue could summon the people, and threaten to dispose of any of his colleagues whenever he felt he had a majority among the tribes. Indeed, why stop at a tribune? Why not remove a praetor, or a consul?'

'We would not create the precedent,' Caesar pointed out impatiently. 'Gracchus created it for us.'

'Exactly,' said Cicero. 'Although the nobles may have murdered him, they did not declare his legislation illegal. I know what Varro means, and to a degree I share his unease. But we are in a desperate struggle, and obliged to take some risks.'

There was a murmur of assent, but in the end the most de-cisive voices in favour were those of Gabinius and Cornelius, the men who would actually have to stand before the people and push the legislation through, and who would, as a consequence, be chiefly liable to the nobles' retaliation, both physical and legal.

'The people overwhelmingly want this supreme command, and they want Pompey to be given it,' declared Gabinius. 'The fact that Crassus's purse is deep enough to buy two tribunes should not be allowed to frustrate their will.'

Afranius wanted to know if Pompey had expressed an opinion.

'This is the dispatch I sent to him this morning,' said Cicero, holding it up, 'and here on the bottom is the reply he sent back instantly, and which reached me here at the same time as you all did.' Everyone could see what Pompey had scrawled, in his large, bold script: the single word, *Agreed*. That settled the matter. Afterwards, Cicero instructed me to burn the letter.

The morning of the assembly was bitterly cold, with an icy wind whipping around the colonnades and temples of the forum. But the chill did not deter a vast assembly from turning out. On major voting days, the tribunes transferred themselves from the rostra to the Temple of Castor, where there was more space to conduct the ballot, and workmen had been busy overnight, erecting the wooden gangways up which the citizens would file to cast their votes. Cicero arrived early and discreetly, with only myself and Quintus in attendance, for as he said as he walked down the hill, he was only the stage manager of this production and not one of its leading performers. He spent a little while conferring with a group of tribal officers, then retreated with me to the portico of the Basilica Aemilia, from where he would have

a good view of proceedings and could issue instructions as necessary.

It was a dramatic sight, and I guess I must be one of the very
few left alive who witnessed it – the ten tribunes lined up on
their bench, among them, like hired gladiators, the two matched
pairs of Gabinius and Cornelius (for Pompey), versus Trebellius
and Roscius (for Crassus); the priests and the augurs all standing
at the top of the steps to the temple; the orange fire on the altar
providing a flickering point of colour in the greyness; and spread
out across the forum the great crowd of voters, red-faced in the
cold, milling around the ten-foot-high standard of their particular tribe. Each standard carried its name proudly in large letters
– *AEMILIA, CAMILIA, FABIA*, and so on – so that its members, if
they wandered off, could see where they were supposed to be.
There was much joking and horse-trading between the groups,
until the trumpet of the herald called them to order. Then the
official crier gave the legislation its second reading in a pene-
trating voice, after which Gabinius stepped forward and made a
short speech. He had joyful news, he said: the news that the
people of Rome had been praying for. Pompey the Great, deeply
moved by the sufferings of the nation, was willing to reconsider
his position, and serve as supreme commander – but only if it
was the unanimous desire of them all. 'And is it your desire?'
demanded Gabinius, to which there was a huge demonstration
of enthusiasm. This went on for some time, thanks to the tribal
officers. In fact, whenever it seemed the volume might be waning,
Cicero would give a discreet signal to a couple of these officers,
who would relay it across the forum, and the tribal standards
would start waving again, rekindling the applause. Eventually
Gabinius motioned them to be quiet. 'Then let us put it to the
vote!'

Slowly – and one had to admire his courage in standing up at all, in the face of so many thousands – Trebellius rose from his place on the tribunes' bench and came forward, his hand raised to signal his desire to intervene. Gabinius regarded him with contempt, and then roared to the crowd, 'Well, citizens, should we let him speak?'

'No!' they screamed in response.

To which Trebellius, in a voice made shrill by nerves, shouted: 'Then I veto the bill!'

At any other time in the past four centuries, excepting the year when Tiberius Gracchus was tribune, this would have been the end of the legislation. But on that fateful morning, Gabinius motioned the jeering crowd to be silent. 'Does Trebellius speak for you all?'

'No!' they chanted back. 'No! No!'

'Does he speak for anyone here?' The only sound was the wind: even the senators who supported Trebellius dared not raise their voices, for they were standing unprotected among their tribes, and would have been set upon by the mob. 'Then, in accordance with the precedent set by Tiberius Gracchus, I propose that Trebellius, having failed to observe the oath of his office and represent the people, be removed as tribune, and that this be voted on immediately!'

Cicero turned to me. 'And now the play begins,' he said.

For a moment, the citizenry simply looked at one another. Then they started nodding, and a sound grew out of the crowd of realisation – that is how I think of it now, at any rate, as I sit in my little study with my eyes closed and try to remember it all – a realisation that they could do this, and that the grandees in the senate were powerless to stop them. Catulus, Hortensius and Crassus, in great alarm, started pushing their way towards the front of the assembly, demanding a hearing, but Gabinius had stationed a few of Pompey's veterans along the bottom steps and they were not allowed to pass. Crassus, in particular, had lost all his usual restraint. His face was red and contorted with rage as he tried to storm the tribunal, but he was pushed back. He noticed Cicero watching and pointed at him, and shouted something, but he was too far away and there was too much noise for us to hear. Cicero smiled at him benignly. The crier read out Gabinius's motion – 'That the people no longer desire Trebellius to be their tribune' – and the electoral clerks dispersed to their stations. As usual, the Suburana were the first to vote, filing up the gangplank two abreast to cast their ballots, then down the stone steps at the side of the temple and back into the forum. The city tribes followed one after the other, and every one of them voted for Trebellius to be stripped of his office. Then the rural tribes started balloting. This all took several hours, and throughout it Trebellius looked grey with anxiety, and frequently conferred with his companion, Roscius. At one point he disappeared from the tribunal. I did not see where he went, but I guess it must have been to plead with Crassus to release him from his obligation. All across the forum, small huddles of senators gathered as their tribes finished voting, and I noticed Catulus and Hortensius going, grim-faced, from group to group. Cicero also did the rounds, leaving me behind as he circulated among the senators, talking to some of those, such as Torquatus and his old ally Marcellinus, whom he had secretly persuaded to switch to Pompey's camp.

At length, after seventeen tribes had voted to oust Trebellius, Gabinius ordered a pause in the balloting. He summoned Trebellius to the front of the tribunal and asked him whether he was prepared now to bow to the will of the people, and by so doing keep his tribunate, or whether it would be necessary to hold an eighteenth ballot and cast him out of office. This was Trebellius's chance to enter history as the hero of his cause, and I have often wondered whether, in his old age, he looked back on his decision with regret. But I suppose he still had hopes of a political career. After a short hesitation, he signalled his assent and his veto was withdrawn. I need hardly add that he was subsequently despised by both sides and never heard of again.

All eyes now turned to Roscius, Crassus's second tribune, and it was at this point, some time in the early afternoon, that Catulus appeared again at the foot of the temple steps, cupped his hands to his mouth, and shouted up to Gabinius, demanding a hearing. As I have mentioned before, Catulus commanded great respect among the people for his patriotism. It was therefore hard for Gabinius to refuse him, not least because he was regarded as the senior ex-consul in the senate. He gestured to the veterans to let him pass, and Catulus, despite his age, shot up the steps like a lizard. 'This is a mistake,' Cicero muttered to me.

Gabinius told Cicero afterwards that he thought the aristocrats, seeing that they had lost, might now be willing to concede in the interests of national unity. But not at all. Catulus railed against the *lex Gabinia* and the illegal tactics being used to drive it through. It was madness, he declared, for the republic to entrust its security to one man. Warfare was a hazardous business, especially at sea: what would happen to this special command if Pompey was killed? Who would be his replacement? A cry went up of 'You!' which, however flattering, was not at all the response that Catulus wanted. He knew he was far too old to go off soldiering. What he really wanted was a dual command – Crassus and Pompey – because even though he detested Crassus personally, he reckoned that the richest man in Rome would at least provide a counterweight to Pompey's power. But by now Gabinius had begun to realise his error in letting Catulus speak. The winter days were short. He needed to finish the voting by sunset. He roughly interrupted the former consul and told him he had had his say: it was time to put the matter to the ballot. Roscius thereupon sprang forward and tried to make a formal proposal splitting the supreme command in two, but the people were becoming exasperated, and refused to give him a hearing. In fact they set up such a defeaning clamour it was said that the noise killed a raven flying overhead and sent it plummeting to the earth. All Roscius could do against the uproar was raise two fingers to veto the legislation and signify his belief that there should be two commanders. Gabinius knew that if he had to call yet another ballot to remove a tribune, he would lose the light, and with it the chance of establishing the supreme command that day – and who could tell what lengths the aristocrats might go to if they had a chance to regroup overnight? So he responded by turning his back on Roscius and ordering the bill to be put regardless.

'That's it,' said Cicero to me, as the voting clerks sprang to their stations. 'It's done. Run up to Pompey's house, and tell them to send a message to the general immediately. Write this down: "The bill is passed. The command is yours. You must set out for Rome at once. Be sure to arrive tonight. Your presence is required to secure the situation. Signed, Cicero."' I checked I had his words correctly, then hurried off on my errand, while Cicero plunged back into the crowded forum to practise his art – cajoling, flattering, sympathising, even occasionally threatening – for there was nothing, according to his philosophy, that could not be made or undone or repaired by words.

*   *   *

Thus was passed, by a unanimous vote of all the tribes, the *lex Gabinia*, a measure which was to have immense consequences – for all those personally concerned, for Rome, and for the world.

As night fell, the forum emptied and the combatants retired to their respective headquarters – the aristocratic diehards to the home of Catulus, on the brow of the Palatine; the adherents of Crassus to his own, more modest dwelling, lower down the same hill; and the victorious Pompeians to the mansion of their chief, on the Esquiline. Success had worked its usual fecund magic, and I should think that at least twenty senators crammed themselves into Pompey's tablinum to drink his wine and await his victorious return. The room was brilliantly illuminated by candelabra, and there was that thick atmosphere of drink and sweat and the noisy racket of masculine conversation which often follows the release of tension. Caesar, Afranius, Palicanus, Varro, Gabinius and Cornelius were all present, but the newcomers outnumbered them. I cannot remember all their names. Lucius Torquatus and his cousin, Aulus, were certainly present, along with another notable young pair of bluebloods, Metellus Nepos and Lentulus Marcellinus. Cornelius Sisenna (who had been one of Verres's most enthusiastic supporters) made himself thoroughly at home, putting his feet up on the furniture, as did the two ex-consuls, Lentulus Clodianus and Gellius Publicola (the same Gellius who was still smarting from Cicero's joke about the philosophy conference). As for Cicero, he sat apart in an adjoining chamber, composing an acceptance speech for Pompey to deliver the next day. At the time, I could not understand his curious quietness, but with hindsight I believe he may have had an intuition that something had just cracked in the commonwealth which it would be hard even for his words to repair. From time to time he sent me out to the vestibule to check on Pompey's whereabouts.

Shortly before midnight, a messenger arrived to say that Pompey was approaching the city along the Via Latina. A score of his veterans had been stationed at the Capena Gate to escort him home by torchlight, in case his enemies resorted to desperate tactics, but Quintus – who had spent much of the night touring the city with the precinct bosses – reported to his brother that the streets were quiet. Eventually, cheering outside announced the great man's arrival, and suddenly there he was among us, bigger than ever, grinning, shaking hands, clapping backs; even I received a friendly punch on the shoulder. The senators clamoured for Pompey to make a speech, at which Cicero remarked, a touch too loudly, 'He cannot speak yet: I have not written what he should say.' Just for a moment I saw a shadow flash across Pompey's face, but yet again Caesar came to Cicero's rescue, howling with laughter, and when Pompey suddenly grinned and wagged his finger in mock-reproach, the atmosphere relaxed into the joshing humour of an officers' mess, where the triumphant commander expects to be ribbed.

Whenever I picture the word *imperium* it is always Pompey who comes into my mind – Pompey that night, hovering over his map of the Mediterranean, distributing dominion over land and sea as casually as he dispensed his wine ('Marcellinus, you can have the Libyan sea, while you, Torquatus, shall have eastern Spain . . .'), and Pompey the following morning, when he went down into the forum to claim his prize. The annalists later reckoned that twenty thousand crammed into the centre of Rome to see him anointed world commander. It was such a throng that even Catulus and Hortensius dared not commit some last act of resistance, although I am sure they would have liked to, but were instead obliged to stand with the other senators, putting the best face on it they could; Crassus, typically, could not even manage that, and stayed away altogether. Pompey did not say much, mostly a few protestations of humble gratitude, crafted by Cicero, and an appeal for national unity. But then he did not have to say anything: his presence alone had caused the price of grain in the markets to halve, such was the confidence he inspired. And he finished with the most wonderful theatrical flourish, which can only have come from Cicero: 'I shall now put on again that uniform once so dear and so familiar to me, the sacred red cloak of a Roman commander in the field, and I shall not take it off again until victory in this war is won – or I shall not survive the outcome!' He raised his hand in salute and left the platform – was wafted from the platform would be a better way of putting it, on a wind of acclamation. The applause was still going on when suddenly, beyond the rostra, he came into view again – steadily climbing the steps of the Capitol, now wearing the *paludamentum*, that bright scarlet cloak which is the mark of every Roman proconsul on active service. As the people went wild with enthusiasm, I glanced across to where Cicero was standing next to Caesar. Cicero's expression was one of amused distaste, but Caesar's was enraptured, as if he were already glimpsing his own future. Pompey carried on into the precincts of the Capitoline Triad, where he sacrificed a bull to Jupiter, and left the city immediately afterwards, without saying goodbye to Cicero or to anyone else. It was to be six years before he returned.

XIII

In the annual elections for praetor that summer, Cicero topped the poll. It was an ugly, scrappy campaign, fought in the aftermath of the struggle over the *lex Gabinia*, when trust between the political factions had broken down. I have before me the letter which Cicero wrote to Atticus that summer, expressing his disgust at all things in public life: 'It is unbelievable in how short a time how much worse you will find them than when you left.' Twice the balloting had to be abandoned halfway through when fighting broke out on the Field of Mars. Cicero suspected Crassus of hiring thugs to disrupt the voting, but could not prove it. Whatever the truth, it was not until September that the eight praetors-elect were finally able to assemble in the senate house to determine which court each would preside over in the coming year. The selection, as usual, was to be settled by drawing lots.

The most coveted office was that of urban praetor, who in those days ran the justice system and was ranked third in the state, behind the two consuls; he also had responsibility for staging the Games of Apollo. If that was the plum, then the post to be avoided at all costs was the embezzlement court, a job of stunning tedium. 'Of course, I should like the urban praetorship,' Cicero confided to me as we walked down to the senate that morning. 'And frankly, I should rather hang myself than sort out embezzlement for a year. But I shall willingly settle for anything in between.' He was in a buoyant mood. The elections were concluded at last and he had won the most votes. Pompey was gone not only from Rome but from Italy, so he had no great man looming over him. And he was getting very close to the consulship now – so close he could almost feel that ivory chair beneath him.

There was always a full chamber for these lot-drawing ceremonies, combining as they did high politics with a game of chance, and by the time we arrived the majority of the senators had already gone in. Cicero entered to a noisy reception, with cheers from his old supporters among the *pedarii* and abusive shouts from the aristocrats. Crassus, stretched out in his usual position on the consular front bench, regarded him through half-closed eyes, like a big cat pretending to be asleep while a little bird hops by. The election had turned out much as Cicero had expected, and if I give you here the names of the other praetors-elect, I believe you will have a good sense of how politics stood at that time. Apart from Cicero, there were only two other men of obvious ability waiting calmly to draw their lots. By far the most talented was Aquilius Gallus, who some say was a better lawyer even than Cicero, and who was already a respected judge; in fact, he was something of a paragon – brilliant, modest, just, kindly, a man of supreme taste, with a magnificent mansion on the Viminal Hill; Cicero had it in mind to approach the older man to be his running-mate for consul. Next to Gallus, at least in gravitas, was Sulpicius Galba, of a distinguished aristocratic family, who had so many consular masks in his atrium, it was inconceivable he would not be one of Cicero's rivals for the consulship; but although he was honest and able, he was also harsh and arrogant – that would count against him in a tight election. Fourth in talent, I suppose, although Cicero sometimes burst out laughing at his absurdities, was Quintus Cornificius, a rich religious fundamentalist, who talked endlessly about the need to revive Rome's declining morals – 'the candidate of the gods', Cicero called him. After that, I am afraid, there was a great shelving-away in ability: remarkably, all the other four praetors-elect were men who had previously been expelled from the senate, for deficiencies in either funds or morals. The oldest of these was Varinius Glaber, one of those clever, bitter men who expect to succeed in life and cannot believe it when they realise they have failed – already a praetor seven years earlier, he had been given an army by the senate to put down the revolt of Spartacus; but his legions were weak and he had been beaten repeatedly by the rebel slaves, eventually retiring from public life in humiliation. Then there was Caius Orchivius – 'all push and no talent', as Cicero characterised him – who had the support of a big voting syndicate. In seventh place when it came to brains Cicero placed Cassius Longinus – 'that barrel of lard' – who was sometimes called the fattest man in Rome. Which left, in eighth, none other than Antonius Hybrida, the drinker who kept a slave girl for a wife, whom Cicero had agreed to help in the elections on the grounds that here, at least, would be one praetor whose ambitions he would not have to worry about. 'Do you know why they call him "Hybrida"?' Cicero asked me one day. 'Because he's half man, half imbecile. I wouldn't award him the half, personally.'

But those gods to whom Cornificius was so devoted have a way of punishing such hubris, and they duly punished Cicero that day. The lots were placed in an ancient urn which had been used for this purpose for centuries, and the presiding consul, Glabrio, called up the candidates in alphabetical order, which meant that Antonius Hybrida went first. He dipped his trembling hand into the urn for a token and gave it to Glabrio, who raised an eyebrow and then read out: 'Urban praetor.' There was a moment of silence, and then the chamber rang with such a shout of laughter that the pigeons roosting in the roof all took off in a great burst of shit and feathers. Hortensius and some of the other aristocrats, knowing that Cicero had helped Hybrida, pointed towards the orator and clapped their sides in mockery. Crassus almost fell off his bench with delight, while Hybrida himself – soon to be the third man in the state – stood beaming all around him, no doubt misinterpreting the derision as pleasure at his good fortune.

I could not see Cicero's face, but I could guess what he was thinking: that his bad luck would surely now be completed by drawing embezzlement. Gallus went next and won the court which administered electoral law; Longinus the fat man received treason; and when candidate-of-the-gods Cornificius was awarded the criminal court, the odds were starting to look decidedly grim – so much so that I was sure the worst was about to happen. But thankfully it was the next man up, Orchivius, who drew embezzlement. When Galba was given responsibility for hearing cases of violence against the state, that meant there were only two possibilities left for Cicero – either his familiar stamping-ground of the extortion court, or the position of foreign praetor, which would have left him effectively the deputy of Hybrida: a grim fate for the cleverest man in the city. As he stepped up to the dais to draw his lot, he gave a rueful shake of his head – you can scheme all you like in politics, the gesture seemed to say, but in the end it all comes down to luck. He thrust his hand into the urn and drew out – extortion. There was a certain pleasing symmetry in that it was Glabrio, the former president of this

very court in which Cicero had made his name, who read out
the announcement. So that left the foreign praetorship to Varinius,
the victim of Spartacus. Thus the courts were settled for the
following year, and the preliminary field lined up for the consulship.

Amid all this rush of political events, I have neglected to mention
that Pomponia had become pregnant in the spring – proof, as
Cicero wrote triumphantly to Atticus when he passed on the
news, that the marriage with Quintus must be working after all.
Not long after the praetorian elections, the child was born, a
healthy boy. It was a matter of great pride to me, and a mark of
my growing standing within the family, that I was invited to
attend the lustrical, on the ninth day following the birth. The
ceremony was held at the Temple of Tellus, next to the family
house, and I doubt whether any nephew could have had a more
doting uncle than Cicero, who insisted on commissioning a
splendid amulet from a silversmith as a naming-present. It was
only after baby Quintus had been blessed by the priest with holy
water, and Cicero took him in his arms, that I realised how much
he missed having a boy of his own. A large part of any man's
motivation in pursuing the consulship must surely have been that
his son, and grandson, and sons of his sons to infinity, could exercise the right of *ius imaginum*, and display his likeness after death
in the family atrium. What was the point in founding a glorious
family name if the line was extinct before it even started? And
glancing across the temple to Terentia, carefully studying her
husband as he stroked the baby's cheek with the back of his little
finger, I could see that the same thought was in her mind.

The arrival of a child often prompts a keen reappraisal of the future, and I am sure this was what led Cicero, shortly after the birth of his nephew, to arrange for Tullia to become betrothed. She was now ten years old, his cynosure as ever, and rare was the day, despite his legal and political work, when he did not clear a little space to read to her or play some game. And it was typical of his mingling of tenderness and cunning that he first raised his plan with her, rather than with Terentia. 'How would you like,' he said to her one morning, when the three of us were in his study, 'to get married one day?' When she replied that she would like that very much, he asked her whom in all the world she would most like to have as a husband.

'Tiro!' she cried, flinging her arms around my waist.

'I am afraid he is much too busy helping me to have time to take a wife,' he replied solemnly. 'Who else?'

Her circle of grown-up male acquaintances was limited, so it was not long before she raised the name of Frugi, who had spent so much time with Cicero since the Verres case, he was almost a part of the family.

'Frugi!' exclaimed Cicero, as if the idea had never before occurred to him. 'What a wonderful thought! And you are sure this is what you want? You are? Then let us go and tell your mama immediately.'

In this way Terentia found herself outmanoeuvred by her husband on her own territory as skilfully as if she had been some cretinous aristocrat in the senate. Not that she could have found much to object to in Frugi, who was a good enough match even for her – a gentle, diligent young man, now aged twenty-one, from an extremely distinguished family. But she was far too shrewd not to see that Cicero, by creating a substitute whom he could train and bring on to a public career, was doing the next best thing to having a son of his own. This realisation no doubt made her feel threatened, and Terentia always reacted violently to threats. The betrothal ceremony in November went smoothly enough, with Frugi – who was very fond of his fiancée, by the way – shyly placing a ring on her finger, under the approving gaze of both families and their households, with the wedding fixed for five years hence, when Tullia would be pubescent. But that night Cicero and Terentia had one of their most ferocious fights. It blew up in the tablinum before I had time to get out of the way. Cicero had made some innocuous remark about the Frugis being very welcoming to Tullia, to which Terentia, who had been ominously quiet for some time, responded that it was indeed very good of them, *considering*.

'Considering what?' asked Cicero wearily. He had obviously decided that arguing with her that night was as inevitable as vomiting after a bad oyster, and that he might as well get it out of the way at once.

'Considering the connection they are making,' she responded, and very quickly she was launched on her favourite line of attack – the shamefulness of Cicero's lackeying towards Pompey and his coterie of provincials, the way that this had set the family in opposition to all who were most honourable in the state, and the rise of mob rule which had been made possible by the illegal passage of the *lex Gabinia*. I cannot remember all of it, and in any case what does it matter? Like most arguments between husband and wife it was not about the thing itself, but a different matter entirely – that is, her failure to produce a son, and Cicero's consequent semi-paternal attachment to Frugi. Nevertheless, I do remember Cicero snapping back that, whatever Pompey's faults, no one disputed that he was a brilliant soldier, and that once he had been awarded his special command and had raised his troops and put to sea, he had wiped out the pirate threat in only forty-nine days. And I also recall her crushing retort, that if the pirates really had been swept from the sea in seven weeks, perhaps they had not been quite the menace that Cicero and his friends had made them out to be in the first place! At that point, I managed to slip out of the room and retreat to my little cubicle, so the rest was lost to me. But the mood in the house during the following days was as fragile as Neapolitan glass.

'You see how hard pressed I am?' Cicero complained to me the next morning, rubbing his forehead with his knuckles. 'There is no respite for me anywhere, either in my business or my leisure.'

As for Terentia, she became increasingly preoccupied with her supposed barrenness, and took to praying daily at the Temple of the Good Goddess on the Aventine Hill, where harmless snakes roamed freely in the precincts to encourage fertility and no man was allowed to set eyes upon the inner sanctum. I also heard from her maid that she had set up a small shrine to Juno in her bedroom.

Secretly, I believe Cicero shared Terentia's opinion of Pompey. There was something suspicious as well as glorious about the speed of his victory ('Organised at the end of winter,' as Cicero put it, 'started at the beginning of spring, and finished by the middle of the summer'), which made one wonder whether the whole enterprise could not have been handled perfectly well by a commander appointed in the normal way. Still, there was no denying his success. The pirates had been rolled up like a carpet, driven from the waters of Sicily and Africa eastwards, through the Illyrian Sea to Achaia, and then purged from the whole of Greece. Finally, they had been trapped by Pompey himself in their last great stronghold, Coracesium, in Cilicia, and in a huge battle on sea and land, ten thousand had been killed and four hundred vessels destroyed. Another twenty thousand had been captured. But rather than have them crucified, as no doubt Crassus would have done, Pompey had ordered the pirates to be resettled inland with their wives and families, in the depopulated towns of Greece and Asia Minor – one of which he renamed, with characteristic modesty, Pompeiopolis. All this he did without reference to the senate.

Cicero followed his patron's fantastic progress with mixed feelings ('Pompeiopolis! Dear gods, the *vulgarity* of it!'), not least because he knew that the more swollen with success Pompey became, the longer the shadow he would cast over his own career. Meticulous planning and overwhelming numerical superiority: these were Pompey's favourite tactics, both on the battlefield and in Rome, and as soon as phase one of his campaign – the destruction of the pirates – was completed, phase two began in the forum, when Gabinius started agitating to have the command of the Eastern legions stripped from Lucullus and awarded to Pompey. He used the same trick as before, employing his powers as tribune to summon witnesses to the rostra, who gave the people a sorry picture of the war against Mithradates. Some of the legions, unpaid for years, had simply refused to leave their winter camp. The poverty of these ordinary fighting men Gabinius contrasted with the immense wealth of their aristocratic commander, who had shipped back so much booty from the campaign that he had bought an entire hill just outside the gates of Rome and was building a great palace there, with all the state rooms named after the gods. Gabinius subpoenaed Lucullus's architects and had them brought to the rostra, where he forced them to show to the people all their plans and models. Lucullus's name from that time on became a synonym for outrageous luxury, and the angry citizens burned his effigy in the forum.

In December, Gabinius and Cornelius stood down as tribunes, and a new creature of Pompey's, the tribune-elect, Caius Manilius, took over the safeguarding of his interests in the popular assemblies. He immediately proposed a law granting command of the war against Mithradates to Pompey, along with the government of the provinces of Asia, Cilicia and Bithynia – the latter two held by Lucullus. Any thin hopes that Cicero might have entertained of lying low on the issue were destroyed when Gabinius came to see him bearing a message from Pompey. This briskly conveyed the general's good wishes, along with his hopes that Cicero would support the *lex Manilia* 'in all its provisions', not only behind the scenes but also in public, from the rostra.

'"In all its provisions",' repeated Gabinius, with a smirk. 'You know what that means.'

'I presume it means the clause which appoints you to the command of the legions on the Euphrates, thus giving you legal immunity from prosecution now that your term as tribune has expired.'

'You have it.' Gabinius grinned and did a passable impersonation of Pompey, drawing himself up and puffing out his cheeks: '"Is he not clever, gentlemen? Did I not tell you he was clever?"'

'Calm youself, Gabinius,' said Cicero wearily. 'I assure you there is no one I would rather see heading off to the Euphrates than you.'

It is dangerous in politics to find oneself a great man's whipping boy. Yet this was the role in which Cicero was now becoming trapped. Men who would never have dared directly to insult or criticise Pompey could instead land blows on his lawyer-surrogate with impunity, knowing that everyone would guess their real target. But there was no escaping a direct order from the commander-in-chief, and so this became the occasion of Cicero's first speech from the rostra. He took immense trouble over it, dictating it to me several days beforehand, and then showing it to Quintus and Frugi for their comments. From Terentia he prudently withheld it, for he knew he would have to send a copy to Pompey and it was therefore necessary for him to ladle on the flattery. (I see from the manuscript, for example, that Pompey's 'superhuman genius as a commander' was amended at Quintus's suggestion to 'Pompey's superhuman *and unbelievable* genius as a commander'.) He hit upon a brilliant slogan to sum up Pompey's success – 'one law, one man, one year' – and fretted over the rest of the speech for hours, conscious that if he failed on the rostra, his career would be set back and his enemies would say he did not have the common touch to move the plebs of Rome. When the morning came to deliver it, he was physically sick with nerves, retching again and again into the latrine while I stood next to him with a towel. He was so white and drawn that I actually wondered if he would have the legs to get all the way down to the forum. But it was his belief that a great performer, however experienced, must always be frightened before going on stage – 'the nerves should be as taut as bowstrings if the arrows are to fly' – and by the time we reached the back of the rostra he was ready. Needless to say, he was carrying no notes. We heard Manilius announce his name and the applause begin. It was a beautiful morning, clear and bright; the crowd was huge. He adjusted his sleeves, drew himself erect, and slowly ascended into the noise and light.

Catulus and Hortensius once again were the leaders of the opposition to Pompey, but they had devised no new arguments since the *lex Gabinia*, and Cicero had some sport with them. 'What is Hortensius saying?' he teased. 'That if one man is to be put in supreme command, the right man is Pompey, but that supreme command ought not to be given to one man? That line of reasoning is now out of date, refuted not so much by words as by events. For it was you, Hortensius, who denounced that courageous man Gabinius for introducing a law to appoint a single commander against the pirates. Now I ask you in Heaven's name – if on that occasion the Roman people had thought more of your opinion than of their own welfare and their true interests, should we today be in possession of our present glory and our worldwide empire?' By the same token, if Pompey wanted Gabinius as one of his legionary commanders, he should have him, for no man had done more, apart from Pompey, to defeat the pirates. 'Speaking for myself,' he concluded, 'whatever devotion, wisdom, energy or talent I possess, whatever I can achieve by virtue of the praetorship which you have conferred upon me, I dedicate to the support of this law. And I call on all the gods to witness – most especially the guardians of this hallowed spot who see clearly into the hearts of all who enter upon public life – that I am acting not as a favour to Pompey, nor in the hope of gaining favour from him, but solely in the cause of my country.' He left the rostra to respectful applause. The law was passed, Lucullus was stripped of his command and Gabinius was given his legateship. As for Cicero, he had surmounted another obstacle in his progress to the consulship, but was more hated than ever by the aristocrats.

Later, he had a letter from Varro, describing Pompey's reaction at the moment when he received the news that he now had complete control of Rome's forces in the East. As his officers crowded round him at his headquarters in Ephesus to congratulate him, he frowned, struck himself on the thigh, and said ('in a weary voice', according to Varro): 'How sad it makes me, this constant succession of labours! Really I would rather be one of those people whom no one has heard about, if I am never to have any relief from military service, and never to be able to escape from being envied so that I can live quietly in the country with my wife.' Such play-acting was hard to stomach, especially when the whole world knew how much he had desired the command.

The praetorship brought an elevation in Cicero's station. Now he had six lictors to guard him whenever he left the house. He did not care for them at all. They were rough fellows, hired for their strength and easy cruelty: if a Roman citizen was sentenced to be punished, they were the ones who carried it out, and they were adept at floggings and beheadings. Because their posts were permanent, some had been used to power for years, and they rather looked down on the magistrates they guarded as mere transitory politicians, here today and gone tomorrow. Cicero hated it when they cleared the crowds out of his way too roughly, or ordered passers-by to remove their headgear or dismount in the presence of a praetor, for the people being so humiliated were his voters. He instructed the lictors to show more politeness, and for a time they would, but they soon snapped back into their old ways. The chief of them, the *proximus lictor*, who was supposed to stand at Cicero's side at all times, was particularly obnoxious. I forget his name now, but he was always bringing Cicero tittle-tattle of what the other praetors were up to, gleaned from his fellow lictors, not realising that this made him deeply suspect in the eyes of Cicero, who was well aware that gossip is a trade, and that reports of his own actions would be being offered as currency in return. 'These people,' Cicero complained to me one morning, 'are a warning of what happens to any state which has a permanent staff of officials. They begin as our servants and end up imagining themselves our masters!'

My own status rose with his. I discovered that to be known as the confidential secretary of a praetor, even if one was a slave, was to enjoy an unaccustomed civility from those one met. Cicero told me beforehand that I could expect to be offered money to use my influence on behalf of petitioners, and when I insisted hotly that I would never accept a bribe, he cut me off. 'No, Tiro, you should have some money of your own. Why not? I ask only that you tell me who has paid you, and that you make it clear to whoever approaches you that my judgements are not to be bought, and that I will decide things on their merits. Aside from that, I trust you to use your own discretion.' This conversation meant a great deal to me. I had always hoped that eventually Cicero would grant me my freedom; permitting me to have some savings of my own I saw as a preparation for that day. The amounts which came in were small – fifty or a hundred here and there – and in return I might be required to bring a document to the praetor's attention, or draft a letter of introduction for him to sign. The money I kept in a small purse, hidden behind a loose brick in the wall of my cubicle.

As praetor, Cicero was expected to take in promising pupils from good families to study law with him, and in May, after the senate recess, a new young intern of sixteen joined his chambers. This was Marcus Caelius Rufus from Interamnia, the son of a wealthy banker and prominent election official of the Velina tribe. Cicero agreed, largely as a political favour, to supervise the boy's training for two years, at the end of which it was fixed that he would move on to complete his apprenticeship in another household – that of Crassus, as it happened, for Crassus was a business associate of Caelius's father, and the banker was anxious that his heir should learn how to manage a fortune. The father was a ghastly money-lending type, short and furtive, who seemed to regard his son as an investment which was failing to show an adequate yield. 'He needs to be beaten regularly,' he announced, just before he brought him in to meet Cicero. 'He is clever enough, but wayward and dissolute. You have my permission to whip him as much as you like.' Cicero looked askance at this, having never whipped anyone in his life, but fortunately as it turned out he got on very well with young Caelius, who was as dissimilar to his father as it was possible to imagine. He was tall and hand-some and quick-witted, with an indifference towards money and business which Cicero found amusing; I less so, for it generally fell to me to do all the humdrum tasks which were Caelius's responsibility, and which he shirked. But still, I must concede, looking back, that he had charm.

I shall not dwell on the details of Cicero's praetorship. This is not a textbook about the law, and I can sense your eagerness for me to get on to the climax of my story – the election for the consulship itself. Suffice it to say that Cicero was considered a fair and honest judge, and that the work was easily within his competence. If he encountered a particularly awkward point of jurisprudence, and needed a second opinion, he would either consult his old friend and fellow pupil of Molon, Servius Sulpicius, or go over to see the distinguished praetor of the election court, Aquilius Gallus, in his mansion on the Viminal Hill. The biggest case over which he had to preside was that of Caius Licinius Macer, a kinsman and supporter of Crassus, who was impeached for his actions as governor of Macedonia. The hearing dragged on for weeks, and at the end of it Cicero summed up very fairly, except that he could not resist one joke. The nub of the pros-ecution case was that Macer had taken half a million in illegal payments. Macer at first denied it. The prosecution then produced proof that the exact same sum had been paid into a money-lending company which he controlled. Macer abruptly changed his story and claimed that, yes, he remembered the payments, but thought that they were legal. 'Now, it may be,' said Cicero to the jury, as he was directing them on points of evidence, 'that the defendant believed this.' He left a pause just long enough for some of them to start laughing, whereupon he put on a mock-stern face. 'No, no, he may have believed it. In which case' – another pause – 'you may reasonably conclude perhaps that he was too *stupid* to be a Roman governor.' I had sat in sufficient courts by then to know from the gale of laughter that Cicero had just convicted the man as surely as if he had been the prosecuting counsel. But Macer – who was not stupid at all, but on the contrary, very clever: so clever that he thought everyone else a fool – did not see the danger, and actually left the tribunal while the jury was balloting in order to go home and change and have a haircut, in anticipation of his victory celebration that night. While he was absent, the jury convicted him, and he was just leaving his house to return to the court when Crassus intercepted him on his doorstep and told him what had happened. Some say he dropped dead on the spot from shock, others that he went straight back indoors and killed himself to spare his son the humiliation of his exile. Either way, he died, and Crassus – as if he needed one – had a whole new reason for hating Cicero.

The Games of Apollo on the sixth day of July traditionally marked the start of the election season, although in truth it always seemed to be election season in those days. No sooner had one campaign come to an end than the candidates began anticipating the start of the next. Cicero joked that the business of governing the state was merely something to occupy the time between polling days. And perhaps this is one of the things that killed the republic: it gorged itself to death on votes. At any rate, the responsibility for honouring Apollo with a programme of public entertainment always fell to the urban praetor, which in this particular year was Antonius Hybrida.

Nobody had been expecting much, or indeed anything at all, for Hybrida was known to have drunk and gambled away all his money. So it was a vast surprise when he staged not only a series of wonderful theatrical productions, but also lavish spectacles in the Circus Maximus, with a full programme of twelve chariot races, athletic competitions and a wild-beast hunt involving panthers and all manner of exotic animals. I did not attend, but Cicero gave me a full account when he came home that evening. Indeed, he could talk of nothing else. He flung himself down on one of the couches in the empty dining room – Terentia was in the country with Tullia – and described the parade into the Circus: the charioteers and the near-naked athletes (the boxers, the wrestlers, the runners, the javelin throwers and the discus men), the flute players and the lyre players, the dancers dressed as Bacchanalians and satyrs, the incense burners, the bulls and the goats and the heifers with their gilded horns plodding to sacrifice, the cages of wild beasts and the gladiators . . . He seemed dizzy with it. 'How much must it have all cost? That is what I kept asking myself. Hybrida must be banking on making it all back when he goes out to his province. You should have heard the cheers they gave to him when he entered and when he left! Well, I see nothing for it, Tiro. Unbelievable as it seems, we shall have to amend the list. Come.'

We went together into the study and I opened the strongbox

and pulled out all the papers relating to Cicero's consular campaign. There were many secret lists in there – lists of backers, of donors, of supporters he had yet to win over, of towns and regions where he was strong and where he was weak. The key list, however, was of the men he had identified as possible rivals, together with a summary of all the information known about them, pro and anti. Galba was at the top of it, with Gallus next to him, and then Cornificius, and finally Palicanus. Now Cicero took my pen and carefully, in his neat and tiny writing, added a fifth, whose name he had never expected to see there: Antonius Hybrida.

And then, a few days later, something happened which was to change Cicero's fortunes and the future of the state entirely, although he did not realise it at the time. I am reminded of one of those harmless-looking specks which one occasionally hears about, that a man discovers on his skin one morning, and thinks little of, only to see it gradually swell over the following months into an enormous tumour. The speck in this instance was a message, received out of the blue, summoning Cicero to see the pontifex maximus, Metellus Pius. Cicero was mightily intrigued by this, since Pius, who was very old (sixty-four, at least) and grand, had never previously deigned even to speak to him, let alone demand his company. Accordingly, we set off at once, with the lictors clearing our way.

In those days, the official residence of the head of the state religion was on the Via Sacra, next to the House of the Vestal Virgins, and I remember that Cicero was pleased to be seen entering the premises, for this really was the sacred heart of Rome, and not many men ever got the chance to cross the threshold.

We were shown to a staircase and conducted along a gallery which looked down into the garden of the vestals' residence. I secretly hoped to catch a glimpse of one of those six mysterious white-clad maidens, but the garden was deserted, and it was not possible to linger as the bow-legged figure of Pius was already waiting for us impatiently at the end of the gallery, tapping his foot, with a couple of priests on either side of him. He had been a soldier all his life and had the cracked and roughened look of something made of leather which has been left outside for years and only lately brought indoors. There was no handshake for Cicero, no invitation to be seated, no preliminaries of any sort. Pius merely said immediately, in his hoarse voice, 'Praetor, I need to talk to you about Sergius Catilina.'

At the mere mention of the name, Cicero stiffened, for Catilina was the man who had tortured to death his distant cousin, the populist politician Gratidianus, by breaking his limbs and gouging out his eyes and tongue. A jagged streak of violent madness ran through Catilina, like lightning across his brain. At one moment he could be charming, cultured, friendly; then a man would make some seemingly innocuous remark, or he would catch another looking at him in a way he thought dis- respectful, and he would lose all self-restraint. During the proscriptions of Sulla, when death lists were posted in the forum, Catilina had been one of the most proficient killers with the hammer and knife – *percussores*, as they were known – and had made a lot of money out of the estates of those he executed. His own brother-in-law was among the men he had murdered. Yet he had an undeniable charisma, and for each person he repulsed by his savagery, he attracted two or three more by his equally reckless displays of generosity. He was also sexually licentious. Seven years previously, he had been prosecuted for having sexual relations with a vestal virgin – none other, in fact, than Terentia's half-sister, Fabia. This was a capital offence, not only for him but for her, and if he had been found guilty she would have suffered the traditional punishment for a vestal virgin who broke her sacred vows of chastity – burial alive in the tiny chamber reserved for the purpose beside the Colline Gate. But the aristocrats, led by Catulus, had rallied around Catilina and secured his acquittal, and his political career had continued uninterrupted. He had been praetor the year before last, and had then gone out to govern Africa, thus missing the turmoil surrounding the *lex Gabinia*. He had only just returned.

'My family,' continued Pius, 'have been the chief patrons of Africa since my father governed the province half a century ago. The people there look to me for protection, and I have to tell you, Praetor, I have never seen them more incensed by any man than they have been by Sergius Catilina. He has plundered that province from end to end – taxed them and murdered them, stolen their temple treasures and raped their wives and daughters. The Sergii!' he exclaimed in disgust, retching up a great gob of yellow phlegm into his mouth and spitting it on to the floor. 'Descended from the Trojans, or so they boast, and not a decent one among them for two hundred years! And now they tell me you are the praetor responsible for bringing his type to book.' He looked Cicero up and down. 'Amazing! I cannot say that I know who the hell you are, but there it is. So what are you going to do about it?'

Cicero was always cool when someone tried to insult him. He merely said, 'Do the Africans have a case prepared?'

'They do. They already have a delegation in Rome seeking a suitable prosecutor. Who should they go to?'

'That is hardly a matter for me. I must remain the impartial president of the court.'

'Blah blah. Spare me the lawyer's talk. Privately. Man-to-man.' Pius beckoned Cicero to come closer. He had left most of his teeth behind on various battlefields and his breath whistled when he tried to whisper. 'You know the courts these days better than I. Who could do it?'

'Frankly, it will not be easy,' said Cicero. 'Catilina's reputation for violence precedes him. It will take a brave man to lay a charge against such a brazen killer. And presumably he will be standing for the consulship next year. There is a powerful enemy in the making.'

'Consul?' Pius suddenly struck himself very hard on the chest. The thump made his priestly attendants jump. 'Sergius Catilina will not be consul – not next year or any year – not as long as this old body has any life left in it! There must be someone in this city who is man enough to bring him to justice. And if not – well, I am not quite such a senile fool that I have forgotten how to fight in Rome. You just make sure, Praetor,' he concluded, 'that you leave enough time in your calendar to hear the case,' and he shuffled off down the corridor, grumbling to himself, pursued by his holy assistants.

As he watched him go, Cicero frowned and shook his head. Not comprehending politics nearly as well as I should have done, even after thirteen years in his service, I was at a loss to understand why he should have found this conversation so troubling. But he certainly was shaken, and as soon as we were back on the Via Sacra, he drew me out of the keen hearing of the *proximus lictor* and said, 'This is a serious development, Tiro. I should have seen this coming.' When I asked why it mattered to him whether Catilina was prosecuted or not, he replied, in a withering tone,

'Because, *bird-brain*, it is illegal to stand for election if you have charges pending against you. Which means that if the Africans do find a champion, and if a charge is laid against Catilina, and if it drags on into next summer, he will be barred from standing for the consulship until the case is resolved. Which means that if by any chance he is acquitted, *I* shall have to fight him in *my* year.'

I doubt whether there was another senator in Rome who would have tried to peer so far into the future – who would have piled up so many *ifs* and discerned a reason for alarm. Certainly, when he explained his anxiety to Quintus, his brother dismissed it with a laugh: 'And *if* you were struck by lightning, Marcus, and *if* Metellus Pius were able to remember what day of the week it was . . .' But Cicero continued to fret, and he made discreet enquiries about the progress of the African delegation as they searched for a credible advocate. However, as he suspected, they were finding it hard going, despite the immense amount of evidence they had collected of Catilina's wrongdoing, and the fact that Pius had carried a resolution in the senate censuring the former governor. No one was anxious to take on such a dangerous opponent, and risk being discovered floating face-down in the Tiber late one night. So, for the time being at least, the prosecution languished, and Cicero put the matter to the back of his mind. Unfortunately, it was not to remain there for long.

XIV

At the end of his term as praetor, Cicero was entitled to go abroad and govern a province for a year. This was the normal practice in the republic. It gave a man the opportunity to gain administrative experience, and also to replenish his coffers after the expense of running for office. Then he would come home, assess the political mood, and if all seemed promising, stand for the consulship that summer: Antonius Hybrida, for example, who had obviously incurred tremendous liabilities by the cost of his Games of Apollo, went off to Cappadocia to see what he could steal. But Cicero did not take this course, and waived his right to a province. For one thing, he did not want to put himself in a position where a trumped-up charge might be laid against him and he would find himself with a special prosecutor dogging his footsteps for months. For another, he was still haunted by that year he had spent as a magistrate in Sicily, and ever afterwards he had hated to be away from Rome for longer than a week or two. There can seldom have been a more urban creature than Cicero. It was from the bustle of the streets and the courts, the senate and the forum that he drew his energy, and the prospect of a year of dreary provincial company, however lucrative, in Cilicia or Macedonia, was anathema to him.

Besides, he had committed himself to an immense amount of advocacy, starting with the defence of Caius Cornelius, Pompey's former tribune, who had been charged with treason by the aristocrats. No fewer than five of the great patrician senators – Hortensius, Catulus, Lepidus, Marcus Lucullus and even old Metellus Pius – lined up to prosecute Cornelius for his part in advancing Pompey's legislation, charging him with illegally ignoring the veto of a fellow tribune. Faced with such an onslaught, I was sure that he was bound to be sent into exile. Cornelius thought so too, and had actually packed up his house and was ready to leave. But Cicero was always inspired by the sight of Hortensius and Catulus on the other side, and he rose to the occasion, making a most effective closing speech for the defence. 'Are we really to be lectured,' he demanded, 'on the traditional rights of the tribunes by five gentlemen, all of whom supported the legislation of Sulla abolishing exactly those rights? Did any of these illustrious figures step forward to support the gallant Gnaeus Pompey when, as the first act of his consulship, he restored the tribunes' power of veto? Ask yourself, finally, this: is it really a new-found concern for the traditions of the tribunes which drags them from their fish-ponds and private porticoes into court? Or is it, rather, the product of certain other "traditions" much dearer to their hearts – their tradition of self-interest and their traditional desire for revenge?'

There was more in a similar vein, and by the time he had finished, the five distinguished litigants (who had made the mistake of all sitting in a row) were looking half their previous size, especially Pius, who obviously found it hard to keep up, and who had his hand cupped to his ear and kept twisting in his seat as his tormentor prowled around the court. This was to be one of the old soldier's last appearances in public before the long twilight of his illness descended upon him. After the jury had voted to acquit Cornelius of all the charges, Pius left the court to jeers and mocking laughter, wearing an expression of elderly bafflement which I fear nowadays I recognise all too well as the natural set of my own features. 'Well,' said Cicero, with a certain satisfaction, as we prepared to walk home, 'at any rate, I believe that now he knows who I am.'

I shall not mention every case which Cicero took on at this time because there were dozens, all part of his strategy to place as many influential men as possible under an obligation to support him at the consular election, and to keep his name constantly in the voters' minds. He certainly chose his clients carefully, and four of them at least were senators: Fundanius, who controlled a big voting syndicate; Orchivius, who had been one of his colleagues as praetor; Gallius, who was planning to run for a praetorship; and Mucius Orestinus, charged with robbery, who was hoping to become tribune, and whose case tied up the practice for many days.

I believe that never before had any candidate approached the business of politics as exactly that – a business – and every week a meeting was convened in Cicero's study to review the campaign's progress. Participants came and went, but the inner core consisted of five: Cicero himself, Quintus, Frugi, myself, and Cicero's legal apprentice, Caelius, who, although still very young (or perhaps because of it), was adept at picking up gossip around the city. Quintus was once again the campaign manager, and insisted on presiding. He liked to suggest, by the occasional indulgent smile or raised eyebrow, that Cicero, genius though he was, could be something of an airy-fairy intellectual, and needed the blunt common sense of his brother to keep his feet on the earth; and Cicero, with a reasonably good grace, played along.

It would make an interesting study, if only I had the life left in me to write it: the story of brothers in politics. There were the Gracchi, of course, Tiberius and Caius, who devoted themselves to distributing wealth from the rich to the poor, and who both perished violently as a result. And then in my own time there were Marcus and Lucius Lucullus, patrician consuls in successive years, as well as any number of siblings from the Metellus and Marcellus clans. In a sphere of human activity in which friendships are transitory and alliances made to be broken, the knowledge that another man's name is forever linked to yours, however the fates may play, must be a powerful source of strength. The relationship between the Ciceros, like that between most brothers, I expect, was a complicated mixture of fondness and resentment, jealousy and loyalty. Without Cicero, Quintus would have been a dull and competent officer in the army, and then a dull and competent farmer in Arpinum, whereas Cicero without Quintus would still have been Cicero. Knowing this, and knowing that his brother knew it too, Cicero went out of his way to conciliate him, generously wrapping him in the glittering mantle of his fame.

Quintus spent a long time that winter compiling an election handbook, a distillation of his fraternal advice to Cicero, which he liked to quote from whenever possible, as if it were Plato's *Republic*. *Consider what city this is*, it began, *what it is you seek, and who you are. Every day, when you go down to the forum, repeat to yourself: 'I am a new man. I seek the consulship. This is Rome.'* I can still recall some of the other little homilies it preached. *All things are full of deceit, snares and treachery. Hold fast to the saying of Epicharmus, that the bone and sinew of wisdom is 'Never trust rashly'*

. . . See to it that you show off both the variety and number of your friends . . . I am very anxious that you should always have a crowd about you . . . If someone asks you to do something, do not decline, even if you cannot do it . . . Lastly, see that your canvass is a fine show, brilliant, resplendent and popular; and also, if it can be managed, that there should be scandalous talk about the crimes, lusts and briberies of your competitors.

Quintus was very proud of his handbook, and many years later he actually had it published, much to the horror of Cicero, who believed that political mastery, like great art, depends for its effects on the concealment of all the cunning which lies behind it.

In the spring Terentia celebrated her thirtieth birthday and Cicero arranged a small dinner party in her honour. Quintus and Pomponia came, and Frugi and his parents, and fussy Servius Sulpicius and his unexpectedly pretty wife, Postumia; there must have been others, but the flow of time has washed them from my memory. The household was assembled briefly by Eros the steward to convey our good wishes, and I remember thinking, when Terentia appeared, that I had never seen her looking quite so fine, or in a more cheerful mood. Her short dark curly hair was lustrous, her eyes bright, and her normally bony frame seemed fuller and softer. I said as much to her maid after the master and mistress had led their guests in to dinner, at which she glanced around to check that no one was observing us, linked her hands and made a circular gesture outwards over her stomach. At first I did not understand, which gave her a fit of the giggles, and it was only after she had run back upstairs, still laughing, that I realised what a fool I had been; and not just me, of course.

A normal husband would surely have noticed the symptoms sooner, but Cicero was invariably up at dawn and back at dusk, and even then there was always a speech to write or a letter to be sent – the miracle was that he should have found time to perform his conjugal duties at all. Anyway, midway through the dinner, a loud shout of excitement, followed by applause, confirmed that Terentia had taken the opportunity of the celebration to announce her pregnancy.

Later that evening, Cicero came into the study with a wide smile. He acknowledged my congratulations with a bow. 'She is certain it is a boy. Apparently, the Good Goddess has informed her of the fact, by means of certain supernatural signs understood only by women.' He rubbed his hands vigorously in anticipation; he really could not stop smiling. 'Always a wonderful addition at election time, Tiro, a baby – suggestive of a virile candidate, and a respectable family man. Talk to Quintus about scheduling the infant's campaign appearances.' He pointed to my notebook. 'I am joking, you idiot!' he said, seeing my dumbstruck expression, and pretended to cuff my ear. But I am undecided whom it says more about, him or me, that I am still not entirely convinced he *was* joking.

From this time on, Terentia became much stricter in her observance of religious rituals, and on the day following her birthday she made Cicero accompany her to the Temple of Juno on Capitol Hill, where she bought a small lamb for the priest to sacrifice, in gratitude for her pregnancy and marriage. Cicero was delighted to oblige her, for he was genuinely overjoyed at the prospect of another child, and besides, he knew how much the voters lapped up these public displays of piety.

★　★　★

And now I fear I must return to the growing tumour that was Sergius Catilina.

A few weeks after Cicero's summons to see Metellus Pius, that year's consular elections were held. But such was the flagrant use of bribery by the winning ticket, the result was swiftly annulled and in October the poll was held again. On this occasion Catilina submitted his name as a candidate. Pius swiftly put a stop to his chances – I suppose it must have been the last successful battle the old warrior fought – and the senate ruled that only those whose names were on the original ballot would be permitted to stand. This drove Catilina into one of his furies, and he began hanging around the forum with his violent friends, making all kinds of threats, which were taken sufficiently seriously by the senate that they voted an armed bodyguard to the consuls. Not surprisingly, no one had been brave enough to come forward and take up the Africans' case in the extortion court. I actually suggested it to Cicero one day, wondering if it might be a popular cause for him to espouse – after all, he had brought down Verres, and that had made him the most famous advocate in the world. But Cicero shook his head. 'Compared to Catilina, Verres was a kitten. Besides, Verres was not a man anyone much liked, whereas Catilina undeniably has a following.'

'Why is he so popular?' I asked.

'Dangerous men always attract a following, although that is not what concerns me. If it were simply a question of the mob in the street, he would be less of a threat. It is the fact that he has widespread aristocratic support – Catulus certainly, which probably also means Hortensius.'

'I should have thought him much too uncouth for Hortensius.'

'Oh, Hortensius knows how to make use of a street fighter

when the occasion demands it. Many a cultured house is protected by a savage dog. And Catilina is also a Sergius, do not forget, so they approve of him on snobbish grounds. The masses and the aristocracy: that is a potent combination in politics. Let us hope he can be stopped in the consular elections this summer. I am only grateful that the task does not look like falling to me.'

I thought at the time that this was the sort of remark which proves there are gods, because whenever, in their celestial orbits, they hear such complacency, it amuses them to show their power. Sure enough, it was not long afterwards that Caelius Rufus brought Cicero some disturbing news. Caelius by this time was seventeen, and, as his father had stated, quite ungovernable. He was tall and well built and could easily have passed for a man in his early twenties, with his deep voice and the small goatee beard which he and his fashionable friends liked to sport. He would slip out of the house when it was dark and Cicero was preoccupied with his work and everyone else was asleep; often he would not return until just before dawn. He knew that I had a little money put by, and was always pestering me to advance him small loans; one evening, after I had refused yet again, I retired to my cubicle to discover that he had found my hiding place and taken everything I possessed. I spent a miserable, sleepless night, but when I confronted him the next morning and threatened to report him to Cicero, tears came into his eyes and he promised to pay me back. And, in fairness to him, he did, and with generous interest; so I changed my hiding place and never said a word about it.

He drank and whored around the city at night with a group of very disreputable young noblemen. One of them was Gaius Curio, a twenty-year-old whose father had been consul and a great supporter of Verres. Another was Mark Antony, the nephew of Hybrida, who I reckon must then have been eighteen. But the real leader of the gang, chiefly because he was the eldest and richest and could show the others ways of getting into mischief they had never even dreamed of, was Clodius Pulcher. He was in his middle twenties and had been away for eight years on military service in the East, getting into all sorts of scrapes, including leading a mutiny against Lucullus – who also happened to be his brother-in-law – and then being captured by the very pirates he was supposed to be fighting. But now he was back in Rome, and looking to make a name for himself, and one night he announced that he knew exactly how he was going to do it – it would be a lark, a dare, risky and amusing (these were his actual words, according to Caelius) – *he would prosecute Catilina.*

When Caelius rushed in to tell Cicero the following morning, the senator at first refused to believe him. All he knew of Clodius were the scandalous rumours, widely circulating, that he had slept with his own sister – indeed these rumours had lately taken on a more substantial form, and had been cited by Lucullus himself as one of the grounds on which he had divorced his wife. 'What would such a creature be doing in the law courts,' scoffed Cicero, 'except as a defendant?' But Caelius, in his cheeky way, retorted that if Cicero wanted proof of what he was saying, he need only pay a visit to the extortion court in the next hour or two, when Clodius was planning to submit his application to prosecute. Needless to say, this was a spectacle Cicero could not resist, and once he had seen his more important clients, he went down to his old haunt at the Temple of Castor, taking me and Caelius with him.

Already, in that mysterious way it does, news that something dramatic was about to happen had spread, and there was a crowd of a hundred or more hanging around the foot of the steps. The current praetor, a man named Orbius, afterwards governor of Asia, had just sat down in his curule chair and was looking around him, no doubt wondering what was up, when a group of six or seven smirking youths appeared, strolling from the direction of the Palatine, apparently without a care between them. They clearly fancied themselves the height of fashion, and I suppose they were, with their long hair and their little beards, and their thick, embroidered belts worn loosely around their waists. 'By heavens, what a spectacle!' muttered Cicero, as they pushed past us, trailing a fragrant wake of crocus oil and saffron unguents. 'They look more like women than men!' One of their number detached himself from the rest and climbed the steps to the praetor. Midway up, he paused, and turned to the crowd. He was, if I may express it vulgarly, 'a pretty boy', with long blond curls, thick, wet red lips and a bronzed skin – a kind of young Apollo. But his voice when he spoke was surprisingly firm and masculine, marred only by his slangy, mock-plebeian accent, which rendered his family name as 'Clodius' instead of 'Claudius': another of his fashionable affectations.

'I am Publius Clodius Pulcher, son of Appius Claudius Pulcher, consul, grandson of consuls in the direct line for the past eight generations, and I come this morning to lay charges in this court against Sergius Catilina for the crimes he lately committed in Africa.'

At the mention of Catilina's name there was some muttering and whistling, and a big brute standing close to us shouted, 'You want to watch your backside, girlie!'

But Clodius did not seem in the least concerned. 'May my

ancestors and the gods bless this undertaking, and bring it to a fruitful conclusion.' He trotted briskly up to Orbius and gave him the *postulatus*, all neatly bound up in a cylinder, with a seal and a red ribbon, while his supporters applauded noisily, Caelius among them, until Cicero silenced him with a look. 'Run and find my brother,' he said to him. 'Inform him of what has happened, and tell him we need to meet at once.'

'That is a job for a slave,' objected Caelius, with a pout, no doubt worried about losing face in front of his friends. 'Surely Tiro here could go and fetch him?'

'Do as you are ordered,' snapped Cicero, 'and while you are at it, find Frugi as well. And be grateful I have not yet told your father of the disreputable company you are keeping.' That made Caelius shift himself, and he disappeared out of the forum towards the Temple of Ceres, where the plebeian aediles were normally to be found at that hour of the morning. 'I have spoiled him,' Cicero said wearily, as we climbed the hill back to the house, 'and do you know why? It is because he has charm, that most cursed of all the gifts, and I never can stop myself indulging someone with charm.'

As punishment, and also because he no longer fully trusted him, Cicero refused to let Caelius attend the day's campaign meeting, but sent him off instead to write up a brief. He waited until he was out of the way before describing the morning's events to Quintus and Frugi. Quintus was inclined to take a sanguine view, but Cicero was absolutely convinced that he would now have to fight Catilina for the consulship. 'I have checked the calendar of the extortion court – you remember what that is like – and the truth is there is simply no chance of Catilina's case being heard until July, which makes it impossible for him to be a consular candidate in this year. Therefore he comes inevitably into mine.' He suddenly pounded his fist on the desk and swore – a thing he rarely did. 'I predicted exactly this outcome a year ago – Tiro is my witness.'

Quintus said, 'Perhaps Catilina will be found guilty and sent into exile?'

'With that perfumed creature as his prosecutor? A man whom every slave in Rome knows to have been the lover of his own sister? No, no – you were right, Tiro. I should have taken down Catilina myself, when I had the chance. He would have been easier to beat in court than he will be in the ballot.'

'Perhaps it is not too late,' I suggested. 'Perhaps Clodius could be persuaded to yield the prosecution to you.'

'No, he will never do that,' said Cicero. 'You had only to look at him – the arrogance of the fellow – a typical Claudian. This is his chance for glory, and he will not let it slip. You had better bring out our list of potential candidates, Tiro. We need to find ourselves a credible running-mate – and quickly.'

In those days consular candidates usually submitted themselves to the electorate in pairs, for each citizen cast two votes for consul and it was obviously good tactics to form an alliance with a man who would complement one's own strengths during the canvass. What Cicero needed to balance his ticket was someone with a distinguished name who had wide appeal among the aristocracy. In return, he could offer them his own popularity among the *pedarii* and the lower classes, and the support of the electoral machine which he had built up in Rome. He had always thought that this would be easy enough to arrange when the time came. But now, as we reviewed the names on the list, I saw why he was becoming so anxious. Palicanus would bring nothing to the ticket. Cornificius was an electoral no-hoper. Hybrida had only half a brain. That left Galba and Gallus. But Galba was so aristocratic, he would have nothing to do with Cicero, and Gallus – despite all Cicero's pleadings – had said firmly that he had no interest in becoming consul.

'Can you believe it?' complained Cicero, as we huddled around his desk, studying the list of likely runners. 'I offer the man the greatest job in the world, and he has to give me nothing in return except to stand at my side for a day or two. Yet he still says he would prefer to concentrate on jurisprudence!' He took up his pen and crossed out Gallus's name, then added Catilina's to the bottom of the list. He tapped his pen beside it idly, underlined it, circled it, then glanced at each of us. 'Of course, there is one other potential partner we have not mentioned.'

'And who is that?' asked Quintus.

'Catilina.'

'*Marcus!*'

'I am perfectly serious,' said Cicero. 'Let's think it through. Suppose, instead of attempting to prosecute him, I offer to defend him. If I secure his acquittal, he will be under an obligation to support me for consul. On the other hand, if he is found guilty, and goes into exile – then that is the end of him. Either outcome is acceptable as far as I am concerned.'

'You would defend *Catilina?*' Quintus was well used to his brother, and it took a great deal to shock him, but on that day he was almost speechless.

'I would defend the blackest devil in hell if he was in need of an advocate. That is our system of law.' Cicero frowned and shook his head irritably. 'But we went over all this with poor Lucius just before he died. Come on, brother – spare me the reproachful face! You wrote the book: "I am a new man. I seek the consulship. This is Rome." Those three things – they say it all. I am a new man, therefore there is no one to help me but myself, and you few friends. I seek the consulship, which is immortality – a prize worth fighting for, yes? And this is Rome – *Rome* – not some abstract place in a work of philosophy, but a city of glory built on a river of filth. So yes, I will defend Catilina, if that is what is necessary, and then I will break with him as soon as I can. And he would do the same to me. That is the world we live in.' Cicero sat back in his chair and raised his hands. 'Rome.'

Cicero did not make a move immediately, preferring to wait and see whether the prosecution of Catilina would definitely go ahead. There was a widespread view that Clodius was simply showing off, or perhaps trying to distract attention from the shame of his sister's divorce. But in the lumbering way of the law, as the summer came on, the process passed through all its various stages – the *postulatio*, *divinatio*, and *nominis delatio* – a jury was selected and a date was fixed for the start of the trial in the last week of July. There was no chance now that Catilina would be free of litigation in time for the consular elections; nominations had already closed.

At this point, Cicero decided to let Catilina know that he might be interested in acting as his advocate. He gave much thought as to how to convey the offer, for he did not wish to lose face by being rebuffed, and he also wanted to be able to deny ever making an approach in case he was challenged in the senate. In the end he hit upon a characteristically subtle scheme. He called Caelius to his study, swore him to secrecy, and announced that he had it in mind to defend Catilina: what did he think? ('But not a word to anyone, mind!') This was exactly the sort of gossip which Caelius most delighted in, and naturally he could not resist sharing the confidence with his friends, among them Mark Antony

– who, as well as being the nephew of Hybrida, was also the adopted son of Catilina's close friend, Lentulus Sura.

I guess it must have taken all of a day and a half for a messenger to turn up on Cicero's doorstep, bearing a letter from Catilina asking him if he would care to visit, and proposing – in the interests of confidentiality – that the rendezvous be conducted after dusk. 'And so the fish bites,' said Cicero, showing me the letter, and he sent back with the slave a verbal reply that he would attend on Catilina in his house that same night.

Terentia was now very close to parturition, and was finding the heat of Rome in July insufferable. She lay, restless and groaning, on a couch in the stifling dining room, Tullia on one side reading to her in a piping voice, a maid with a fan on the other. Her temper, warm in the best of circumstances, was in these days permanently inflamed. As darkness fell and the candelabra were lit, she saw that Cicero was preparing to leave, and immediately demanded to know where he was going. When he gave a vague reply, she tearfully insisted that he must have taken a concubine and was visiting her, for why else would a respectable man go out of doors at this hour? And so, reluctantly, he told her the truth, that he was calling on Catilina. Of course this did not mollify her in the slightest, but only enraged her further. She demanded to know how he could bear to spend a moment in the company of the monster who had debauched her own sister, a vestal virgin, to which Cicero responded with some quip about Fabia having always been 'more vestal than virgin'. Terentia struggled to rise but failed and her furious invective pursued us all the way out of the house, much to Cicero's amusement.

It was a night very like the one on the eve of the elections for aedile, when he had gone to see Pompey. There was the same oppressive heat and feverish moonlight; the same slight breeze stirred the smell of putrefaction from the burial fields beyond the Esquiline Gate and spread it over the city like an invisible moist dust. We went down into the forum, where the slaves were lighting the street lamps, past the silent, darkened temples, and up on to the Palatine, where Catilina had his house. I was carrying a document case, as usual, and Cicero had his hands clasped behind his back and was walking with his head bowed in thought. Back then the Palatine was less built up than it is today, and the buildings were spaced further apart. I could hear the sound of a stream nearby and there was a scent of honeysuckle and dog rose. 'This is the place to live, Tiro,' said Cicero, halting on the steps. 'This is where we shall come when there are no more elections to be fought, and I need take less account of what the people think. A place with a garden to read in – imagine that – and where the children can play.' He glanced back in the direction of the Esquiline. 'It will be a relief to all concerned when this baby arrives. It is like waiting for a storm to break.'

Catilina's house was easy to find, for it was close by the Temple of Luna, which was painted white and lit up at night by torches, in honour of the moon goddess. A slave was waiting in the street to guide us, and he took us straight into the vestibule of the mansion of the Sergii, where a most beautiful woman greeted Cicero. This was Aurelia Orestilla, the wife of Catilina, whose daughter he was supposed to have seduced initially, before moving on to the mother, and for whose sake, it was rumoured, he had murdered his own son by his first marriage (the lad having threatened to kill Aurelia rather than accept such a notorious courtesan into the family). Cicero knew all about her, and cut off her effusive greeting with a curt nod. 'Madame,' he said, 'it is your husband I have come to see, not you,' at which she bit her lip and fell silent. It was one of the most ancient houses in Rome, and its timbers creaked as we followed the slave into the interior, which smelled of dusty old drapes and incense. One curious feature I remember was that it had been stripped almost bare, and obviously recently, for one could see the blurred rectangular outlines of where pictures had once hung, and circles of dust on the floor marked the absence of statues. All that remained in the atrium were the dingy wax effigies of Catilina's ancestors, jaundiced by generations of smoke. This was where Catilina himself was standing. The first surprise was how tall he was when one got close up – at least a head higher than Cicero – and the second was the presence behind him of Clodius. This must have been a terrific shock to Cicero, but he was far too cool a lawyer to show it. He shook hands quickly with Catilina, and then with Clodius, politely refused an offer of wine, and the three men turned straight to business.

Looking back, I am struck by how alike Catilina and Clodius were. This was the only time I ever saw them in a room together, and they might have been father and son, with their drawling voices, and the way they stood together so languidly, as if the world was theirs to own. I suppose this is what is called 'breeding'. It had taken four hundred years of intermarriage between the finest families in Rome to produce those two villains – as thoroughbred as Arab bloodstock, and just as quick and headstrong and dangerous.

'This is the deal as we see it,' said Catilina. 'Young Clodius here will make a brilliant speech for the prosecution and everyone will say he is the new Cicero and I am bound to be convicted. But then you, Cicero, will make an even more brilliant argument for the defence in reply, and therefore no one will be surprised when I am acquitted. At the end of it, we shall have put on a good show and we shall all emerge with our positions enhanced.

I am declared innocent before the people of Rome. Clodius is acknowledged as the brave and coming man. And you will have won yet another splendid triumph in the courts, defending someone a cut above your usual run of clients.'

'And what if the jury decides differently?'

'You need not be concerned about them.' Catilina patted his pocket. 'I have taken care of the jury.'

'The law is *so* expensive,' said Clodius with a smile. 'Poor Catilina has had to sell his heirlooms to be sure of justice. It really is a scandal. How *do* people manage?'

'I shall need to see the trial documents,' said Cicero. 'How soon before the hearing opens?'

'Three days,' said Catilina, and he gestured to a slave who was standing at the door. 'Does that give you long enough to prepare?'

'If the jury has already been convinced, I can make the speech in six words: "Here is Catilina. Let him go."'

'Oh, but I want the full Ciceronian production!' protested Catilina. 'I want: "This n-n-noble m-m-man . . . the b-b-blood of centuries . . . behold the tears of his w-w-wife and f-f-friends . . ."' He had his hand in the air and was twirling it expressively, crudely imitating Cicero's almost imperceptible stutter. Clodius was laughing; they were both slightly drunk. 'I want "African s-s-savages s-s-sullying this ancient c-c-court . . ." I want Carthage and Troy to be conjured before us, and Dido and Aeneas—'

'You will get,' said Cicero, coldly cutting him off, 'a professional job.' The slave had returned with the papers for the trial and I began rapidly piling them into my document case, for I could sense the atmosphere beginning to worsen as the drink took hold and I was anxious to get Cicero out of there. 'We shall need to meet to discuss your evidence,' he continued, in the same chilly tone. 'Tomorrow it had better be, if that is convenient to you.'

'By all means. I have nothing better to do. I had been expecting to stand for the consulship this summer, as you well know, until this young mischief-maker put a stop to it.'

It was the agility that was so shocking in a man of such height. He suddenly lunged forward and wrapped his powerful right arm around Clodius's neck and dragged the younger man's head down, so that Clodius was bent double. Poor Clodius – who was no weakling, incidentally – let out a muffled cry, and his fingers clawed feebly at Catilina's arm. But the strength of Catilina was appalling, and I wonder if he might not have broken his visitor's neck with a quick upward flick of his forearm, if Cicero had not said calmly, 'I must advise you, Catilina, as your defence attorney, that it would be a grievous mistake to murder your prosecutor.'

On hearing that, Catilina swung round and frowned at him, as if he had momentarily forgotten who Cicero was. Then he started laughing. He ruffled Clodius's blond curls and let him go. Clodius staggered backwards, coughing and massaging the side of his head and throat, and for an instant he gave Catilina a look of pure murder, but then he too started laughing, and straightened up. They embraced, Catilina called for some more wine, and we left them to it. 'What a pair,' exclaimed Cicero, as we passed by the Temple of Luna on our way back home. 'With any luck they will have killed one another by morning.'

By the time we had returned to Cicero's house, Terentia was in labour. There was no mistaking it. We could hear the screams from the street. Cicero stood in the atrium, white with shock and alarm, for he had been away when Tullia was born, and nothing in his philosophy books had prepared him for what was happening. 'Dear heavens, it sounds as though she is being tortured. Terentia!' He started towards the staircase which led to her room, but one of the midwives intercepted him.

We passed a long vigil in the dining room. He asked me to stay with him, but was at first too anxious to do any work. Sometimes he lay stretched out on the same couch Terentia had been occupying when we left, and then, when he heard another scream, he would jump up and pace around. The air was hot and heavy, the candle flames motionless, their black threads of smoke as rigid as plumb-lines suspended from the ceiling. I busied myself by emptying my case of the court papers I had carried back from Catilina's house and sorting them into categories – charges, depositions, summaries of documentary evidence. Eventually, to distract himself, Cicero, still prone on the couch, stretched out a hand and started reading, picking up one roll after another and holding it to the lamp which I placed beside him. He kept flinching and wincing, but I could not tell whether it was the continuing howls from upstairs or the horrific allegations against Catilina, for these were indeed the most appalling accounts of violence and rape, dispatched by almost every town in Africa, from Utica to Thaenae, and from Thapsus to Thelepte. After an hour or two, he tossed them aside in disgust and asked me to fetch some paper so that he could dictate a few letters, beginning with one to Atticus. He lay back and closed his eyes in an effort to concentrate. I have the very document before me now.

It is a long time since I had a line from you. I have already written to you in detail about my election campaign. At the moment I am proposing to defend my fellow candidate Catilina.

We have the jury we want, with full cooperation from the prosecution. If he is acquitted I hope he will be more inclined to work with me in the campaign. But should it go otherwise, I shall bear it philosophically.

'Ha! That is certainly true enough.' He closed his eyes again.

I need you home pretty soon. There is a decidedly strong belief going around that your noble friends are going to oppose my election.

And at that point my writing stops, because instead of a scream we heard a different sound from above us – the gurgling cry of a baby. Cicero sprang from the couch and ran upstairs to Terentia's room. It was some time before he reappeared, and when he did he silently took the letter from me and wrote across the top in his own hand:

I have the honour to inform you that I have become the father of a little son. Terentia is well.

How transformed a house is by the presence of a healthy newborn baby! I believe, although it is seldom acknowledged, that this must be because it is a double blessing. The unspoken dreads which attend all births – of agony, death and deformity – are banished, and in their place comes this miracle of a fresh life. Relief and joy are intertwined.

Naturally, I was not permitted upstairs to see Terentia, but a few hours later Cicero brought his son down and proudly showed him off to the household and his clients. To be frank, there was not much that was visible, apart from an angry little red face and a lick of fine dark hair. He was wrapped up tight in the woollen swaddling clothes which had performed the same service for Cicero more than forty years earlier. The senator also had a silver rattle preserved from his infancy which he tinkled above the tiny face. He carried him tenderly into the atrium and pointed to the spot where he dreamed that one day his consular image would hang. 'And then,' he whispered, 'you will be Marcus Tullius Cicero, son of Marcus Tullius Cicero the *consul* – how does that sound? Not bad, eh? There will be no taunts of "new man" for you! Here you are, Tiro – make the acquaintance of a whole new political dynasty.' He offered the bundle to me, and I held it nervously, in that way the childless do when handed a baby, and was relieved when the nurse took him from me.

Cicero meanwhile was once again contemplating the blank spot on his atrium wall, and had fallen into one of his reveries. I wonder what it was he was seeing there: his death mask, perhaps, staring back at him, like a face in the mirror? I enquired after the health of Terentia, and he said, distractedly, 'Oh, she is very well. Very strong. You know what she is like. Strong enough, at least, to resume belabouring me for making an alliance with Catilina.' He dragged his gaze away from the empty wall. 'And now,' he sighed, 'I suppose we had better keep our appointment with the villain.'

When we reached the house of Catilina, we found the former governor of Africa in a charming humour. Cicero later made a list of his 'paradoxical qualities' and I give it here, for it was nicely put: 'To attach many by friendship, and to retain them by devotion; to share what he possessed with all, and to be at the service of all his friends in time of need, with money, influence, effort, and – if necessary – with reckless crime; to control his natural temper as occasion required, and to bend and turn it this way and that; to be serious with the strict, easy with the liberal, grave with the old, amiable with the young, daring with criminals, dissolute with the depraved . . .' This was the Catilina who was waiting for us that day. He had already heard about the birth of Cicero's son, and pumped his advocate's hand in warm congratulation, and then produced a beautiful calfskin box, which he insisted Cicero open. Inside was a baby's silver amulet which Catilina had acquired in Utica. 'It is merely a local trinket to ward off ill health and evil spirits,' he explained. 'Please give it to your lad with my blessing.'

'Well,' replied Cicero, 'this is handsome of you, Catilina.' And it was indeed quite exquisitely engraved, certainly no mere trinket: when Cicero held it to the light I saw all manner of exotic wild animals chasing each another, linked by a motif of curling serpents. For one last moment he toyed with it, and weighed it in his palm, but then he replaced it in its box and handed it back to Catilina. 'I am afraid I cannot accept it.'

'Why?' asked Catilina, with a puzzled smile. 'Because you are my advocate, and advocates cannot be paid? Such integrity! But this is only a trifle for a baby!'

'Actually,' said Cicero, drawing in his breath, 'I have come to tell you I am not going to be your advocate.'

I was in the act of unpacking all the legal documents on to a small table which stood between the two men. I had been watching them in a sideways fashion but now I put my head down and carried on. After what seemed to me a long silence, I heard Catilina say, in a quiet voice, 'And why is that?'

'To speak frankly: because you are so obviously guilty.'

Another silence, and then Catilina's voice, when it came, was once again very calm. 'But Fonteius was guilty of extortion against the Gauls, and you represented him.'

'Yes. But there are degrees of guilt. Fonteius was corrupt but harmless. You are corrupt and something else entirely.'

'That is for the court to decide.'

'Normally I would agree. But you have purchased the verdict in advance, and that is not a charade I wish to be a part of. You have made it impossible for me to convince myself that I am acting honourably. And if I cannot convince myself, then I cannot convince anyone else – my wife, my brother, and now, perhaps more importantly, my son, when he is old enough to understand.'

At this point I risked a look at Catilina. He was standing completely motionless, his arms hanging loosely by his sides, and I was reminded of an animal that has suddenly come across a rival – it was a type of predatory stillness: watchful and ready to fight. He said lightly, but it seemed to me the lightness was now more strained: 'You realise this is of no consquence to me, but only to yourself? It does not matter who is my advocate; nothing changes for me. I shall be acquitted. But for you now – instead of my friendship, you will have my enmity.'

Cicero shrugged. 'I prefer not to have the enmity of any man, but when it is unavoidable, I shall endure it.'

'You will never have endured an enmity such as mine, I promise you that. Ask the Africans.' He grinned. 'Ask Gratidianus.'

'You removed his tongue, Catilina. Conversation would be difficult.'

Catilina swayed forward slightly, and I thought he might do to Cicero what he had only half done to Clodius the previous evening, but that would have been an act of madness, and Catilina was never wholly mad: things would have been far easier if he had been. Instead he checked himself and said, 'Well then, I suppose I must let you go.'

Cicero nodded. 'You must. Leave the papers, Tiro. We have no need of them now.'

I cannot remember if there was any further conversation; I do not believe there was. Catilina and Cicero simply turned their backs on one another, which was the traditional means of signalling enmity, and so we left that ancient, empty, creaking mansion, and went out into the heat of the Roman summer.

XV

Now began a most difficult and anxious period in Cicero's life, during which I am sure he often regretted that he had made such an enemy of Catilina, and had not simply found some excuse to wriggle out of his commitment to defend him. For there were, as he often observed, only three possible outcomes to the coming election, and none was pleasant. Either he would be consul and Catilina would not – in which case who could tell what lengths his resentful and defeated rival might be willing to go to? Or Catilina would be consul and he would not, and all the resources of the office would be turned against him. Or – and this, I think, alarmed him most of all – he and Catilina might be consuls together, in which case his dream of supreme *imperium* would degenerate into a year-long running battle, and the business of the republic would be paralysed by their acrimony.

The first shock came when the trial of Catilina opened a couple of days later, because who should step forward to act as chief defence advocate but the senior consul himself, Lucius Manlius Torquatus, head of one of the oldest and most respected patrician families in Rome. Catilina was escorted into court by all the traditional old guard of the aristocracy – Catulus, of course, but also Hortensius, Lepidus and the elder Curio. The only consolation for Cicero was that Catilina's guilt was utterly manifest, and Clodius, who had his own reputation to consider, actually made quite a decent job of drawing out the evidence. Although Torquatus was an urbane and precise attorney, he could only (to use the crude phrase of the time) apply so much perfume to this particular turd. The jury had been bribed, but the record of Catilina's behaviour in Africa was sufficiently shocking that they very nearly found him guilty, and he was only acquitted *per infamiam* – that is, he was dishonourably discharged from the court. Clodius, fearful of retaliation from Catilina and his supporters, departed the city soon afterwards, to serve on the staff of Lucius Murena, the new governor of Further Gaul. 'If only I had prosecuted Catilina myself!' groaned Cicero. 'He would be with Verres in Massilia by now, watching the waves coming in!' But at least he had avoided the dishonour of serving as Catilina's defender – for which, incidentally, he gave much credit to Terentia, and thereafter he was always more willing to listen to her advice.

Cicero's campaign strategy now called for him to leave Rome for four months, and travel north to canvass, all the way up to the borders of Italy in Nearer Gaul. No consular candidate, as far as I am aware, had ever done such a thing before, but Cicero, even though he loathed to leave the city for so long, was convinced it was worth it. When he stood for aedile, the number of registered electors was some four hundred thousand; but now those rolls had been revised by the censors, and with the extension of the franchise as far north as the River Po, the electorate had increased to almost one million. Very few of these citizens would ever bother to travel all the way to Rome to cast their votes in person. But Cicero reckoned that if he could only persuade just one in ten of those he met to make the effort, it could give him a decisive edge on the Field of Mars.

He fixed his departure for after the Roman Games, which began that year as usual on the fifth day of September. And now came Cicero's second – I will not call it a shock exactly, but it was certainly more troubling than a mere surprise. The Roman Games were always given by the curule aediles, one of whom was Caesar. As with Antonius Hybrida, nothing much was expected of him, for he was known to be hard up. But Caesar took the whole production over, and in his lordly way declared that the games were in honour not only of Jupiter, but of his dead father. For days beforehand he had workmen in the forum building colonnades, so that people could stroll around and see the wild beasts he had imported, and the gladiators he had bought – no fewer than three hundred and twenty pairs, clad in silver armour: the greatest number ever produced for a public spectacle. He laid on banquets, held processions, staged plays, and on the morning of the games themselves the citizens of Rome woke to discover that he had, overnight, erected a statue of the populist hero, Marius – the aristocrats' great hate-figure – within the precincts of the Capitol.

Catulus immediately insisted that a session of the senate be called, and tabled a motion demanding that the statue be removed at once. But Caesar replied to him with contempt, and such was his popularity in Rome, the senate did not dare to press the matter further. Everyone knew that the only man who could possibly have lent Caesar the money for such an extravaganza was Crassus, and I remember how Cicero returned from the Roman Games in the same dejected manner that he had come back from Hybrida's Games of Apollo. It was not that Caesar, six years his junior, was ever likely to run against him personally in an election, but rather that Crassus was clearly up to something, and he could not work out what. Cicero described to me that night a part of the entertainment. 'Some poor wretch, a criminal, was led out naked into the centre of the Circus, armed with a wooden sword, and then they released a panther and a lion to attack him, which no doubt they had starved for weeks. And actually he put on a reasonable show, using the only advantage he had – his brains – dashing this way and that, and for a while it looked as though he might succeed in making the beasts attack one another instead of him. The crowd were cheering him on. But then he tripped and the creatures tore him to pieces. And I looked to one side of me at Hortensius and the aristocrats, all laughing and applauding, and at Crassus and Caesar side by side on the other, and I thought to myself, Cicero: that man is you.'

His personal relations with Caesar were always cordial, not least because Caesar enjoyed his jokes, but he had never trusted him, and now that he suspected he was in alliance with Crassus, he began to keep a greater distance. There is another story I should tell about Caesar. Around this time Palicanus came to call, seeking Cicero's support for his own bid for the consulship. Oh dear – poor Palicanus! He was a cautionary lesson in what can happen in politics if one becomes too dependent on the favour of a great man. He had been Pompey's loyal tribune, and then his loyal praetor, but he had never been given his share of the spoils once Pompey had achieved his special commands, for the simple reason there was nothing left he could offer in return; he had been bled dry. I picture him, day after day sitting in his house, staring at his gigantic bust of Pompey, or dining alone beneath that mural of Pompey as Jupiter – truthfully, he had about as much chance of becoming consul as I did. But Cicero tried to let him down kindly, and said that although he could not form an electoral alliance with him, he would at least try to do something for him in the future (of course, he never did). At the end of the interview, just as Palicanus was rising, Cicero, keen to end on a friendly note, asked to be remembered to his daughter, the blowsy Lollia, who was married to Gabinius.

'Oh, do not talk to me about that whore!' responded Palicanus. 'You must have heard? The whole city is talking about it! She is being screwed every day by Caesar!'

Cicero assured him he had not heard.

'Caesar,' said Palicanus bitterly. 'Now there is a duplicitous bastard! I ask you: is that any time to bed a comrade's wife – when he is a thousand miles away, fighting for his country?'

'Disgraceful,' agreed Cicero. 'Mind you,' he observed to me after Palicanus had gone, 'if you are going to do such a thing, I should have thought that was the ideal time. Not that I am an expert on such matters.' He shook his head. 'Really, though, one has to wonder about Caesar. If a man would steal your wife, what else wouldn't he take from you?'

Yet again I almost told him what I had witnessed in Pompey's house; and yet again I thought the better of it.

It was on a clear autumn morning that Cicero bade a tearful goodbye to Terentia, Tullia and little Marcus, and we left the city to begin his great campaign tour of the north. Quintus, as usual, remained behind to nurse his brother's political interests, while Frugi was entrusted with the legal casework. As for young Caelius, this became the occasion of his finally leaving Cicero and going to the household of Crassus to complete his internship.

We travelled in a convoy of three four-wheeled carriages, pulled by teams of mules – one carriage for Cicero to sleep in, another specially fitted out as an office, and a third full of luggage and documents; other, smaller vehicles trailed behind for the use of the senator's retinue of secretaries, valets, muleteers, cooks, and heaven knows who else, including several thick-set men who acted as bodyguards. We left by the Fontinalian Gate, with no one to see us off. In those days, the hills to the north of Rome were still pine-clad, apart from the one on which Lucullus was just completing his notorious palace. The patrician general had now come back from the East, but was unable to enter the city proper without forfeiting his military *imperium* and with it his right to a triumph. So he was lingering out here amid his spoils of war, waiting for his aristocratic cronies to assemble a majority in the senate to vote him *triumphator*, but the supporters of Pompey, among them Cicero, kept blocking it. Mind you, even Cicero glanced up from his letters long enough to take a look at this colossal structure, the roof of which was just visible over the treetops, and I secretly hoped that we might catch a glimpse of the great man himself, but of course he was nowhere to be seen. (Incidentally, Quintus Metellus, the sole survivor of the three Metelli brothers, had also recently returned from Crete, and was also holed up outside the city in anticipation of a triumph which, again, the ever jealous Pompey would not allow. The plight of Lucullus and Metellus was a source of endless amusement to Cicero: 'A traffic jam of generals,' he called them, 'all trying to get into Rome through the Triumphal Gate!') At the Mulvian Bridge we paused while Cicero dashed off a final note of farewell to Terentia. Then we crossed the swollen waters of the Tiber and turned north on to the Flaminian Way.

We made extremely good time on that first day, and shortly before nightfall we reached Ocriculum, about thirty miles north of the city. Here we were met by a prominent local citizen who had agreed to give Cicero hospitality, and the following morning the senator went into the forum to begin his canvass. The secret of effective electioneering lies in the quality of the staff work done in advance, and here Cicero was very fortunate to have attached to his campaign two professional agents, Ranunculus and Filum, who travelled ahead of the candidate to ensure that a decent crowd of supporters would always be waiting in each town when we arrived. There was nothing about the electoral map of Italy which these two rascals did not know: who among the local knights would be offended if Cicero did not stop to pay his respects, and who should be avoided; which were the most important tribes and centuries in each particular district, and which were most likely to come his way; what were the issues which most concerned the citizens, and what were the promises they expected in return for their votes. They had no other topic of conversation except politics, yet Cicero could sit with them late into the night swapping facts and stories, as happily as he could converse with a philosopher or a wit.

I would not weary you with all the details of the campaign, even if I could remember them. Dear gods! What a heap of ash most political careers amount to, when one really stops to consider them! I used to be able to name every consul for the past one hundred years, and most praetors for the past forty. Now, they have almost entirely faded out of my memory, quenched like lights at midnight around the Bay of Naples. Little wonder that the towns and crowds of Cicero's consular campaign have all merged into one generalised impression of hands shaken, stories listened to, bores endured, petitions received, jokes told, under-takings given, and local worthies smoothed and flattered. The name of Cicero was famous by this time, even outside Rome, and people turned out to see him en masse, especially in the larger towns where law was practised, for the speeches he had prepared for the prosecution of Verres – even those he had not delivered – had been extensively copied and circulated. He was a hero to both the lower classes and the respectable knights, who saw him as a champion against the rapacity and snobbery of the aristocracy. For this reason, there were not many grand houses which opened their doors to him, and we had to endure taunts and even occasionally missiles whenever we passed close to the estates of one or other of the great patricians.

We pressed on up the Flaminian Way, devoting a day to each of the decent-sized towns – Narnia, Carsulae, Mevania, Fulginiae, Nuceria, Tadinae and Cales – before finally reaching the Adriatic coast about two weeks after leaving Rome. It was some years since I had gazed upon the sea, and when that line of glittering blue appeared above the dust and scrub I felt as thrilled as a child. The afternoon was cloudless and balmy, a straggler left behind by a distant summer which had long since retreated. On impulse, Cicero ordered that the wagons be halted so that we could all walk on the beach. How odd the things which *do* lodge in one's mind, for although I cannot now recall much of the serious politics, I can still remember every detail of that hour-long interlude – the smell of the seaweed and the taste of salt spray on my lips, the warmth of the sun on my cheeks, the rattle of the shingle as the waves broke and the hiss as they receded, and Cicero laughing as he tried to demonstrate how Demosthenes was supposed to have improved his elocution by rehearsing his speeches with a mouth full of pebbles.

A few days later, at Ariminum, we picked up the Aemilian Way and swung west, away from the sea, and into the province of Nearer Gaul. Here we could feel the nip of winter coming on. The black and purple mountains of the Apenninus rose sheer to our left, while to our right, the Po delta stretched grey and flat to the horizon. I had a curious sensation that we were mere insects, creeping along the foot of a wall at the edge of some great room. The passionate political issue in Nearer Gaul at that time was the franchise. Those who lived to the south of the River Po had been given the vote; those who lived to the north had not. The populists, led by Pompey and Caesar, favoured extending citizenship across the river, all the way to the Alps; the aristocrats, whose spokesman was Catulus, suspected a plot further to dilute their power, and opposed it. Cicero, naturally, was in favour of widening the franchise to the greatest extent possible, and this was the issue he campaigned on.

They had never seen a consular candidate up here before, and in every little town crowds of several hundred would turn out to listen to him. Cicero usually spoke from the back of one of the wagons, and gave the same speech at every stop, so that after a while I could move my lips in synchronicity with his. He denounced as nonsense the logic which said that a man who lived on one side of a stretch of water was a Roman and that his cousin on the other was a barbarian, even though they both spoke Latin. 'Rome is not merely a matter of geography,' he would proclaim. 'Rome is not defined by rivers, or mountains, or even seas; Rome is not a question of blood, or race, or religion; Rome is an ideal. Rome is the highest embodiment of liberty and law that mankind has yet achieved in the ten thousand years since our ancestors came down from those mountains and learned how to live as communities under the rule of law.' So if his listeners had the vote, he would conclude, they must be sure to use it on behalf of those who had not, for that was their fragment of civilisation, their special gift, as precious as the secret of fire. Every man should see Rome once before he died. They should go next summer, when the travelling was easy, and cast their ballots on the Field of Mars, and if anyone asked them why

they had come so far, 'You can tell them Marcus Cicero sent you!'
Then he would jump down, and pass among the crowd while
they were still applauding, doling out handfuls of chickpeas from
a sack carried by one of his attendants, and I would make sure
I was just behind him, to catch his instructions and write down
names.

I learned much about Cicero while he was out campaigning.
Indeed, I would say that despite all the years we had spent together
I never really knew him until I saw him in one of those small
towns south of the Po – Faventia, say, or Claterna – with the late
autumn light just starting to fade, and a cold wind blowing off
the mountains, and the lamps being lit in the little shops along
the main street, and the upturned faces of the local farmers gazing
in awe at this famous senator on the back of his wagon, with his
three fingers outstretched, pointing towards the glory of Rome.
I realised then that, for all his sophistication, he was really still
one of them – a man from a small provincial town with an
idealised dream of the republic and what it meant to be a citizen,
which burned all the fiercer within him because he, too, was an
outsider.

For the next two months Cicero devoted himself entirely to
the electors of Nearer Gaul, especially those around the provincial capital of Placentia, which actually lies on the banks of the
Po and where whole families were divided by the vexed question of citizenship. He was given great assistance in his
campaigning by the governor, Piso – that same Piso, curiously
enough, who had threatened Pompey with the fate of Romulus
if he pressed ahead with his desire for the special command. But
Piso was a pragmatist, and besides, his family had commercial
interests beyond the Po. He was thus in favour of extending the
vote; he even gave Cicero a special commission on his staff, to

enable him to travel more freely. We spent the festival of Saturnalia at Piso's headquarters, imprisoned by snow, and I could see the governor becoming more and more charmed by Cicero's manners and wit, to the extent that one evening, after plenty of wine, he clapped him on the shoulder and declared, 'Cicero, you are a good fellow after all. A better fellow and a better patriot than I realised. Speaking for myself, I would be willing to see you as consul. It is only a pity it will never happen.'

Cicero looked taken aback. 'And why are you so sure of that?'

'Because the aristocrats will never stand for it, and they control too many votes.'

'It is true they have great influence,' conceded Cicero. 'But I have the support of Pompey.'

Piso roared with laughter. 'And much good may it do you! He is lording it around at the other end of the world, and besides – haven't you noticed? – he never stirs for anyone except himself. Do you know who I would watch out for if I were you?'

'Catilina?'

'Yes, him too. But the one who should really worry you is Antonius Hybrida.'

'But the man is a halfwit!'

'Cicero, you disappoint me. Since when has idiocy been a bar to advancement in politics? You take it from me – Hybrida is the man the aristocrats will rally around, and then you and Catilina will be left to fight it out for second place, and do not look to Pompey for help.'

Cicero smiled and affected unconcern, but Piso's remarks had obviously struck home, and as soon as the snowfall melted we set off back to Rome at maximum speed.

★　★　★

We reached the city in the middle of January, and to begin with all seemed well. Cicero resumed his hectic round of advocacy in the courts, and his campaign team once again met weekly under the supervision of Quintus, who assured him his support was holding firm. We were minus young Caelius, but his absence was more than made up for by the addition of Cicero's oldest and closest friend, Atticus, who had returned to live in Rome after an absence in Greece of some twenty years.

I must tell you a little about Atticus, whose importance in Cicero's life I have so far only hinted at, and who was about to become extremely significant indeed. Already rich, he had recently inherited a fine house on the Quirinal Hill together with twenty million in cash from his uncle, Quintus Caecilius, one of the most loathed and misanthropic money-lenders in Rome, and it says much about Atticus that he alone remained on reasonable terms with this repulsive old man right up to his death. Some might have suspected opportunism, but the truth was that Atticus, because of his philosophy, had made it a principle never to fall out with anyone. He was a devoted follower of the teachings of Epicurus – 'that pleasure is the beginning and end of living happily' – although I hasten to add that he was an Epicurean not in the commonly misunderstood sense, as a seeker after luxury, but in the true meaning, as a pursuer of what the Greeks call *ataraxia*, or freedom from disturbance. He consequently avoided arguments and unpleasantness of any kind (needless to say, he was unmarried) and desired only to contemplate philosophy by day and dine by night with his cultured friends. He believed that all mankind should have similar aims, and was baffled that they did not: he tended to forget, as Cicero occasionally reminded him, that not everyone had inherited a fortune. He never for an instant contemplated undertaking anything as upsetting or dangerous as a political career, yet at the same time, as an insurance against future mishap, he had taken pains to cultivate every aristocrat who passed through Athens – which, over two decades, was a lot – by drawing up their family trees, and presenting them as gifts, beautifully illustrated by his slaves. He was also extremely shrewd with money. In short, there can never have been anyone quite so worldly in their pursuit of unworldliness as Titus Pomponius Atticus.

He was three years older than Cicero, who stood somewhat in awe of him, not only because of his wealth but also because of his social connections, for if there is one man guaranteed to enjoy an automatic entrée into smart society it is a rich and witty bachelor in his middle forties with an unfeigned interest in the genealogy of his host and hostess. This made him invaluable as a source of political intelligence, and it was from Atticus that Cicero now began to realise how formidable was the opposition to his candidacy. First, Atticus heard over dinner from his great friend Servilia – the half-sister of Cato – that Antonius Hybrida was definitely running for the consulship. A few weeks after that, Atticus reported a comment of Hortensius (another of his acquaintances) to the effect that Hybrida and Catilina were planning to run on a joint ticket. This was a serious blow, and although Cicero tried to make light of it – 'Oh well, a target that is double the size is twice as easy to hit' – nevertheless I could see that he was shaken, for he had no running-mate of his own, and no serious prospect at this stage of finding one.

But the really bad news came just after the senatorial recess in the late spring. Atticus sent a message that he needed to see the Cicero brothers urgently, so when the courts had closed for the day all three of us made our way up to his house. This was a perfect bachelor set-up, built on a promontory next to the

Temple of Salus – not large, but with the most wonderful views across the city, especially from the library, which Atticus had made the centrepiece of the house. There were busts of the great philosophers around the walls, and many little cushioned benches to sit on, for Atticus's rule was that while he would never lend a book, any of his friends were free whenever they liked to come up and read or even make their own copies. And it was here, beneath a head of Aristotle, that we found Atticus reclining that afternoon, dressed in the loose white tunic of a Greek, and reading, if I remember rightly, a volume of *Kyriai doxai*, the principal doctrines of Epicurus.

He came straight to the point. 'I was at dinner last night on the Palatine, at the home of Metellus Celer and the Lady Clodia, and among the other guests was our former consul, no less an aristocrat than' – he blew on an imaginary trumpet – 'Publius Cornelius Lentulus Sura.'

'By heavens,' said Cicero with a smile, 'the company you keep!'

'Did you know that Lentulus is trying to make a comeback, by standing for a praetorship this summer?'

'Is he really?' Cicero frowned and rubbed his forehead. 'He is of course a great friend of Catilina. I suppose they must be in alliance. See how the gang of rascals grows?'

'Oh yes, it is quite a political movement – he, and Catilina and Hybrida, and I got the impression there were others, but he would not give me their names. At one point, he produced a piece of paper with the prediction of some oracle written upon it, that he would be the third of the Cornelii to rule as dictator in Rome.'

'Old Sleepy-Head? Dictator? I trust you laughed in his face.'

'No, I did not,' replied Atticus. 'I took him very seriously. You ought to try it some time, Cicero, instead of just delivering one of your crushing witticisms which simply shuts everybody up. No, I encouraged him to ramble on, and he drank more of Celer's excellent wine, and I listened more, and he drank more, and eventually he swore me to secrecy and he told me his great secret.'

'Which is?' said Cicero, leaning forward in his seat, for he knew that Atticus would not have summoned us for nothing.

'They are being backed by Crassus.'

There was a silence.

'Crassus is voting for them?' asked Cicero, which I think was the first time I had ever heard him say something seriously stupid: I ascribe it to the shock.

'No,' said Atticus irritably. 'He is backing them. You know what I mean. Financing them. Buying them the whole election, according to Lentulus.'

Cicero seemed temporarily deprived of the power of speech. After another long pause it was Quintus who spoke up. 'I do not believe it. Lentulus must have been well in his cups to make such a ridiculous boast. What possible reason would Crassus have for wanting to see such men in power?'

'To spite me,' said Cicero, recovering his voice.

'Nonsense!' exclaimed Quintus angrily. (Why was he so angry? I suppose because he was frightened that the story was true, in which case he would look a fool, especially in the light of all the assurances he had given his brother that the campaign was in the bag.) 'Absolute nonsense!' he repeated, although with slightly less certainty. 'We already know that Crassus is investing heavily in Caesar's future. How much would it cost him in addition to buy two consulships and a praetorship? You are talking not just about a million, but four million, five million. He hates you, Marcus, everyone knows it. But does he hate you so much more than he loves his money? I doubt it.'

'No,' said Cicero firmly, 'I am afraid you are wrong, Quintus. This story has the ring of truth, and I blame myself for not recognising the danger earlier.' He was on his feet now, and pacing around, as he always did when he was thinking hard. 'It started with those Games of Apollo given by Hybrida – Crassus must have paid for those. The games were what brought Hybrida back from the political dead. And could Catilina really have raised the funds to bribe his jury simply by selling a few statues and pictures? Of course not. And even if he did, who is paying his campaign expenses now? Because I have been inside his house and I can tell you: that man is bankrupt.' He wheeled around, his gaze darting to right and left, bright and unseeing, his eyes working as rapidly as his thoughts. 'I have always known in my bones that there was something wrong about this election. I have sensed some invisible force against me from the very outset. Hybrida and Catilina! These creatures should never even have been *candidates* in any normal canvass, let alone the front-runners. They are merely the tools of someone else.'

'So we are fighting Crassus?' said Quintus, sounding resigned to it at last.

'Crassus, yes. Or is it really Caesar, using Crassus's money? Every time I look around, I seem to see a flash of Caesar's cloak, just disappearing out of view. He thinks he is cleverer than anyone, and perhaps he is. But not on this occasion. Atticus –' Cicero stopped in front of him, and took his hands in both of his '– my old friend. I cannot thank you enough.'

'For what? I merely listened to a bore, and then plied him with a little drink. It was hardly anything.'

'On the contrary, the ability to listen to bores requires stamina, and such stamina is the essence of politics. It is from the bores that you really find things out.' Cicero squeezed his hands warmly, then swung around to his brother. 'We need to find some evidence, Quintus. Ranunculus and Filum are the men who can sniff it out – not much moves at election time in this city that those two are not aware of.'

Quintus agreed, and in this way the shadow-boxing of the consular election finally ended, and the real fight began.

XVI

To discover what was going on, Cicero devised a trap. Rather than simply asking around about what Crassus was up to – which would have got him nowhere, and would also have alerted his enemies that he was suspicious – he called Ranunculus and Filum to him, and told them to go out into the city and let it be known that they were representing a certain anonymous senator who was worried about his prospects in the forthcoming consular ballot, and was willing to pay fifty sesterces per vote to the right electoral syndicate.

Ranunculus was a runtish, almost half-formed creature, with a flat, round face at the end of a feeble body, who well deserved his nickname of 'Tadpole'. Filum was a giant spindle, an animated candlestick. Their fathers and grandfathers had been bribery agents before them. They knew the score. They disappeared into the back streets and bars, and a week or so later reported back to Cicero that something very strange was going on. All the usual bribery agents were refusing to cooperate. 'Which means,' as Ranunculus put it, in his squeaky voice, 'either that Rome is full of honest men for the first time in three hundred years, or that every vote that was up for sale has already been bought.'

'There must be someone who will crack for a higher price,'

insisted Cicero. 'You had better do the rounds again, and this
time offer a hundred.'

So back they went, and back they returned after another week
with the same story. Such was the huge amount that the bribery
agents were already being paid, and such was their nervousness
about antagonising their mysterious client, that there was not a
single vote to be had, and not a breath of rumour as to who that
client might be. Now you might well wonder, given the thousands of votes involved, how such an immense operation could
remain so tight a secret. The answer is that it was very cleverly
organised, with perhaps only a dozen agents, or *interpretes* as they
were called, knowing the identity of the buyer (I regret to say
that both Ranunculus and Filum had acted as *interpretes* in the
past). These men would contact the officials of the voting syndicates and strike the initial bargain – such-and-such a price for fifty
votes, say, or five hundred, depending on the size of the syndicate. Because naturally no one trusted anyone else in this game,
the money would then be deposited with a second category of
agent, known as the *sequestres*, who would hold the cash available
for inspection. And finally, when the election was over and it was
time to settle up, a third species of criminal, the so-called *divi-
sores*, would distribute it. This made it extremely difficult to bring
a successful prosecution, for even if a man was arrested in the
very act of handing over a bribe, he might genuinely have no idea
of who had commissioned the corruption in the first place. But
still Cicero refused to accept that someone would not talk. 'We
are dealing with bribery agents,' he shouted, in a rare show of
anger, 'not an ancient order of Roman knights! Somewhere you
will find a man who will betray even as dangerous a paymaster
as Crassus, if the money is good enough. Go and track him down
and find his price – or must I do everything myself?'

By this time – I suppose it must have been well into June, about a month before the election – everyone knew that something strange was going on. It was turning into one of the most memorable and closely fought campaigns in living memory, with a field of no fewer than seven for the consulship, a reflection of the fact that many men fancied their chances that year. The three front-runners were reckoned to be Catilina, Hybrida and Cicero. Then came the snobbish and acerbic Galba, and the deeply religious Cornificius. The two no-hopers were the corpulent ex-praetor Cassius Longinus, and Gaius Licinius Sacerdos, who had been governor of Sicily even before Verres, and who was at least a decade older than his rivals. (Sacerdos was one of those irritating candidates who enter elections 'not out of any personal ambition', as they like to say, but solely with the intention of 'raising issues' – 'Always beware of the man who says he is not seeking office for himself,' said Cicero, 'for he is the vainest of the lot.') Realising that the bribery agents were unusually active, the senior consul, Marcius Figulus, was prevailed upon by several of these candidates to bring before the senate a severe new law against electoral malpractice: what he hoped would become the *lex Figula*. It was already illegal for a candidate to offer a bribe; the new bill also made it a criminal offence for a voter to accept one.

When the time came for the measure to be debated in the senate, the consul first went round each of the candidates in turn to ask for his opinion. Sacerdos, as the senior man, spoke first, and made a pious speech in favour; I could see Cicero squirming with irritation at his platitudes. Hybrida naturally spoke against, but in his usual bumbling and unmemorable way – no one would ever have believed his father had once been the most eagerly sought advocate in Rome. Galba, who was going to lose badly in any case, took this opportunity to withdraw from the election, loftily announcing that there was no glory in participating in such a squalid contest, which disgraced the memory of his ancestors. Catilina, for obvious reasons, also spoke against the *lex Figula*, and I must concede that he was impressive. Utterly without nerves, he towered over the benches around him, and when he came to the end of his remarks he pointed at Cicero and roared that the only men who would benefit from yet another new piece of legislation were the lawyers, which drew the usual cheers from the aristocrats. Cicero was in a delicate position, and as he rose I wondered what he would say, because obviously he did not wish to see the legislation fail, but nor, on the eve of the most important election of his life, did he want to alienate the voting syndicates, who naturally regarded the bill as an attack on their honour. His response was adroit.

'In general I welcome this bill,' he said, 'which can only be a terror to those who are guilty. The honest citizen has nothing to fear from a law against bribery, and the dishonest should be reminded that a vote is a sacred trust, not a voucher to be cashed in once a year. But there is one thing wrong with it: an imbalance which needs to be redressed. Are we really saying that the poor man who succumbs to temptation is more to be condemned than the rich man who deliberately places temptation in his way? I say the opposite: that if we are to legislate against the one, we must strengthen the sanctions against the other. With your permission, therefore, Figulus, I wish to propose an amendment to your bill: *That any person who solicits, or seeks to solicit, or causes to be solicited, the votes of any citizen in return for money should be liable to a penalty of ten years' exile.*' That produced an excited and long-drawn-out 'Oohh!' from all around the chamber.

I could not see Crassus's face from where I was standing, but

Cicero delightedly assured me afterwards that it turned bright red, for that phrase, *or causes to be solicited*, was aimed directly at him, and everyone knew it. The consul placidly accepted the amendment, and asked if any member wished to speak against it. But the majority of the house were too surprised to react, and those such as Crassus who stood to lose most dared not expose themselves in public by openly opposing it. Accordingly, the amendment was carried without opposition, and when the house divided on the main bill, it was passed by a large margin. Figulus, preceded by his lictors, left the chamber, and all the senators filed out into the sunshine to watch him mount the rostra and give the bill to the herald for an immediate first reading. I saw Hybrida make a move towards Crassus, but Catilina caught his arm, and Crassus walked rapidly away from the forum, to avoid being seen with his nominees. The usual three weekly market days would now have to elapse before the bill could be voted upon, which meant that the people would have their say almost on the eve of the consular election.

Cicero was pleased with his day's work, for the possibility now opened up that if the *lex Figula* passed, and if he lost the election because of bribery, he might be in a position to launch a prosecution not only against Catilina and Hybrida, but also against his arch-enemy Crassus himself. It was only two years, after all, since a previous pair of consuls-elect had been stripped of their offices for electoral malpractice. But to succeed in such an action he would require evidence, and the pressure to find it became even more intense. Every waking hour he now spent canvassing, going about with a great crowd of supporters, but never with a *nomenclator* at his elbow to whisper the names of the voters: unlike his opponents Cicero took great pride in being able to remember thousands of names, and on the rare occasion when he met someone whose identity he had forgotten, he could always bluff his way through.

I admired him greatly at this time, for he must have known that the odds were heavily against him and the chances were that he was going to lose. Piso's prediction about Pompey had proved amply correct, and the great man had not lifted a finger to assist Cicero during the campaign. He had established himself at Amisus, on the eastern edge of the Black Sea – which is about as far away from Rome as it is possible to get – and there, like some great Eastern potentate, he was receiving homage from no fewer than twelve native kings. Syria had been annexed. Mithradates was in headlong retreat. Pompey's house on the Esquiline had been decorated with the captured beaks of fifty pirate triremes and was nowadays known as the *domus rostra* – a shrine to his admirers all across Italy. What did Pompey care any more about the pygmy struggles of mere civilians? Cicero's letters to him went unanswered. Quintus railed against his ingratitude, but Cicero was fatalistic: 'If it is gratitude you want, get a dog.'

Three days before the consular election, and on the eve of the vote on the bribery law, there was at last a breakthrough. Ranunculus came rushing in to see Cicero with the news that he had found a bribery agent named Gaius Salinator, who claimed to be in a position to sell three hundred votes for five hundred sesterces apiece. He owned a bar in the Subura called the Bacchante, and it had been agreed that Ranunculus would go to see him that very night, give him the name of the candidate for whom the bribed electors were to vote, and at the same time hand over the money to one of the *sequestres*, who was trusted by them both. When Cicero heard about this he became very excited, and insisted that he would accompany Ranunculus to the meeting, with a hood pulled down to conceal his well-known face. Quintus was against the plan, considering it too dangerous, but Cicero was insistent that he needed to gather evidence at first hand. 'I shall have Ranunculus and Tiro with me for protection,' he said (I assume this was one of his jokes), 'but perhaps you could arrange for a few loyal supporters to be drinking in the neighbourhood, just in case we need more assist-ance.'

I was by this time almost forty, and after a life devoted exclu-sively to clerical duties my hands were as soft as a maiden's. In the event of trouble it would be Cicero, whose daily exercises had given him an imposing physique, who would be called upon to protect me. Nevertheless, I opened up the safe in his study and began counting out the cash we needed in silver coin. (He had a well-stocked campaign fund, made up of gifts from his admirers, which he drew on to pay for such expenses as his tour of Nearer Gaul: this money was not bribes, as such, although obviously it was comforting for the donors to know that Cicero was a man who famously never forgot a name.) Anyway, this silver was fitted into a money belt which I had to strap around my waist, and with a heavy tread, in both senses of the phrase, I descended with Cicero at dusk into the Subura. He cut a curious figure wearing a hooded tunic borrowed from one of his slaves, for the night was very warm. But in the crowded slums of the poor, the bizarrely dressed are an everyday sight, and when people saw a man with a hood pulled down low over his face they gave him a wide berth, perhaps fearing that he had leprosy or some disfig-uring complaint which they might catch. We followed Ranunculus, who darted, appropriately tadpole-like, through the labyrinth of narrow, squalid alleys which were his natural habitat, until at last we came to a corner where men were sitting leaning against the wall, passing back and forth a jar of wine. Above their heads, beside the door, was a painting of Bacchus with his groin thrust out, relieving himself, and the spot had the smell to match the sign. Ranunculus stepped inside and led us behind the counter and up some narrow wooden stairs to a raftered room, where Salinator was waiting, along with another man, the *sequester*, whose name I never learned.

They were so anxious to see the money, they paid little attention to the hooded figure behind me. I had to take off my belt and show them a handful of coins, whereupon the *sequester* produced a small pair of scales and began weighing the silver. Salinator, who was a flabby, lank-haired, pot-bellied creature, watched this for a while, then said to Ranunculus, 'That seems well enough. Now you had better give me the name of your client.'

'I am his client,' said Cicero, throwing back his hood. Needless to say, Salinator recognised him at once, and stepped back in alarm, crashing into the *sequester* and his scales. The bribery agent struggled to recover, hopelessly trying to turn his stumble into a sequence of bows, and began some improvised speech about what an honour it was and so forth to help the senator in his campaign, but Cicero shut him up quickly. 'I do not require any help from the likes of you, wretch! All I require is information.'

Salinator had just begun to whine that he knew nothing when suddenly the *sequester* dropped his scales and made a dive for the staircase. He must have got about halfway down before he ran into the solid figure of Quintus, who spun him around, hauled him up by his collar and the seat of his tunic and threw him back into the room. I was relieved to see, coming up the stairs behind Quintus, a couple of stout young lads who often served as Cicero's attendants. At the sight of so many, and confronted by the most famous advocate in Rome, Salinator's resistance began to weaken. What finished it altogether was when Cicero threatened to hand him over to Crassus for trying to sell the same votes twice. He was more scared of retribution at Crassus's hands than of anything, and I was reminded of that phrase about Old Baldhead which Cicero had repeated years before: 'the most dangerous bull in the herd'.

'Your client is Crassus, then?' asked Cicero. 'Think carefully before you deny it.'

Salinator's chin twitched slightly: the nearest he dared come to a nod.

'And you were to deliver three hundred votes to Hybrida and Catilina for the consulship?'

Again he gave the ghost of a nod. 'For them,' he said, 'and the others.'

'Others? You mean Lentulus Sura for praetor?'

'Yes. Him. And the others.'

'You keep saying "the others",' said Cicero, frowning. 'Who are these "others"?'

'Keep your mouth shut!' shouted the *sequester*, but Quintus kicked him in the stomach and he groaned and rolled over.

'Ignore him,' said Cicero affably. 'He is a bad influence. I know the type. You can tell me.' He put an encouraging hand on the bribery agent's arm. 'The others?'

'Cosconius,' said Salinator, casting a nervous glance at the figure writhing on the floor. Then he took a breath and said rapidly, in a quiet voice: 'Pomptinus. Balbus. Caecilius. Labienus. Faberius. Gutta. Bulbus. Calidius. Tudicius. Valgius. And Rullus.'

As each new name was mentioned, Cicero looked more and more astonished. 'Is that it?' he said, when Salinator had finished.

'You are sure there is no one left in the senate you have forgotten?' He glanced across at Quintus, who was looking equally amazed.

'That is not just two candidates for consul,' said Quintus. 'That is three candidates for praetor and *ten* for tribune. Crassus is trying to buy the entire government!'

Cicero was not a man who liked to show surprise, but even he could not disguise it that night. 'This is completely absurd,' he protested. 'How much is each of these votes costing?'

'Five hundred for consul,' replied Salinator, as if he were selling pigs at market. 'Two hundred for praetor. One hundred for tribune.'

'So you are telling me,' said Cicero, frowning as he performed the calculation, 'that Crassus is willing to pay three quarters of a million merely for the three hundred votes in your syndicate?'

Salinator nodded, this time more vigorously, even happily, and with a certain professional pride. 'It has been the most magnificent canvass anyone can remember.'

Cicero turned to Ranunculus, who had been keeping watch at the window in case of any trouble in the street. 'How many votes do you think Crassus will have bought altogether at this sort of price?'

'To feel confident of victory?' replied Ranunculus. He pondered the matter judiciously. 'It must be seven or eight thousand.'

'*Eight thousand?*' repeated Cicero. 'Eight thousand would cost him *twenty million*. Have you ever heard the like? And at the end of it, he is not even in office himself, but has filled the magistracies with ninnies like Hybrida and Lentulus Sura.' He turned back to Salinator. 'Did he give you any reason for such an immense exercise?'

'No, Senator. Crassus is not a man much given to answering questions.'

Quintus swore. 'Well, he will answer some fucking questions now,' he said, and to relieve his frustration he aimed another kick at the belly of the *sequester*, who had just started to rise, and sent the fellow groaning and crashing back to the floor.

Quintus was all for beating the last scrap of information out of the two hapless agents, and then either marching them round to the house of Crassus and demanding that he put a stop to his schemes, or dragging them before the senate, reading out their confessions, and calling for the elections to be postponed. But Cicero kept a cooler head. With a straight face he thanked Salinator for his honesty, told Quintus to have a cup of wine and calm down, and me to gather up our silver. Later, when we had returned home, he sat in his study and tossed that little leather exercise ball of his from one hand to the other, while Quintus raged that he had been a fool to let the two bribery agents go, that they would surely now alert Crassus or flee the city.

'They will not do either,' replied Cicero. 'To go to Crassus and tell him what has happened would be to sign their own death warrants. Crassus would never leave such incriminating witnesses alive, and they know it. And flight would merely bring about the same result, except that it would take him longer to track them down.' Back and forth, back and forth went the ball. 'Besides, no crime has been committed. Bribery is hard enough to prove at the best of times – impossible to establish when not a vote has been cast. Crassus and the senate would merely laugh at us. No, the best thing is to leave them at liberty, where at least we know where to find them again, and be ready to subpoena them if we lose the election.' He threw the ball higher and caught it with a swiping motion. 'You were right about one thing, though, Quintus.'

'Was I really?' said Quintus bitterly. 'How kind of you to say so.'

'Crassus's action has nothing to do with his enmity for me. He would not spend twenty million simply to frustrate *my* hopes. He would only invest twenty million if the likely return were *huge*. What can it be? On that issue I must confess myself baffled.' He stared at the wall for a while. 'Tiro, you always got on well with young Caelius Rufus, didn't you?'

I remembered the shirked tasks which I had been obliged to complete for him, the lies I had told to keep him out of trouble, the day he stole my savings and persuaded me not to report his thieving to Cicero. 'Reasonably well, Senator,' I replied cautiously.

'Go and talk to him tomorrrow morning. Be subtle about it. See if you can extract any clues from him about what Crassus is up to. He lives under the same roof, after all. He must know something.'

I lay awake long into the night, pondering all of this, and feeling increasingly anxious for the future. Cicero did not sleep much either. I could hear him pacing around upstairs. The force of his concentration seemed almost to penetrate the floorboards, and when sleep did at last come to me, it was restless and full of portents.

The following morning I left Laurea to deal with Cicero's press of visitors and set off to walk the mile or so to the house of Crassus. Even today, when the sky is cloudless and the mid-July heat feels oppressive even before the sun is up, I whisper to myself, 'Election weather!' and feel again that familiar clench of excitement in my stomach. The sound of hammering and sawing rose from the forum, where the workmen were finishing the erection of the ramps and fences around the Temple of Castor, for this was the day on which the bribery bill was to be put to the vote of the people. I cut through behind the temple and paused to take a drink from the tepid waters of the fountain of Juturna. I had no idea what I was going to say to Caelius. I am a most inexpert liar – I always have been – and I realised I should have asked Cicero to advise me on some line to take, but it was too late now. I climbed the path to the Palatine, and when I reached the house of Crassus I told the porter that I had an urgent message for Caelius Rufus. He offered to let me wait inside but I declined. Instead, while he went off to fetch the young man, I crossed the street and tried to make myself as inconspicuous as possible.

Crassus's house, like the man himself, presented a very modest façade to the world, although I had been told that this was deceptive, and that once you got inside it went back a long way. The door was dark, low and narrow, but stout, flanked by two small, barred windows. Ivy climbed across peeling walls of light ochre. The terracotta roof was also ancient, and the edges of the tiles where they overhung the pavement were cracked and black, like a row of broken teeth. It might have been the home of an unwise banker, or some hard-up country landowner who had allowed his town house to fall into disrepair. I suppose this was Crassus's way of showing that he was so fabulously rich, he had no need to keep up a smart appearance, but of course in that street of millionaires it only drew attention to his wealth, and there was something almost vulgar in this studied lack of vulgarity. The dark little door was constantly opening and shutting as visitors scurried in and out, revealing the extent of the activity within: it put me in mind of a buzzing wasps' nest, which shows itself only as a tiny hole in the masonry. None of these men was recognisable to me until Julius Caesar stepped out. He did not see me, but walked straight off down the street in the direction of the forum, trailed by a secretary carrying a document case. Shortly afterwards, the door opened again and Caelius appeared. He paused on the threshold, cupped his hand above his eyes to shield them from the sun and squinted across the street towards me. I could see at once that he had been out all night as usual, and was not in a good humour at being woken. Thick stubble covered his handsome chin, and he kept sticking out his tongue, swallowing and wincing, as if the taste of it was too horrible to hold it in his mouth. He walked carefully towards me, and when he asked me what in the name of the gods I wanted, I blurted out that I needed to borrow some money.

He squinted at me in disbelief. 'What for?'

'There is a girl,' I replied helplessly, simply because it was the sort of thing he used to say to me when he wanted money and I had not the wit to come up with anything else. I tried to steer him along the street a little way, anxious that Crassus might come out and see us together. But he shook me off and stood swaying in the gutter.

'A girl?' he repeated incredulously. 'You?' And then he began to laugh, but that obviously hurt his head, so he stopped and put his fingers gently to his temple. 'If I had any money, Tiro, I should give it to you willingly – it would be a gift, bestowed simply for the pleasure of seeing you with any living person other than Cicero. But that could never happen. You are not the type for girls. Poor Tiro – you are not any kind of type, that I can see.' He peered at me closely. 'What do you really need it for?' I could smell the stale wine hot on his breath, and could not prevent myself flinching, which he mistook for an admission of guilt. 'You are lying,' he said, and then a grin spread slowly across his stubbled face. 'Cicero sent you to find out something.'

I pleaded with him to move away from the house, and this time he did. But the motion of walking evidently did not agree with him. He halted again, turned very white and held up a warning finger. Then his eyes and throat bulged, he gave an alarming groan, and out came such a heavy gush of vomit it reminded me of a chambermaid emptying a bucket out of an upstairs window into the street. (Forgive these details, but the scene just came entirely back into my mind after an absence of sixty years, and I could not help but laugh at the memory.) Anyway, this seemed to act as a purge; his colour returned and he became much brighter. He asked me what it was that Cicero wanted to know.

'What do you think?' I replied, a little impatiently.

'I wish I could help you, Tiro,' he said, wiping his mouth with the back of his hand. 'You know I would if I could. It is not nearly as pleasant living with Crassus as it was with Cicero. Old Baldhead is the most awful shit – worse even than my father. He has me learning accountancy all day, and a duller business was never invented, except for commercial law, which was last month's torture. As for politics, which does amuse me, he is careful to keep me away from all that side of things.'

I tried asking him a few more questions, for instance about Caesar's visit that morning, but it quickly became clear that he was genuinely ignorant of Crassus's plans. (I suppose he might have been lying, but given his habitual garrulity, I doubted it.) When I thanked him anyway and turned to leave, he grabbed my elbow. 'Cicero must be really desperate,' he said, with an expression of unaccustomed seriousness, 'to ask for help from me. Tell him I am sorry to hear it. He is worth a dozen of Crassus and my father put together.'

I did not expect to be seeing Caelius again for a while, and banished him from my mind for the remainder of the day, which was entirely given over to the vote on the bribery bill. Cicero was very active among the tribes in the forum, going from one to another with his entourage, and urging the merits of Figula's proposal. He was especially pleased to find, under the standard marked *VETURIA*, several hundred citizens from Nearer Gaul, who had responded to his campaign and turned out to vote for the first time. He talked to them for a long while about the importance of stamping out bribery, and as he turned away he had the glint of tears in his eyes. 'Poor people,' he muttered, 'to have come so far, only to be mocked by Crassus's money. But if we can get this bill through, I may yet have a weapon to bring the villain down.'

My impression was that his canvassing was proving effective, and that when it came to a vote the *lex Figula* would pass, for the majority were not corrupt. But simply because a measure is honest and sensible does not guarantee that it will be adopted; rather the opposite, in my experience. Early in the afternoon, the populist tribune Mucius Orestinus – he, you may remember, who had formerly been a client of Cicero's on a charge of robbery – came to the front of the rostra and denounced the measure as an attack by the aristocrats on the integrity of the plebs. He actually singled out Cicero by name as a man 'unfit to be consul' – those were his precise words – who posed as a friend of the people, but never did anything for them unless it furthered his own selfish interests. That set half the crowd booing and jeering and the other half – presumably those who were accustomed to selling their votes, and wished to continue doing so – yelling their approval.

This was too much for Cicero. He had, after all, only the year before, secured Mucius's acquittal, and if such a glossy rat as this was leaving his sinking ship, it really must be halfway to the sea bed already. He shouldered his way to the steps of the temple, his face red with the heat and with anger, and demanded to be allowed to answer. 'Who is paying for *your* vote, Mucius?' he shouted, but Mucius pretended not to hear. The crowd around us were now pointing to Cicero, pushing him forward and calling on the tribune to let him speak, but obviously that was the last thing Mucius wanted. Nor did he want a vote on the bill which he might lose. Raising his arm, he solemnly announced that he was vetoing the legislation, and amid scenes of pandemonium, with scuffles between the rival factions, the *lex Figula* was lost. Figulus immediately announced that he would summon a meeting of the senate the following day to debate what should be done.

It was a bitter moment for Cicero, and when at last we reached his house and he was able to close the door on the crowd of his supporters in the street, I thought he might collapse again, as on the eve of the elections for aedile. For once he was too tired to play with Tullia. And even when Terentia came down with little Marcus, and showed him how the infant had learned to take a wobbly step or two unaided, he did not hoist him up and toss him into the air, which was his usual greeting, but simply patted his cheek and squeezed his ear in an absent-minded way, and then passed on towards his study – only to stop dead in surprise on the threshold, for who should be sitting at his desk but Caelius Rufus.

Laurea, who was waiting just inside the door, apologised to Cicero and explained that he would have told Caelius to wait in the tablinum, like every other visitor, but he had been insistent that his business was so confidential he could not be seen in the public rooms.

'That is all right, Laurea. I am always pleased to see young Caelius. Although I fear,' he added, shaking Caelius's hand, 'that you will find me dull company at the end of a long and dispiriting day.'

'Well then,' said Caelius with a grin, 'perhaps I might have just the news to cheer you up.'

'Crassus is dead?'

'On the contrary,' laughed Caelius, 'very much alive, and planning a great conference tonight in anticipation of his triumph at the polls.'

'Is he indeed?' said Cicero, and immediately, at this touch of gossip, I saw him start to revive a little, like some wilted flower after a sprinkle of rain. 'And who will be at this conference?'

'Catilina. Hybrida. Caesar. I am not sure who else. But the chairs were being set out as I left. I have all this from one of Crassus's secretaries, who went around the city with the invitations while the popular assembly was in progress.'

'Well, well,' murmured Cicero. 'What I would not give to have an ear at that keyhole!'

'But you could have,' responded Caelius. 'This meeting is in the chamber where Crassus transacts all his business affairs. Often – but not tonight, I am told by my informant – he likes to keep a secretary close at hand, to make a note of what is said, but without the other person being aware of it. For that purpose he has had a small listening post constructed. It is just a simple cubicle, hidden behind a tapestry. He showed it to me when he was giving me lessons in how to be a man of business.'

'You mean to tell me that Crassus eavesdrops on *himself*?' asked Cicero in wonder. 'What sort of statesman would do that?'

'"There is many a rash promise made by a man who thinks there are no witnesses" – that was what he said.'

'So you think that you could hide yourself in there, and make an account of what is said?'

'Not me,' scoffed Caelius. 'I am no secretary. I was thinking of Tiro here,' he said, clapping me on the shoulder, 'with his miraculous shorthand.'

I would like to be able to boast that I volunteered readily for this suicidal assignment. But it would not be true. On the contrary, I threw up all manner of practical objections to Caelius's scheme. How would I enter Crassus's house undetected? How would I leave it? How would I determine which speaker was which from the babble of voices if I was concealed behind a screen? But to all my questions Caelius had answers. The essential fact was that I was terrified. 'What if I am caught,' I protested to Cicero, finally coming to the crux of what really bothered me, 'and tortured? I cannot claim to be so courageous that I would not betray you.'

'Cicero can simply deny any knowledge of what you were doing,' said Caelius – unhelpfully, I thought, from my point of view. 'Besides, everyone knows that evidence obtained under torture is unreliable.'

'I am beginning to feel faint,' I joked feebly.

'Compose yourself, Tiro,' said Cicero, who had become increasingly excited the more he heard. 'There would be no torture and

no trial. I would make sure of that. If you were detected, I would
negotiate your release, and I would pay any price to see that you
were unharmed.' He took both my hands in that sincere double
grip of his, and looked deep into my eyes. 'You are more my
second brother than my slave, Tiro, and have been ever since we
sat and learned philosophy together in Athens all those years ago
– do you remember? I should have discussed your freedom with
you before now, but somehow there has always seemed to be
some fresh crisis to distract me. So let me tell you now, with
Caellus here as my witness, that it is my intention to give you
your liberty – yes, and that simple life in the country you have
long desired so much. And I see a day when I shall ride over from
my place to your little farm, and sit in your garden, and as we
watch the sun go down over some distant, dusty olive grove or
vineyard, we shall discuss the great adventures we have had
together.' He let go of my hands, and this rustic vision trembled
on the warm dusky air an instant longer, then faded. 'Now,' he
said briskly, 'this offer of mine is not conditional in any way on
your undertaking this mission – let me make that clear: you have
earned it many times over already. I would never order you to
put yourself in danger. You know how badly my cause stands
tonight. You must do whatever you think best.'

Those were very nearly his exact words: how could I forget
them?

XVII

The conference was set for nightfall, which meant there was no time to be lost. As the sun vanished behind the brow of the Esquiline, and as I climbed the slope of the Palatine Hill for the second time that day, I had a disturbing premonition that I was walking into a trap. For how could I, or Cicero for that matter, be certain that Caelius had not transferred his loyalty to Crassus? Indeed, was 'loyalty' not an absurd word to apply to whatever shifting, temporary focus of amusement seized the fancy of my young companion? But there was nothing to be done about it now. Caelius was already leading me down a small alley towards the back of Crassus's house. Pulling aside a thick curtain of trailing ivy, he uncovered a tiny, iron-studded door, which looked to have long since rusted shut. But a sharp jab from his shoulder caused it to swing silently open and we jumped down into an empty storeroom.

Like Catilina's, the house was very old, and had been added to over the centuries, so that I quickly lost track of our route as we followed the winding passages. Crassus was famous for the number of highly skilled slaves he owned – he hired them out, as a kind of employment agent – and with so many swarming around on duty it seemed impossible that we could reach our destination undetected. But if Caelius had developed any skill during his years of legal study in Rome, it was for illicit entry and exit. We cut across an inner courtyard, hid in an antechamber while a maid went by, then stepped into a big, deserted room, hung with fine tapestries from Babylon and Corinth. Perhaps twenty gilt chairs had been arranged in the centre in a semicircle, and numerous lamps and candelabra were lit around the perimeter. Caelius quickly seized one of the lamps, crossed the floor and lifted the edge of a heavy woollen tapestry depicting Diana bringing down a stag with a spear. Behind it was an alcove, of the sort in which a statue might stand, just high enough and deep enough to take a man, with a little ledge near the top for a lamp. I stepped inside smartly, for I could hear loud male voices coming closer. Caelius put a finger to his lips, winked at me, and carefully replaced the tapestry. His rapid footsteps faded and I was alone.

To begin with I was blind, but gradually I became used to the weak glow of the oil lamp just behind my shoulder. When I put my eye to the tapestry I found that there were tiny spyholes, bored through the thick material in such a way as to give me a complete view of the room. I heard more footsteps, and then abruptly my vision was obscured by the back of a wrinkled bald pink head, and Crassus's voice rang very loud in my ears – so loud I almost stumbled forward in shock – calling genially to his visitors to follow him. He moved away, and the shapes of other men passed by on their way to take their places: the loose-limbed Catilina; Hybrida, with his drinker's face; Caesar, looking sleek and dandified; the impeccable Lentulus Sura; Mucius, the hero of the afternoon; and a couple of notorious bribery agents – these I recognised, together with various other senators who were seeking the tribuneship. They all seemed in an excellent mood, joking with one another, and Crassus had to clap his hands to get their attention.

'Gentlemen,' he said, standing before them with his back to me, 'thank you for attending. We have much to discuss and not long in which to do it. The first item on the agenda is Egypt. Caesar?'

Crassus sat, and Caesar stood. He stroked back a stray sparse hair and tucked it behind his ear with his index finger. Very carefully, so as not to make a sound, I opened my notebook, withdrew my stylus, and, as Caesar started to speak in that unmistakable harsh voice of his, started to write.

It is, if you will forgive a little immodesty at this juncture, the most wonderful invention, my shorthand system. Although I concede that Xenophon had some primitive version nearly four centuries before me, that was more of a private aid to composition than proper stenography, and besides, it was only suitable for Greek, whereas mine compresses the whole of Latin, with its large vocabulary and complex grammar, into four thousand symbols. And it does so, moreover, in such a way that the system can be taught to any willing pupil; in theory even a woman could become a stenographer.

As those who have the skill will know, few things wreak greater havoc with shorthand than trembling fingers. Anxiety renders the digits as dextrous as Lucanian sausages, and I had feared my nervousness that night would be an impediment to a fast script. But once I was underway I found the process oddly soothing. I did not have time to stop and consider what I was writing. I heard the words – Egypt, colonists, public land, commissioners – without remotely comprehending their meaning; my ambition was merely to keep pace with their delivery. In fact, the greatest practical difficulty I had was the heat: it was like a furnace in that confined place; the sweat ran in stinging rivulets into my eyes and the perspiration from my palms made my stylus slippery to grip. Only occasionally, when I had to lean forward and press my eye to the fabric to check the identity of the speaker, did I realise the enormity of the risk I was taking. Then I experienced a sensation of terrifying vulnerability, made worse by the fact that the audience often seemed to be staring directly at me. Catilina in particular appeared fascinated by the scene on the tapestry which concealed me, and my worst moment of the night by far came right at the end, when Crassus declared the conference over. 'And when we meet again,' he said, 'the destiny of all of us, and of Rome, will have been changed for ever.' The moment the applause was finished, Catilina rose from his seat and walked directly towards me, and as I shrank back against the wall, he ran his palm down the tapestry, barely a hand's breadth from my sweating face. The way that bulge travelled before my gaze still has the power to wake me in the night with a shout. But all he wished to do was compliment Crassus on the workmanship, and after a brief discussion about where it had been purchased, and – inevitably with Crassus – how much it had cost, the two men moved away.

I waited a long time, and when at last I dared to look out through my spyhole, I saw that the room was empty. Only the disarrangement of the chairs proved that there had been a meeting at all. It took an effort to restrain myself from wrenching aside the tapestry and making a run for the door. But the agreement was that I would wait for Caelius, so I forced myself to sit hunched in that narrow space, my back to the wall, my knees drawn up and my arms clasped around them. I have no idea how long the conference had lasted, except that it was long enough to fill the four notebooks I had brought with me, nor how long I sat there.

It is even possible I fell asleep, because when Caelius returned, the lamps and candles, including my own, had all burned away to darkness. I jumped when he pulled back the tapestry. Without speaking, he put out his hand to help me, and together we crept back through the sleeping house to the storeroom. After I had scrambled up stiffly into the alley, I turned to whisper my thanks.

'No need,' he whispered in return. I could just make out the excited gleam of his eyes in the moonlight – eyes so wide and bright that when he added, 'I enjoyed it,' I knew that it was not mere bravado, but that the young fool was telling the truth.

It was well after midnight when I finally returned home. Everyone else was asleep, but Cicero was waiting up for me in the dining room. I could tell he had been there for hours by the scattering of books around the couch. He sprang up the moment I appeared. 'Well?' he said, and when I nodded to signify my mission had succeeded, he pinched my cheek and declared me the bravest and cleverest secretary any statesman ever had. I pulled the notebooks from my pocket to show him. He flipped one open and held it to the light. 'Ah, of course, they are all your damned hieroglyphics,' he said with a wink. 'Come and sit down and I shall fetch you some wine, and you can tell me everything. Would you like something to eat?' He looked around vaguely; the role of waiter was not one which came naturally to him. Soon I was sitting opposite him with an untouched cup of wine and an apple, my notebooks spread before me, like a schoolboy called to recite his lesson.

I no longer possess those wax tablets, but Cicero kept my subsequent transcription among his most secret papers, and looking at it now I am not surprised that I could not follow the original discussion. The conspirators had obviously met many times before, and their deliberations that night presupposed a good deal of knowledge. There was much talk of legislative timetables, and amendments to drafts of bills, and divisions of responsibilities. So you must not imagine that I simply read out what I had written and all was clear. It took the two of us many hours of puzzling over various cryptic remarks, and fitting this to that, until at last we had the whole thing plainly in sight. Every so often Cicero would exclaim something like 'Clever devils! They are such clever devils!' and get up and prowl around, then return to work some more. And to cut it short, and give you the gist, it turned out that the plot which Caesar and Crassus must have been hatching over many months fell into four parts. First, they aimed to seize control of the state by sweeping the board in the general elections, securing not only both consulships, but also all ten tribunates, and a couple of praetorships besides: the bribery agents reported that the thing was more or less a fait accompli, with Cicero's support slipping daily. The second stage called for the introduction by the tribunes of a great land reform bill in December, which would demand the breaking up of the big publicly owned estates, in particular the fertile plains of Campania, and their immediate redistribution as farms to five thousand of the urban plebs. The third step involved the election in March of ten commissioners, headed by Crassus and Caesar, who would be given immense powers to sell off conquered land abroad, and to use the funds thereby released to compulsorily purchase further vast estates in Italy, for an even greater programme of resettlement. The final stage demanded nothing less than the annexation of Egypt the following summer, using as a pretext the disputed will of one of its dead rulers, King Ptolemy the something-or-other, drawn up some seventeen years earlier, by which he had supposedly bequeathed his entire country to the Roman people; again, the revenue from this was to be given to the commissioners, for further acquisition of land in Italy.

'Dear gods: it is a *coup d'état* disguised as an agrarian reform bill!' cried Cicero, when we finally reached the end of my record. 'This commission of ten, led by Crassus and Caesar, will be the real masters of the country; the consuls and the other magistrates will be mere ciphers. And their domination at home will be maintained in perpetuity by the proceeds of extortion abroad.' He sat back and was silent for a long while, his arms folded, his chin on his chest.

I was drained by what I had endured and longed only for sleep. Yet the early summer light now beginning to seep into the room showed we had worked right through the night and it was already election eve. I was aware of the dawn chorus starting up outside, and soon after that heard the tread of someone coming down the stairs. It was Terentia in her nightdress, her hair awry, her unmade-up face soft with sleep, a shawl drawn around her narrow shoulders. I stood respectfully and looked away in embarrassment. 'Cicero!' she exclaimed, taking no notice of me. 'What on earth are you doing down here at this hour?'

He looked up at her and wearily explained what had happened. She had a very quick mind for anything political or financial – had she not been born a woman, and given her spirit, there is no telling what she might have done – and naturally, the moment she grasped it, she was horrified, for Terentia was an aristocrat to her core, and the notion of privatising state land and giving it to the plebs was, to her, a step on the road to the destruction of Rome.

'You must lead the fight against it,' she urged Cicero. 'This could win you the election. All the decent men will rally to you.'

'Ah, but will they?' Cicero picked up one of my notebooks. 'Outright opposition to this could rebound on me badly. A large faction in the senate, half of them patriotic and the other half just plain greedy, has always favoured seizing Egypt. And out on the streets, the cry of "Free farms for all!" is far more likely to gain Catilina and Hybrida votes than cost them. No, I am trapped.' He stared at the transcript of the conference and shook his head slowly, like an artist ruefully contemplating the work of some talented rival. 'It really is an extraordinary scheme – a stroke of true political genius. Only Caesar could have dreamed it up. And as for Crassus – for a down-payment of just twenty million, he can expect to gain control of most of Italy and the whole of Egypt. Even you would concede that that is a good return on your investment.'

'But you have to do *something*,' persisted Terentia. 'You cannot simply allow it to happen.'

'And what exactly would you have me do?'

'And you are supposed to be the cleverest man in Rome?' she asked in exasperation. 'Is it not obvious? Go to the senate this morning and expose what they are plotting. Denounce them!'

'A brilliant tactic, Terentia,' responded Cicero sarcastically. (I was beginning to find my position between them increasingly uncomfortable.) 'I both reveal the existence of a popular measure and denounce it at the same time. You are not listening to me: the people who stand to benefit the most from this are *my* supporters.'

'Well then, you have only yourself to blame for depending on such a rabble in the first place! This is the problem with your demagoguery, Cicero – you may think you can control the mob, but the mob will always end up devouring you. Did you seriously believe you could beat men like Crassus and Catilina when

it came to a public auction of principles?' Cicero grunted irritably; however, I noticed he did not argue with her. 'But tell me,'
she continued, needling away at him, 'if this "extraordinary
scheme", as you call it – or "criminal enterprise", as I should
prefer it – really is as popular as you say, why all this skulking
around at night? Why do they not come out with it openly?'

'Because, my dear Terentia, the aristocrats think like you. They
would never stand for it. First it will be the great public estates
that are broken up and redistributed, next it will be their private
domains. Every time Caesar and Crassus give a man a farm, they
will create another client for themselves. And once the patricians
start to lose control of the land, they are finished. Besides, how
do you think Catulus or Hortensius would react to being ordered
around by a ten-man commission elected by the people? The
people! To them it would seem like a revolution – Tiberius
Gracchus all over again.' Cicero threw the notebook back on to
the dining table. 'No, they would scheme and bribe and kill to
preserve the status quo, just as they always have done.'

'And they would be right!' Terentia glowered down at him.
Her fists were clenched; I almost expected her to hit him. 'They
were right to take away the powers of the tribunes, just as they
were right to try to stop that provincial parvenu Pompey. And if
you had any sense, you would go to them now with this, and
you would say to them, "Gentlemen, this is what Crassus and
Caesar are proposing to do – support me and I shall try to put
a stop to it!"'

Cicero sighed in exasperation and slumped back on to the
couch. For a while he was silent. But then he suddenly glanced
up at her. 'By heavens, Terentia,' he said quietly, 'what a clever
shrew you are.' He jumped up and kissed her on the cheek. 'My
brilliant, clever shrew – you are quite correct. Or rather, half

correct, for there is actually no need for *me* to do anything with
it at all. I should simply pass it to Hortensius. Tiro, how long
would it take you to make a fair copy of this transcript – not of
all of it necessarily, just enough to whet Hortensius's appetite?'

'A few hours,' I said, bewildered by his dramatic change of
mood.

'Quick!' he said, more alive with excitement than I can ever
remember seeing him. 'Fetch me a pen and paper!'

I did as I was ordered. He dipped the nib in the inkpot, thought
about it for a moment, and then wrote the following, as Terentia
and I watched over his shoulder:

From: Marcus Tullius Cicero
To: Quintus Hortensius Hortalus
Greetings!
I feel it is my patriotic duty to share with you in confidence this
record of a meeting held last night at the home of M. Crassus,
involving G. Caesar, L. Catilina, G. Hybrida, P. Sura, and
various candidates for the tribuneship whose names will be
familiar to you. I intend to tackle certain of these gentlemen in
a speech to the senate today, and if you would care to discuss
the matter further, I shall be afterwards at the home of our
esteemed mutual friend T. Atticus.

'That should do the trick,' he said, blowing on the ink to dry
it. 'Now, Tiro, make as full a copy of your notes as you can,
being sure to include all the passages which will make their blue
blood run cold, and deliver it, together with my letter, personally into the hands of Hortensius – personally, mark you: not to
any aide – at least an hour before the senate meets. Also, send
one of the lads with a message to Atticus, asking him to call on

me before I leave.' He gave me the letter and hurried out of the door.

'Do you want me to ask Sositheus or Laurea to bring in your clients?' I called after him, for by now I could hear them queuing outside in the street. 'When do you want the doors opened?'

'No clients in the house this morning!' he shouted in reply, already halfway up the stairs. 'They can accompany me to the senate if they wish. You have work to do and I have a speech to compose.'

His footsteps thumped along the boards above our heads to his room and I found myself alone with Terentia. She touched her hand to her cheek where her husband had kissed her and looked at me in puzzlement. 'Speech?' she said. 'What speech is he talking about?'

But I had to confess that I had no idea, and thus can claim no hand in, or even prior knowledge of, that extraordinary piece of invective which all the world knows by the name of *In toga candida*.

I wrote as quickly and as neatly as my tiredness would allow, setting out my document like the script of a play, with the name of the speaker first, and then his remarks. I excised a great deal of what I considered irrelevant material, but then at the end I wondered if I was really competent enough to judge. Therefore I decided to keep my notebooks with me, in case I might need to refer to them during the day. Once it was done, I sealed it and placed it in a cylinder, and set off. I had to push my way through the throng of clients and well-wishers blocking the street, who clutched at my tunic and demanded to know when the senator would appear.

Hortensius's house on the Palatine was subsequently bought,

many years later, by our dear and beloved emperor, so that gives you an idea of how fine it was. I had never been to it before and I had to stop several times and ask for directions. It was right at the top of the hill, on the south-western side overlooking the Tiber, and one might have been in the country rather than the city, with its view over the dark green trees to the gentle silver curve of the river and the fields beyond. His brother-in-law Catulus, as I think I have mentioned, owned the house next door, and the whole spot – fragrant with the scent of honeysuckle and myrtle, and silent save for the twittering of the birds – was redolent of good taste and old money. Even the steward looked like an aristocrat, and when I said I had a personal message for his master from Senator Cicero, you might have thought I had farted, such an exquisite expression of distaste spread across his bony face at the mention of the name. He wanted to take the cylinder from me, but I refused, so he bade me wait in the atrium, where the masks of all Hortensius's consular ancestors stared down at me with their blank, dead eyes. Displayed on a three-legged table in the corner was a sphinx, wonderfully carved from a single huge piece of ivory, and I realised that this must be the very sphinx which Verres had given to his advocate all those years ago, and which Cicero had made his joke about. I was just stooping to examine it when Hortensius came into the room behind me.

'Well,' he said, as I stood up, feeling guilty, 'I never thought to see a representative of Marcus Cicero under the roof of my ancestors. What is all this about?'

He was wearing his full senatorial rig, but with slippers on his feet instead of shoes, and was obviously still getting ready to depart for the morning's debate. It seemed strange to me, too, to see the old enemy unarmoured, as it were, outside the arena.

I gave him Cicero's letter, which he broke open and read in front of me. Immediately he saw the names it mentioned he gave me a sharp glance, and I could tell that he was hooked, although he was too well bred to show it.

'Tell him I shall inspect it at my leisure,' he said, taking the document from me, and strolled back the way he had come, as if nothing less interesting had ever been placed in his manicured hands – although I am sure that the moment he was out of sight he must have run to his library and broken open the seal. For myself, I went back out into the fresh air and descended to the city by the Caci Steps, partly because I had time to kill before the senate convened and could afford to take a long way round, and partly because the other route took me nearer to the house of Crassus than I cared to go. I came out into that district on the Etruscan road where all the perfume and incense shops are located, and the scented air and the weight of my tiredness combined to make me feel almost drugged. My mood was oddly separated from the real world and its concerns. By this time tomorrow, I remember thinking, the voting on the Field of Mars would be well underway, and we would probably know whether Cicero was to be consul or not, and in either event the sun would shine and in the autumn it would rain. I lingered in the Forum Boarium and watched the people buying their flowers and their fruit and all the rest of it, and wondered what it would be like not to have any interest in politics, but simply to live, as the poet has it, *vita umbratilis*, 'a life in the shade'. That was what I planned to do when Cicero gave me my freedom and my farm. I would eat the fruit I grew and drink the milk of the goats I reared; I would shut my gate at night and never give a fig for another election. It was the closest to wisdom I have ever come.

By the time I eventually reached the forum, two hundred or

more senators had assembled in the senaculum and were being watched by a crowd of curious gawpers – out-of-towners to judge by their rustic dress, who had come to Rome for the elections. Figulus was sitting on his consular chair in the doorway of the senate house, the augurs beside him, waiting for a quorum, and every so often there was a minor commotion as a candidate erupted into the forum with his corona of supporters. I saw Catilina arrive, with his curious mixture of young aristocrats and the dregs of the streets, and then Hybrida, whose rackety assemblage of debtors and gamblers, such as Sabidius and Panthera, seemed quite respectable by comparison. The senators began to file into the chamber, and I was just beginning to wonder if some mishap had befallen Cicero when, from the direction of the Argiletum, came the noise of drums and flutes and then two columns of young men rounded the corner into the forum, carrying freshly cut boughs above their heads, with children scampering excitedly all around them. These were followed by a mass of respectable Roman knights led by Atticus, and then came Quintus with a dozen or so backbench senators. Some maids were scattering rose petals. It was a vastly better show than any of its rivals had managed, and the crowd around me greeted it with applause. At the centre of all this whirling activity, as in the eye of a tornado, walked the candidate himself, clad in the gleaming *toga candida* which had already seen him through three victorious election campaigns. It was rare that I was able to watch him from a distance – usually I was tucked in behind him – and for the first time I appreciated what a natural actor he was, in that when he donned his costume he found his character. All those qualities which the traditional whiteness was supposed to symbolise – clarity, honesty, purity – seemed to be personified in his solid frame and steady gaze as he walked, unseeing, past me. I could tell by the way he moved, and his air of detachment, that he was heavy with a speech. I fell in at the back of the procession and heard the cheers from his supporters as he entered the chamber, and the answering cat-calls of his opponents.

We were kept back until the last of the senators had gone in, and then permitted to run to the bar of the house. I secured myself my usual decent vantage point beside the door jamb and was immediately aware of someone squeezing in beside me. It was Atticus, looking white with nerves. 'How does he find it within himself to do this?' he asked, but before I could say anything, Figulus got up to report on the failure of his bill at the popular assembly. He droned on for a while, and then called on Mucius to explain his conduct in vetoing a measure which had been adopted by the house. There was an oppressive, restless air in the chamber. I could see Catilina and Hybrida among the aristocrats, with Catulus seated just in front of them on the consular bench, and Crassus a few places along from him. Caesar was on the same side of the chamber, on the bench reserved for ex-aediles. Mucius got up and in a dignified way explained that his sacred office called on him to act in the interests of the people, and that the *lex Figula*, far from protecting those interests, was a threat to their safety and an insult to their honour.

'Nonsense!' shouted a voice from the opposite side of the aisle, which I recognised at once as Cicero's. 'You were bought!'

Atticus gripped my arm. 'Here he goes!' he whispered.

'My conscience—' continued Mucius.

'Your conscience had nothing to do with it, you liar! You sold yourself like a whore!'

There came that low grumble of noise which is caused by several hundred men all muttering to one another at once, and suddenly Cicero was on his feet, his arm outstretched, demanding the floor. At that same moment I heard a voice behind me calling to be let through, and we shuffled out of the way to allow a late-arriving senator, who proved to be Hortensius, access to the chamber. He hurried down the aisle, bowed to the consul, and took his place next to Catulus, with whom he quickly struck up a whispered conversation. By this time Cicero's supporters among the *pedarii* were bellowing that he should be allowed to speak, which, given that he was a praetorian, and outranked Mucius, he was undeniably entitled to do. Very reluctantly, Mucius allowed himself to be pulled down by the senators seated around him, whereupon Cicero pointed at him – his white-draped arm held out straight and rigid, like some statue of avenging Justice – and declared: 'A whore you are, Mucius – yes, and a treacherous one at that, for only yesterday you declared to the popular assembly that I was not fit to be consul – I, the first man to whom you turned when you were prosecuted for robbery! Good enough to defend you, Mucius, but not good enough to defend the Roman people, is that it? But why should I care what you say about me, when the whole world knows you were paid to slander me?'

Mucius turned scarlet. He shook his fist and started shouting insults in return, but I could not make them out over the general tumult. Cicero regarded him with contempt, then held up his hand for silence. 'But who is Mucius in any case?' he said, spitting out the name and dismissing it with a flick of his fingers. 'Mucius is just one solitary whore in a whole hired troupe of common prostitutes. Their master is a man of noble birth, bribery his chosen instrument – and believe me, gentlemen, he plays it like a flute! He is a briber of juries, a briber of voters and a briber of tribunes. Little wonder he loathed our bill against bribery, and that the method he used to stop it should have been – bribery!'

He paused and lowered his voice. 'I should like to share some information with the house.' The senate now went very quiet. 'Last night, Antonius Hybrida and Sergius Catilina met, together with others, at the house of this man of noble birth—'

'Name him!' shouted someone, and for a moment I thought that Cicero might actually do so. He stared across the aisle at Crassus with such calculated intensity that he might as well have gone over and touched him on the shoulder, so clear was it whom he had in mind. Crassus sat up slightly in his seat and slowly leaned forward, never taking his eyes from Cicero: he must have wondered what was coming. One could feel the entire chamber holding its breath. But Cicero had different quarry to chase, and with an almost palpable effort of will, he dragged his gaze away from Crassus.

'This man, as I say, of noble birth, having bribed away the bribery bill, has a new scheme in mind. He intends now to bribe his way to the consulship, not for himself but for his two creatures, Hybrida and Catilina.'

Naturally, both men instantly jumped up to protest, as Cicero must have calculated they would. But as their rank was no higher than his, he was entitled to leave them standing. 'Well, there they are,' he said, turning to the benches behind him, 'the best that money can buy!' He let the laughter build and chose the perfect moment to add: 'As we lawyers say – *caveat emptor!*'

Nothing is more injurious to a politician's dignity and authority than to be mocked, and if it happens it is vitally important to appear entirely unconcerned. But Hybrida and Catilina, buffeted by gusts of merriment from every side, could not decide whether to remain defiantly standing or to sit and feign indifference. They ended up trying to do both, bobbing up and down like a pair of workmen at either end of a pump-handle, which only increased the general hilarity. Catilina in particular was obviously losing his temper, for like many arrogant men the one thing he could not abide was to be teased. Caesar tried to come to their rescue, rising to demand what point Cicero was trying to make, but Cicero refused to acknowledge his intervention and the consul, enjoying himself like everyone else, declined to call Cicero to order.

'Let us take the lesser first,' continued Cicero, after both his targets had finally sunk back in to their seats. 'You, Hybrida, should never even have been elected praetor, and would not have been had I not taken pity on you, and recommended you to the centuries. You live openly with a courtesan, you cannot speak in public, you can barely remember your own name without the assistance of a *nomenclator*. You were a thief under Sulla, and a drunkard thereafter. You are, in short, a joke; but a joke of the worst sort – a joke that has gone on too long.'

The chamber was much quieter now, for these were insults which would oblige a man to be your enemy for life, and as Cicero turned towards Catilina, Atticus's anxious grip on my arm tightened. 'As for you, Catilina, is it not a prodigy and a portent of evil times that you should hope for, or even think of, the consulship? For from whom do you ask it? From the chiefs of the state, who, two years ago, refused even to allow you to stand for it? Do you ask it from the order of knights which you have slaughtered? Or from the people, who still remember the monstrous cruelty with which you butchered their leader – my kinsman – Gratidianus, and carried his still-breathing head through the streets to the Temple of Apollo? Do you ask it from the senators, who by their own authority had almost stripped you of all your honours, and surrendered you in chains to the Africans?'

'I was acquitted!' roared Catilina, leaping back to his feet.

'Acquitted!' mocked Cicero. 'You? Acquitted? You – who disgraced yourself by every sort of sexual perversion and profligacy; who dyed your hands in the wickedest murder, who plundered the allies, who violated the laws and the courts of justice? You, who married in adultery the mother of the daughter you first debauched? Acquitted? Then I can only imagine that Roman knights must have been liars; that the documentary evidence of a most honourable city was false; that Quintus Metellus Pius told lies; that Africa told lies. Acquitted! O wretched man, not to see that you were not acquitted by that decision, but only reserved for some more severe tribunal, and some more fearful punishment!'

This would have been too much even for an equable man to sit through, but in Catilina it induced nothing short of murderous insanity. He gave an animal's bellow of primitive rage and launched himself over the bench in front of him, crashing between Hortensius and Catulus, and diving across the aisle in an effort to reach his tormentor. But of course this was precisely the reaction Cicero had been trying to goad him into. He flinched but stood his ground as Quintus and a few other ex-soldiers scrambled to form a cordon around him – not that there was any need, for Catilina, big though he was, had been seized at once by the consul's lictors. His friends, among them Crassus and Caesar, quickly had him by the arms and started dragging him back to his seat as he writhed and roared and kicked in fury. The whole of the senate was on its feet, trying to see what was happening, and Figulus had to suspend the session until order was restored.

When the sitting resumed, Hybrida and Catilina, as custom dictated, were given the opportunity to respond, and each man, quivering with outrage, tipped a bucketful of the usual insults over Cicero's head – ambitious, untrustworthy, scheming, 'new man', foreigner, evader of military service, coward – while their supporters cheered them dutifully. But neither had Cicero's flair for invective, and even their most dedicated partisans must have been dismayed by their failure to answer his central charge: that their candidacies were based on bribery by a mysterious third party. It was noticeable that Hortensius and even Catulus offered them only the most half-hearted applause. As for Cicero, he put on a professional mask and sat smiling and unconcerned throughout their shrill tirades, seemingly no more concerned than a duck in a rainstorm. Only afterwards – after Quintus and his military friends had escorted him rapidly out of the chamber to prevent a further assault by Catilina, and only after we had reached the safety of Atticus's house on the Quirinal and the door had been locked and barred – only then did he appear to realise the enormity of what he had done.

XVIII

There was nothing left for Cicero now except to wait for the reaction of Hortensius. We passed the hours in the dry stillness of Atticus's library, surrounded by all that ancient wisdom, under the gaze of the great philosophers, while beyond the terrace the day ripened and faded and the view over the city became yellower and dustier in the heat of the July afternoon. I should like to record that we took down the occasional volume and spent the time swapping the thoughts of Epicurus or Zeno or Aristotle, or that Cicero said something profound about democracy. But in truth no one was much in the mood for political theory, least of all Quintus, who had scheduled a campaign appearance in the busy Porticus Aemilia and fretted that his brother was losing valuable canvassing time. We relived the drama of Cicero's speech – 'You should have seen Crassus's face when he thought I was about to name him!' – and pondered the likely response of the aristocrats. If they did not take the bait, Cicero had placed himself in a highly dangerous position. Every so often, he would ask me if I was absolutely certain that Hortensius had read his letter, and yet again I would reply that I had no doubt, for he had done so right in front of me. 'Then we shall give him another hour,' Cicero would say, and resume his restless pacing, occasionally stopping to make some cutting remark to Atticus: 'Are they always this punctual, these smart friends of yours?' or 'Tell me, is it considered a crime against good breeding to consult a clock?'

It was the tenth hour by Atticus's exquisite sundial when at last one of his slaves came into the library to announce that Hortensius's steward had arrived.

'So now we are supposed to negotiate with his servants?' muttered Cicero. But he was so anxious for news that he hurried out into the atrium himself, and we all went with him. Waiting there was the same bony, supercilious fellow whom I had encoun tered at Hortensius's house that morning; he was not much more polite now. His message was that he had come in Hortensius's two-seater carriage to collect Cicero and convey him to a meeting with his master.

'But I must accompany him,' protested Quintus.

'My orders are simply to bring Senator Cicero,' responded the steward. 'The meeting is highly sensitive and confidential. Only one other person is required – that secretary of his, who has the quick way with words.'

I was not at all happy about this, and nor was Quintus – I out of a cowardly desire to avoid being cross-examined by Hortensius, he because it was a snub, and also perhaps (to be more charit- able) because he was worried for his brother's safety. 'What if it is a trap?' he asked. 'What if Catilina is there, or intercepts you on your journey?'

'You will be under the protection of Senator Hortensius,' said the steward stiffly. 'I give you his word of honour in the pres- ence of all these witnesses.'

'It will be all right, Quintus,' said Cicero, laying a reassuring hand on his brother's arm. 'It is not in Hortensius's interests for any injury to befall me. Besides,' he smiled, 'I am a friend of Atticus here, and what better guarantee of safe passage is there than that? Come along, Tiro. Let us find out what he has to say.'

We left the relative safety of the library and went down into the street, where a smart *carpentum* was waiting, with Hortensius's livery painted on its side. The steward sat up at the front next to the driver, while I sat in the back with Cicero and we lurched off down the hill. But instead of turning south towards the Palatine, as we had expected, we headed north, towards the Fontinalian Gate, joining the stream of traffic leaving the city at the end of the day. Cicero had pulled the folds of his white toga up over his head, ostensibly to shield himself from the clouds of dust thrown up by the wheels, but actually to avoid any of his voters seeing him travelling in a vehicle belonging to Hortensius. Once we were out of the city, however, he pulled his hood down. He was clearly not at all happy to be leaving the precincts of Rome, for despite his brave words he knew that a fatal accident out here would be very easy to arrange. The sun was big and low, just beginning to set behind those massive family tombs which line the road. The poplars threw elongated shadows which fell jet black across our path, like crevasses. For a while we were stuck behind a plodding bullock cart. But then the coachman cracked his whip and we raced forward, just narrowly managing to overtake it before a chariot rattled past us, heading towards the city. I guess we both must have realised by then where we were going, and Cicero pulled his hood up again and folded his arms, his head down. What thoughts must have been spinning through his mind! We turned off the road and began climbing a steep hillside, following a driveway freshly laid with gravel. It took us on a winding journey over gushing brooks and through gloomy, scented pine groves where pigeons called to one another in the dusk, until eventually we came to a huge pair of open gates, and beyond them an immense villa set in its own park, which I recognised from the model Gabinius had displayed to the jealous mob in the forum as the palace of Lucullus.

For years thereafter, whenever I smelt fresh cement and wet paint, I would think of Lucullus and that echoing mausoleum he had built for himself beyond the walls of Rome. What a brilliant, melancholy figure he was – perhaps the greatest general the aristocrats had produced for fifty years, yet robbed of ultimate victory in the East by the arrival of Pompey, and doomed by the political intrigues of his enemies, among them Cicero, to linger outside Rome for years, unhonoured and unable even to attend the senate, for by crossing the city's boundaries he would forfeit his right to a triumph. Because he still retained military *imperium*, there were sentries in the grounds, and lictors with their bundles of rods and axes waited sullenly in the hall – so many lictors, in fact, that Cicero calculated that a second general on active service must be on the premises. 'Do you think it's possible that Quintus Metellus is here as well?' he whispered, as we followed the steward into the cavernous interior. 'Dear gods, I think he must be!'

We passed through various rooms stuffed with loot from the war until at last we reached the great chamber known as the Room of Apollo, where a group of six were talking beneath a mural of the deity shooting a fiery arrow from his golden bow. At the sound of our footsteps on the marble floor, the conversation ceased and there was a loud silence. Quintus Metellus was indeed among them – stouter, greyer and more weather-beaten following his years of command in Crete, but still very much the same man who had attempted to intimidate the Sicilians into dropping their case against Verres. On one side of Metellus was his old courtroom ally Hortensius, whose bland and handsome face was expressionless, and on the other, Catulus, as thin and sharp as a blade. Isauricus, the grand old man of the senate, was also present – seventy years old he must have been on that July evening, but he did not look it (he was one of those types who never look it: he was to live to be ninety, and attend the funerals of almost everyone else in the room); I noticed he was holding the transcript I had delivered to Hortensius. The two Lucullus brothers completed the sextet. Marcus, the younger, I knew as a familiar figure from the senate front bench. Lucius, the famous general, paradoxically I did not recognise at all, for he had been away fighting for eighteen out of the past twenty-three years. He was in his middle fifties, and I quickly saw why Pompey was so passionately jealous of him – why they had literally come to blows when they met in Galatia to effect the handover in the Eastern command – for Lucullus had a chilly grandeur which made even Catulus seem slightly common.

It was Hortensius who ended the embarrassment, and who stepped forward to introduce Cicero to Lucullus. Cicero extended his hand, and for a moment I thought Lucullus might refuse to shake it, for he would only have known Cicero as a partisan of Pompey, and as one of those populist politicians who had helped engineer his dismissal. But finally he took it, very gingerly, as one might pick up a soiled sponge in a latrine. 'Imperator,' said Cicero, bowing politely. He nodded to Metellus as well: 'Imperator.'

'And who is that?' demanded Isauricus, pointing at me.

'That is my secretary, Tiro,' said Cicero, 'who recorded the meeting at the house of Crassus.'

'Well, I for one do not believe a word of it,' replied Isauricus, brandishing the transcript at me. 'No one could have written down all of this as it was uttered. It is beyond human capacity.'

'Tiro has developed his own system of stenography,' explained Cicero. 'Let him show you the actual records he made last night.'

I pulled out the notebooks from my pocket and handed them around.

'Remarkable,' said Hortensius, examining my script intently. 'So these symbols substitute for sounds, do they? Or for entire words?'

'Words mostly,' I replied, 'and common phrases.'

'Prove it,' said Catulus belligerently. 'Take down what I say.' And giving me barely a moment to open a fresh notebook and take up my stylus, he went on rapidly: 'If what I have read here is true, the state is threatened with civil war as a result of a criminal conspiracy. If what I have read is false, it is the wickedest forgery in our history. For my own part, I do not believe it is true, because I do not believe such a record could have been produced by a living hand. That Catilina is a hothead, we all know well enough, but he is a true and noble Roman, not a devious and ambitious outsider, and I will take his word over that of a new man – always! What is it you want from us, Cicero? You cannot seriously believe, after all that has happened between us, that I could possibly support you for the consulship? So what is it?'

'Nothing,' replied Cicero pleasantly. 'I came across some information which I thought might be of interest to you. I passed it along to Hortensius, that is all. You brought me out here, remember? I did not ask to come. I might more appropriately ask: What do *you* gentlemen want? Do you want to be trapped between Pompey and his armies in the East, and Crassus and Caesar and the urban mob in Italy, and gradually have the life squeezed out of you? Do you want to rely for your protection on the two men you are backing for consul – the one stupid, the other insane – who cannot even manage their own households, let alone the affairs of the nation? Is that what you want? Well, good then. I at least have an easy conscience. I have done my patriotic duty by alerting you to what is happening, even though you have never been any friends of mine. I also believe I have demonstrated by my courage in the senate today my willingness to stand up to these criminals. No other candidate for consul has done it, or will in the future. I have made them my enemies and shown you what they are like. But from you, Catulus, and from all of you, I want *nothing,* and if all you wish to do is insult me, I bid you a good evening.'

He spun around and began walking towards the door, with me in tow, and I guess that must have felt to him like the longest walk he ever took, because we had almost reached the shadowy antechamber – and with it, surely, the black void of political oblivion – when a voice (it was that of Lucullus himself) shouted out: 'Read it back!' Cicero halted, and we both turned around. 'Read it back,' repeated Lucullus. 'What Catulus said just now.'

Cicero nodded at me, and I fumbled for my notebook. '"If what I have read here is true",' I began, reciting in that flat, strange way of stenography being read back, '"the state is threatened with civil war as a result of a criminal conspiracy if what I have read is false it is the wickedest forgery in our history for my own part I do not believe it is true because I do not believe such a record could have been produced by a living hand—"'

'He could have memorised that,' objected Catulus. 'It is all just a cheap trick, of the sort you might see done by a conjuror in the forum.'

'And the latter part,' persisted Lucullus. 'Read out the last thing your master said.'

I ran my finger down my notation. '". . . never been any friends of mine I also believe I have demonstrated by my courage in the senate today my willingess to stand up to these criminals no other candidate for consul has done it or will in the future I have made them my enemies and shown you what they are like but from you Catulus and from all of you I want nothing and if all you wish to do is insult me I bid you a good evening."'

Isauricus whistled. Hortensius nodded, and said something like 'I told you' or 'I warned you' – I cannot remember exactly – to which Metellus responded, 'Yes, well, I have to say, that is proof enough for me.' Catulus merely glared at me.

'Come back, Cicero,' said Lucullus, beckoning to him. 'I am satisfied. The record is genuine. Let us put aside for the time being the question of who needs whom the most, and start from the premise that each of us needs the other.'

'I am still not convinced,' grumbled Catulus.

'Then let me convince you with a single word,' said Hortensius impatiently. 'Caesar. Caesar – with Crassus's gold, two consuls and ten tribunes behind him!'

'So, really, we must talk with such people?' Catulus sighed. 'Well, Cicero perhaps,' he conceded. 'But we certainly do not need *you*,' he snapped, pointing at me, just as I was moving, as always, to follow my master. 'I do not want that creature and his tricks within a mile of me, listening to what we say, and writing everything down in his damned untrustworthy way. If anything is to pass between us, it must never be divulged.'

Cicero hesitated. 'All right,' he said reluctantly, and he gave me an apologetic look. 'Wait outside, Tiro.'

I had no business to feel aggrieved. I was merely a slave, after all: an extra hand, a tool – a 'creature', as Catulus put it. But nevertheless I felt my humiliation keenly. I folded up my note-book and walked into the antechamber, and then kept on walking, through all those echoing, freshly stuccoed state rooms – Venus, Mercury, Mars, Jupiter – as the slaves in their cushioned slippers moved silently with their glowing tapers among the gods, lighting the lamps and candelabra. I went out into the soft warm dusk of the park, where the cicadas were singing, and for reasons which I cannot even now articulate I found that I was weeping, but I suppose I must have been very tired.

It was almost dawn when I awoke, stiff in my limbs and damp with cold from the dew. For a moment I had no idea where I was or how I had got there, but then I realised I was on a stone bench close to the front of the house, and that it was Cicero who had woken me. His face looming over me was grim. 'We have finished here,' he said. 'We must get back to the city quickly.' He glanced across to where the carriage was waiting, and put his finger to his lips to warn me not to say anything in front of Hortensius's steward. So it was in silence that we clambered into the *carpentum*, and as we left the park I remember turning for a final look at the great villa, the torches still burning along its terraces, but losing their sharpness now as the pale morning light came up; of the other aristocrats there was no sign.

Cicero, conscious that in little more than two hours he would have to leave his house to go down to the Field of Mars for

the election, kept urging the driver to make better speed, and
those poor horses must have been whipped until their hides
were raw. But we were lucky that the roads were empty, save
for a few very early voters walking into town for the election,
and we hurtled along at a great speed, reaching the Fontinalian
Gate just as it was opening, and then rattled up the paved
slopes of the Esquiline Hill faster than a man could sprint. Just
before the Temple of Tellus, Cicero told the driver to stop and
let us out, so that we could walk the last part of the way – an
order which puzzled me, until I realised that he wanted to
avoid being seen by the crowd of his supporters which was
already beginning to assemble in the street outside his front
door. He strode on ahead of me in that way of his, with his
hands clasped behind his back, still keeping his thoughts to
himself, and I noticed that his once-brilliant white toga was
stained with dirt. We went down the side of the house and
through the little door at the back which the servants used,
and there we bumped into Terentia's business manager, the
odious Philotimus, who was obviously on his way back from
some nocturnal assignation with one of the slave girls. Cicero
did not even see him, so preoccupied was he with what had
happened and what was to come. His eyes were red with tiredness, his face and hair brown with dust from the journey. He
told me to go and open up the door and let the people in.
Then he went upstairs.

Among the first across the threshold was Quintus, who naturally demanded to know what was happening. He and the others
had waited for our return in Atticus's library until nearly
midnight, and he was furious and anxious in equal measure.
This put me in an awkward spot, and I could only stammer
that I would prefer it if he addressed his questions directly to

his brother. To be honest, seeing Cicero and his bitterest enemies all together in such a setting now seemed so unreal to me, I could almost have believed I had dreamed it. Quintus was not satisfied, but fortunately I was saved further embarrassment by the sheer number of visitors pouring through the door. I escaped by pretending I had to check everything was ready in the tablinum, and from there I slipped into my little cubicle and rinsed my neck and face with tepid water from my basin.

When I next saw Cicero, an hour later, he once again demonstrated those remarkable powers of recuperation which I have observed to be the distinguishing mark of all successful politicians. Watching him come down the stairs in a freshly laundered white toga, his face washed and shaved and his hair combed and scented, no one could have guessed that he had not slept for the past two nights. The cramped house by this time was packed with his supporters. Cicero had the infant Marcus, whose first birthday it was, carefully balanced on his shoulders, and such a cheer went up when the two of them appeared, it must have shaken off several roof tiles: no wonder the poor child started crying. Cicero quickly lifted him down, lest this be seen as a bad omen for the day, and handed him to Terentia, who was standing behind him on the stairs. He smiled at her, and said something, and at that moment I realised for the first time just how close they had become over the years: that what had started as a marriage of convenience was now a most formidable partnership. I could not hear what passed between them, and then he came down into the crowd.

So many people had turned out it was hard for him to struggle through the tablinum to the atrium, where Quintus, Frugi and Atticus were surrounded by a very decent showing of senators.

Among those present to demonstrate their support were Cicero's old friend Servius Sulpicius; Gallus, the renowned scholar of judisprudence, who had refused to run himself; the elder Frugi, with whom Cicero was forming a family connection; Marcellinus, who had supported him ever since the Verres trial; and all those senators he had represented in the courts, such as Cornelius, Fundanius, Orchivius, and also Fonteius, the corrupt ex-governor of Gaul. Indeed, as I struggled through the rooms after Cicero, it was as if the past ten years had all sprung back to life, so many half-forgotten courtroom struggles were represented there; even Popillius Laenas, whose nephew Cicero had rescued from a charge of parricide on the day Sthenius came to see us. The atmosphere was more akin to a family festival than an election day, and Cicero as ever was in his element on these occasions: I doubt if there was one supporter whose hand he did not shake, and with whom he did not establish one brief moment of rapport, sufficient to leave the other man feeling he had been specially singled out.

Just before we left, Quintus pulled him to one side to ask, quite angrily as I recall it, where on earth he had been all night – he had almost sent men out looking for him – to which Cicero, conscious of the people all around him, replied quietly that he would tell him later. But that only made Quintus more aggrieved. 'Who do you think I am?' he demanded. 'Your maid? Tell me now!' And so Cicero told him then very rapidly about the journey out to the palace of Lucullus and the presence there of Metellus and Catulus, as well as Hortensius and Isauricus.

'The whole patrician gang!' whispered Quintus excitedly, his irritation entirely forgotten. 'My gods, whoever would have thought it? And are they going to support us?'

'We talked for hour after hour, but in the end they would

not commit themselves until they had spoken to the other great families,' replied Cicero, glancing nervously around in case anyone was listening, but the din was too great for him to be overheard. 'Hortensius, I think, would have agreed on the spot. Catulus remains instinctively opposed. The others will do what self-interest dictates. We shall just have to wait and see.'

Atticus, who had heard all this, said, 'But they believed in the truth of the evidence you showed them?'

'I think so, yes. Thanks to Tiro. But we can discuss all this later. Put on your bravest faces, gentlemen,' he said, gripping the hands of each of us in turn, 'we have an election to win!'

Seldom can a candidate have staged a more splendid show than Cicero did during his walk down to the Field of Mars, and for that much credit must go to Quintus. We made up a parade of three or four hundred, with musicians, young men carrying green boughs wound with ribbons, girls with rose petals, actor friends of Cicero's from the theatre, senators, knights, merchants, stall-holders, regular spectators from the law courts, guild officers, legal clerks, representatives from the Roman communities in Sicily and Nearer Gaul. We set up a terrific noise of cheering and whistling as we came on to the campus and there was a great surge of voters towards us. It is always said of elections, in my experience, that whichever one is in progress at the time is the most significant there has ever been, and on that day, at least, it was arguably true, with the added excitement that no one knew how it would turn out, given the activity among the bribery agents, the sheer number of candidates and the enmity between them following Cicero's attack on Catilina and Hybrida in the senate.

We had anticipated trouble, and Quintus had taken the

precaution of stationing some of our heftier supporters immediately behind and in front of his brother. As we approached the
voting pens I felt increasingly worried, for I could see Catilina
and his followers up ahead, waiting beside the returning officer's
tent. Some of these ruffians jeered us as we arrived at the enclosure, but Catilina himself, after a brief and contemptuous glance
in Cicero's direction, resumed talking to Hybrida. I muttered to
young Frugi that I was surprised he did not at least put on a
show of intimidation – that, after all, was his usual tactic – to
which Frugi, who was no fool, responded. 'He does not feel he
needs to – he is so confident of victory.' His words filled me with
unease.

But then a very remarkable thing happened. Cicero and all
the other senators seeking either the consulship or the praetorship – perhaps two dozen men – were standing in the small
area reserved for the candidates, surrounded by a low sheep
fence to separate them from their supporters. The presiding
consul, Marcius Figulus, was talking to the augur, checking
that all was propitious for the ballot to begin, when just at that
moment Hortensius appeared, followed by a retinue of about
twenty men. The crowd parted to let him through. He
approached the fence and called to Cicero, who interrupted
his conversation with one of the other candidates – Cornificius,
I think it was – and went over to him. This in itself surprised
people, for it was known that there was little love lost between
the two old rivals, and there was a stir among the onlookers;
Catilina and Hybrida certainly both turned to stare. For a
moment or two, Cicero and Hortensius regarded one another,
then simultaneously they nodded, and each reached out and
slowly shook the hand of the other. No word was uttered, and
with the handclasp still in place, Hortensius half turned to the

men behind him and raised Cicero's arm above his head. A great shout of applause, mingled with some boos and groans, broke out from the watching crowd, for there was no doubt what the gesture meant: I certainly never expected to see anything like it. *The aristocrats were supporting Cicero!* Immediately, Hortensius's attendants turned and disappeared into the throng, presumably to spread the word among the nobles' agents in the centuries that they were to switch their support. I risked a look at Catilina and saw on his face an expression of puzzlement rather than anything else, for the incident, though obviously significant – people were still buzzing about it – was so fleeting that Hortensius was already walking away. An instant later, Figulus called to the candidates to follow him to the platform so that the voting could begin.

You can always spot a fool, for he is the man who will tell you he knows who is going to win an election. But an election is a living thing – you might almost say, the most vigorously alive thing there is – with thousands upon thousands of brains and limbs and eyes and thoughts and desires, and it will wriggle and turn and run off in directions no one ever predicted, some-times just for the joy of proving the wiseacres wrong. This much I learnt on the Field of Mars that day, when the entrails were inspected, the skies were checked for suspicious flights of birds, the blessings of the gods were invoked, all epileptics were asked to leave the field (for in those days an attack of epilepsy, or *morbus comitialis*, automatically rendered proceed-ings void), a legion was deployed on the approaches to Rome to prevent a surprise attack, the list of candidates was read, the trumpets were sounded, the red flag was hoisted over the

Janiculum Hill, and the Roman people began to cast their ballots.

The honour of being the first of the one hundred and ninety-three centuries to vote was decided by lot, and to be a member of this *centuria praerogativa*, as it was known, was considered a rare blessing, for its decision often set the pattern for what followed. Only the richest centuries were eligible for the draw, and I remember how I stood and watched as that year's winners, a stalwart collection of merchants and bankers, filed self-importantly over the wooden bridge and disappeared behind the screens. Their ballots were quickly counted, Figulus came to the front of his tribunal and announced that they had put Cicero in first place and Catilina second. At once a gasp went up, for all those fools I was speaking of had predicted it would be Catilina first and Hybrida second, and then the gasp quickly turned into cheers as Cicero's supporters, realising what had happened, began a noisy demonstration which spread across the Field of Mars. Cicero was standing under the awning beneath the consul's platform. He permitted himself only the most fleeting of smiles, and then, such was the actor in the man, he composed his features into an expression of dignity and authority appropriate to a Roman consul. Catilina – who was as far away from Cicero as it was possible to get, with all the other candidates lined up between them – looked as if he had been struck in the face. Only Hybrida's expression was blank – whether because he was drunk as usual or too stupid to realise what was happening I cannot say. As for Crassus and Caesar, they had been loitering and chatting together near to the place where the voters emerged after casting their ballots, and I could have laughed aloud as they looked at one another in disbelief. They held a hurried consultation and then darted off in different directions, no doubt to demand how the expenditure of twenty million sesterces had failed to secure the *centuria praerogativa*.

If Crassus really had purchased the eight thousand votes which Ranunculus had estimated, that would normally have been enough to swing the election. But this ballot was unusually heavy, thanks to the interest aroused all across Italy, and as the voting went on throughout the morning it became apparent that the briber-in-chief had fallen just short of his target. Cicero had always had the equestrian order firmly behind him, plus the Pompeians and the lower orders. Now that Hortensius, Catulus, Metellus, Isauricus and the Lucullus brothers were delivering the blocs of voters controlled by the aristocrats, he was winning a vote from every century, either as their first or second preference, and soon the only question was who would be his consular colleague. Throughout the morning, it looked as if it would be Catilina, with my notes (which I found the other day) showing that at noon the voting was:

Cicero	81 centuries
Catilina	34 centuries
Hybrida	29 centuries
Sacerdos	9 centuries
Longinus	5 centuries
Cornificius	2 centuries

But then came the voting of the six centuries composed exclusively of the aristocrats, the *sex suffragia*, and they really put the knife into Catilina, so that if I retain one image above all from that memorable day it is of the patricians, having cast their ballots, filing past the candidates. Because the Field of

Mars lies outside the city limits, there was nothing to stop Lucius Lucullus, and Quintus Metellus with him, both in their scarlet cloaks and military uniforms, turning out to vote, and their appearance caused a sensation – but nothing like as great an uproar as greeted the announcement that their century had voted Cicero first and then Hybrida. After them came Isauricus, the elder Curio, Aemilius Alba, Claudius Pulcher, Junius Servilius – the husband of Cato's sister, Servilia – old Metellus Pius, the pontifex maximus, too sick to walk but carried in a litter, followed by his adopted son, Scipio Nasica . . . And again and again the announcement was the same: Cicero first, and next Hybrida; Cicero first, and next Hybrida; Cicero first . . . When, finally, Hortensius and Catulus passed by, it was noticeable that neither man could bring himself to look Catilina in the eye, and once it was declared that their century, too, had voted for Cicero and Hybrida, Catilina must have realised his chances were finished. At that point Cicero had eighty-seven centuries to Hybrida's thirty-five and Catilina's thirty-four – for the first time in the day, Hybrida had eased in front of his running-mate, but more importantly, the aristocrats had publicly turned on one of their own, and in the most brutal manner. After that, Catilina's candidacy was effectively dead, although one had to give him high marks for his conduct. I had anticipated that he would storm off in a rage, or lunge at Cicero and try to murder him with his bare hands. But instead he stood throughout that long, hot day, as the citizens went past him and his hopes of the consulship sank with the sun, and he maintained a look of imperturbable calm, even when Figulus came forward for the final time to read the result of the election:

Cicero	193 centuries
Hybrida	102 centuries
Catilina	65 centuries
Sacerdos	12 centuries
Longinus	9 centuries
Cornificius	5 centuries

We cheered until our throats ached, although Cicero himself seemed very preoccupied for a man who had just achieved his life's ambition, and I felt oddly uneasy. He was now permanently wearing what I later came to recognise as his 'consular look': his chin held ever-so-slightly high, his mouth set in a determined line, and his eyes seemingly directed towards some glorious point in the distance. Hybrida held out his hand to Catilina, but Catilina ignored it, and stepped down from the podium like a man in a trance. He was ruined, bankrupt – surely it would be only a year or two before he was thrown out of the senate altogether. I searched around for Crassus and Caesar, but they had quit the field hours earlier, once Cicero had passed the number of centuries needed for victory. So, too, had the aristocrats. They had gone home for the day the instant Catilina had been safely disposed of, like men who had been required to perform some distasteful duty – put down a favourite hunting-dog, say, which had become rabid – and who now wanted nothing more than the quiet comfort of their own hearths.

Thus did Marcus Tullius Cicero, at forty-two, the youngest age allowable, achieve the supreme *imperium* of the Roman consulship – and achieve it, amazingly, by a unanimous vote of the centuries, and as a 'new man', without family, fortune or force of arms to assist him: a feat never accomplished before or afterwards. We returned that evening from the Field of Mars to his modest home, and once he had thanked his supporters and sent them away, and received the congratulations of his slaves, he ordered that the couches from the dining room be carried up on to the roof, so that he could dine beneath the open sky, as he had done on that night – so long ago it seemed – when he had first disclosed his ambition to become consul. I was honoured to be invited to join the family group, for Cicero was insistent that he would never have achieved his goal without me. For a delirious moment I thought he might be about to award me my freedom and give me that farm right there and then, but he said nothing about it, and it did not seem the appropriate time or setting to bring it up. He was on one couch with Terentia, Quintus was with Pomponia, Tullia was with her fiancé, Frugi, and I reclined with Atticus. I can recall little at my great age of what we ate or drank, or any of that, but I do remember that we each went over our particular memories of the day, and especially of that extraordinary spectacle of the aristocracy voting en masse for Cicero.

'Tell me, Marcus,' said Atticus, in his worldly way, once plenty of good wine had been consumed, 'how did you manage to persuade them? Because, although I know you are a genius with words, these men despised you – absolutely loathed everything you said and stood for. What did you offer them, besides stopping Catilina?'

'Obviously,' replied Cicero, 'I had to promise that I will lead the opposition to Crassus and Caesar and the tribunes when they publish this land reform bill of theirs.'

'That will be quite a task,' said Quintus.

'And that is all?' persisted Atticus. (It is my belief, looking back, that he was behaving like a good cross-examiner, and that he knew the answer to the question before he asked it, probably from his friend Hortensius.) 'You really agreed to nothing else? Because you were in there for many hours.'

Cicero winced. 'Well, I did have to undertake,' he said reluctantly, 'to propose in the senate, as consul, that Lucullus should be awarded a triumph, and also Quintus Metellus.'

Now at last I understood why Cicero had seemed so grim and preoccupied when he left his conference with the aristocrats. Quintus put down his plate and regarded him with undisguised horror. 'So first they want you to turn the people against you by blocking land reform, and then they demand that you should make an enemy out of Pompey by awarding triumphs to his greatest rivals?'

'I am afraid, brother,' said Cicero wearily, 'that the aristocracy did not acquire their wealth without knowing how to drive a hard bargain. I held out as long as I could.'

'But why did you agree?'

'Because I needed to win.'

'But to win what, exactly?'

Cicero was silent.

'Good,' said Terentia, patting her husband's knee. 'I think all those policies are good.'

'Well, you would!' protested Quintus. 'But within weeks of taking office, Marcus will have no supporters left. The people will accuse him of betrayal. The Pompeians will do the same. And the aristocrats will drop him just as soon as he has served his purpose. Who will be left to defend him?'

'I shall defend you,' said Tullia, but for once no one laughed at her precocious loyalty, and even Cicero could only manage a faint smile. But then he rallied.

'Really, Quintus,' he said, 'you are spoiling the whole evening. Between two extremes there is always a third way. Crassus and Caesar have to be stopped: I can make that case. And when it comes to Lucullus, everyone accepts that he deserves a triumph a hundred times over for what he achieved in the war against Mithradates.'

'And Metellus?' cut in Quintus.

'I am sure I shall be able to find something to praise even in Metellus, if you give me sufficient time.'

'And Pompey?'

'Pompey, as we all know, is simply a humble servant of the republic,' replied Cicero, with an airy wave of his hand. 'More importantly,' he added, deadpan, 'he is not here.'

There was a pause, and then, reluctantly, Quintus started to laugh. 'He is not here,' he repeated. 'Well, that is true.' After a while, we all laughed; one had to laugh, really.

'That is better!' Cicero smiled at us. 'The art of life is to deal with problems as they arise, rather than destroy one's spirit by worrying about them too far in advance. Especially tonight.' And then a tear came into his eye. 'Do you know who we should drink to? I believe we should raise a toast to the memory of our dear cousin, Lucius, who was here on this roof when we first talked of the consulship, and who would so much have wanted to see this day.' He raised his cup, and we all raised ours with him, although I could not help remembering the last remark Lucius ever made to him: *Words, words, words. Is there no end to the tricks you can make them perform?*

Later, after everyone had gone, either to their home or to their bed, Cicero lay on his back on one of the couches, with his hands clasped behind his head, staring up at the stars. I sat quietly on the opposite couch with my notebook ready in case he needed anything. I tried to stay alert. But the night was warm and I was swooning with tiredness, and when my head nodded forward for the fourth or fifth time, he looked across at me and told me to go and get some rest: 'You are the private secretary of a consul-elect now. You will need to keep your wits as sharp as your pen.' As I stood to take my leave, he settled back into his contemplation of the heavens. 'How will posterity judge us, eh, Tiro?' he said. 'That is the only question for a statesman. But before it can judge us, it must first remember who we are.' I waited for a while in case he wanted to add something else, but he seemed to have forgotten my existence, so I went away and left him to it.

AUTHOR'S NOTE

Although *Imperium* is a novel, the majority of the events it describes did actually happen; the remainder at least *could* have happened; and nothing, I hope (a hostage to fortune, this), demonstrably *did not* happen. That Tiro wrote a life of Cicero is attested both by Plutarch and Asconius; it vanished in the general collapse of the Roman Empire.

My principal debt is to the twenty-nine volumes of Cicero's speeches and letters collected in the Loeb Classical Library and published by Harvard University Press. Another invaluable aid has been *The Magistrates of the Roman Republic, Volume II, 99 B.C.–31 B.C.* by T. Robert S. Broughton, published by the American Philological Association. I should also like to salute Sir William Smith (1813–93), who edited the *Dictionary of Greek and Roman Biography and Mythology*, the *Dictionary of Greek and Roman Antiquities* and the *Dictionary of Greek and Roman Geography* – three immense and unsurpassed monuments to Victorian classical scholarship. There are, of course, many other works of more recent authorship which I hope to acknowledge in due course.

R.H.

16 May 2006